FINDING THE LOVE-LIGHT
(Hayah Series 2)

By Richard P. Matthews

Revitalizing In-sight
Simrishamn, Sweden

PUBLISHED BY REVITALIZING IN-SIGHT

Copyright © 2019 by Richard P. Matthews

This book is a work of fiction, although many of the event may have happened in reality. Names, characters, businesses, organizations, places, events, and incidents either are the product of the author's imagination or are messages from the 'I Am' within. Any resemblance to actual persons, living or dead, or events, is entirely conveyed by the 'Great I Am' within us and all of creation. The fiction debate should not be carried into future happenings.

The Bible translations quoted here are translations of the author.

Published in Simrishamn, Sweden by Revitalizing In-sight.

www.revitalizingin-sight.com

The portrayal of the Infinite Love logo is a registered trademark of Revitalizing In-sight.

U.S. Library of Congress Control Number: 2007932585

Cataloging Data.

Matthews, Richard P.

Finding the Love-light/Richard P. Matthews. — 1st ed.

p. cm.

1. FINDING THE LOVE-LIGHT—Fiction. 2. Inspirational

3. Body-mind-spirit-earth 4. Spirituality 5. New Life

I. Title. II. Matthews, Richard P.

ISBN: 978-0-9798106-8-8

PRINTED IN POLAND by Amazon Fulfillment

10 8 6 4 2 0 1 3 5 7 9

First Edition

CONTENTS

4

FORWARD
Choosing

Sometimes, the wakeup call comes before we sleep. The wakeup call is now! So, wake up and connect with the 'Great I Am' within you. There is no time like the present.

CHAPTER 1
Telekinesis

The 'Great I Am' says to me, "Now that you are listening. Listen to your purpose in this moment. Listen, and go with Me."

I no sooner settle into my seat on the plane until 'I Am' starts to talk to me. It is a long flight home from Israel. The first leg of the mission is complete. The New Curtain is Open.

I'm Hoss Proxetter, and I'm listening to the 'Great I Am' within me.

The 'I Am' responds, "Hoss, you are getting as good at reading Me as I am at reading you. Only a few of those connected to Me are able to do that. You make our connection personal. Or should I say, you make it a relationship. I like that."

"So where are we going? Do I have to get off the plane?" I sense the 'I Am's urgency. I unfold myself from my seat and stand in the aisle.

'I Am' laughs, "Sit down in your seat and go into your meditation."

I do as 'I Am' asks and crawl back into my window seat. Fortunately, the two passengers sitting next to me haven't boarded yet. I arrange all my travel gear and settle into my seat. Within seconds, I'm in a deep meditation. I feel my breathing saying the unutterable syllable. Slowly, 'I Am's light fills me, and I feel like a speck floating on the Light. I am traveling on the Love-light. I listen and wait. My awareness fills with 'I Am's presence.

'I Am' explains, "You have an important mission that cannot wait."

Suddenly, I find myself sitting behind Dan and

Nan on their MAF (Mission Aviation Fellowship) airplane. I'm now Hayah.

The two-way radio is blasting away. "MAF base to Dan, come in please. MAF base to Dan, come in please. MAF base to Dan, come in please. Dan, Nan come in, come in. This is important." The caller starts to talk to someone else, but we can still hear him. "They're not answering. They could be away from the plane. They could be in trouble. What do you want me to do?"

"Keep trying!" the other voice says .

The radio keeps blasting, "Dan, Nan come in. Dan, Nan come in, this is MAF base, come in please. Dan, Nan come in, this is MAF base, come in please..."

I say to Nan and Dan, "Aren't you going to answer that?

Nan and Dan nearly jump out of their skin, with their heads spinning around to look at me. They both say at the same time, "How did you get here?"

I smile and laugh, "I don't know."

In an instant 'I Am' is in our heads, "I Am always with you, especially, when you need help. You know that. Nan, I will let you fill Hayah in on what you are up to."

Nan looks at Dan, who smiles and nods. She then looks at me, "The refugee camps on the western border of Chad are in a stalemate. We got them in order, but we could not get them to connect to the 'Great I Am' within them no matter what we did or said. That still remains a mystery to us. But Sudan is a non-functional country, and peace is a distant hope for now. When I explain that if they connect, they will receive 'I Am's protection, it is as if they are ignoring my words.

"Then 'I Am' sends us off to Baga in Nigeria, near Lake Chad. A rebel leader of the Boko Haram, Abubakar Shekau, is emerging, with a demonic plan.

The 'Great I Am' asks us to nip it in the bud. We try to correct his faulty brain chatter and ego. But just when we begin to make some progress, the Mission Aviation Fellowship pulls us out saying, 'You need to get out of harm's way.'

"The next thing we know, the MAF is keeping us busy by sending us hither and thither with nonsense missions."

Here the 'Great I Am' adds, "I of course know that the leaders at MAF are thinking, 'it is not part of our Christian mission.' I see this as one more disappointment in the blind Christian institution. However, Dan and Nan had no choice but to do as they ordered."

Nan pauses and then continues, "Then a couple of days ago 'I Am' gives us a report that the Boko Haram has kidnaped 276 young girls from the girl's school in Chibok, Baga, Nigeria. When 'I Am' gives us the intelligence that Abubakar Shekau has taken them to some of the islands on Lake Chad, Dan and I realize we must do something. Just moments ago, both Dan and I were silently wishing that you were here to help."

The radio starts squawking again, "MAF base to Dan, come..." Klick! Dan turns off the radio.

Dan turns to me and smiles, "Now that you are here, we are a force to be reckoned with."

"What's your plan?" I ask.

The 'Great I Am' is giving Dan a message, which we also hear, "The girls are scattered all over the islands. Many of them do not even know where they are, so they can be of little help to you. Abubakar is shifting constantly from island to island, with a small band of men. The rest of his men are divided up among the islands as their rulers. You need to pick each island at random. I can only guide you to the ones where there is the most conflict, be it family or terrorists. You need to find the girls and liberate them from Boko Haram."

Dan starts his approach from the north to Lake Chad and points it out.

I look, but don't see a 1,350 square kilometer lake. I'm shocked. All I see is a small lake and a huge marsh, with thousands of raised patches of land. Most of these are less than a kilometer wide and three kilometers long. There are thousands of these so-called islands, about twenty-three in every ten square kilometers. The majority of these little islands have only one small village. The small lake in the south-west end of the area has a few real islands. These support small fishing villages or farming villages. However, the huge Lake Chad of 1963 is gone.

None of this is any surprise to Nan and Dan. They are enjoying the beauty as it slides beneath us. And beautiful it is, with lush greens, colorful birds, thatch huts, domestic animals and the largest horned cattle I have ever seen.

Dan passes over the lake and then banks to the right and follows it to the north-east. We are all looking for the same thing. The military presence of the Boko Haram.

As we reach the end of the Lake area, Nan says, "I don't see any military activity or anything out of the ordinary." Neither did we.

Dan circles the plane and heads back south-west to make another pass.

I ask Dan, "Where are you going to set the plane down? I saw only one patch that looked like it had a landing strip. How are we going to get to the other islands?"

"There is one other that has a small landing strip. We can take those first, but they are the least likely to have any of the girls or Boko Haram terrorists. But we know the people on those islands, and they may be able to point us in the right direction." Dan explains. "There are a few small villages on the edge of the Lake that have landing strips. We can secure the plane there and take a canoe to several islands that are accessible. Hayah, how are you with a canoe?"

"I love canoeing. In Boy scouts, I once did a two-hundred-mile canoe trip. Great experience! Does that count?"

"Is there anything you haven't done?"

"I was never able to learn how to play the piano."

Nan laughs, "Well then you will just be useless on this assignment. I'll have to leave the piano home." Everyone laughs with her, which releases the tension.

Dan circles one of the little islands, "Anybody see anything down there?"

I call out, "I see a dog, but it looks friendly."

Nan says, "She is."

Dan lines up with the landing strip and starts our approach. Suddenly, several kids come in view and start waving and cheering. The landing is a bit bouncy, but professionally managed. Nan and I wave to the kids racing alongside us, as we come to a stop.

Dan says, "The take-off is a bit scarier."

The spontaneous welcome of the inhabitants of the island is overwhelming. They surround Dan and Nan, who speak their language. There is a joyful exchange between them. The sound of their voices grows louder as they all start talking at once. At first, I'm standing by myself. Then Momo, the dog comes up to me. We immediately start communicating, and I start loving on her and she returns the affection with enthusiasm. Her tail is going a mile a minute. I start to play with her. Soon the children gather round, and we all start to play together.

After a while, a woman, in the crowd around Nan and Dan, steps outside the circle and watches us with a broad glowing smile on her face. When the voices of the crowd start to quiet down, she calls out to Nan while motioning to me, "Who is that man? Momo is never that friendly with any stranger."

Nan calls back, "That's Hayah."

Instantly, the group freezes and grows silent, slowly turning to look at me. The children pause and step back in silence. Momo leaps into my arms, and I cradle her like a lamb. When I look up, the woman is slowly walking toward me, with her eyes and face glowing with light. Some of the others in the group start to follow her. They stop just five meters away and start to kneel.

I quickly put Momo down and rush to her with open arms, "Please, please, please no. I'm just a messenger. The 'Great I Am' is within you. You can connect." I scoop her up and hug her. I gesture to the others to please stand. They slowly comply but stand frozen in their tracks.

A small boy begins to tug my hand. I look down into his little face beaming with innocence. He asks, "Mister, are you the elephant man?"

Dan steps forward, "Yes he is. And he can help you all to find the 'Great I Am' within you." A buzz starts to move through the group. The 'Great I Am' tells us what they are thinking. They are all expecting a Billy Graham evangelical slap on the forehead and a zap your saved. Dan smiles, "OK, everybody lay down on your back."

The children are on their backs in a nanosecond. Most of the adults lie down hesitantly. A few stand and watch. I go into action walking among them.

'I Am' helps me to speak to them in their language. "Everybody fold your hands on your upper belly and relaxes." Soon, they are all breathing naturally, and their hands are going up and down. I point this out and continue, "Close your eyes and focus on your breathing. Shut down all the silly things your brain is saying. Go into the peaceful darkness within you, relax and enjoy it, focus on your breathing. Right now, you are the only thing in the universe. You are breathing. You are alive, feel your breath of life. Now you can see a speck of light in the darkness, move toward it. Go into it." I pause and wait. I look over all those who are lying down. 'I Am' tells me how close some of them are right now and stops me over Chinwe, a little girl about six or seven years old.

To my surprise she leaps to her feet and sings out, "Mommy, the 'Great I Am' is inside me. The 'I Am's Love-light is filling me. 'I Am' is telling me we must stop that man. Hayah will protect us." She races to her mother, who is now on her feet, and throws her arms around her legs.

Dan, Nan and I are getting the same message and turn toward the thatch hut on the far end of the clearing, about fifty meters away. A man, over two meters tall, emerges from the hut. He is wearing military camouflage fatigues and carrying an assault rifle. His face is badly scared and sporting a three-day beard. His body is muscular and fills out his uniform tightly.

He shouts as he strides toward us, "Kneel down you PIGS! Kneel to your GOD! KNEEL!

I walk toward him. Dan and Nan move in front of the people to shield them. They cower in a tight group behind them. Chinwe steps out beside Nan, ignoring the plea of her mother. Nan turns to her mother and nods in the affirmative, with a slight smile.

The man hesitates as I continue to walk toward him. He shouts, "What do you want?"

Still stepping forward, I call back, "Give yourself up like a man, and we will turn you over to the authorities unharmed. You don't want to do this."

The man laughs and shouts back, "You don't

even have a gun. How do you plan on doing that? Neel down or I'll blow off your head!" He pauses. He takes aim, "Maybe I'll do it any way!"

I keep walking forward, "I wouldn't do that, you will only be committing suicide." I open my arms in Love, free of hatred.

He shouts, "Who do you think you are, Hayah!" He fires. The BANG rings out.

I call out as I go into slow-motion perception, "Yes, -I -am." I watch the bullet flying in at my head. Suddenly, it boomerangs back on its own path from which it came. I see the expression on his face change, as my words reach his ears, to surprise and regret. In that instant the bullet passes through his forehead over his sighting eye and the back of his head explodes. I come out of my slow-motion perception.

Slowly, I continue walking toward the hut. 'I Am' is telling me to prepare for the worst. Unfortunately, 'I Am' is not telling me what that means.

When I reach the hut, I step to the side and open the door carefully. I hear nothing and peek inside. Seeing no threat, I step inside.

On the ground I see a half-naked little girl. She is savagely beaten, bloody, and molested. The 'Great I Am' tells me "I have her now. She is free." But out of reflex, I reach down to check her life-signs anyway. She is dead. I cover her with a blanket lying nearby and scoop her up in my arms.

As I carry her back to the others; I pause over the killer. For a moment, I wonder why I feel no remorse over his death. Then 'I Am' says only two words, "Lost forever." I know what that means. I have seen it before with Osama bin Laden.

When I reach the group, and they learn of the little girl's death, there is a buzz about what to do. At first, they feel that they will be held responsible for her death, and they should bury her.

I refuse, and say, "She needs to go back to her parents. What would you want if she were your daughter?" They quickly agreed. I ask, "Why do you feel responsible?"

Dede, Chinwe's mother, steps forward and explains, "The day they kidnap the girls Abubakar Shekau comes here and holds us captive. Early the next morning, thirty canoes arrive. They each load two men and two or three girls in a canoe and shove off to islands Abubakar has marked on a map. This goes on for the whole day, until each canoe has made nine or ten trips. The next morning Abubakar leaves that monster (She points to the dead terrorist) and takes five men in two canoes and heads North. He threatens that if we say anything or go anywhere, we will all be killed." By this time, she is shaking all over and begins to cry.

Chinwe pulls on her mother's sleeve to get her attention. It takes a full minute before her mother responds. Her mother bends down and listens; as Chinwe whispers something in her ear.

Dede looks up at me, then back at Chinwe. Chinwe steps back, and stares at her mother, standing strong and tall with both closed hands on her hips.

Dede looks at me again. I smile knowingly. She walks over to me and says, "You already know what she asked me; don't you?"

"Yes, I do."

"Is that possible; can you teach all of us how to connect to G..." She gets stuck on the G word.

"The 'Great I Am' mommy. 'I Am's the one inside you, not the one up there." Chinwe points into the heavens.

I look at Chinwe, Nan and Dan and we all say at the same time, "The 'I Am' says you can!" I give each of them a high five. Dede's face lights up, and the light spreads.

I carefully lay the body of the little girl in the MAF plane, and Dan flies her to Chibok.

Chinwe, Nan and I start to teach villagers to connect to the 'Great I Am' within themselves. Everyone lies down, and we go through the same steps. The 'Great I Am' is carefully guiding Chinwe and taking advantage of the innocence and lack of baggage. The others actually learn more quickly from her than they do from us. When she lays her little hand on someone, her love of them melts their resistance and they move quickly toward the Love-light.

In less than an hour everyone, but one man, is leaping with a lightness of being and connecting one after another. The one man left, Abdu, is the most educated and a devout Christian worshiper. It is obvious that his brain chatter and ego are getting the best of him and he cannot shut them down. The 'Great I Am' tells the three of us that his doctrine and dogma are consuming him, and he feels he is losing his control over the others. Chinwe doesn't see why they are so important. Nan tries to explain it but fails. Chinwe's face lights up and I motion to Nan.

Chinwe goes over to Abdu's hut and brings out his Bible. She walks right up to Abdu and says simply, "It is all right for you to listen to your brain chatter and protect your ego, but when the bullets start flying you can hold up your Bible for protection. The rest of us will be connected and protected." She hands him his Bible and gives him a big hug, pouring her love into him. In that instant he sees the Love-light and embraces it.

Now everyone, children and adults, sit down in a circle. As always, the 'Great I Am' takes charge, "Your connection creates a new purpose for all of

you. We now have an option we did not have before."
(Everyone in the circle can see that the others are
also hearing the 'I Am'.) "Will you go out in groups
of three to find the kidnaped girls and bring them
home?" They all say yes. "It will take time, but
together we can do this, and we shall find them all.
You are connected and protected as long as you have
no hatred and violence in your heart." There is a
cheer goes up among them all.

When Dan comes back, we leave for their MAF
base in Chad. As soon as we are in the air, the radio
squawks, "MAF base to Dan, come in please."

I say, "You better take that." And...

And I find myself sitting on the plan, flying home
from Israel. As I come out of my meditation, I have
an incredible feeling about the dream I just had.

'I Am' says, "Our connection is incredible. It was
not a dream. Hayah was there."

I'm confused, "How can that be?" I can feel his
smile.

"You experienced telekinesis. When we are
connected, your brain has 100% of its power. Your
inner awareness, with My help, can project your
physical presence anywhere on the planet, or the
universe for that matter. Do you remember the time
you saw yourself grocery shopping and thought it was
a dream? Only to have your neighbor knock on the
door and ask why you left your full cart in the isle."

"Yes. Was that you?"

"Yes. You had no money, and we decided to get
the brain-chatter about food out of your head. I wish
more of these people were connected, like you."

As I look around the plane and study the mass of
humanity, 'I Am's words sink in. I wonder how many
of these people are connecting to the 'I Am'. The next
moment, 'I Am' makes me aware of the answer,
"Unfortunately, you are the only one connected, but

two are close and a lot of good people are looking in the wrong place."

I see the seatbelt light come on and hear the flight attendant announce that they are preparing for landing. I'm more than surprised. That is the longest meditation I have ever had.

'I Am' says, "Now, you need to get us home, and you need to get some sleep. We have a lot of work to do to untie the knot from creation."

CHAPTER 2
Mission Update

'I Am's Light is pouring into my inner Being. Slowly, I awaken from a deep sleep. The closed blinds and heavy curtains darken the room, but bits of sunlight are sneaking in through many spaces.

I rub my eyes and greet the day. As I sit-up and get out of bed, I say naturally, "Good morning."

From deep within, 'I Am's words fill my inner Being, with a soothing voice, "Welcome to a new day, Hoss."

I glanced at the digital clock. To my surprise, I had slept for over 13 hours.

'I Am' laughs and says, "Your old body needs the rest."

"What old body?" I respond, "I have the body of a thirty-year-old." I glance in the mirror and see that I'm no longer Hayah. I'm back in Hoss' body. "OK, you old fart," I say to the mirror. "Let's give this body a workout." I start to exercise my body with stretches and workout routines.

"Can I talk to you while you're working out?" 'I Am' says.

"What do you mean? You're the reason I'm working out. Fire away, I'll just listen." I continue to do my routine in slow motion with deep breathing.

"We need to go over your trip and make some plans. The elephants are back in their bais (a natural open clearing in a tropical forest where the wildlife comes to water, eat minerals and graze; NGM), but they are not doing well. Very few of the cows are pregnant. Now, they are in real danger of extinction. They really want to help the humans, but the boomerang effect is wiping out the poachers and littering the tropical forests with human bodies. The good news is the elephants all made it home safely.

"You already know about Dan and Nan, MAF and the rebel leader, Abu-Baku Shrekau.

"Reid is having some success with the Rangers at Zakouma National Park in Chad. Only one of the Rangers has lost his connection with Me, and many more are showing an interest in the job. Reid is ecstatic and the word is spreading throughout Africa.

"Dick and Abby are having the ultimate love relationship beyond anything since Adam and Eve. And I must say that I'm really enjoying it. From the beginning, I meant it to be this way.

"On the downside, National Geographic Magazine (NGM) is laughing at and ridiculing his pictures and story on the animals. Every time I try to find the underlying cause of this, I'm led to a dead end. They have also rejected all the articles of Dr. James, Dr. Spike, and Dr. Kathrin, which Dick sent in."

"What about Phyllis?" I ask.

"No, there is nothing from Phyllis. I haven't been able to get through to her either. Maybe you can help?"

"Sure," I say. "I plan on calling her anyway."

'I Am' laughs and continues, "The one person who is a major surprise, is Bosco. What an incredible 14-year-old boy! He is still connected and doing everything I ask him to do. On top of that, he has helped twelve of his friends connect to Me, seven boys and five girls. They are a major force in Kinigi. They make sure no more traps are set for the Mountain Gorillas or other game. Their connection is so strong, they know every time the baby gorilla, his mother and the Silverback come down to the bamboo rim, and they all go up to meet them. They all play together, and the Silverback has adopted them all. Dr. Kathrin and Dr. Spike, the co-directors of GorillaDoctors, are pleasantly amazed and constantly seeking their help on the mountain.

Jasper is teaching them how to hunt game for food.

"Many of the Rhinos decided to stay in the Reserve at Tsavo West National Park in Kenya, creating a respectable heard. Those that headed home made it with only one incident, which did not turn out well for the perpetrator.

"President Zahur of Kenya is holding his own with the political opposition, and our connection is stronger.

"Then there is Odis from Tanzania. I never dreamed that this man would be connected, let-a-lone a mover and shaker in Tanzania. Now he is, like Paul, a force to be reckoned with. He broke up six al-Qaeda training camps and crushed two want-a-be terrorist groups, with only a little help from Me. He is fearless and never gives up."

I finish my Yoga routine and meditation. 'I Am' continues to bring me up to date. At this point, I can hear a new lightness in his voice. I smile because it actually sounds like joy. The 'I Am's light grows brighter within me as I feel 'I Am's Love.

"India is going through a major transformation. As you would expect, Rohan, the Conservator of Forest & Field Director of Nagarjunsagar-Srisailam Tiger Reserve (NSTR), is revolutionizing the forestry industry with his Special Beat Officers (SBO). In one week, they wiped out deforestation in their area. Now there are plans to train other SBO teams for all the Nature reserves in India. And there is more. The India military is sending observers to look into the work of the SBO's. They're considering the creation of Special Forces for their national defense. That will be the first non-violent Special Forces in the history of the world.

"Here comes the biggest surprise of all. Uddatla and Shaik T are growing their connected following by thousands every day. You met some of them on your flight to Israel. Uddatla organized the Women's

Liberation Force. The women are taking charge of
their destiny. And crimes against women are down
40%. It is a good start; we need to work on the
judicial system. I want to talk to you about a
boomerang response that may turn the whole
situation around in a hurry. Also, Shaik T organized
the New Earth Community, with a sharp vision of the
Crystal City. Between the two of them, they could
realize the 1% of the huge Indian population within
the next three years. Then Love, My Spirit Host, and
I will build the first Crystal City."

The light within me is now so bright, I feel like a
speck within it. The 'I Am's joy and Love are
overflowing. Then the intensity of the light lessens. I
wonder what is happening.

There is a long silence before 'I Am' continues,
"That brings us to the Philippines. Because of the
influence of the Roman Catholic hierarchy in the
Philippines, we are now on the ten most wanted list.
In spite of the video that Sjuto, of the National
Bureau of Investigation (NBI), took, the politicians
will see what they want to see. They won't see that
the hatred and violence is coming from the attacker."

I interrupt passionately, "What do you mean,
We? I'm the one they have on tape!"

"I Am the one causing the boomerang effect. But
this is not the first time I have been declared dead by
the people who worship Me. Nor will I hesitate to
reject them."

"What are you planning?"

"Nothing. When the Crystal Cities start
emerging all over the planet, these people will be left
to destroy themselves." 'I Am' pauses in sadness for
a moment and then continues. "The corruption in
Thailand is also very deep. We are wanted there as
well. And that little knot of phony monks is behind it
and the attempt to bring down your plane. Make no
mistake, our mission will not be easy. Even the

Royals have lost their connection to Me already."

"What? They seemed so sincere."

"I heard Lord Whosiewut, their advisor, say, 'You did the right thing, offend no one, do what you must, and walk away looking good as the monarchy of England. I only wish Harry could learn that simple truth. But whatever you do, don't take any of it seriously. This creature, Hayah, is just another lowlife.'

"There is a positive note on which to end this update and another surprise. China is taking the warning seriously and is planning a public burning of their ivory stockpile."

"What? I'll believe that when I see it!"

"As, you plan your trip back to Israel, do what you have to do, but be prepared these people may be difficult."

"They're your Chosen People. You have had a connection with them."

"The operative word there is 'had' and then only with a few. Right now, I Am more interested in those people who are **choosing** to connect with Me and want to stay connected.

"Go ahead and make those phone calls you are eager to make, but do not forget to do your laundry."

As always, 'I Am' is the one who knows the one thing we are most likely to forget. Let me explain, 'I Am' is the little voice inside us, to whom we need to learn to listen. I consider it a sixth sense, which is just as real as the other five. Let's call it 'awareness'. It has been called many other things like, 'insight', 'instinct', 'intuition', 'a gut feeling', 'it came to me', or 'inspiration', which are often discredited and looked down upon. Awareness is the sixth sense, which is consciousness and being aware of the 'Great I Am' within you. It becomes stronger when we connect with the 'I Am'.

For those of you who are reading this story without having read *A New Curtain Opens*, I'm Hoss Proxetter. I discovered that the 'Great I Am' was inside me when I was only twelve years old. I connected with the 'I Am', and my life changed. The 'I Am' had a purpose for me, which I accepted. A lifetime later, 'I Am' sends me on a mission as Hayah, a young man of thirty-five, with some really incredible superpowers. (OK, they are only incredible, and they are powers that everybody can have when they connect to the 'I Am'.)

Besides the mission updates, which you just overheard Him tell me about, there are some important parts you may want to know. Embedded in the action and adventure of the story are explanations as to why we need to connect to the 'Great I Am', where to find the 'I Am', how to meditate, how to get past the peaceful center within you and into 'I Am's Love-light and how to deal with your life's purpose when 'I Am' reveals it to you. Most importantly, you get to learn about the potential love of my life, Phyllis.

"Speaking of Phyllis, I need to call her and build a fire under her to get her article written and delivered to Dick." I gesture to you, my reader, to hold on a minute.

I dial the phone and wait while it rings, and rings, and rings. My impatience is written all over my face as it rings for the tenth time. Slowly, my impatience turns into concern. I check my voice mail. There are no messages. I ask the 'I Am', "What did you mean; You haven't been able to get through to her?"

'I Am' responds with a concerned tone, "I mean she is blocking Me. And I mean blocking me completely. I do not even know where she is right now."

I react, "That's unusual."

"Very unusual! I do not remember it happening before. At least not since..." 'I Am' stops in mid-sentence.

"Since when?"

"Could you call Dick and Dr. James at Harvard? And ask them if they know anything. Right now, Phyllis is totally off their radar. I'll try and check around to see who she has had contact with in the last 24 hours."

I turn back to you, my reader, with a question on my face, "There you have it. Already, we are up to our eyeballs in a mystery. 'Wait a minute,' you're thinking, the 'I Am's supposed to be all knowing!' Well, the 'I Am' is. 'I Am' knows everything we are doing all the time, even if we are not aware of 'I Am's presence. For example, 'I Am' told me what you were thinking just now. 'I Am' even knows what you are planning on doing, but because of freewill, 'I Am' doesn't know what you do until you do it. Until now, you may have been able to program your rational mind and ego that the 'I Am' doesn't exist. You may simply ignore the 'I Am'. But the 'I Am' is right there inside you, waiting for you to connect. So, what is happening to Phyllis is not normal. I do hope that she is all right. Please excuse me while I make some phone calls."

I walk over to my computer and boot it up. While it whirrs and beeps into action, I take out my address book and look up Dick's number. With one click, Skype flies up onto the screen, and I type in Dick's number and ad him to my contact list. I slip on my headset and double-click to call his number, with a boop-boopidy-boo. We can hear the boop and see the bubble going from my picture to his number. After seven boops, he picks up.

Dick's cheery voice says, "Mr. Click at your service."

In an instant, 'I Am' changes me into Hayah. "Hi, Dick, Hayah here."

"Hello, Hayah! How is public enemy number one?"

"The 'I Am' just told me. And 'I Am' is taking most of the responsibility even though the hatred and violence is all in the actions of the perpetrators. But I'm still trying to get used to the idea. Right now, I'm missing Phyllis and longing to see her. We kind-of got a thing started in Israel.

"Speaking of romance, how are you and Abby doing?"

"My friend, there aren't words to describe it. All I can say is the poets got it all wrong. What we have now gives a whole new meaning to the word Love. Have you ever experienced this?"

"No, I wish I could say I did."

"Maybe you and Phyllis..."

I cut him off, "She's the reason I'm calling. What have you heard from her?"

"Nothing, no articles, no response to my phone calls, her school hasn't heard from her since she got back, it is like she dropped off the face of the earth."

My heart is aching, "I hope she's alright."

"The police and hospitals knew nothing. The airlines said she was on the flight from Israel, but then nothing. I share your concern. We really need her input. Her report could break-up the logjam."

"Tell me about that," I sense his concern.

Dick is pensive, "When I got back, my editor at NGM gave me a cold shoulder. The next day he called me into his office and laid it all out for me. After reviewing all my pictures and footage, he took it up with the legal department. There was a flood of negative comments and calls from influential people. How they got wind of it so quickly, I don't know. However, the strangest thing is they interpret what they see in the pictures and footage to be the opposite of what actually happened. Instead of seeing the solders attacking the elephants, they see the elephants and you attacking the solders."

"What?!!" I'm flabbergasted and outraged.

"They do that with every sequence. When your Most Wanted posters comes out of the Philippines and Thailand your image and credibility is fried. You are some powerful evil wizard, who is using the animals to destroy the planet and humankind."

"You're kidding!" I'm shocked. The 'Great I Am' is present but noticeably quiet.

Dick's voice is sadly cautious, "And that is not the worst of it. They want me to help them entrap you. Of course, you and the 'Great I Am' know that will never happen." He pauses and then asks cautiously, "You do know that?!!"

I smile and answer confidently, "Yes! Of course, we do." A strong feeling swells up from deep within me and I add, "Dick, we will figure this out and develop a plan. Meanwhile find out what ever you can as to whom these influential people are and who are the negative voices behind this. Once we know their names, the 'I Am' will know everything about them. Remember, you can take things like this directly to the 'I Am'. I learned a long time ago that 'I Am' needs our help to pull this off"

"Thanks, Hayah; I'll get right on it."

"I'll talk to you soon, Dick. Goodbye."

"Till then, my friend."

The line closes with a boop.

I look up Dr. James number, at Harvard, and enter it into my Skype numbers. I click the phone icon and here the boop-boopidy-boo. After one boop, he answers.

Instantly he says, "Hello, Hayah. The 'I Am' told me you were about to call."

"Hi, James, we need your help."

"So, 'I Am' says. I'm surprised I didn't see this

coming; I'm such a cynic. Who do you think is behind your character assassination? I've seen it here at Harvard before, with faculty members but never on this scale."

I say, "The main person behind it will be the hardest to learn. We'll get many minor names that are responsible for a small piece of the deception, but someone, with a lot of political know-how, is masterminding this hate campaign. Our biggest problem is how to reverse it once we figure it out."

James becomes extremely excited, "I have an idea that might help us on both fronts. I'll have Dick send me the pictures and videos, and I'll show them to the students in one of my classes. I'll ask them for an objective evaluation of the material to determine all the possible interpretations of the message. This will tell us **how** they are twisting the truth and may lead us to the **who**. Then, I'll have the students focus on the truth and create a plan to bring the truth of the issue into the limelight."

"That's an incredible idea. You're brilliant!"

"Not anymore," James says humbly. "We both know where it comes from though." We both laugh.

"Do it! And I'll go to work on the 'who list'. Call me when you have the details worked out."

"Will do." James and I disconnect with a boop.

CHAPTER 3
Connecting Tree Begins

I sit down in my chair and relax. I look at four books next to me, the Upanishads, the Avesta, the Bible, and the Qur'an. My mind is racing through the creation story, Adam and Eve, and the human disconnect with the 'Great I Am'. I wonder how the reconnect began and with whom. Just as I reach out for a book, the 'Great I Am' begins to describe what the 'I Am' calls 'The Connecting Tree'.

The 'I Am' says, "Many millenniums pass, but finally, a middle-aged woman, with seven children, becomes aware of My Love-light within her. On her own, she learns how to shut down her irrational left-brain chatter and discovers an inner peace. Her name is Devaki, and she is married to Vasudeva. He is not on the same path as Devaki, but he accepts and supports her. He can feel the profound changes occurring within her.

"One morning, before the rest of the family is awake, Devaki is moving deeper and deeper in her meditation. She moves past the moment of inner peace and finds herself bathing in what she calls, 'the dark sea of nothingness'. She embraces the nothingness and soaks up the serenity.

"I appear as a speck of light floating through the vast nothingness within her. She sees Me and moves closer. She embraces the Light, and My Love-light quickly fills her entire body and mind. I call her by name, 'Devaki, can you hear Me?'"

"She responds, 'Yes, Master. I'm listening.'"

"My joy explodes in a bedazzling Light, and I say, 'I Am here within you. Connect with me and we can bring the Love-light back into the world.'"

"She answers, 'Yes, Master...' At that moment she hears her infant cry, and she quickly comes out of her meditation.

"She walks over and picks up a one-year-old baby. She comforts him. Just when I assume the connection is broken, she says, 'Master, this is my son Balarama.' The connection is secure.

"I assure her, 'He shall always have my protection.' I'm filled with joy.

"Without hesitation, she says, 'Thank you, Master.'

"My connection with her is a new beginning. Now, I start to put together a plan.

"For the next two days, our connection continues for most of the time. The Love-light grows within her, and she grows increasingly positive, pushing back her Dark-side with Love. She tries to tell her husband about Me, but he finds it hard to believe. Fortunately, he encourages her to continue and promises to keep an open mind.

"On the third day, I have a plan. During the early morning, I appear to Devaki and Vasudeva in a dream. I explain that I will help them conceive their eighth son. He will be my first prophet, and they are to call him Krishna. He will bring the human race back to the Love-light and help people to connect with Me within them. He will neutralize the Dark-side in all humans. I let my Love overflow within both of them. They awaken and experience their most passionate lovemaking, and Krishna is conceived.

"From that moment on, Devaki bares in her womb her lotus-eyed son. All those who gaze upon her must turn their heads away from the blinding Light that fills her. Those who can stand to look on her radiance can feel the darkness in their irrational left-brain minds turn and run away.

"Krishna is a pure delight from the day he is born in 3228 BCE. We connect, and he willingly fulfills his purpose. His Light is powerful, and he can drive off a dev creating a Dark-side in another human from a hundred paces. He nurtures the honor and equality of both men and women and insists on its acceptance. He becomes a living example of what it means to connect to Me, right up to his premature death.

"My hopes are that his Love-light and life shall be an endless number of ripples on a quiet sea, which reaches and changes distant shores. Unfortunately, it is a small pebble thrown into an angry sea, which creates no ripples at all. At least that is the way it is until now.

"After Krishna, the planet is in a steady decline. The Dark-side is totally corrupting the human left-brain irrational mind. All of nature is pleading for me to do something. That is when I decide on the Great Flood. Plants and rocks can survive. All I have to protect is one human family and one animal family from each species. I let the animals sort things out for themselves to send the strongest family, and I go to the only human who is connected with Me, Noah. I ask Noah to build the arch. Every culture in the world has one form or another of this story, and we all know how it ends.

"Shortly after the Flood, Abraham connects with Me. He becomes my new hope for humanity. He goes wherever I send him, without question. He does whatever I ask of him. His wife, Sarah, is as faithful to him as he is to Me. She only connects to Me on a few occasions and doesn't know that I Am inside her listening to her every thought and watching her every action. To lie to Me is useless.

"From Abraham comes My chosen people, which branches into two separate nations. Hagar gives birth to Ishmael, who becomes the Father of My Islamic people. Sarah gives birth to Isaac, who becomes the Father of My Hebrew people. These two great nations produce both leaders who are connected to Me and those who are consumed by their Dark-side.

"A few people start to discover they can control their Dark-side. A few of them learn how to develop their positive nature and become a constructive influence on others. A few manage to find the Love-light within, but become secretive and protective of their discovery, sharing it with only a few. I constantly nudge these people to connect with Me, but still find it extremely hard to get through to them.

"Then Zarathustra brakes through and we connect. The Love-light produces a total transformation in him as a human being. He withdraws from society and we live in a cave for many years. He becomes very aware of his irrational left-brain chatter and shuts down his Dark-side, with My Love-light. He reconnects to nature and the natural order of the universe. When he leaves the cave to start his journey to fulfill My purpose for him, I Am right there within him. He helps millions of people to connect with Me and starts a major movement, which spreads throughout the land."

I interrupt again, "This is a great history lesson, but why are you leaving out all the empires and dynasties?"

"This is the family tree of My choosing people. I Am focusing on those connecting with Me. Your history books do an adequate job of covering the falsely assumed great accomplishments of the human race. As you know, Hoss, our purpose in these books is to help people shut down their Dark-side, their left-brain irrational mind and connect with the Love-light and Me.

"There is something in the left-brain Dark-side of the human mind that likes to create tangible Temples, shrines and icons for worship. When the irrational left-brain mind has an abstract idea, the irrational left-brain mind thinks it will be real if it can give it form. The irrational left-brain mind then pretends it has life when it is only a lifeless idol or thing.

"Even in the positive side, the Since and Spiritual side, of the human right-brain mind, there is a resistance to connecting with Me. The Hebrew people told Moses, 'You listen to God and then tell us.' To them, I become the invisible God instead of the 'I Am' within them.

"My choosing people shut down their irrational left-brain chatter and look inside their real bodies, which has form and awareness. Within the body, there is empty space or blackness. In that blackness, there is a speck of Light, which is Me. Once they find Me, they have a choice, to connect or not connect.

"This tree is about those who choose to connect," the 'I Am' says.

"This is a unique experience," I confirm 'I Am's purpose.

CHAPTER 4
As a Rat

That night, I fall into a deep sleep.

In the middle of the night, I start tossing and turning for 90 seconds, I sit up in bed, wide-awake. The room is dark. I walk to my desk, turn on the lamp and boot up my computer.

I turn to you, my reader, "Whenever I have a dream, I get up immediately and write it down. At that moment, I can remember every detail of the dream. If I wait until morning, I won't remember more than 10%, or may not even remember that I dreamed. With the 'Great I Am' within me, the 'I Am' often uses me to go places where the 'I Am' is being blocked, or where the 'I Am' wants me to learn something firsthand. This may be one of them. You're welcome to look over my shoulder as I write it out."

I can hear voices and footsteps above me. I'm inside the walls of an incredibly old house or mansion, which is well over a hundred and fifty years old. I can see that because I can see the wooden lath and hardened plaster oozing between them. I can also see the old posts and beams, the iron piping for gas lighting and the points of hand-cut steel nails. I climb up the high wall to the second floor and make my way down a long beam until I come to a natural hole in the wall. I measure its size with my whiskers. It will be a tight fit, but I can squeeze through it.

I peek out of the hole. I see the back of a throne like chair, and a man standing next to it with alligator shoes and wool-silk trousers of a suit. I can't see the ceiling. In fact, I can barely see the arm of the chair. The hole opens out under a bookcase, which will give me great cover.

With a little effort, I squeeze through the hole and run down the wall under the bottom shelf of the bookcase. Soon, I come to a corner of the room, but the bookcase turns to the left, and I follow it about one and half meters down the sidewall. This gives me a great vantage point where I can see the side of the chair and the shiny heels of the man's shoes. The chair is about two meters from the bookcase. I resist the temptation to move out to the front edge of the bookcase in order to get a full view of the room and see their faces. I stay close to the wall.

The person in the chair is a woman. Her stiletto-heeled shoes are on the floor beside the chair. I study her feet. They seem to be exceptionally long. But as I look closely, they are bony. The skin and tissue are like leather. Her toes appear to be as long as fingers. Her nails are like long curved talons. The hand that is resting on the arm of the chair is similar in appearance. It rarely moves except to tighten and flex the fingers or thump a fingernail on the arm of the chair. While her feet seem to dance on the floor as she speaks. Then, I realize that she is gesturing with her feet the way some people talk with their hands.

They are having a heated discussion. The woman screams at the man. "Are you forgetting the time when sex was the religion in India? And you let that slip away from us." Her voice is so shrill that it hurts my ears. "Now you're telling me that you let the little darling plead guilty to raping the girl. The girl should just keep quiet and let him do it. What kind of a man are you? Grow a pair! Sex is power! Sex is control! You are nothing but a pathetic little worm! If you let India slip through our grasp, you will experience the full force of my wrath! Do you hear me? Do...You...Hear...Me?!!"

The man turns and steps toward the bookcase.
His toes turn in.

"DON'T YOU TURN YOUR BACK ON ME!!!"

The man turns back, slowly. His toes still turn
in.

"Where is your fury?! Where is your hatred?!
Without hatred we are nothing! Hate is the
backbone of violence! Hate is the lifeblood of
vengeance the salvation of religion!"

Slowly the man's feet straighten again, and he
takes a wider, stronger stance. He answers with a
powerful base voice, "Yes, Your Eminence!"

Her voice becomes calmer, but still shrill, "There,
what do you think you should do now, Angra
Mainyu?"

"I shall sow destruction among them. I shall
inflate the male egos to our purpose. They shall
dominate! They shall stalk their prey and obliterate
them," he responds with confidence.

"Very good! That is more worthy of you." Her
toes uncurl and her feet relax. "We cannot afford to
lose India! Where are we with the other countries?"

Angra Mainyu begins to walk from one side of
her chair to the other and back. As he walks, he gains
swagger and confidence. Her feet dance with
excitement. Every negative victory is punctuated
with a stomp of her left foot.

He begins his report, "I have some powerful devs
strategically placed with very influential leaders.
Most of these leaders are thoroughly corrupt and
under our control. We now have control of 166
countries, which includes 29 of the monarchies."

She interrupts him, "Details, Angra Mainyu,
details! Statistics bore me!"

"All of our leaders are basking in a show of
wealth and grandeur. Their greed and passions are
in complete control of all their decisions. They all
secretly worship sex and practice sexual abuse as

power and domination. Each of them has a boogeyman, of their own making, which kindles their hatred and violence toward innocent do-gooders, as well as racial and ethnic groups. Also, I take great pride in the fact that they all value themselves and their superior intellect over all others. Every one of them listens to and obeys the devs that are running them.

"Right now, I'm working on a small group of warrior leaders. They are so radicalized religiously, ethically, intellectually and emotionally that they will make the Christian Crusades, the Islamic Conquests and both World Wars look like a day at the beach. They do anything I put in their precious left-brain minds and consider me their God. Since the God they grew up with was some mythical unseen God, they don't know the difference.

"I can't wait for the day, Your Eminence, when you can reveal yourself to your subjects and take over this planet. You are the real power in the universe! You are the true creator! You are the..."

"Enough!" She cuts him off, "Stick to your report. Tell me what you are doing to stop this Hayah, nobody."

"He is totally discredited. The lie is always much more dramatic and interesting than the truth. My devs are running all the people he needs to help him get out the word. The video technician at NGM has re-edited Dicks' footage so it appears that Hayah is using sorcery to attack the solders and massacre them. The headline reads, 'Animal Life is More Important Than Human Life.' When these were bumped up to legal, our woman there had no problem selling the others that this position was indefensible.

"With the mountain gorillas, my devs simply edited the footage and reversed it in places, so now it appears that Hayah is using sorcery to wound and cripple the healthy animals. The NGM staff is so infuriated that they are drafting new articles to condemn this new enemy as a monster in the eyes of animal activists.

"The Rhino footage now shows a vicious Rhino attacking an innocent man trying to defend himself. Their natural anger and hostility is so pervasive that (even though they are my favorite above all other creatures) they should be exterminated, like many other dangerous species.

"I'm taking a two-step approach with the 'Warning'. On the one hand, if the warning never goes out then the repercussions will be unrelated to events and mean nothing. The cause of a health epidemic of any kind or the cause of an Ebola Virus will simply be unknown. My second approach is to have the people ignore the warning by making it unimportant and not urgent. We have pulled off this approach for one hundred years regarding global warming. The stupid people still refuse to accept that the burning of their precious fossil fuels, the driving of their gas guzzling cars and the dumping of their nuclear waste is choking them to death. Now it is too late to reverse it by human intervention, and you and I get to enjoy watching them die a miserable and painful death.

"I must say how much I enjoyed making Hayah into 'Public Enemy Number One'. He didn't see it coming, and now he can't stop it. It has a life of its own. He will not be able to show his face in public again. He is so stupid; he is not worth a minute of my time. He has no real power without you know who. I could squash..."

Her voice takes on a hissing quality, "You don't get it. Do you? You bloody fool! It's not his powers that will destroy us. It is hiss's MESSAGE! He

knows the secret! He is making left-brain
intelligence secondary and ego an enemy."

"But what I have done is working! He doesn't
have a clue and will never be able to stop it."

Shouting, "That's what you said about The Son
and look at what his death did, you stupid idiot! Now
this man is about to finish what That Son started.
You watch, you moron, this man will flip all your
superficial efforts around before you have a chance to
wipe your ass."

"But..."

"Don't but Me! I'll be lucky if I can salvage this
mess myself..."

At this point, I see a hair from her head floating
down past her arm and landing on the arm of her
chair.

Her rage continues, "...Sometimes, you are totally
bloody useless! You have no idea what he is up to, do
you? Well, I do! And the loser here will not be
me...," she waves her arm in the air for the first time.

The motion sends the hair floating down from
the arm of the chair. It seems to take forever. Angra
Mainyu crosses to the right side of the chair.

Still screaming, she says, "I will not hesitate to
through you under the bus! So, contact your devs
and figure out a way to stop this message, and don't
forget you cannot fail again!"

The hair is about to reach the floor, when Angra
Mainyu almost steps on it. His motion stirs it up and
it floats toward me.

"Yes, Your Eminence."

She offers her assistance, "I'll see what I can do.
Like all men, he must have a weakness."

Her long toes and claw like nails curl like a fist.
Her hair continues to flutter toward me like a feather
responding to every movement in the air around it.

"If anyone can find it you can," he says.

"Have your devs been able to even get close to

him?"

"No, Your Eminence. Thirteen have tried and thirteen have failed."

With each of his movements, the hair inches toward me. I don't dare stick my head out any further. The hair has my full attention now. I already know where this conversation is going.

Her foot fist clinches tighter. "I tried to take him twice when he was very young. The first time was after he had a vision of me in creation. His reaction to me was so compassionate and understanding it softened my resolve. Only one other has ever done that. The second time, I broke through his defenses; at least I thought I did. I shot an electrical bolt into his right eye and injured it, but he opened his heart and poured out a powerful Love-light that could only have come from the 'Great One'. I fled for my life. After that, I could never get close."

I blink my right eye and watch her hair move under the bookcase as Angra Mainyu steps closer to her.

"You are the powerful creator, My Lady. I will follow you anywhere."

Her voice is reflective, "I did my part and lost it all."

I sniff her hair and draw the aroma deep within me. I remember that smell... But cannot place it. She begins to scream, which grows in intensity. I turn and run down the wall toward the hole. I dive through the hole and finally feel safe as I land on my pillow.

I turn to you; there you have it. Now, I'm going back to bed. I don't have to figure out what it means until I have a few more winks. Ok, I will answer those two questions but no more.

Angra Mainyu (destructive mind/ego) can be

found on Wikipedia. The devs are his Fallen Spirits, from the human Dark-side.

I sit down on my bed and swing my feet up. Slowly, I let my head sink into my pillow.

As I close my eyes, I tell you. "You don't need to wish me any more sweet-dreams."

CHAPTER 5
Love-light

After my morning workout routine, I sit down to meditate. I quickly move into the center of my being and connect with 'I Am's presence. I sit in silence, shutting down my left-brain chattering irrational mind and ego. Slowly, I'm filled with 'I Am's Love-light and peace until my whole body seems to be glowing. 'I Am' is silent, and I sense that the 'I Am' wants me to just soak up the Love-light and be at peace within myself. All the thoughts about last night's dream fade away. The right-brain rational thoughts take over.

> *All there is*
> *Is Love*
> *And Light*
> *Awareness in every cell*
> *Wholeness of Being*
> *Eternal presence*
> *Unity with all creation*
> *Harmony with everything*
> *Absolute peace*
> *Total oneness*
> *This is the*
> *Love-light*

This moment is free of time, yet I want it to last forever.

And ever...

And ever...

Suddenly, I realize. This is the Second part of the 'Great I Am', Love. The Second Being in creation.

The 'Great I Am' breaks the silence, "I want you to remember the power of the Love part of Me. That

Love is the greatest power of all. This is the Love, of the one you call the Devine Mother, the Love part of Me; this is the Love that made us One; this is the Love that gave life to My Word, My Light; this is the Love-light My Son used to bring all My images into Being; this is Love-light. The Light, Love and Word are one. We are the Love-light.

"What are you feeling?"

"The Love-light is filling me with compassion," I respond. "I totally understand your Love together and can comprehend why You want Love to come back to you. But I don't understand why and how Love could turn to Hate and walk away from You and the Love-light?"

There is a surge of energy before the Love-light speaks, "The Light wants me to answer your question."

I quickly ask, "Is this Yeshua talking to me?"

"Yes, I Am the Word of the 'Great I Am'. In my physical form, you know me as Yeshua. I Am the one who is always talking to you. The 'I Am' gives me the words and I say them to you. They are 'I Am's words, but it is always my voice.

"In this case, to answer your question as to why and how Love could leave, I was the one working with Love in creation and we experienced the same things. It's a little like the time you let me take over your body to deal with the Rhinos. (Thank you very much for that.) Now, only you and I really know what makes the Rhinos tick, or in this case 'gets them ticked off'."

"How do I know when it's you or when it's the 'I Am', to whom I'm talking?" I ask.

"Does it matter?"

"Of course not," I realized the instant I asked the question. They are one. Of course, the 'I Am' knows what is in my right-brain mind.

Yeshua continues, "That's right. Let's get on with

the real question here. As Yeshua, I could realize how difficult it is for humans to understand or even begin to comprehend what happened in creation. You, however, saw and experienced a little piece of that in your healing of the mountain gorillas. That will at least help you to get a handle on what I Am about to tell you.

"This you have already experienced, the Love-light between The Light and Love which produced me. As you say, We are all one, but We each have incredibly unique functions. For now, look at these functions separately.

"The Light, the 'Great I Am', has an image of everything 'I Am' wants to create. (Note that I Am avoiding the word 'idea', because what is happening is beyond any thought process. Any artist knows exactly what I mean by that.) I clearly see everything the 'I Am' wants to create, large or small, in every detail from genetic structure/instructions (DNA), molecular composition, multiple components, heart, lungs, brain, all the way up to a finished work or entity.

"I then can see every image in all its details and word it into being. Through me, it takes on physical form. I build it element by element, molecule by molecule, piece by piece. Everything is *worded* into being in a specific order and in balance with the whole of creation. I Am literally seeing something emerge out of nothing. Imagine, if you can, what that must feel like.

"The Love fills every image with Love, creating a life-giving fluid in everything, like the Cambium layer and xylem tracheid in trees, veins in plants and blood vessels and arteries in all living creatures, fish, fowl, reptile, mammal and human. The Love then pumps the energy, fluids or blood through them.

"Finally, the Light, the 'Great I Am', breaths into everything the breath of life. The 'I Am' fills them with Light and becomes part of their being. Every part of creation can now feel the 'Great I Am's presence as the Love-Light.

"The Three Parts actually experience the birth of everything. It is one thing to see The Light's image of something come into being, but it is quite another to see something become alive. When The Love adds Love, there is an exciting attachment of the Love-light when it becomes one. Together, we feel the fulfillment of what We created.

"Over thousands of millenniums, We were all hooked on what We were creating. The Love-light flowed through us, and We were filling the planet with Love-light. Most of what We created were wonderful successes, with only a few failures. But those were easily corrected."

"Are humans one of those?" I ask.

"Man and Woman are our crowning accomplishment. If we could, however, there are a few adjustments We would make, which brings me to why We cannot.

"As our creation neared the end of its first phase, Love began to have many ideas of creatures to create by Love's self: Unicorn, a horse with a long spiral horn; Pegasus, a winged horse; Phoenix, a bird born and reborn from fire; Centaur, half man – half horse; Mermaid, half woman – half fish and many more. Love knew what they looked like and planed on making them out of pieces of what We already made. Unfortunately, it was impossible to end up with a living creature. The Light would have to put the image together from scratch, each with its own DNA. I would then put it together, and Love would put the blood into it. Then Light would need to fill it with Light and life. The 'I Am' was very fond of two of Loves' creatures, the Unicorn and the Phoenix. The 'I Am' even started on the DNA for the Unicorn.

"Hoss, you alone know the awesome power of

that feeling of creation. Your experience of making the limb for the mountain gorilla filled you with it. The Light and I were doing our part, but it was your hands. It came to life in your hands. That is why Love wants all the power.

"But how? It is not only that The Love turns away from The Light, and it is more than The Love flipping to its opposite, Hate. Hate is the one with a irrational left-brain mind and ego. Two qualities The Light and I do not need. The Light pictures everything. I, The Word, do or act. Examine the story of my life as Yeshua and see for yourself.

"Hate's irrational left-brain mind thinks it knows everything. Hate's ego is shouting seize the power. Hate's irrational left-brain mind and ego are saying seize control of everything. That is how Hate is thinking.

"That is how all irrational left-brain thinking works. It will lead you away from what you cannot understand or accept. Believe Me, I experienced that firsthand after feeding the multitude. I fed them. Yet, how could they walk away? Their irrational left-brain minds told them to turn their backs on me. It was just lunch. They could not connect. They could not find the Love-light within themselves. Not even Peter! To him I was just another irrational left-brain thought, the mythical Messiah.

"After Hate turned away from Us, Hate came down here to rule the human domain. Hate gave the irrational left-brain mind and ego to Eve and Adam. And humans are the only thing Hate has control of, because of their irrational left-brain mind and ego. If Hate shall continue, the human race will destroy the planet earth. Their 'Age of Reason' is already doing it.

"But we are going to prevent that from happening by bringing Hate back to be Love again; The Love from the beginning. Aren't we?"

"You bet!" is my confident affirmation.

"I know this is difficult for you to grasp, but Our Love is from the same woman you saw in your dream last night; the woman you call the 'Dragon Lady'. I want you to feel it while we unravel your dream."

I feel a change in energy again, and say, "This is the first time since I saw Love in the creation vision that she is taking on human/dragon form. It is most disturbing. The times Hate attacked me, I only saw the fiery pupil of Hate's eye swirling and pulling everything into it. Hate entered my head and tried to hide in all the dark places in my mind, but I poured out her own Love-light toward her eye, which made her scream and flee. I do wish I could bring Love back to you, but I don't understand why _you_ can't bring Love back."

"Because humans have the only power that will convince Our Love to return. You have the power to shut down your Dark-side and choose the Love-light within you, which is Me. That simple act demonstrates that Our Love, the original Love, is a key building block to all creation and the irrational mind and ego are only creating a myth. When 1% of the people make that Love-light connection, Hate will get the message, loud and clear. We know you can do it, but right now, your Dragon Lady, Hate, is the cause of our problems. We need to turn this around."

I'm aware of what the 'Great I Am' wants me to do, "OK, I'll contact Dick and fill him in on what we know. Then, I'll call James. Do you need any help with the problem in India? I sense you want to ask me something."

"I do," The 'I Am' says, "but let Me work it out a little more. It has been a problem for thousands of years. Now, I want to put an end to it.

"I Am going to let you and Dick manage the editing problems. I do not do computers and technical stuff.

"I will analyze the 'Warning' problem and see if I can produce a new solution. I have faced this problem far too often when it comes to humans. With the rest of the animal kingdom, cause and effect produces an instant correction. But not with humans. They **think** they can alter the cause and produce a different effect. They **think** they can rewrite the rules to win every time. Do not worry, I will produce something.

"Let's get to work, so we can start dealing with the growing disaster in the Middle-East!"

I walk over to my computer and boot it up. It whirrs into action and races through its start-up menu with beeps and pops. In my head, I'm already going over the things I need to discuss with Dick. I wander if he is aware of any of the things that the Dragon Lady is doing. It is extremely difficult for me to talk about the things of which Hate is capable.

Before Skype can load, my landline rings. I cross to the phone, pick up and check the display. It is a secret number. I answer with a cautious tone in my voice, "Hello?"

"Hi, stranger," a woman's voice says in a soft sultry tone on the other end.

It takes me a full five seconds for the sound of her voice to register. Then in a flash, my caution flips to pure joy, "Phyllis! I've been trying to reach you!"

"I've had some family business to take care of, after I got back."

I ask, "Anything serious?"

"No, pretty dull and boring, mostly accounting stuff, you know."

"I'm glad for that. I was starting to worry about you."

"Really, I'm not used to someone worrying about me. It feels nice. I could get used to it."

"Dick is trying to reach you too."

"Oh, yes, I owe him an article. Just haven't had time, you know; got distracted by someone in Israel," she laughs, which slowly becomes a giggle.

I laugh, "Anybody I know?"

"I'll never tell. It was a secret rendezvous." She is still giggling.

"Speaking of rendezvous, when can we do it again?"

"Why, do you miss me?" She says coyly.

"You might say that." I'm grinning from ear to ear.

"I'm not used to that ether. It's one of the pitfalls of a solitary lifestyle."

"I know what you mean," I say.

"Well, let's remedy that. I'm longing to see you. You know what they say, 'You can never get too much of a good thing.' And I consider you a good thing."

"I must say I feel the same way about you. I just hope this old body is up for the adventure."

"I'm sure it is. Fortunately, this body of mine still knows a trick or two."

"Unfortunately, I have spent a lifetime looking for Love in all the wrong places. I would really like to find the real thing," I say with deep sincerity.

"Do you know anyone who has ever found the 'real thing'? (She pauses.) I doubt it." She says with skepticism.

"Dick and Abby have it! Dan and Nan are on their way to finding it!"

"How do you know?" Her skepticism deepens.

"I'm surprised you didn't notice. You can see it on them, but they don't talk about it. In fact, they are very secretive about it."

"I say again. How do you know? What is this 'real thing' you want to find? How will you know this 'real thing' when you find it? You may be searching for something that doesn't exist." Her sultry tone is gone.

Her change in tone is making me cautious, although I must say I really like the sultry voice. There is a primal excitement in it. "Nan shared some very interesting details when I spoke to her about their Love life. She said that their Love has gone to a whole new level. They were both feeling an incredible oneness of Being growing between them. Dick said, 'All the poets are not even close!'"

"That's pretty vague don't you think. I don't want to see you tilting at windmills. What I can give you is real!"

"What's that?"

"I can give you passion, devotion, fulfillment and the best sex of your life."

"I love the sound of that." I'm tempted to just go with the flow. But... "There was a time when I would have shut up and raced to hold you in my arms. But I have been there and done that. What happens when the passion is spent, and the luster faces challenging times? What happens when you have enough, and the sex loses its thrill?"

"That would never happen with me. There are always ways to make it new. You have never been with the right woman before."

"Oh, you make it so tempting. And I know I could make your body sing as it has never sung before. But where is the unconditional caring? Where is the unity of two souls who can't live apart? Where is the joy of knowing that someone else really loves you and wants to spend the rest of their days with you?"

"Let's just talk about you making my body sing." The sultry tone is sliding back into her voice. "The rest we can worry about latter."

I can feel the presence of the 'Great I Am' within me, but the 'I Am' is quiet. I need help, but I have to blunder along on my own. "Phyllis, our attraction for each other is a beautiful thing. I deeply feel that the 'I Am' has brought us together, and we have a mutual connection to the 'I Am'. Dick and Abby's connection with the 'I Am' has produced the most perfect Love relationship since creation."

"Who says so?"

"The 'Great I Am' told me that this was the way it was intended for a Man and a Woman to come together."

Phyllis is silent on the other end of the phone line. I can barely hear her breathing.

I continue, "It is their connection with the 'I Am' that has made all the difference. That same connection could work for us. I have met only a few women that I could live with, but at this point, I'm looking for a woman I can't live without, emotionally. I feel that you could be that woman."

There is a short pause before Phyllis responds. Her tone is now friendly, "When can we get together? Then we can see how things work out."

"I have a lot to deal with in the next couple of days. I'm sure the 'Great I Am' is keeping you up to date. After that, I can see you, or we can meet some place."

"I would really like to have you come here; this is where I have all my toys."

"Now, that sounds like fun!" My mind is filling with all kinds of fantasies, and I struggle to stay focused and get back to business. "I almost forgot. Dick wants me to ask you to send him your article. Have you sent it yet? If you're stuck, I'm sure the 'Great I Am' could help you with it."

She lets out a large sigh and then begins to explain, "The first article I wrote was too long, over a hundred pages. Plus, the fact that it was extremely dull and boring. I tried to edit it, but that made it vague, so I trashed it and started again. I focused only on the mountain gorillas, which is my field of expertise. Then I bogged down in the healing of the wounded gorillas. No matter how hard I tried, I could not make it sound believable, so I trashed that one. This is turning out to be the most difficult article to write of my entire carrier."

"Why don't you ask the 'I Am' to help you?"

"I want it to be scientific and logical not spiritual."

"It's no wonder you're having problems. The 'Great I Am' is the source of all science!"

Phyllis screams in frustration. Then there is a long silence again. Finally, she says, "Ok, ok, I'll see what I can do! But tell Dick not to hold things up waiting for my article. I'll call you in a couple of days to set up a time for our meeting."

"Grea...," I start, but there is a click on the other end.

I'm left with a sea of doubts and other emotions running through my mind and body. What did I say? What should I have said? My burgeoning love is under attack. I listen for 'I Am's comments, but there is only silence.

CHAPTER 6
Connecting Tree Grows

I'm walking in the woods. A silent stillness
engulfs me. My chattering left-brain mind and ego
are attacking my awareness. I blow them a kiss of
love and they flee into nothingness. I slowly move
toward 'I Am's inner presence. Finally, I connect and
become acutely aware of the Love-light within me.
For a moment, I simply bask in the joy of being with
the 'I Am'.

My awareness tells me, without words, that 'I
Am' is working on something. I wonder what it is. I
assume that the 'I Am' is working on the India
problem. However, my assumptions are usually
wrong.

The 'Great I Am' starts to describe the early
Connecting Tree again, "From the very beginning of
his life, Moses is a difficult baby driving his mother
and Me nuts. Only part of this can be blamed on the
society in which he was born, which is irrationally
super left-brain intellectual and totally immersed in
their Dark-side, to the point of making it an art form.
With babies and young children, I usually have a
particularly good connection until their irrational
mind takes over. But Moses is a different story. He
is crying all the time, never content at his mother's
breast and often bites her nipple savagely.

"As a young boy, growing up in the royal palace,
he is angry all the time and downright mean to other
children. To answer the question in your mind, no it
is not a dev. It feels like he already knows My
purpose for him and wants to get as far away from
Me as possible.

"As a man, he has a terrible temper. He grows
into a royal bully, which the Pharaoh praises as part

of his royal linage. He is brutal with women and has no love. His left-brain Dark-side is consuming him. It is no surprise when his hot temper flashes and he kills another nobleman. I Am surprised when the Pharaoh orders his arrest and execution. I do what I can do to help with his escape, with little hope of ever connecting with him.

"In the desert, his arrogance, hatred and left-brain thoughts of revenge drive him like a madman. The Dark-side of his left-brain brain taunts him and belittles him. Finally, he collapses face down in the sand and begs for death.

"Now, his left-brain irrational brain chatter lets him go, and he slides into the peace of his inner Being. The sun bakes down on the back of his head, and all his anger, frustration and doubts melt away. In that stillness the Love-light fills him. I can finally reach out to him.

"In a rush of emotions, he embraces Me with his whole Being, and we make a connection. He goes limp in my arms and begins to weep. I ask him, 'Why do you weep?'

"'My Lord, I thought you were dead. Now I'm dead!'

"I smile and say, 'Moses, you are not dead, but you better kneel up before you create another flood with your tears.' He sits up and takes a deep breath. He wipes the sand and tears from his face.

"Thus, begins one of the most powerful connections with Me. I can appear to him in many forms, but most importantly, he finds Me at his very center. He has serious struggles with his left-brain Dark-side, but our connection is never broken, and the Love-light always prevails."

The 'Great I Am' is reliving the moment in silence. I say nothing.

CHAPTER 7
Unraveling Hate's Web

Suddenly, I become aware that the 'Great I Am' wants me to get down to business. Of course, I have a web to unravel, which Angra Mainyu and the Dragon Lady created.

I quickly emerge from my meditation and find myself on my front steps. I walk in and head for my tablet, activating it. Skype is loaded and running. I scroll down and click on Dick's name.

After three boops, Abby picks up with video. As my cursor moves toward the video button, I turn into Hayah.

Abby is beaming, "Hello, Hayah, I was hoping you would call. It seems we have run into a sticky-wicket."

"Not in your beautiful Love relationship, I hope!"

"No!" Abby laughs in a barely audible breathy tone, "So you know about that."

"Only that the 'Great I Am' says it is the best without telling me the details."

"The BEST doesn't begin to describe it! Every day we grow closer to each other. I learn more about myself and Dick, and the same with Dick. For the first time in our lives, we know we have something permanent."

"When we have time, I really want to hear all about it. Right now, we have to fix a problem."

"I know. Dick is sliding into a funk. He has no idea what is going on. If you can wait a minute, I'll get him." She gets up and leaves the room.

The video camera is still on, and I can see a large print of an old elephant with tusks that are one-and-a-half meters long. The expression in its eyes is sheer joy as it poses for the photographer, Dick. The animals really do love him; as he loves them.

Abby and Dick return and pull up a second chair. Dick adjusts the camera to zoom out for the twofer shot. I can see that Dick is not a happy camper.

When he is done adjusting the camera, he looks at me and says, "I'm glad you called buddy and hope you know what is going on. This attack is a first for me; I feel wounded. Abby's love is the only thing holding me together. And the 'Great I Am' says you will call and explain, so explain away and don't gild the lily."

I start slowly, "This is difficult for me to explain, because it's my first time explaining it to someone else, so bear with me. This may be hard for the two of you, because you both have been on the peak of your life. Your connection to the 'Great I Am' is perfect, and the connection to each other is perfect. Fortunately, that is now a constant for eternity.

"Unfortunately, there is a downside, which can't change the connections you have, but it can make your life damn difficult. You are both aware that there is a left-brain Dark-side at work in the human mind and know how to shut down your left-brain chattering mind. What you don't know is that the dark left-brain chatter is something more than an abstract 'pain-body'. It is a real entity, a dev, at work in the human mind, trying to push us to our Dark-side. Fortunately, they have no power over us. The dev's scary show is only an allusion. Many good people, like yourselves, control them and live in the Love-light. When you're connected, you simply blow them a kiss of Love and poof they vanish. However, there are many people being controlled by their left-brain dev and living in their Dark-side. These people are manipulating and trashing your work. But the devs driving them are minor entities.

"I'll give you the condensed version. At the top of the hierarchy is the woman I call the 'Dragon Lady' or Hate, who is The Love from the beginning of creation. The Love made us. You feel The Love between each other. But The Love walked away from that Love, became Hate, who wanted to create solo and couldn't. The only thing Hate had to give, was given to Eve and Adam, and that was a 'irrational mind and ego'. Through those 'gifts', Hate has influence over humanity since the beginning of the human downfall. It is the downfall of Hate and the downfall of humanity. It is the creation of the Dark-side in us all.

"Hate's accomplice is Angra Mainyu, which literally means 'destructive mind and ego', or 'destroyer'. He goes by different names in every culture. His workers are the 'devs', which are the Dark-spirits from the downfall. I am sure that they are real experiences for you. In the last few days, you faced Angra Mainyu, with all his slimy tricks and deception.

"That's the condensed version. I know it must be difficult and frightening for you to hear all this. It was for me the first time I faced the Dragon Lady. But when I opened my arms and poured out the Love-light the Hate vanished in a blink of an eye. Before we get into the details of what they did, what is your reaction?"

Abby is the first to chime in, as she looks at Dick, "I feel I'm speaking for both of us when I say that this is basically what we expected. But we didn't know who the entities were. What do we call them?"

"They would like you to believe they have real power, but they don't. Call them by name. That diminishes a great deal of the hold they have over you and diminishes your fear of them. I call the Dragon Lady, 'my Lady', because of who The Love was in the beginning, and our goal is to bring The Love back to the 'Great I Am' because The Love is the second piece of the three in creation."

Abby asks, "Is that why 'I Am' doesn't destroy

evil?"

"Bingo!" I say smiling from ear to ear. "Angra Mainyu doesn't deserve a nickname and he will forever reign over the world of Darkness and constant torment."

Dick looks better, but there is concern written all over his face. He says, "My big concern here is what power is the 'I Am' going to give us to fight them off? This is the war between Good and Evil! Isn't it?"

"The war between Good and Evil is a left-brain myth created by the irrational mind and ego, and the Dragon Lady has used it to pit humanity against humanity since the creation of Adam and Eve. In every war each side considers the enemy evil and themselves good. When one side wins, the peace never lasts long and a new pseudo evil enemy emerges, while the real evil is lurking beneath the surface. All war is fueled by human hatred, lust for power and greed, which are part of the left-brain irrational mind and ego of every humans' Dark-side, the two gifts from the Dragon Lady in the beginning.

"There is no cosmic conflict. All in creation is in harmony: light and darkness; birth and death; up and down. There is only Love-light in the 'Great I Am'. When 1% of the people connect to the 'I Am', the crystal city will emerge, and the Dark-side of the left-brain irrational mind and ego will be left to destroy itself.

"As for the power, you already have it. The Love-light **is** the greatest power. If they attack you, connect with the 'I Am' in your center and pour out the Love-light on the attacker, and they will flee in a flash. Remember, as long as you are connected, you are protected."

Dick is smiling now, "Wow, this gets better and better. OK, I can feel that you have something else."

"Yes, I do. We have intelligence on them, and they have nothing on us."

"What?!" They both say at the same time.

"Right! Last night I visited them as a rat inside the walls of their mansion and learned everything they have done. All we have to do is unravel the mess. But it's a P-r-e-t-t-y BIG Mess."

Abby is shocked, "You're not kidding! Are You?"

"I would like to get shots of that the next time," Dick adds. "Maybe, I can invent a rat-cam and go with you the next time." His laughter removes the remaining stress.

We all share in the humor for a moment and then return to the serious business of unraveling the mess.

CHAPTER 8
The BIG Mess

I consider for a moment where to begin. "Let me start with what Angra Mainyu did, or I should say, what his devs did, because he has some devs running some well-placed people at NGM. One is in the editing room. The other is on the legal staff."

Dick responds, "I don't know the people on the legal staff, and the only person I trust with my footage in the editing room is Dudley. No way is a dev running him. I have had a good working relationship with him for years, and he's a really nice guy. I'll have to see if anyone else has worked on my stuff."

"Ask the 'Great I Am' if Dudley did the editing."

Abby joins in, "The 'I Am' is giving me the name of the woman in legal, who is handling the case. Her name is Lilly. I'll see what I can find out about her."

"Oh boy, the 'I Am' is telling me that Dudley is blocking Him, or the dev running him is doing the blocking. Woe, this is scary. I thought I could trust him." Dick is growing angry, "I'm going down there and have it out with him."

"Slow down Dick. The devs feed on anger. Anger is a great emotional release valve to let loose of resentment as long as it doesn't lead to wrath, violence and hatred. Confrontation will gain you nothing and let them know we are on to them. We should channel your anger energy into a positive action plan."

Dick is calming down, "Now, I know why you are always so cool in crisis moments. I have to keep telling myself; Love is my weapon; Love is my tool."

Abby asks, "Do you know what we should be looking for and what we should do when we find it?"

"Let's figure that out," I say. "Dick, do you have a list of the prints you turned over to Dudley, and did you Photoshop any of them?"

"First of all, the pictures are all digital. There are no prints. I have a separate file with all the images I selected, so that would be the same as a list. Regarding Photoshop, I never Photoshop any of my pictures. If the image isn't perfect, I don't use it."

"Excellent! That makes it easy. Make hard copy prints of everything you sent. Then you can put them side by side, to what they have. You will then be able to pick out the alterations in two seconds and prove your case."

Abby makes a note for Dick.

"Next, did you create a story board and edit the raw video footage yourself?"

Dick responds confidently, "Yes, I always story board any event so it is an accurate representation of what happened. I then select the raw footage to tell the story with the best visual images I have."

I continue, "Did you touch up or manipulate any of the frames in the final footage?"

"I never do, and I never will. That's why my stuff wins awards."

"Perfect, make sure to back up your computer and protect your data. Do you have a safety-deposit box?"

Abby is still making notes for Dick. She responds, "We backup everything and keep it in our safe."

"That's too easy to crack and a thief will know what to look for. A safety-deposit box is a little more secure if you keep the number and key hidden."

Dick says, "We'll do it. And I have the perfect secret hiding place."

"Now, let me tell you what they have done, if you haven't figured that out already." I continue, "They have Photoshopped all your images, so they tell a totally different story. They have re-edited the video footage, so it tells the opposite story. What they show now is mad angry elephants attacking innocent soldiers and destroying them. It shows me willfully injuring baby mountain gorillas and cutting off a young gorillas' leg. It shows a Rhino rushing and goring an innocent rancher. It shows tigers attacking innocent villagers and forest workers. They are rewriting the articles to attack wildlife conservation and promote the legal right to hunt the animals to extinction and harvest their body parts."

Dick cries out, "Stop, we have to do something!"

Abby asks calmly, "How do we confront the perpetrators and NGM?"

"Let's talk about that. A confrontation would be a full-frontal assault, and I'm sure that is exactly what Angra Mainyu is expecting. Yes, it is winnable because you have everything to disprove the lie. However, with the legal department involved, we will need a lawyer. Now you are talking years to settle, and that is a win for the Dragon Lady even if NGM has to pay you in the end."

"So, what other choices do we have?" Abby asks.

"Let's look at choice B. Dick, what stuff did you send to James?"

"The same stuff I sent to NGM."

I ask, "Did you sign any kind of contract with NGM on this job, or get an advance or expenses?"

"No, this was strictly freelance and out of pocket."

"Great!" I continue, "Are you prepared to walk away from getting any money out of NGM?"

Abby and Dick look at each other and both answer at the same time, "Yes! What's important is the truth gets out." They look at each other and laugh.

"Well, this is choice B. I haven't spoken to James today, but I'm already getting great messages. James has presented your pictures and videos to one of his large classes. The students' first reaction is wonder and disbelief. Their second reaction is awe, and they hope that it is true. Their third reaction is excitement and a desire to investigate. His class wants to meet us. When I call, we will get the invitation."

Dick's shyness speaks up, "You know I'm not good at public speaking!"

"I know, but you are excellent at Q&A. Your pictures can give the students millions of words. I'll do the speaking and we can field the Q&A together.

"If I'm reading this situation correctly, just one of these students could send this message viral in less than a minute. Before the day is out the press will be all over us. By morning, You Tube will be climbing the walls to get your videos. All the real footage will be out there, and the bosses of NGM will see the lies in the stuff they have, and heads will roll. You get all that without confronting anybody. And it will all happen so fast, Angra Mainyu won't know what hit him."

Dick says, "I once heard you tell the 'Great I Am', "You never do anything in a small way. Well, brother, you are a lot like the 'I Am'."

Abby asks, "Does this mean I get to come along?"

I respond, "Of course, we can't do it without you. You are two peas in the same pod."

On this joyous note, we say our goodbyes and press the red button.

CHAPTER 9
The Young People

I scroll down and tap on James' name. His window opens and I hear the 'boop-boopidy-boo'; then the boop and bubble begin. After many boops, James finally accepts the call, without video.

"Hi, Hayah, 'I Am' told me you were going to call and filled you in on the class. As you know, the response of the class was fantastic. The 'I Am' also explained how Angra Mainyu altered the originals. I was wondering when he was going to show up. You don't need to explain because he has already attacked me six times in my life. Only now, I have the tool to fight back. Have you seen any of the altered pictures or video footage?"

"No, I haven't. But from Angra Mainyu's description, the message is reversed to support his agenda."

"Oh boy. Is it true you snuck in on him as a rat?"

I laugh, "That will raise some eyebrows. Yes, I did."

James explains, "As a kid, I had an aversion and deep fear of rats, after a friend of mine told me that his baby brother almost had his arm chewed off by a rat. A month later, he invited me over to see the rats. I was really scared, but I went anyway. He took me into his bedroom, which was also the baby's room, to watch for the rat. There was so much trash and garbage in his room; it was no wonder that a rat would come in to eat it. I then looked in the crib to see the injured baby. There was only a single bite on his arm. I turned to my friend and said, 'You do know that it is all your trash and garbage attracting the rats, don't you?' After that, we cleaned up the room, and he never saw the rat again. Fortunately, it gave me a profound respect for rats."

"That's a delightful story. They are just part of nature's balancing of our ecosystem."

"Precisely," says James.

"I see why you're so popular with your students."

"Speaking of students, can Abby, Dick and you come to my class on Thursday, the day after tomorrow?"

"Yes, I've been speaking to Abby and Dick and their eager to come as well. What approach should we take in talking with them?"

I can feel that James is anxious to say what he has to say. "Let me give you my take on what happened in this morning's class. Over 95% of the students are shutting themselves off from anything that remotely resembles a religious ideology of any kind; so, I presented the pictures and video footage as part of a conservation action to save the endangered species. That captured the attention of everyone in the class. I didn't mention the 'Great I Am', or meditation, or connecting with their inner Being. I simply asked them to look at the pictures and footage and tell me what they saw. I assured them, the pictures and footage were authentic, without special effects, or CG animation and untouched. Since there is no soundtrack on the video, I was concerned that they would lose interest quickly. Instead, after the first three minutes, they started commenting on what they saw, and their interactions became the soundtrack. Without me saying anything, they suspended their own disbelief and began to realize they were watching a miracle. When they saw Abby learning and developing the power, they fell in love with her. You, they saw as the invincible superhero. You were not human; you couldn't be. After the showing, they wanted to know who the photographer is. I told them Dick from NGM and they flipped out. I had no idea his name was a household word. I became brazen as brass and told them I would invite Abby, Dick and you for Thursday's class. I asked them to continue the discussion of the pictures and footage and be prepared to make suggestions for a presentation. I suspect the lecture hall will be packed.

"Can you deal with all that?"

I'm a bit overwhelmed, "I can manage everything but the part about not being human."

"When you meet that will take care of itself... I hope."

"Me too. Fantastic job James. This is the perfect way to reach kids. Humm, I need to see them as young adults."

James laughs, "That would help."

CHAPTER 10
Awakening

Dick, Abby and I met at James' office a half hour before the lecture. When I arrive, James is completing his briefing on Tuesday's class with Abby and Dick. Dick is so excited about Abby's recognition; it is very touching. He suggests that we let Abby go first in our presentation. I agree whole-heartedly.

I then mention our major problem, "How can we explain to the students our connection to the 'Great I Am' within us? This is what the 'I Am' and I concluded, and we need your input, James. Following your biological approach on Tuesday, we can focus on DNA awareness; the one sense shared by all things. We can start with a tiny celery seed and work our way up to humans."

James agrees, "I like that. It is in keeping with what most of them are studying."

Abby lights up, "That's right down my alley. Wow, I finally get to use all that stuff I crammed into my head."

Dick is concerned, "What about me. I'm a photographer, not a scientist."

"We already discussed your approach, Dick." I reassured him, "Your point of view is incredibly special. You see and study the behavior of everything, from a plant to an elephant. Listen to the 'I Am' and be guided through it."

"You're right," Dick says confidently.

James asks Dick, "Would you like to make your pictures and video footage available to the students? I can post them to my website, and you can announce the link in the class. That way the students can share them with friends if you like."

Dick looks at me, "This is what you meant." I

nod my head, yes. He turns to James, "Do it! They need to go out, ASAP. Write down the link for me."

The lecture hall is in one of the old Harvard buildings. It is much bigger than I imagined, with seating for over 250 people. The seats tier sharply above the lecture floor containing a table and podium. The large screen is on the front wall. We all stand in awe as a steady stream of people file in and take their seats. The hall is already over half full. James places a reserved sign on three of the front and center seats. He then scans the audience for his students and acknowledges them. A security guard comes down and speaks to him and then leaves, checking the exit lights at all the doors as he leaves.

We huddle for a brief moment in front of the table. I ask, "Is everyone centered and connected?" Everyone answers, with a yes. Then beneath the murmur of the gathering crowd, we all hear 'I Am's voice, "Yes." We all break out laughing at the same time. James gestures for us to take our seats in the front row, and we go and sit down, with Abby in the middle. Dick sits for only a minute, takes out his camera and starts to take pictures of James. A minute later, he is on his feet and moving around taking pictures of the audience. Now he is totally relaxed.

Abby and I look at each other. She says, "You got to Love him!" As she says this, Dick takes a shot of Abby and smiles as though he heard what she said.

A techie comes down and puts a mic on each of us. After putting a mic on James, he goes back to his booth. James starts to quiet down the audience, which is no easy task. On the hour he starts.

"Welcome everyone, students and guests. I must confess; I'm not accustomed to having one hundred percent of my class in attendance, not to mention so many guests. For those standing at the rail, there are

three seats down here." He points them out. "Two
seats over here, and one seat in the middle of these
friendly folks.

"Security wants me to remind you of where the
exit doors are located." He gestures in the direction
of each one. "Now, if you will all please fasten your
seatbelts, we will blast off to the unknown planet."
There is a chuckle that rolls through the audience.

"This is a class on 'Endangered Species and
Wildlife Habitats'. Tuesday, we viewed some
unpublished pictures and videos from an event I
attended last week. To summarize what we saw, I
put together a slideshow of 1000 pictures, which will
last ten minutes. It is only fair that I warn you; every
time you blink, you will miss one slide. After the
slideshow, we will start the discussion."

James gestures to the projection booth. The
lights dim and the slideshow begins. Within five
seconds, there is absolute silence and stillness in the
auditorium. The heart rate and breathing of the
audience quicken to the pace of the slideshow. Three
minutes in, the 'Great I Am' starts to tell us what they
are feeling. "They are wondering how the
'boomerang effect' is working. Where does Hayah get
his healing power? If Rhinos can get past their
anger, why can't humans? In the Abby class, did she
really find the power so quickly? Why are the
habitats so important?" The slideshow ends, and
James waits until he hears movement before starting.

"Those images should give us a place to start our
discussion. Now, I give you Abby the newest member
of the team." The audience applauds vigorously.
James stays on the lecture floor to field the
questions.

Abby comes forward and stands in the center of
the lecture floor. She is radiant and unprepared for
the positive reception. She thanks them repeatedly.
The applause continues. She gestures for them to

quiet down. The applause continues. She looks at James, and he shrugs his shoulders. As Abby is about to give up and sit down, she hears 'I Am's voice inside her, "They are truly overjoyed with your being here. To gain control, get your first question and start to speak in a low calm voice, so they have to be quiet to hear you."

James calls for the first question. Only a person in the front row can hear him. She asks, "Where does your superpower come from?" No one can hear the question. The 'Great I Am' repeats the question for James and Abby, "Where does your superpower come from?"

Abby begins to speak in a low calm voice, "It is not really a superpower. It exists within everything. It is part of the DNA in everything." Before she says the word DNA, you can hear a pin drop in the lecture hall. She repeats the question, "Where does my superpower come from? It is not a superpower. It is in the DNA of everything. As humans we are overpowered by our left-brain irrational minds and ego. Because we think with the left-brain, we think, we assume we are superior to all other things. Our ego calls it higher intelligence. When in reality it is neither higher nor intelligent. It is left-brain chatter. Consider a tiny celery seed. It is smaller than a pinhead.

"Does it have a brain? No. Does it have intelligence? Yes. In its DNA it is aware of what it is. It is aware of what it will be. It is aware of how it will become what it is to be. It is aware of how to make more celery seeds. I can see what you are thinking, 'We know how to make more humans!' And we can all laugh together. But who are you? What is the purpose of your life? How will you become that person? Wow, you just scored 25% on your intelligence test. You know how to make more humans. It's no wonder we have a population problem. In academia, what is a score of 25%? A score of 50% would be failing. Meanwhile, every animal on the planet knows more than we do, as does every plant and every stone. Yet we destroy everything else with our stupidity.

"My power comes from listening to my DNA awareness. I'm right-brain aware of myself. I'm aware of the purpose of my life. I'm aware of how to attain that purpose. I'm aware of the Love-light in all procreation.

"You can call that a superpower if you want. But you can have the power just as easily as I can."

The audience applauds her as she returns to her seat. Dick and I come up to the table and stand in front of it. James calls for the next question. A young man in the back row speaks up, "Dick, what are you doing that makes your pictures and videos so much better than anyone else?"

Dick timidly takes a step forward and snaps a picture of the young man in the back row. I sit on the edge of the table. With his camera in one hand, he begins to explain. "As my charming wife says, the secret is in listening to our DNA awareness and the DNA awareness of everything else. You can learn about photography, composition, and light. But, to me a picture is much more. I connect with my subjects and study their behavior. Let me continue with my wife's analogy, only with a flower. The flower's blossom is full and ready to open. It is hanging on the curved stem with its head hung down. The heavy due is beading on it leaves. Right now, the sun is hiding behind a cloud, which will move off in a few minutes. I position myself so the sun will be over my shoulder. I frame and focus on the flower, and I wait. The cloud moves off, and I wait. The sun shines on the flower, and I wait. Sun is glistening in the due drops, but I wait. Slowly the flower lifts its head and turns its leaves to the sun, but I wait. Then very subtly, the flower takes a breath, click. That breath captures everything the flower is and its joy of life. The picture captures that moment, and everyone wonders why it looks so different from all the other pictures of the same flower."

He looks up to the young man who asked the question, "Just as the picture I just took of you will show you at your best, because you were filled with confidence and pride for asking such a good question. I'm glad to send it to you through James."

James picks out a young woman on the right side of the audience. She asks, "Dick, in your video of the military assault on the elephants it appears that the bullets are bouncing off the elephants and flying back to kill the soldiers. How is that possible without CG animation?"

Dick looks at me and then turns back to the young woman, "Miss, the full experience of what we call the 'boomerang effect' is best seen in the uncut video. I'm pleased to make all the pictures and video footage available to everyone here." Dick then reads out the web address twice. He continues, "Hayah is the best person to answer what you see technically but let me describe it in more general terms. The 'boomerang effect' has existed for thousands of years. History proves, if we do a destructive or stupid thing to our planet, we will pay for it in the end. My favorite example happened in Chicago on Lake Michigan, and I have pictures of this. One year they had a major Alewives problem, with millions of the small fish washing up on the beaches. It caused major pollution and sanitation problems, as well as closing down the beaches. Some brilliant marine biologist introduced the clever idea of introducing Coho Salmon into the Lake, which would feed on the Alewives. For two years it appeared to have solved the problem. Three years later, Chicago was having problems pumping in their water from the Lake. The divers discovered barnacles growing on the water intake screens off the shore. The cost of the constant removal of the barnacles was ten times greater than the cost of the Alewives removal. Oopps, it was the Alewives that were eating the barnacles and keeping the screens clean. Yes, it looks like we are ooppsing ourselves right out of existence.

"I'll turn it over to Hayah to explain what is happening with the elephants."

I step forward as Dick takes up his camera again. "The boomerang effect is an extension of Newton's law of motion; 'for every action, there is an equal and opposite reaction.' If there is a protective shield around an animal or person, any act of violence against them will bounce off the shield and travel back on the same path with equal velocity to the perpetrator. Thus, the perpetrator is destroying his or herself."

James recognizes another plain looking woman, with dark-rimmed glasses. She asks, "Are you the one giving this protective shield to the animals and your team?"

"The direct answer to your question is no," I state bluntly. "My role here is limited. I'll start with the animals, which are already aware of and connected to their inner Being, the scientifically uninteresting part of their DNA. They are also free of hatred. With those two qualities, they have the shield and are protected. As Abby so beautifully pointed out, most humans are unaware and don't have a clue about connecting with anything but their irrational left-brain mind and ego, and only a few are free of hatred. My role here is to help my team and others to be aware of and to make that connection."

The woman with the dark-rimmed glasses wants to ask a follow-up question. "What is the 'uninteresting part of DNA' of which I'm supposed to be aware?"

"Let me ask you a question, what makes up 95% of any DNA chain and molecule?"

She responds quickly, "Space."

"And what is in that Space?"

"Nothing!"

I continue, "Most scientists would consider that pretty uninteresting. But what if I told you there is something in that space."

"What?" she asks.

"When you or anyone else here is ready, Dr. James will help you become aware of what is there."

The 'Great I Am' cuts in and the four of us here loud and clear, "I Am checking everyone. There are a few that are close, and some are blocking me completely. The young man behind you, Abby, over your left shoulder, is a major question mark."

The woman presses the issue, "I'm ready."

The man behind Abby starts to sing.

> Gat-a-tat, Tat, Tat
> Six specks on a zat
> My mind is supreme overall.
> My ego makes me ten feet tall.
> Anger and hate shall always reign.
> Nothing tastes better than disdain.
> A lie and deceit
> Are oh so sweet.
> Maiming and killing
> Are oh so thrilling.
> Pure joy I get from causing pain.
> To take a life my greatest gain.
> Gat-a-tat, Tat, Tat

Instantly, the 'I Am' says, "That's a dev rhyme. Get ready!"

We immediately go into 'slow-motion perception'. (This is a natural state, which a rescuer experiences in a crisis. They feel like everything around them is in slow-motion, while their speed is normal. To the victim it is the opposite, where their speed is normal, and the rescuer's is a blur. We use this to our advantage.)

The young man starts his chant again.

> *Gat-a-tat, Tat, Tat*
> *Six specks on a zat*
> *My mind is supreme overall.*
> *My ego makes me ten feet tall.*

I step toward the young man and glance at Abby.

> *Anger and hate shall always reign.*
> *Nothing tastes better than disdain.*
> *A lie and deceit*
> *Are oh so sweet.*
> *Maiming and killing*
> *Are oh so thrilling.*

The young man pulls out a gun and points it at Abby's head. Three people scream, "GUN!" People franticly move back. James pushes the security button.

> *Pure joy I get from causing pain.*
> *To take a life my greatest gain.*
> *Gat-a-tat, Tat, Tat*

I take another slow step closer to the young man.

He screams at me, "Take one more step and I'll blow her head off!"

I stand still, "Look Timmy, don't do this. You can shut down the chattering dev in your head."

He screams again, "I don't want to!" Timmy shouts. "He gives me power! He makes me feel important! He's the best computer game I ever played."

"Oh? I know him. His name is Wormwood. He has no power. He is playing with your rational mind and ego."

Wormwood lies, using Timmy's voice, "I don't know you." He laughs maniacally, "And now you're going to tell me if I pull this trigger, I'll be blowing my own brains out. Well, daaaaaa, I'll be blowing Timmy's brains out." His maniacal laugh is out of control. Timmy grins.

While he is speaking, I take advantage of the slow-motion perception. I move quickly to him in a blur and back to my place. I start to laugh at him, "Wormwood, is this what you're going to blow Timmy's brains out with?" I hold up the gun by the barrel, hanging between two fingers, and walk it over to the security guard.

Timmy looks at his empty hand and screams, "How did you do that!"

I walk back to stand in front of Timmy. Abby stands and James comes forward. Dick films the incident. I reach out my hand toward Timmy's chest saying, "Wormwood, here is the Love-light." I blow him a kiss. Instantly, Wormwood flies out and up into a large lecture hall light.

Wormwood screams, "TAT, TAT, TAT..."

The light sputters and spits sparks as he enters it. Then it explodes.

Timmy is looking at us with hatred in his eyes, "You stupid people. He is the best thing that ever happened to me. I have not lost a computer game tournament since he came to help me. You have no idea what you have done. I enjoy the Dark-side and the dark arts. I want to feel the thrill of the kill." He spits in my face, but it bounces back on his face. His expression changes to one of shock.

The security guard comes over, cuffs him and drags Timmy out struggling and screaming obscenities.

Abby and I sit down, and James motions for the audience to sit. After a moment, the young woman, with the dark-rimmed glasses stands and says loudly, "Sir, Sir, Sir?" Everyone looks up at her.

She says, "Sir, on second thought, I'm not ready." The audience laughs, releasing their tension.

That evening, everyone present downloads Dick's pictures and video footage. Within hours, they go viral, with over ten million hits worldwide.

CHAPTER 11
Connecting Tree, Prophets

The next morning, I start my journey to Israel. I will have a layover in London for a day or so. This will give me a chance to meet a certain someone. Then I'll go on to Tel Aviv-Yafo. As soon as the plain is airborne, 'I Am' continues to describe 'The Connecting Tree'.

The 'Great I Am' starts with Samuel, "My connection with Samuel is a natural one. From his early boyhood, we are two words in the same sentence. He openly embraces My purpose for him and never considers anything else. I often feel that his connection with Me is everything that Adam and Eve's could have been. His Dark-side is shut down completely. Yet he becomes an expert at dealing with the Dark-side in others, especially as a Judge. As a Prophet, he speaks only my words. He is the first to listen carefully to Me so I can communicate to him what others are thinking before they act. This makes him valuable to David.

"As Elijah grows into manhood, he spends most of his time out in nature. It is the animals, plants and rivers that bring him to Me. First, he becomes one with them; then he becomes aware of My presence within them. On his own, he learns their languages and begins communicating with them. All of nature embraces him as they did Adam and Eve in the beginning. Slowly they draw him away from his left-brain brain chatter and into a state of oneness. There he finds boundless joy free from the human murder and mayhem of those times.

"That night, as all nature is singing Elijah asleep, he slowly slides into what he experiences as a dark pool of water. He finds it warm and calming. Then he sees My Light glistening beneath the water. He swims toward the Light and dives down to see what it is. We connect, and as natural as a sunrise we become one.

"Because of his communion with nature, no drought can leave him hungry or thirsty. Together, we work many miracles. When the widow's son stops breathing, he takes him to his cot and asks, 'O.K. Lord what do I do now?' I have him put his hand on the boy's upper abdomen, and I fill the boy with My Light. Then I tell Elijah to push down hard. He does and the air rushes out of the boy's mouth. Then all by itself, the boy's body takes a breath.

"During our struggle with the false Baal prophets, he sets up a sacrifice on the altar. They can't light the fire. But he dowses the altar with water three times and says to Me in a light tone, 'I did as you asked. Now it is your turn to reveal yourself to these people. However, it is beyond me why you want to give them a second chance.' Like nature, he doesn't want to give humans a second chance.

"My connection with Isaiah gives Me a unique insight into the workings of the human mind. Our connection is deep and personal from the start. He examines everything I give him, and I react. Before I can say anything, he senses My reaction and explains, 'Every Prophet must examine the validity of his or her vision. The human left-brain mind is a trickster and can hide the true images of you, The Holly.'

"He takes the false image of Me as the unseen 'I Am' on the mountain and turns it into a powerful metaphor. He says, 'The Mountain is within you. You are 'I Am's House. The choice is clear; I know

You are alive within me, and not a learned knowledge of You.' Isaiah once tells the High Priest of Israel, 'If you want to build a monument to The Holly, then connect to the 'I Am' and let your life be that monument.'

"Isaiah shows Me his Darkest-side and reveals the arduous process of shutting down his hatred and wrath to move back to My Love-light. His pain nearly breaks My heart, but his love for his people fills My heart with joy.

"Hosea connects with Me and accepts My purpose for him to turn his whole life into a metaphor of Israel's broken relationship to Me and their misuse of My Love.

"What is a Love relationship with Me or another? My Love is everlasting, an eternal bond between all things. It is the bases of My connection with everything. I want everything, everyone, to feel the Love-light within and connect with Me just like all Nature is doing. Adam and Eve experienced the bond of this Love in their daily life and all their lovemaking but the Dragon Lady made them walk away from it.

"Except for precious few, humans are the whores in the Hosea metaphor. Sex without Love is nothing but a brief erotic pleasure, a moment of passion, a spent desire without fulfillment, a lie the Irrational Mind calls love. It is sexual lust when people turn sex into a religion, or religion into the passionate worship of idols, greed, power or an unseen God; they are all whores and disconnected from My Love-light.

"I Am, the 'Great I Am', within everything. Everything you need is to be found in Me. 'I Am' your essence of being! I warn My Hebrew people, wake up and please do not turn your backs on Me again.

"Hosea wants you to choose to walk the path of My purpose for you, and you will get where you want to go. He says, 'Right-living people will walk their path easily; wrong-living people are always tripping and stumbling.'

"My Prophet Jeremiah is able to connect with Me against all odds. He is both able to fight off his active Dark-side in a Dark-Time, and deal with the collective left-brain Dark-side of most people working against him. He achieves the impossible; he connects with Me and positively fulfills My purpose for him.

"He confronts My Hebrew people with their sex-and-religion, calling them experts at chasing the left-brain Dark-side. He points out that they are not looking for Me or listening for My voice within. Plus, he coins the perfect phrase to describe their 'unseen god' by calling it a 'sky-god'.

"Jeremiah creates the perfect image to describe Me within all things. He calls Me, 'the straw to the wheat'. I Am the straw within you that holds you up. I Am the straw that feeds you. I Am the straw that connects you to the earth. The straw and the wheat are one. I Am one within everything.

"To him, I Am Love. Connect with Me and you can expect Love, Love and more Love. I want you to know Me firsthand. Left-brain knowledge of Me is empty and easily corrupted.

"As you know Hoss, Jeremiah calls the 'Dragon Lady' the 'Queen of Heaven' and her manipulation of the human left-brain mind is with 'goddess cookies'.

"I assured you, My boomerang-effect will always occur:

> 'The Dark-side produces its own destruction.'
> 'Hatred poisons the one who hates.'
> 'Greed impoverishes the one who

desires too much.'
'Power corrupts the one who seeks it or
has it.'
'Violence kills the one who holds the
sword.'

"My connection with Ezekiel is more than a presence within him. Ezekiel sees My presence at work in the Babylonian catastrophe. He sees My presence in others, whether they're connected to Me or not. He works to help people connect to Me, or at least feel My presence within.

"Ezekiel is more than a man of visions. When I tell him to 'Eat this book', he takes every Word inside him and digests it. While others study it to gain an understanding, he experiences the Word and makes it part of who he is.

"To him, 'I Am' a blazing presence. He listens. He sees. He experiences the 'Endtime'. The 'Endtime' is more than an apocalyptic event. It is the turning point when the human left-brain Irrational Mind recognizes its own Dark-side. It is the moment you first say NO to the left-brain Dark-side and positively turn toward the Love-Light. After this 'Endtime', every day that you can say no to the left-brain Irrational Mind's Dark-side, it becomes easier and easier, because 'I Am' here to help you. The 'Endtime' is not about death; it is about a new Life with Me within you.

"To Ezekiel, 'I Am' here; 'I Am' now; 'I Am' within. Yes, I call him 'Son of man'. He is that close to My heart. He is My watchman.

"The only difficulty Ezekiel has is confronting Israel and Judah with their obscenities. When he gets going, he quotes Me word for word without making Me a monster.

"Finally, I tire of the corrupt leadership in the

Middle East and make Ezekiel My voice against
them. I declare, 'The Land is My Land! Forever!'
Why are the American Indians the only ones to
remain faithful to that decree?"

Again, the 'Great I Am' becomes silent. I can feel
a sadness growing in the 'I Am'. Then I realize that
the reason for 'I Am's sadness will not be spoken.
This is a book about 'Finding the Love-light', and this
list is 'The Connecting Tree'. You'll have to read
between the lines.

CHAPTER 12
Connecting Tree Blooms

The 'Great I Am' is quiet within me. I feel the Love-light, but the 'I Am' says nothing.

Finally, the 'Great I Am' opens up, "Hoss, I know you can sympathize with the difficulties which followed My last summary of the Connecting Tree. Unfortunately, after Ezekiel very few are listening, and no one is connecting. The left-brain human 'Irrational Mind and Ego' are being dominated by the Dark-side. A feeling of deep sadness begins to overtake Me. I wonder; what can I do?

"Krishna's Spirit is the first to sense My despair, and he fears another Great Flood or something worse. He says, 'Light of my Life, may I be so bold as to suggest something?'

"I smile at his radiant presence, 'Yes, of course.'

"He lets out a deep sigh and begins to explain, 'There is a young man who is now discovering my message in the VEDAS and UPANISHADS. He is on a serious search to find the Love-light and You.'

"I ask, 'Are you referring to Siddhartha Gautama?'

"He replies, 'Yes, do you know him?'

"I laugh, 'Of course, I know him. Would you like to give him a few nudges in the right direction?' The idea was making Me feel better, so I added, 'He has real potential. If anyone can break through his Dark-side, it will be him. He won't give up.'

"Krishna lights up with enthusiasm, 'I'll get right on it!'

"Krishna has many setbacks. Siddhartha starts in many false directions, like the desire to attain a higher intelligence. But Krishna brings him back. Finally, Siddhartha finds the 'Middle Way' and begins to focus on meditation. First, he shuts down his chattering rational mind and ego in his Dark-side. Next, he starts to feed his body, where he finds his inner blackness, which he calls Nirvana. In that state, he rejoices in his success at reaching his goal. However, he cannot see my Love-light and is unaware of My presence.

"Krishna presses him on. Siddhartha goes deeper within himself. Finally, after 49 days of continuous meditation, he embraces the black emptiness, becomes aware of My Light and cautiously approaches. He hesitates and then reaches out to take the speck of light in his hand. As he opens his closed hand, he sees a lotus flower with a glowing center. Suddenly he goes into the glowing center and becomes part of Me. I fill him with My Love-light and we meet for the first time. Krishna embraces him.

"That is the beginning of my connection with Gautama Buddha, and he Awakens to My purpose for his life. He fills us all with hope."

The 'Great I Am' pauses in telling the story of the Connecting Tree. I sit in silence, looking out the plane window. I wonder why so few are connecting to the 'I Am'. I have no idea how long I was staring out into the black sky, but now I'm seeing land light below us.

The 'I Am' says, "That is enough for now. It should help you with the people you are going to meet in the Middle East and Israel. I hope something good comes out of your visit with Phyllis. I will be within you as always."

My daydreaming is on one track now.

CHAPTER 13
The Rendezvous

After collecting my backpack and going through customs, I emerge as Hayah through the security doors, expecting to see Phyllis. There is a crowd of people holding up name signs for those who are arriving. I scan the crowd and don't see Phyllis. I scan again hoping to find her. Only by chance do I notice a man holding a sign, which says, 'Hoss'. He is a tall good-looking man in his mid to late fifties. He has blond hair and deep brown eyes. He is wearing a black suit, starched white shirt and tie. He is sporting a chauffeur's hat, which is pushed back on his head. He is studying the arrivals carefully but does not notice me.

I carefully approach him, "Are you working for Phyllis?"

"Yes Sir," he answers curtly and looks me over from head to toe. He breaks a slight grin and shakes his head slightly. "Are you him? You're not much."

"I'm the one here to see Phyllis. Who are you?" I say, trying to be friendly.

He slides the hat on properly, "Excuse me Sir. I'm Argna, her chauffeur and man Friday. I thought you were older and taller. Can I take your... backpack?"

I'm 183 centimeters, but not as tall as this guy. I already have the backpack on. "No thank you. Where's Phyllis? I thought she was going to meet me."

He starts to walk toward the exit. "She is taking care of some last-minute details and arranging a very special reception and meal for you."

I fallow without saying anything.

We walk out the exit and across to an area where a line of limos is parked.

I look up at Argna and ask, "Are you sure we have the right Phyllis, who teaches at the university?"

Argna laughs, "That's her. She is independently wealthy and definitely a fine Lady."

I react on his use of the term Lady. "What do you mean Lady? Is she a royal?"

He takes on an air, but says, "Not in the British sense, but noble just the same. She is every inch a Lady."

I'm not sure what he means, but assume he has an extremely high opinion of her too, "That she is; that she is!"

He opens the left rear door of the limo. I take off my backpack and throw it in. I slap him on the back saying, "Thanks, my good man."

Then I open the left front door, get in and close the door. He stands there, still holding the rear door. He is shocked at my casualness, while expecting me to play along and put on airs. Slowly, he closes the rear door, walks around the front of the limo and gets in behind the wheel.

He glares at me for a moment and then starts the limo. He pulls out, saying nothing.

We weave through the streets in silence working our way East from the airport.

Finally, I break the silence, "Look, old chap, my family has spent several generations playing down our royal linage." His mouth falls open. "We prefer to be one of the people. In fact, royalty is a myth. There is no such thing as the Devine right of kings."

He stammers out, "You're a British royal?"

"Not anymore!" I quickly respond. "I'm just another Joe trying to navigate my way through this complicated world. It was never the 'Great I Am's intention to make any man or woman a king or queen. The 'I Am' has the same Love for everybody. Don't you agree?" I turn and look at him.

He turns away in silence, focusing on the road.

There is a distance in his eyes and a blank expression on his face.

I can't read it, and the 'Great I Am' within me is not giving me any help.

We sit in silence for several minutes. Then, I notice we are pulling into Fulham. I admire the beautiful old homes, "This sure is a beautiful area."

Argna does not respond.

I ask, "I hope I haven't offended you, old chap."

He says nothing.

We start to drive past Hurlingham Park, the polo field. To my surprise, we turn up a side street and immediately stop in front of an entrance to a large Victorian Mansion.

Argna gets out, and I get out. He opens the left rear door and I take out my backpack. We walk under a white canopy to the front door. He opens the door for me, and I step inside.

I admire the beautiful foyer and the winged staircase.

Argna says briskly, "Wait here; Phyllis will be down directly. I must go and put the car up."

Without another word, he turns and leaves.

I take off my backpack, set it down in front of me and continue to admire the architecture. I don't know how long I wait, but I turn 360° several times.

Finally, I hear a woman's footsteps on the gallery going around three-quarters of the upper level. I look up but can see no one. Then I see Phyllis at the head of the stairs. She slowly descended to the upper landing.

She is wearing a tight fitting, full-length gown. It is in purplish gray and black sections. The fabric is shimmering velvet with a swirling pattern of sparkling sequins or jewels that accents her figure in a star-like pattern. She looks fantastic. The gown is low cut and boldly reveals her cleavage. She is absolutely stunning.

As she pauses on the landing to descend one of the wing-like staircases, we make eye contact for the first time. Her eyes are sparkling and full of excitement. I can see her anticipation building in the depth of her eyes. They are already flirting with me.

Her face is glowing. Her smile is warm and inviting. Her expression has a quality I have never seen before. I'm drawn to it. I struggle to figure it out. The closer she gets the more alluring it becomes. It is a combination of joy, mystery, pleasure, romance and something else. What is it?

She seems to be floating down the stairs, with dance like movements. Every curve in her body teases my imagination. Every movement is seductive. I'm longing to hold her in my arms.

I start to move toward her.

Her pace quickens.

My heart is pounding. My stomach is in knots.

She opens her arms and flies into mine.

Our bodies come together in a passionate embrace.

Our kiss is deep and full of longing.

With our bodies pressed tightly together, our heads pull back and we stare into each other's eyes.

Her hair is glistening and exceptionally long, almost to her waist. It falls freely about her shoulders and down her back. My fingers play in it across her bare back.

She is the first to speak, "I miss you so much!"

"And I you," I say warmly. "You look so fantastic. You know, I'm falling in Love with you."

In a seductive voice, she says, "You have no idea how much I have been longing for this."

I look deep into her eyes and enjoy her beauty. Then suddenly I realize what it is. There is a naughty glimmer emerging from deep within her. Oh, it looks so sexy. I slowly break the moment, "We better cool this down or we won't get to that dinner you made."

"Oh, the dinner! I almost forgot." She pulls apart quickly, but I hold onto her hand. When her arm is at full length, she turns back.

I say, "I feel very under dressed for the occasion."

She laughs, "Not under dressed enough. Just take those off and come as you are."

"What?"

Her laughter is playful, "If you must, I laid out a change of clothes in your room. It is up the stairs to the right, down the hall and the sixth room on the left." She comes back and gives me a kiss. She starts to rush off; then she turns around walking backwards and pointing at a door in the corner of the room, "The dining room is through there." She disappears through a large door between the two stair wings.

I stand there for a moment holding on to the vision of her exit. "Wow, what a woman!" I say to myself.

I collect my backpack and head up to my room.

CHAPTER 14
Dinner for Two

My room is large and elegant, with a nice masculine touch. There are two large windows, with heavy fringed drapes. There is a round tile stove in the corner, with a shiny brass door. The furniture set includes a large inlaid walnut wardrobe, a dresser with an oval mirror over it, a large bed with a headboard and footboard as tall as me, two night-tables, two fiddle backed chairs and a standing full-length dressing mirror. The huge down pillow is as wide as the bed. The down comforter is 25 centimeters thick. The bed sheets and duvet-cover are a natural-colored extra-soft linen.

Laid out neatly on the bed is a sharply pressed tuxedo, a starched formal shirt, a pair of white braces, a purplish gray cummerbund and black socks. On the floor in front of the arrangement is a pair of black patent leather shoes. I turn and look at the dresser, and there sits the black bowtie and a pair of silver cufflinks.

I take off my travel clothes, shower and quickly dress. To my surprise, everything fits perfectly, including the shoes. Tying the bowtie takes a little fussing to get it perfect. When I finish, I put on the jacket and look at myself in the full-length mirror. Instead of admiring the look, I can't help thinking, "This is no longer me."

But it will give Phyllis joy, and I'm willing to do anything for her. I can feel my love for her swelling up inside me. My heart is pounding like a steam engine.

I leave my room and head downstairs. I cautiously open the door that Phyllis pointed out. It is not a dining room, but there is a circular staircase. I take the stairs up. At each landing, I check the doors, but they are locked. I continue up.

At the top of the stairs, I find a small round dining room, with a round table. The table is set for two with a fine white linen tablecloth, and each place setting is arranged perfectly with fine china and sterling silver. The centerpiece is an arrangement of dried twisted hazel branches covered with gold dust. There are six large candle stands around the room, with large unlit candles on them.

I walk over to look out the windows that surround over half of the room. The panorama is beautiful and includes part of the London skyline, Hurlingham Park, the River Thames and the many rooftops of Fulham. It is all quite breathtaking. I become lost in the view.

Slowly, I become aware that I'm all alone. I start wondering where Phyllis may be. I turn around and see that there is a door in the back of the room and next to it an empty sideboard with only two warming trays. My heart is so filled with images of Phyllis that I start to long for her. I have to shut down my brain chatter and stop worrying.

I wish Phyllis could fall in love with me. I can feel her attraction and driving passion. But I sense that she is filled with Love and suppressing it, and I don't know why. I hope beyond hope that she will unlock her heart and share my Love for her. I become lost in a daydream of that moment, and an inner longing takes me over.

Then without warning, the door opens, and Phyllis comes in carrying a large tray of food. Argna is fallowing her with another tray. They set them down on the sideboard, and Argna starts arranging things.

Phyllis rushes over and throws her arms around me. We embrace passionately, pressing our bodies into each other. After a wonderfully long moment, she steps back and holds me at arm's length.

She looks me over from head to toe, and says, "My how grand you look! I don't think I have ever seen you look so handsome. You were born for elegance."

I'm slightly embarrassed, "It may be in my blood, but I was born for something else."

She gives me a kiss and takes my arm, "Shall we have our dinner while it is still warm?"

She takes my arm, and I walk her over to the table. I pull out her chair; she sits, and I move her in. I walk around and take my seat. We both sit looking at each other for a moment. I feel very loving. She looks coy and flirtatious.

Argna walks around the room lighting the candles and returns to the sideboard. He starts to serve the food.

I say to Phyllis, "This is such a beautiful place. How did you ever manage to find it?"

"It's been in the family for hundreds of years," she replies matter-of-factly. "I'm glad you like it."

I say, "The view is spectacular. Do you eat up here often?

"No, just on special occasions," she says while raising her eyebrows.

I must say I do find her flirtations fun and try to return them as best I can. The flirtations and banter continue throughout the three-course meal, with a lot of humor thrown in. Phyllis enjoys playing up the royal line. While I enjoy playing it down. It is all done in such a lighthearted way that we both are caught up in uncontrollable laughter.

At first, I feel a little awkward with Argna in the room, but he is incredibly good at serving and virtually disappears into the background. He knows exactly what he is doing, and Phyllis never has to give him an order. He is so skilled at it that after he clears the last course, I don't even notice that he is gone.

After pushing the twisted hazel aside, Phyllis and

I are holdings hands over the table. The conversation is about our likes and dislikes, our favorite and lest favorite foods, our favorite art, theatre, dance, and movies. We are both amazed at how similar our tastes are.

I notice that it is now dark outside and turn to Phyllis, "Could we blow out the candles and look at the lights? It is a clear night, and it should be spectacular." I stand.

She is out of her seat before me. "That's a brilliant idea! Ever since I was little, I would come up here to look at the lights. It's like being on top of the world."

She starts on one side, and I start on the other. In less than a minute, we meet in the middle and embrace. It is soft and tender, as we turn to look out the windows while clinging to each other.

We stand there in silence for a long time. My arm is around her waist, and her arm around mine and her head on my chest. This begins to feel like the Love for which I'm hoping. With every micro movement, she snuggles in closer. And I hold her tighter. Together, we survey her domain. In that moment, we begin to feel like one.

She says very quietly, "You feel like a rock. You are so grounded, so strong. I have never met anyone like you. You would make any woman feel safe." She turns her head up to look in my face.

Our eyes lock, and each of us is drawn deep into the other person. My heart pounds with Love for her. I can feel her heart pounding too.

She slowly twists in my arms and coils her body around mine. We embrace with a passionate kiss. Her tongue is darting in and out of my mouth. Her hands slide down to my buttocks, and she pulls my hips tight against her own. She grinds her pelvis into my groin.

My hands softly explore her naked back. With

one finger, I gently trace the plunging edge of her gown. Then, I trace it again with my finger sliding slightly under the edge of the fabric. The third time, all my fingers are gliding on her soft skin beneath the fabric.

Our hearts race. Our breathing quickens.

As she continues to grind her pelvis against mine, she raps one leg around my leg, and her gown starts to creep up her legs. Then she switches legs and her gown creeps up further.

I continue to explore with my hands, exploring the contour of her buttocks. It is firm and sensual. Finally, each of my hands cup each of her cheeks, and I help her slide up my body.

Now she raps her legs around my hips, and her gown slides up higher and higher. She continues to grind into me. She kisses my neck, nibbling and kissing.

I nibble on her earlobe. Then, I blow on her bear shoulder and down the front of her gown.

She moans with ecstasy.

I continue to blow a fine stream of air tracing the perfect contours of her face.

She leans her head back and soaks up the pleasure.

I trace the outline of her mouth.

She opens her eyes, now glassy with joy. She slowly puts a finger over my blowing mouth. She whispers in a trembling voice, "You weren't kidding when you said you would make my body tingle all over with pleasure. I'm so wet. I want you so bad, and I want you now."

I breath out, "Here?"

"In my playroom," she breaths seductively. She slowly uncoils her legs, sliding down my body. She slowly runs her hand down my chest, to my waist and then cups my crotch over the front of my pants. "It looks like you're up for that." She smiles up at me.

In a playful tone now, she says, "In your wardrobe there is a robe for you. Go to your room and change into it. That is all you will need. I'll send Argna to bring you to my playroom." She turns to leave and looks back, "By the way, could you come as Hoss, the real man?" In an instant she is out the door, but not gone.

Her fragrance, both perfume and passion, lingers in the room. Her presence fills my heart. My body is longing to hold her again. My imagination wants to make mad passionate love with her.

With that thought, I dance down the spiral staircase and back to my room, changing into Hoss on the way.

CHAPTER 15
The Playroom

I find the robe in the wardrobe. It is pure silk in a deep red paisley pattern, with black satin lapels. In the bottom of the wardrobe, there is also a pair of slippers. I quickly undress, slide into the robe and put on the slippers. The robe feels so good next to my skin. It is very sensual.

I check myself in the mirror. I'm ready.

As I wait for Argna, I connect with the 'Great I Am' within me. The 'I Am's Love-light is super bright, perhaps the brightest in all my experience.

'I Am' asks me, "Are you ready for this?"

I respond, "Why shouldn't I be? I've been waiting for this my whole life. I think she really does Love me."

The 'I Am' continues, "Then you do not know? Your emotions are blocking your awareness."

"My awareness is telling me that you feel this is a wonderful opportunity," I say slightly confused.

"It is, but not about her love for you. She is setting you up. You are being lured into a trap."

"No way!" I exclaim.

"Then you're not getting any of my messages? I wondered why you were not responding." The 'I Am' says.

"What messages?!"

"Oh, boy! She is more clever than I thought. My first message was when she didn't show up at the airport. I said, 'Look at the shoes.' My second message was when you were examining the architecture while waiting for her, 'This is the place.' My third message was, 'Where is all the staff to run this place?' Then there is her remark, 'You would make any woman feel safe.' 'She is not saying you make her feel safe.' Then she coiled herself around your body and I asked, 'Who does that remind you of.' Let us skip to the end, 'Why do you have to come as Hoss?'"

My left-brain deception is complete, as I hear myself say, "You're misinterpreting everything. This is Phyllis we are talking about."

The 'I Am' says emphatically, "This is not Phyllis we are talking about! I overheard her discussing with Angra, 'which way would he be the weakest, as Hayah or Hoss.' They think Hayah is a Superhero, all-powerful. They do not get it. Your connection is the same."

I hesitate, then start to argue, "No..."

At that moment there is a knock at the door.

I call out, "Come in."

Argna opens the door and steps into the room.

The 'Great I Am' says to me, "Look at his shoes."

I look. They are alligator shoes. The realization hits me like a ton of bricks. A say in a very calm voice, "Now, I'm ready for this." Now it is Angra's turn to be in the dark.

I follow Argna (Angra Mainyu) out of the room. There is a sadness inside me. It is not a sadness for a lost love, because you cannot lose what you didn't have in the first place. My sadness is for yet another failed attempt. It is for all the mistakes in my youth.

Argna leads me downstairs and through a door opposite the dining room door. It leads to another spiral staircase, only down.

I remember a special young woman; I was dating. We were in a love-lust relationship. I wanted her to find the Love-light within her and told her about the 'Great I Am' within her. A few days later, I called on her at her dorm. We met in the foyer, and she told me, "I never want to see you again. You don't just want my body. You want my soul!" She turned and walked away.

Argna passes the first subbasement and opens the door to the second subbasement. I follow.

In this crazy world we live in, real Love is so hard to find. In reality, it is safe to say, "We don't find Love. Love finds us."

Argna leads me through a maze of dimly light stone corridors. I carefully note each one as we pass.

The 'Great I Am' within me is now quiet. It is important that I deal with this crisis myself. It would mean nothing to the 'Dragon Lady' to hear it from the 'I Am'. She has to hear it from us mere mortals.

Argna stops and opens a heavy wooden door, which swings in. He steps aside.

I stoop and step into the room. The door swings closed behind me. I can hear the lock throwing the bolt into place.

The room is dimly lit with candles. The stone walls are dank and dark. In several places there are rings securely fastened to the wall. Hanging from them are lengths of iron chains with cuffs attached. The ring next to the door is empty. I assume that the chain on the floor was once hanging from it. Around the room are several iron sexual torture devices. Some of them are hanging from the ceiling. Others are fastened to wooden planks or elaborate mechanical contraptions.

At the far end of the room, there is a slightly raised area. In the center is what looks like an altar. Its surface is shiny with blood or other bodily fluids. There are six tall candle stands around it with wide burning candles.

Standing in front of the altar is Phyllis (the 'Dragon Lady'). She is dressed from head to toe in a black skintight leather suit, with holes cut for the eyes and mouth. The jeweled/sequin pattern that was on her gown is also on the leather suit. She is holding a riding crop.

She snaps the riding crop in the air and commands loudly, "Come here!"

"No thank you, my Lady," I respond calmly.

She turns slightly to the altar and sharply cracks the riding crop on it, "Come here, I say!"

Again, I respond calmly, "This is beneath you, my Lady, taking the perfect Love that is within you and pushing it to the Dark-side of the puny human left-brain irrational mind."

She explodes in a rage. In an instant, she is standing in front of me. She shouts, "You do as I tell you and shut your impudent mouth!" She grins and whacks the riding crop across my face.

I smile.

She winces in pain, stepping back, feeling the blow on her own face.

I say comfortingly, "Its time, my Lady, to give all this up. It all adds up to nothing. Let me tell..."

Her wrath flies out of control and she starts pounding me repeatedly with the riding crop, screaming, "You! You! You..." With each blow her body twitches in pain.

Finally, she throws the riding crop against the wall and starts to slap me, scratch me and pound me with her fists. The results all boomerang back on her. The scratches tear open the leather suit and draw blood. She winces from the sting.

I continue, "Let me tell you, my Lady, how much we need you, how much we need your Love." I reach out and touch her bleeding wound. It heals beneath my hand. I know she can heal herself, but it means more coming from me. "I don't want you to go through eternity with a scar there." I take her claw hand and kiss it.

In that instant, her image starts to flicker back and forth between the woman in black leather and The Love in creation. The Love is beautiful. She is naked from the waist up, with a sheer fabric billowing out and hanging low on her hips, held in place by a belt of stars. Her hair cascades down past her feet and frames her image.

I step back and open my arms out to her. I reach inside and bring out his Love-light. The Love-light starts to fill the room and engulf the Dragon Lady.

She starts to say very softly, "No, no, no..."

I explain, "It is your Love-light, my Lady, from the beginning. Be part of it once more, so your creation can continue. Come, my Lady, let us send it to all the world, the world which You as Three parts made."

The Love-light is very bright now and the leather clad Dragon Lady disappears.

"No, no, no..."

However, smoke begins to rise from beneath her feet. It swirls around behind her, rising higher and higher.

I keep pouring out the Love-light saying, "It is yours, my Lady. Come, take it up again."

Then I notice the smoke is taking the shape of a dragon. In an instant, The Love is gone, and a huge dragon stands before me.

I continue to pour out the Love-light.

The dragon opens its mouth and spews out fire on me.

The flames surround me, but I give her the Love-light.

The image of the dragon flickers, and I see that the hair of Love is now singed.

The dragon opens its mouth again, and I see a ball of flame forming in its mouth. Then in the next instant, the dragon inhales drawing the ball of flame inside itself. And I hear her scream, "Nooooooo..."

In a puff of smoke, she is gone.

I stand there alone and unharmed.

As I take a deep breath, I hear the bolt on the door lock open. I turn to face the door. It swings open quickly and I kick the chain into the doorway.

A huge beast bursts into the room, with a loud roar. It is the ugliest, meanest, scariest thing I have ever seen. I'm not going to diminish any of my friends in the animal kingdom by trying to describe him. But it is the worst looking creature that Stephen King could ever dream up.

His roar is still ringing in my ears when I say, relaxed and calm, "Come now, Angra Mainyu, you can do better than that."

He roars again and threatens me with one of his appendages. "I'm going to eat you for a midnight snack," he says in a very deep threatening voice.

I smile, "Now that was fairly good. I'm sure it would scare some of the naughty children and unconnected people but come now. Don't you have anything for those of us who are connected to the 'Great I Am'?"

He pauses and then starts another roar, showing his teeth, "Roooaaarrr..."

I cut him off, "Look Angra, or should I call you Heylel, because that is who you really are, the Shining Light, the Light Bearer. Do you recognize this?" I open my arms and pour out the Love-light.

His image flickers back and forth between the beast and a bright shining Spirit.

I continue while pouring out the Love-light, "Help her come back, Heylel, your reward would be great. It is much better to be a Shining Light than a Destroyer of human rational minds."

His image continues to flicker as he starts to leave. He tries to close the door behind him, but the chain is in the way. He abandons the effort and starts up the hall.

I call after him, "We Love you, Heylel."

I make my way out of the maze and back to my guestroom. I hang up the robe and the tuxedo.

While hanging up the shirt, I notice a lipstick mark on the collar. I say to her, "This is from the 'I Am'," and I kiss the stain. The color of the stain turns bright red and then slowly fades away. I say to her, "Buy for now, my Lady."

I dress in my travel clothes again and throw on my backpack. After a short deliberation, I decide to hike back to Heathrow airport tonight.

As soon as I'm out of the mansion and turn West on Hurlingham Road, I hear the 'Great I Am' within me. The 'I Am' says, "Wow, that was a major step forward, Hoss. You are only the second person in history to be able to get through to her, and Yeshua says his attempt did not have such a powerful impact. For the first time We are of the opinion that this can really work. Connected humans can bring Love home."

I walk in silence for a moment shielding my ego from the praise. "There are two things that made it easy for me. She actually let me feel the Love for you that is within her. That by itself is extraordinary. Then beneath your urgency to get through to me, you let me feel the Love you have for her. Now, I can fully understand why creation was so special, with the Three parts of you all. It makes my mission worth the effort."

The 'I Am' asks, "Are you really going to walk to Heathrow?"

I sense 'I Am's concern, "I can't sleep right now, and it is only about 13 miles. I can do that in four hours. It will do me good."

I cross the River Thames and set my course for due West to use the small streets and parks.

CHAPTER 16
The Word and the Tree

After about an hour, I hear the 'Great I Am', "I can feel that you need to hear the next part of the 'The Connecting Tree'. You need to know that you are not the only one struggling here. You are not alone. I'll take you back and let you experience personally what I experienced." 'I Am' pauses; then I sense that the 'I Am' is comforting someone else. Slowly, I'm allowed to see what is happening.

The Buddha is weeping, and all Nature is weeping with him. The 'Great I Am' says to them, "You did all you could do. You were right. They were not ready to hear your message. I must come up with something else." There is a deep silence and no one breaths. They all share the same image of an explosive apocalypse. Then the 'I Am' continues, "That is not a choice. It is not enough that I am only a part of everyone and everything. I must become one of them. I must experience this struggle with the Dark-side of the human left-brain Irrational Mind and Ego. My Word must become flesh. I must live their life and die their death." Obviously, Isaiah and Ezekiel are helping the 'I Am' cook up this idea.

Now the 'Great I Am' continues the story, "I briefly connect to two women, Elizabeth, who is married to Zachariah, and Mary, who is not yet married to Joseph. I help Elizabeth and Zachariah to conceive a son, named John. He is my messenger to prepare the way for My arrival. Then, I enter Mary's womb and experience, for the first time, firsthand, the fetal development and childbirth. My name is to be Yeshua." (Jesus is the Greek translation of the Aramaic. No one likes to hear their given name translated into another language. It is simply not your name. In this case the Greeks cannot say the 'sh' sound. They also say a 'J' with a 'Ye' sound. So, what you end up with is 'Yesus'.)

"John connects to Me from birth. As a young boy, he also connects to all of Nature. This combination gives him enormous strength to fight off the Dark-side. By the time he is in his late teens, his Dark-side is totally under control, and his ego is shut down. His voice is My voice.

"As a man in his early thirties, he is not only powerful in appearance, he is powerful in every other way. His voice is like thunder. His words shake the religious and Hebrew establishments. His Love-light comforts the high and low.

"His use of water to cleanse the human rational mind and spirit is unique. My experience of it is also immensely powerful."

The 'Great I Am' pauses and reflects on that moment and then continues, "As the 'I Am', I am aware of every feeling and thought you have, but I do not actually experience the feeling sensations. As Yeshua, I have these sensations for the first time, the sheer pleasure of nursing at my mother's breast, the sheer joy of childhood. I learn to walk, run and play. I share in the daily chores of life. I learn to read.

"While still a boy, I experience what it means to work and have tired mussels. What a wondrous feeling! I even feel sorry for those in the leisurely class. Then Joseph begins to teach me the cabinetmaking trade. This is the closest thing to creation, only I get to have the image of the cabinet in My own head, instead of taking the image from the 'Great I Am'. To take a couple of logs and cut and shape the wood with My hands until I have a door or table is a comforting and rewarding feeling.

"As a young man, I start to experience the Dark-side of my Left-brain Irrational Mind and Ego. I call it the 'LIM&E'. I'm expecting it to be a dark pit of swirling molten rock. Instead, I discover it is nothing more than bad choices. I can feel the "LIM&E" trying to push anger into violence, wrath and hatred; it is pushing want and need into greed for more; it is pushing strength into power and domination; it is pushing Love and affection into the worship of sexual pleasure. Worst of all, it is pushing constructive, rational, and positive thought into blind irrational and deceptive conclusions, turning reality into a myth and an abstract idea into a reality. Fortunately, the body is not affected by or controlled by the 'LIM&E', and I can use the body to stay in control. The devs are chattering in my head all the time to make bad choices, but there is no force behind it. I simply stay focused in my body center and stay in control. My body never lies to me. The 'LIM&E' lie to me all the time. When they put on their scary show and threaten Me with bodily harm, it is laughable, and I simply blow them a kiss of Love and they disappear. This is something any human can do. The truth is **they have no power over you**. That is why it is so easy to cast out the devs, just give the person and dev a loving hug and poof the dev will vanish. They then can go on to chatter at someone else, who is silly enough to pay attention.

"All those who choose to listen to their devs, and become angry with them, are making their situation worse. The devs feed on anger. Those people who choose to embrace their Dark-side, are the ones who make wars, become greedy, poison themselves with hatred, seek power, and domination. They have only themselves to blame; it is all about their bad choices.

"There are only two points I want to make about my mission and message. I knew going in, as Isaiah foretold and I said repeatedly, that I would be tried, found guilty, suffer immensely, be executed, die and be raised up. The heart of My message is that 'I Am' within you, and you are in Me'. Yet, after feeding the more than 5000 people and driving that point home, everyone turns their back on Me and walks away, including most of my Apostles. That breaks My heart. It destroys My whole reason for coming. To this day, most people prefer to worship a 'Sky god' than connect with Me and My Love-light within."

Yeshua pauses again. All the Spirits and I get ready for the 'Great I Am's Judgment, which doesn't come. Yeshua continues.

"Mary Magdalena connects to me and casts out her own devs. She helps Me heal My broken heart and gets Me through the ordeal of My mission. She is always faithful.

"My Apostle John connects with Me, and I fill him with My Love-light. He is the only one to see sin as missing the mark. Thus, to worship a 'Sky god' instead of connecting to Me is to miss the mark and sin. To follow all the rules but fail to discover and follow My purpose for you in life is to miss the mark and sin. To read all the prayers and participate in all the rituals but fail to listen for My voice within is to miss the mark and sin.

"My Apostle Bartholomew connects after My death. His description of that moment is immensely powerful. He says, 'My mind explodes into a million pieces. My heart leapt from my breast into the hand of the 'Great I Am'. I felt a Love so great, that I felt my Heart would burst. I felt a Light so strong; it washed all the sins from my soul.' He makes it clear that it is pointless to ask Me or anyone else to forgive your sins, because they are already forgiven. What you must do is realize that you missed the mark, correct it and forgive yourself.

"Judas is a beloved friend who connects with Me when we are boys, long before I ask him to be My Apostle. He totally understands my mission and does everything I ask him to do. Without him, My mission would not be fulfilled. I'll leave it to you to see the real betrayers and those that altered the texts.

"My Apostle Paul's connection is incredible. We still laugh about it. He falls off his horse, hits his head on a stone, sees a blinding light and connects with Me. In 49 seconds, he accomplishes what it takes The Buddha 49 days to do. I wish it were that easy for everybody."

The Buddha starts one of his deep belly-laughs.

The 'Great I Am' is silent again and reflects on the life as Yeshua. Finally, Yeshua summarizes, "My greatest joy was the experience of human life. My greatest pain and suffering was not on the cross but watching 5000 people walk away from Me within them. My presence within them is as real as the food they ate. It is as real as the bread and wine in our last meal together. But no, they have to turn it into a symbol, a magical conversion of substances, a myth."

The 'I Am' is silent for a few minutes, then says, "Hoss, I cannot begin to tell you how much your success means to us here. You are giving us all hope."

"Thanks, the Yeshua story helps me a lot," I say simply and change the subject. "I see the airport ahead. I'm going to check in and rest before my flight."

116

CHAPTER 17
Connecting Tree Continues

After a long nap on the floor of the boarding area, I board my flight for Tel Aviv-Yafo. I settle into my seat and look out the window. My head is full of all the conflicts now arising in the Middle East. The moment I stop the left-brain chatter and put all these irrational thoughts out of my head, my mind wanders to thoughts of The Connecting Tree. There must be another peace about those connecting after Yeshua. I wander if that is a lengthy list.

Sometimes when the 'Great I Am' really wants me to listen intently, the Love-light becomes brighter, and the 'I Am' becomes quiet. This is one of those times.

Eventually, the 'Great I Am' says, "Patanjali, who wrote the Yoga Sūtras, from the teachings of Krishna, develops a strong connection with Me by simply using the unutterable syllable ॐ (OM) as a breathing mantra in meditation. He clearly defines the ॐ syllable from the ancient Sanskrit and discovers its silent presence in his breathing. It turns out to be the most powerful mantra to settle the left-brain chattering irrational mind and reach the peaceful center ready to awaken to My Love-light within. A few are able to follow him.

"My Messenger Muhammad is a good man who, by sheer will, manages to live his life in the positive side of his rational brain, remaining honest and trustworthy. He worships in the cave of Hira and is aware of My presence within but finds it difficult to break through. He is 40 when he finally connects, and I present his life's purpose. He experiences amazement, joy, doubts and many questions all at once. If I say it once, I say it a hundred times, 'Be positive. Do not say no; connect and be one with Me!' Muhammad struggles with his decision for three years, and thanks to his wife Khadijah he chooses positively. He accepts his purpose to unite all the Arab tribes and accomplishes it before his death.

"To My surprise, the Benedictine monk and philosopher, Anselm connects to Me. After connecting, he writes, with great humor, an ontological argument proving my existence, by basing each premise of the argument on his connection with Me, 'I Believe the 'I Am' to be...' The irrational part that follows is the left-brain mind trap, meaning nothing. We both enjoy a good laugh while writing it.

"The next person to connect is no surprise at all. His parents could feel the Spirit at work in him when he was born and named him after Bartholomew. As a young boy he heard the stories of Yeshua at his mother's knee and finds Me within by the time he is ten. As a man, Bartholomew Legate is a rough looking black man working as a cloth merchant in London. On the side, he takes My message as Yeshua and becomes a street preacher. He smilingly and joyfully accepts My purpose for him knowing full well, it will lead to his being burned at the stake by King James for his unorthodox message.
"It is through Bartholomew Legate that Roger Williams connects with Me when he is only 7 years old. While Bartholomew Legate is selling cloth in the shop of Roger's father, he simply lays his hand on Roger's head. The next moment Roger exclaims, 'I feel the Father of Light within me.' Throughout his often-perilous journey, he clings to that mantra and never loses his connection to Me. The two words that best describe his life with Me are Love and Hope. He

also takes the message to the North American continent, establishes the first democratic colony and helps three American Indian chiefs recognize their connection to Me.

"Those American Indian chiefs are Sachem Massasoit, Sachem Canonicus and Sachem Philip. I Am a constant voice within them, and the Spirits of Truth and Peace becomes their guardian angels. All humanity would do well to learn from them.

"Two more philosophers connect with Me. Immanuel Kant turns all philosophy right side up to experience My presence within and connect. Søren Kierkegaard connects with Me while walking the streets of Copenhagen. He then describes the entire process in his collective works before his early death at 42. The message is clear only when you digest the full body of his work.

"In the Islamic community, Bahá'u'lláh connects with Me while imprisoned in the 'black pit' (Síyáh-Chál). He anticipates My purpose for him and immediately embraces it. He faithfully writes all I give to him, and writes, and writes. I see the futility of the faith politics and encourage him to become a hermit in the mountains of the Kurdish-inhabited area to continue his writing. His exile to Constantinople gradually leads to his long-term imprisonment in the penal colony of Akká, Palestine (now Acre, Israel). While there, he writes his greatest body of work for Me. 'The message is now: 'I Am' one and within everyone; there is but one race, the human race; all religions must unite; and complete unity is the goal. The earth is but one country and humankind its citizens.'

"The connection I have with Mohandas Gandhi is

unique. He finds Me and connects early in his life, and I become the Love-light within him. We are in constant communication with each other. The uniqueness is that his purpose takes him into the social, political and civil behavior areas. His primary purpose is to find the basic goodness in everyone. Yet, his honest view penetrated all institutional masks. A priest once asked him, 'Mohandas, your words and works are more like Jesus' than anyone I have ever met. Why are you not a Christian?'

"Mohandas answers him, 'Because I never met one.'

"Those are not my words; but I cannot have said it better," says the 'Great I Am'.

I hear the 'I Am' laughing so hard that the plane shakes. Then I realize the plane is landing.

The 'I Am' says, "Hoss, thank you for listening to all this, but I know you will find it helpful on this leg of our journey."

Lord Vishnu, the 'Great I Am', the Ahura-Mazda, Allah, God, the Holly, the Master, Father, Lord of the Heavenly Hosts, no matter what you call the 'I Am', 'I Am' is your Inner Being. 'I Am' says to Moses, "'I Am', Hayah, 'I Am'." The 'I Am' is telling you not only 'who' or 'what' 'I Am' is; 'I Am' is telling you where 'I Am' is. "'I Am', your Essence of Being, 'I Am'. 'I Am' here inside you, listen. Listen and connect with Me."

CHAPTER 18
A Walk Together

I check into the Gordon Inn in Tell Aviv. I put
my backpack in my room and walk down to the
beach, which is in front of the hostel. It is late in the
afternoon. The beach is empty, except for a few
lovers who are oblivious to anything else but the now
and their own little patch on the sand. The red beach
parasols are folded closed. The red chairs and
lounges sit empty. I'm alone as I walk along the
beach meeting only the occasional person out for a
stroll like me. The Tel Aviv skyline stands towering
in the near distance.

It is difficult to keep my left-brain chattering
mind at bay. Isn't it strange that the one woman that
I should fall in love with is the same woman that
brought the Love to the Light in the beginning? The
same woman that 'I Am' Love's to this day and will
always Love. I begin to laugh to myself and say,
"Take heart husbands of the earth, even the 'Great I
Am' has a problem reading the Woman of Creation!"

I can hear the 'Great I Am' laughing as well.

The chatter starts me thinking about finding the
right woman. Then the old cliché pops into my mind,
"The right woman will find you." The person who
started that cliché did know what they were talking
about. What are the odds, ten million to one?

The 'I Am' says, "More than that."

Of course, the 'I Am' is listening to my inner
thoughts. I respond, "Don't you have anything better
to do?"

"I enjoy listening to your inner thoughts. It
reminds me of my inner thoughts as Yeshua and how
much I entertained Abba." Yeshua's laugh has an
echo.

The funny thing here is I don't really mind his

constant presence and the lack of privacy. There is no such thing as having a secret or wondering if the 'Great I Am' is watching. 'I Am's presence is constant. The 'I Am' is in your essence of being. Now you, my reader, are thinking, "If that is the case, I never want to connect to the 'I Am'." And that is really funny, because 'I Am' is still your inner being weather you recognize it or not. Ignorance is only bliss as long as you are ignorant.

I turn around and start to walk back toward the hostel. I shut down the inner thoughts and we walk in silence. I study the shoreline looking for crinoids (a small, petrified segment, the size of a fingernail, of a marine invertebrate with a cup-shaped body and five or more feathery flexible and active arms). These have always had a fascination for me since I was six years old, and my collection is numerous and faithfully stored in my treasure box. My body is a hundred percent present now. My focus is keen.

Alas, there are no Crinoids. Then, hello, what's this. A black bit of iron is sticking up out of the sand. That won't do; it could seriously injure someone. I reach down and pluck it up, while looking for the nearest trash container. It feels heavier than I expected for its size. I look down at what is in my hand. It is a hand tooled iron arrowhead. I look more closely. There is no machine tooling and it looks very old. I've seen a lot of flint Indian arrow heads and modern steel ones, but never one of iron. I'll have to check it out; I slip it in my pocket.

When I get back to the beach front of the hostel, I cross up the beach to the beach walk, passing two young guys scanning the beach with metal detectors. I say, "Hi," with a smile and a friendly tone, as I always do. They don't respond and look at me as if I were some weirdo. This is the typical response in a modern unsocial culture, where social contact is on the social media, which is not social by any stretch of the imagination.

I sit on the retaining wall overlooking the beach and water to watch the sunset. I feel 'I Am's presence within me, as always. My natural breathing relaxes my body completely and brings the 'I Am' into focus. I ask the 'I Am', "Why is it that I never get tired of watching sunsets and sunrises?"

'I Am' says, "That would be like getting tired of breathing. Constants always feels comfortable." The 'I Am' pauses, then changes the subject to my purpose of being here. "By the way, those two young men out there are the ones you are supposed to meet at the University tomorrow."

"Great, they already think I'm a weirdo. This isn't going to be easy."

"Is it ever?" 'I Am' says with a grin.

Yes, in our awareness we can experience 'I Am's smiles, grins, frowns and eye twinkles. I respond, "Not lately! But it was much easier when I was a kid."

"Now that you mention it, it sure was, especially with you. And you were a lot of fun. With you, I got to experience borderline naughty in a highly creative way," 'I Am' smiles.

The two young men are having a pow-wow and glancing in my direction. Then they go back to scanning the beach. Or it's just my paranoia after being public enemy number one.

Now 'I Am' laughs aloud, "At the time that was pretty scary, but now it's very funny. Picture your Wanted Poster, with the scariest picture they can find of you, saying, 'Wanted for stopping a Cardinal from wiping out the elephant population.' Only the President of the Philippines could take that seriously."

The two young men are working themselves closer to me. I close my eyes and soak up the rays of the setting sun.

He starts to alert me, "Maybe I should introduce you to these boys. The one with the long hair and beard is Jacob. The one with the skin head and lower lip beard is Abbud, son of Abdul 'Adl. They are the two young men you are supposed to meet tomorrow when you go to Abram's ecology class. James and his friend Abram have them all fired up with the pictures and videos."

I ask, talking to the 'I Am' silently, "How strong is their friendship with each other?"

"They are best friends since they met here at the University three years ago."

I'm surprised, "Even though one is an Israeli and the other a Palestinian?"

"They are determined to find peace between their people, and both are actually close to connecting with me. There is no hatred in them." The 'I Am's joy is strong.

Jacob and Abbud are now only five meters away, and 'I Am' lets me hear their conversation.

Jacob whispers to Abbud, "Are you sure it's him. He looks so normal. I mean, he doesn't look like a superhero."

"I'm telling you it is Hayah. He's the one with the mountain gorillas." Abbud assures him.

"Wow, Let's go ask him," Jacob says as he starts to move toward me.

Abbud grabs him by the arm, "You can't do that. He's meditating; he's got his eyes closed."

They are now only four meters away. They stand silently, watching me and blocking the rays of the sunset. I say without opening my eyes, "Jacob, could you move a meter to your right? And Abbud, could you move a meter to your left?" They look at each other shocked. "I don't mean to separate you, but you are blocking the rays of the sunset."

They both move to the right. The light baths my face again, and I smile.

The boys stand very still and silent. Abbud thinks, "he can see with his eyes closed." Jacob thinks, "There is a Divine power lighting up his face."

I say aloud, "No, I can't see with my eyes closed, and it is the setting sun that is lighting up my face."

They both say at the same time, "I was only thinking that! How do you know my name?"

I continue, "The 'Great I Am' within me is telling me who you are and what you're thinking."

The boys turn and look at each other, with big question marks on their faces. As the sun's intensity diminishes, I slowly open my eyes. I answer their question before they ask it, "Yes, I'm Hayah."

They look at each other and are speechless for a moment. Then they both start talking at the same time.

Abbud, "What did it feel like to heal the baby gorilla?"

Jacob, "How can you move so fast?"

Abbud, "How does the boomerang effect work?"

Jacob, "Who is the 'Great I Am'?"

Abbud, "Can you fly?"

Jacob, "What other superpowers do you have?"

Together, "How can we find the Love-light?"

I hold up my hand for them to be silent and gesture to the sunset. They stop and turn to watch the sun disappear below the horizon. Their bodies are relaxed now, and their breathing is natural and in unison.

I point to the sunset glow on the horizon and ask, "How often does that happen?"

Abbud answers, "every day."

I ask, "and for how long?"

Jacob says, "since the beginning of creation."

I press the point, "and how long will it continue?"

Abbud says, "The scientific theory is, a few billion years, give or take a billion years." The boys laugh.

"That is a convenient answer, 'give or take a

billion years.' So, what is the answer to my first question in one word?"

Jacob say, "Always.?"

"Both of you are sons of Abraham and I'm here to bring your families together."

Abbud reacts sarcastically, "Good luck on that pal. Our families have been hating each other for millenniums!"

Now, the 'Great I Am' starts to take over the conversation, so my words are 'I Am's words. "Somehow, the two of you are free from that hatred. I feel the loving friendship within you. How would you like to bring that feeling to your families?"

Jacob jumps in, "Yes, Yes, Yes!"

Abbud is more cautious, "How are just the two of us going to do that?"

I can feel 'I Am's excitement, "That is why I'm here. That is why I want to meet with your class tomorrow. I want to find those who will work to achieve this goal. Are you interested?"

"Of course," Jacob says quickly. "Are you going to give us the Superpowers?"

"You already have those," 'I Am' says, smiling.

Abbud interjects, "Even with Superpowers it is no easy job. Understand me; I'm all for it, but it was easier to discover a new planet than to bring our families together will be."

"Believe me, I know! Both your families have drifted the furthest they have ever been from Me. But I know We can do this if you connect with me."

'I Am' turns things over to me again.

Abbud hesitantly asks, "Was... Was that... Was that the 'Great I Am' talking to us?"

"Yes, it was. When you connect to the 'I Am', 'I Am' will talk directly to you.

Jacob and Abbud respond, "Sign me up!"

CHAPTER 19
Science vs. Theology

After a sound night's sleep, I awake to another beautiful day at 5 am and the calming sounds of the Mediterranean Sea's surf. I greet the 'Great I Am' as always and head down to the beach to do my morning workout and meditation. This is a special experience for me, and the sand and sea have many stories to share.

The breakfast is also special, and I enjoy watching the international travelers making plans for their day of sightseeing. Then the 'Great I Am' starts to prepare me for my presentation at Tel Aviv University (TAU).

The 'I Am' is pleased with the direction TAU has taken. It is ranked as one of the top 14 universities in the world and is primarily known for its humanitarian, scientific and environmental programs. I'm sure you can see that this all sounds great, but then the 'I Am' reveals a major disappointment, "I wish the politicians and religious leaders were as awake and aware as many of the students and faculty." Now 'I Am's mood shifts, "However, you will discover that many are close to connecting with Me. There are many potentially great leaders who accept that I Am here within them, but do not know how to get to Me. Together, we will find them in the group today.

"It is thanks to Twitter spreading the pictures and videos and James' contact with Professor Hanna Katsmum that we have this opportunity. BUT Hanna has major reservations about you. She would much rather have Abby. To her, Abby made it look so easy to connect and she would like it to be easy. It was only because of Dick that Abby was physically prepared. Unfortunately, Abby is not ready to start training others with their body preparation and physical awareness. This is a major obstacle for many who want to teach the process. It is only because of James' positive report that Hanna agreed to have you.

"Be prepared, Hanna may be overly critical of everything you do or say. She was emotionally and physically abused by three different men and still carries the scars. However, she wants to connect to Me, and I have great plans for her when she connects. I Am sure that you can turn her around, but you may have to make some extra effort to awaken her inner body awareness. Of course, I will help where I can."

I say to you, my reader, "Don't panic! I know this sounds like an attack is imminent, but it is not. Even if it were, the 'Great I Am' has just given me a heads up, and I'm now forewarned and preparing. In this case, the 'I Am' is letting me know what someone is thinking so I can avoid conflict and nurture Hanna in a positive direction. This is one of the greatest rewards of being connected with the 'Great I Am' in any situation. The only way you can make a mistake is not to listen to the 'I Am' or let your left-brain ego convince you that you know best. Believe me; I've been there, done that.

I decide to walk the 5 K to the Porter School of Environmental Studies (PSES) on the TAU campus, where today's event is to take place. I enjoy exploring Tel Aviv and checking out the houses and parks, of which there are many, including the park along the Yarkon River.

As I walk up Dr. George Wise Street and approach the rotary, the spectacular PSES building comes into view. I stop and admire it for a minute. It is no wonder that this building won so many awards, and to realize it is totally environmentally friendly. This is going to be a pleasure.

The closer I get the more I'm impressed. I open the front door and step inside the glass enclosed atrium. It is truly a work of art. I could spend the entire day exploring every detail, but I catch a glimpse of Hanna out of the corner of my eye. She is standing some thirty meters away and studying my every move. Slowly, I turn to her and lock eye contact, with a broad smile. I quickly cross the distance as 'I Am's Love-light fills me. She is a tall, attractive, well-trained woman, who looks like a person in charge.

I extend my hand in friendship, saying, "Thank you for having me, Professor Katsmum. I'm Hayah."

Suddenly, she seems off balance, "How do you know my name? We have never met. Have we?"

"No ma'am," I say warmly shaking her hand slowly. She returns the handshake in the same manner. Her eyes study me carefully. I add as usual, "A little birdy told me."

She finally breaks a smile, "Welcome! So, James has been telling you stories."

"No, he didn't tell me he was going to contact you, but I'm glad he did," I say, as she continues the handshake.

She asks, "Then who is the 'Little Birdy' that told you about me?" She stops shaking my hand but does not let it go. She studies my eyes and face as I study hers.

"The 'Great I Am' tells me you're not acquainted yet, but hopefully, you will be soon." I gently squeeze her hand as she lets go.

Her face looks puzzled, not knowing what I mean. She changes the subject, "Let's see the lecture hall where you will meet the students and some guests. Then we can go to my office to discuss the media that James sent."

"Great!" I offer her my arm. Naturally, she

smiles and takes it. Two steps later, she thinks better of it and let's go.

The classroom is typical and will work perfectly. Next, Hanna takes me up to the Green Roof and explains along the way that she thinks it would be a perfect place for the Meditation class. The image in my mind is a pure disaster, with people falling off the roof to their death. My left-brain chatter continues, telling me she is going to push me off the roof. The 'Great I Am' laughs.

The 'I Am' says, "You better shutdown your left-brain chatter, because you are in for a major surprise."

Hanna swings open the door to the roof and steps out and to one side, holding the door open for me. I step out and freeze in my tracks. I stand there in awe for over a minute. This is the most beautiful roof garden I have ever seen. All the plants are succulents, with every variety of cactus I have ever seen. They are in full bloom, flaunting every color in the rainbow. I mumble with tears in my eyes, "This is a wonderful tribute to Your creation!"

Hanna responds, "It's not my creation, but it sure is lovely." I give her a warm smile, and she continues. "I think that the center deck would be a beautiful place to meditate. It is wide enough for a mat and chair for each person. The canopy will protect us from the sun. What do you think? Is this a possibility?"

"Wow, I have never seen anything so perfect. This will help make it an awesome experience for everyone. I can't thank you enough."

Now, Hanna gives me a genuine smile, and says, "Good, let's go down to my office."

When we get to her office, Hanna explains how she wants to focus on three segments from Dick's videos. Oddly enough they are not the ones James' students chose to focus on in his class or what they tweeted. One is the elephant dance. The second is the baby gorilla trapped in the snare and Bosco's heroism. The third is the female Rhino who chases me. The only hint she gives me, as to her motivation, is the effect that human behavior has on wild animals. I react on this antiquated them but say nothing.

The 'Great I Am' is in my ear instantly, "She is totally left-brain blocking the fact that I Am present in humans, the animals and nature. The DNA theme is out the window. Now I know why she is having such a challenging time connecting."

"Don't panic, I believe I can get through to her," I say comforting the 'I Am'. "She is just trying to get a typical male reaction out of me and start an argument."

I hear the 'I Am's hum, "You are getting exceptionally good at this. Tell our readers how you will manage it."

I explain, "I will simply agree and move on. It would be nice to know who and what is influencing her. However, if she doesn't stop playing games, I recommend that we forget about including her in the meditation at this time."

"Fair enough," the 'I Am' says reluctantly.

In the class, as people are coming in and settling down, I can feel a positive and exciting energy in the students. The classroom is packed with two rows of students and faculty standing in the back. The noise level grows extremely high, but Professor Hanna Katsmum takes command and orders silence. The group instantly complies, and the mood becomes very formal. She cordially welcomes me and there is a restrained round of applause, which she quickly cuts off.

Without further ado, she calls for the first video segment. Not surprisingly, it starts with the elephants already gathered together in a massive herd of over ten thousand. The music starts to blast from our enemy's trucks. The elephants start to sway and move their feet to the music. As I'm standing in front of them, I start to copy them doing the steps in a Line Dance. Within a moment, all the onlookers come down to the front and join the Line Dance. The earth shakes and everyone bounces to the rhythm, including the trucks in the distance.

During the video clip, the audience in the classroom begins to laugh and the laughter builds until the end of clip. Professor Katsmum barks for silence, and the laughter is cut off immediately. She then turns to me and asks, "Hayah, do you think it is appropriate for humans to train wild animals to mimic human behavior?"

I respond with a warm smile, "First of all, Professor Katsmum, I want to thank you for giving me the opportunity to speak to your class and for showing these wonderful video clips." I turn to the students and faculty, "I want you all to know that the moment in that clip was just as exciting for me as it was for you. Now, Professor Katsmum, to answer your question. In a word, NO! You are absolutely correct; it is not appropriate for humans to train wild animals to mimic human behavior. "However, let's look at the clip again." I call up to the projectionist, "Please run that clip again and be prepared to pause it when I raise my hand." I start to narrate over the clip, "The ten thousand wild elephants you see here, have migrated to Chad from all over Africa. They make up hundreds of families but note how precious few calves there are. The music you hear is coming from the poacher's scouting trucks. The elephants know the poachers are there to kill them, yet the elephants start to dance." I hold up my hand and the picture freezes. "Note that I'm not dancing yet. Look at their faces as I did at that moment. Look in their eyes. There is no anger there. There is only love and joy. They are filled with the Love-light of the 'Great I Am' within them. They want you to feel 'I Am's presence within you. They want their enemy to feel the Love-light and go home." I lower my hand and the clip continues. "I'm moved by what I see, and I start to dance. Soon we are all dancing. Feel the love and joy. Move your feet. You in the back can dance. Laugh if you want. Feel the 'I Am's presence in your joy. Feel the room shake as we felt the earth move. Learn what the elephants are trying to <u>teach you</u>." I raise my hand again and the clip freezes on the last frame of the poacher's trucks.

The dance and joy continues for a moment. Even Hanna started to get into it. Slowly they quit down as they recognize the details in the last frame. "That is what I learned from the elephants. Now, learn from your fellow human beings in this one picture. Note the six gunships flying in behind the trucks. Within seconds, they will insert their troops and open fire on us. Professor Katsmum has spared you the gory details. The air is filled with flying bullets, blood and destruction. Then the silence of death. Because of the boomerang effect and the elephants' connection to the 'Great I Am' it was not our death, but all those who came to kill us died that day. It was tragic." I lower my hand and the screen goes blank.

"The message the 'Great I Am' is sending us is, 'If you are connected, you are protected.' Let the animals **teach you**. Thank you, Professor Katsmum." I sit down.

Hanna is off balance but calls for the next clip. It opens with Bosco's dramatic entrance, screaming and crying that his leg is being injured. His mother comforts him, but she is slow to notice the fact that the injury is the result of his own doing, and her own plan to stop the warning from getting out. As the wound gets increasingly serious, the people and

Bosco wise up that it is their snares that are causing the injury. The boomerang effect bounces the pain and damage back on those that set the snares.

When Bosco leads everybody to where he set his snare, we can see a baby gorilla, who's leg is caught in the snare. He feels no pain, and tugs hard at the snare. Increasing the pain and severity of Bosco's wound. When the baby gorilla sees Bosco's pain he holds very still. Bosco begs me to let the baby gorilla loose, which I do. Bosco's pain subsides and the wound grows no worse. The clip ends.

Professor Katsmum, ask me, "Hayah, do you think it is appropriate to use the black magic of a boomerang effect to achieve your purpose?" She grins with a got-ja look.

The 'Great I Am' tells me that her Grandfather is behind these questions and attacks.

I call up to the projectionist to reset the clip, and he informs me that he already has. I then turn to Professor Katsmum, "Thank you Professor for sharing your perception with the class. Again, my answer is an emphatic NO! Now let's examine your perceptions." I raise my hand and the clip starts to roll. "Look carefully at Bosco's mother. She is using black magic to try and heal Bosco with no success. The Professor has edited out where she also has used black magic to prevent the warning from going out, so the community is totally unaware of the danger they are facing." I lower my hand, "Now let's deal with your perception that the boomerang effect is black magic as your Grandfather has told you. Which is surprising since he is a scholar of the Torah. Is Samuel using black magic when he says, 'let Nabal's evil boomerang back on him.' (1 Samuel 25:39b)? Of course not! Is Joel saying that the 'I Am' is using black magic when He says, 'you do something to them, they do something to you, forget it. I'll see to it that it boomerangs on you.' (Joel 3:4)? No! On the contrary, He is saying that it is the 'I Am's tool of justice. Is Obadiah revealing the boomerang effect as the 'I Am's tool of black magic or judgement when 'I Am' says, 'As you have done, it will be done to you. / What you did will boomerang back and hit your own head.' (Obadiah vs.15b)? Of course, it is 'I Am's tool of judgement! Which shows you that religious scholars are not always aware; even though they think they know. Unlike science, all their conclusions are based on myth, theory and deductive logic. Science, on the other hand, is based on observations, events, test results and inductive logic."

I raise my hand to stat the clip again. "Note Bosco's change of heart in comparison to his mother and the other women. Professor Katsmum, this is not a gender thing. These women are practicing voodoo; there's your black magic." The clip ends. "Unfortunately, Professor, you have cut out the best part. At this point Bosco goes through a complete revelation, connecting to the 'Great I Am' within him, and the park rangers collect 288 snares with the aid of him and the other boys. All that in one day, which is more than the two previous years combined."

I study Hanna's angry face and the 'Great I Am' tries to get a read on where she is going next. The 'I Am' is far from pleased and finds that the love in her is deeply suppressed.

Hanna calls for the next clip and shoots me a hostile stare. The clip begins with the angry female Rhino pawing the ground and snorting at me. Then she starts her charge toward me, and I turn and run at top speed. The video goes back and forth between her charge and my flight. As she gets closer and closer, my peril becomes obvious, and the back and forth between us becomes shorter and shorter. Now, we are in the same frame, and I can almost feel the warmth of her snort on my calves. I start making sharp turns and dodging around bushes. This slows her down, but she charges ahead with her hoofs pounding the earth like thunder in my ears. Finally, I throw my hat in the air and dive in the shelter escape hole. The clip is cut here. The students and faculty are relieved and pleasantly amused.

I look at Hanna's harsh stare, and ask, "Professor Katsmum, let me tell you exactly what your question is."

With a maniacal smirk she flippantly fires back, "If your so clever, go ahead." The students start to chuckle, because they know, but the faculty is dead silent, because they don't.

I say to everyone in the hall, "Your question is, 'If your 'Great I Am' is so powerful, why couldn't the 'I Am' stop the Rhino from attacking you?' Well, Professor Katsmum?"

Hanna is shocked. She looks at her notes. Then she timidly responds, "That's it word for word." The faculty gasps, and the students continue to chuckle, because they have seen all these tapes online.

I respond lightheartedly, "To answer your question, Professor, the 'I Am' could, but doesn't! The Rhino has the same free-will that you have. She can choose to attack me with all her rage, just as you can. However, the difference between you is that her rage is a matter of taste, but your rage is an assumed intellectual superiority. Your left-brain irrational mind is playing games with you. It is lying to you. And you think you know when you don't know. The 'Great I Am' is within you and if you are connected you are protected, but the 'I Am' cannot protect you from yourself.

"Now, the 'Great I Am' knew what was in the Rhino's mind, and the 'I Am' told me to run. Why did she attack me?" Hanna is silent. "Class, why did the Rhino attack me?"

The students say together, "She didn't like your hat!"

The students and faculty have a good laugh. Hanna finally starts to laugh as well.

When the laughter starts to calm down, I continue, "Let's get down to the main reason I'm here, which is the Middle-East crisis. And Israel is part of that crisis.

"I need six people who will work to connect to the 'Great I Am' within and are willing to accept 'I Am's purpose for you for the rest of your lives. Who would like to connect?"

A sea of hands goes up, even Hanna's.

"OK, we need to narrow this down." I pause and listen to the 'I Am'. "Very good, the 'I Am' is going to give me six names. I would like to meet with these people as soon as we finish here; Talia, Ori, Noya, Jacob, Abbud and Hanna. The rest of you will be invited to a series of meditation groups to help you nurture your interest in connecting with the 'Great I Am' within you. I will schedule these before I leave.

CHAPTER 20
The Class Assembles

The next morning, after my meditation, the 'Great I Am' fills me in on the three new people in the meditation group. "Talia comes from a prominent conservative political family, who are descendants from Levi. From the age of ten she has been a rebellious youth in constant conflict with her father over political and religious issues. She has never meditated and seldom attends worship. Yet, she is instinctively aware of My presence and often acts on a message I give her. She emphatically believes that you are opening a new way of life, and she wants to be part of it.

"Ori is a quite shy soul, who is living a life off the radar. He has never taken a meditation or yoga class, yet he has read dozens of books on the subject and tried to train himself. Many times, he has been close to breaking through to Me, but his left-brain irrational mind always tricks him to move away. Within him is an enormous power, a sensitive heart and an incredible focus of will. If he can connect with Me, he will be a force to be reckoned with.

"Noya may be small in size, but she is a major powerhouse. She is an experienced meditator and yoga practitioner, and she actually thinks she is connected to Me, but is not. She mistakenly believes that I'm talking to her when she is in a state of inner peace. In actuality, it is her left-brain ego driving her. She has been easily misled by several false meditation 'experts' and thinks she knows best. She will have major problems connecting with her body, but I think you can help her redirect and overcome. I have great plans for her if she can break through.

"I should also update you about Hanna. She has had a major row with her Grandfather, defending you and attacking his misperception of you and your mission. I think she has turned a corner."

I'm always blown away with 'I Am's intimate understanding of everyone. Of course, if 'I Am' is right here inside us, 'I Am' knows everything we feel, think, or do.

We all gather outside the door to the roof-garden and wait for Hanna to come and open. I take the time to check their clothing, mats and sittables. Everyone is well prepared for the day's work. Then the questions start, which reminds me that they are accepting all this on blind faith.

The first question is, 'What is it like to be connected with the 'Great I Am'?"

"Fare enough, we will start at the end goal," I say with a smile. "When you connect with the 'Great I Am' within you, 'I Am' will tell you what your life's purpose is. Then you have a choice to accept or decline. If you decline, you simply go your own way. If you accept, the 'I Am' will be with you every step of your life's journey; knowing that because you are connected you are protected."

Abbud asks, "What if I change my mind?"

I smile as the 'Great I Am' expresses annoyance with indecisive people, "If you go your own way, you can still connect with the 'Great I Am' at any time when you are ready. However, if you connect, accept your life's purpose, and then walk away (which you are free to do), your left-brain irrational mind will move you deep into your dark-side. From there it is exceedingly difficult to return. I might add, there are many that have done just that, but they all have deeply regretted it."

Hanna has come up behind me after the students start to ask their questions. She asks, "Can you explain exactly how the boomerang effect is working, and how those connected are now protected?"

I turn and draw Hanna into the group. "The traditional boomerang effect has always been in operation if you do an unlawful thing it will always come back on your own head. In modern terms, we call it by many names: What goes around comes around; Treat others as you would have them treat you; or Bad Karma. Now, when you connect to the 'Great I Am' your protection occurs in three ways. First, you will hear 'I Am's voice clearly telling you what your enemy is about to do before they do it, so you are totally prepared. Second, when needed, you will go into what I call slow-motion perception. This is a natural phenomenon that animals and people experience in moments of extreme danger or crisis. When you are connected, it can be controlled at will. When you are in it, you perceive that everyone else is moving in slow-motion, but in actuality to others, you are only a blur. Third, as long as there is no hate or violence in your heart, 'I Am' will create an invisible force-field around you. Thus, all acts of violence will bounce off you and back on the exact same path to the perpetrator, with equal speed and force."

Hanna responds, "That explains a lot!"

"Yes," I respond to 'I Am's message, "To answer the question you are all thinking. When you connect you will all have that ability." 'I Am' continues to tell me that, for the first time Abbud has no doubts.

Hanna opens the door to the roof-garden. We all file out with our things, and Hanna closes the door. Immediately, those in front stop and the rest of us start to jam-up together. Those in front start to whisper and slowly they pass it back to Hanna and me. "There is a baby bird in the middle of the deck."

I leave my stuff and work my way to the front of the group. I motion for everyone to be very silent and relax. I then talk very softly to the baby bird and approach. She turns to look at me and does the baby wing flutter. I glance around to see if there is a nest nearby. There is none. I slowly crouch down and put the back of my point finger on the deck and slide it forward until it is right in front of her. Confidently, she steps up on my finger with one foot. Then she steps up with the other foot. Slowly, I lift her up until she is in front of my face.

We start to have a conversation. I narrate for you and the class, "Of course, the 'Great I Am' is helping me understand everything she says. She tells me how this is her first flight, and she tried to go higher and farther than her brothers and sisters. But when she got up this far, she was exhausted and landed on the deck, because it was big and easy. Now she has a problem. She says, 'I can't hop high enough to get into flight.' I tell her, 'I will hold you up and launch you, but you must promise to fly to the nearest tree.' She agrees nodding her head."

She then gives me a kiss on my lips, and I hold her up and give my wrist a snap. She launches into the air, drops a little bit and then catches the air under her wings and flies to the nearest tree. She chirps and sings to us all.

Jacob asks, "Is that part of the superpowers?"

"Not really," I say warmly. "That is part of me. But it can be part of who you are as well."

CHAPTER 21
Meditation - The Body

I have each person in the group find their spot on the deck and setup to use their sittables first. I ask everyone to do their own stretches and warmup routines. It is interesting to see the variety of warmups, everything from yoga to calisthenics. I do my own stretches, body toning and meditation. Then, I have them sit down and relax.

While walking around between them, I begin to narrate what they are to do. To avoid continuous chatter, I insert lengthy pauses to allow them to listen to their bodies.

"Your body is talking to you all the time. So is your left-brain irrational mind and ego. The purpose of this class is to shut down your chattering left-brain mind and ego and learn to listen to your body.

"Listen carefully to what I'm saying. Follow the directions, without thinking about them. Simply dismiss any left-brain thoughts that pop in your head. Relax.

"Put both feet flat on the deck. Let your hands rest in your lap, palms up. Keep your back straight and head up."

I notice that Noya has her middle finger and thumb together, in a classic Hindu pose. I bend down and gently open her fingers and smooth out her hand, whispering, "Relax, listen to your body."

I say to the group, "Listen to your body. What do your hands feel like? Is the energy in them openly outward or inwardly closed? Listen to their message.

"Now turn your hands over, palms down on your legs. Feel what they are saying. Are they openly outward or inwardly closed?"

Several respond, "Inwardly closed, wow!"

"Right, and you are all getting the same message.

Turn them over again."

Jacob responds with amazement, "Now, I feel the energy flowing in and out openly."

The others chime in with similar observations. I go over to Noya and bring her middle finger up to her thumb. I ask, "Where is the Divinity you're seeking?"

She responds, "Above and behind my head."

I answer, "That is your left-brain irrational mind telling you that. Open your hands and listen to your body. The 'I Am' is your essence of being. You will find the 'I Am' inside you. 'I Am' is waiting there for you."

She looks up into my eyes, and I can see her surprise. I put my hand on her shoulder and smile warmly.

I say to the group, "Start to become aware of your feet (avoid thinking about them, just be aware). What are they trying to tell you? Are you aware of any discomfort, like pinching shoes, too cold, too hot, or tiredness? Correct the problem. Be aware of them again."

I watch as they all start to deal with their feet. Those wearing shoes take them off. Everyone is now rubbing their feet. Some use acupressure. 'I Am' tells me that Hanna has pain in her neck and where to press on her feet. I gently take her feet in each hand and press with my thumb on that spot. She lets out a deep sigh and says, "Oooh! That feels good. How did you know?"

I smile as I stand up and look around. Everyone else is now holding their feet up. The 'I Am' picks the order and tells me where to press on each person's feet. By the time I finish, each person is deep into their body awareness.

I continue, "Now move your awareness up your lower legs to your knee. If you experience any discomfort, give it a rub. Be aware of the difference between the two legs. If you gave a rub to one, the

other one may be telling you that it wants a rub too."
This goes more smoothly.

"Move your awareness up your legs to the pelvis
area, then up your back and neck to the head, making
whatever adjustments the body asks you to make to
be more comfortable and relaxed."

Most everyone needs to work out kinks in the
back, neck, or shoulders. They are all tuning into
their bodies.

"Now move your awareness down your arms to
your hands, doing the same thing. When your hands
are comfortable, just sit for a few minutes and be
aware of your whole body."

I pause for a few minutes.

"What is it telling you? Enjoy the feeling! Note
that the ego is silent, and you turned off your left-
brain irrational mind. Now without breaking your
awareness, how does that feel?"

Each person responds, speaking as though from
a great distance. Ori says, "I never knew."

Abbud says, "I not only can feel my body; I can
see it from the inside out."

Talia says, "I feel the greatest sense of presence
ever."

Jacob witnesses, "In the midst of the calmness, I
see a floating blue-black sphere. Now a star meets
it."

Hanna starts a healing process, "At first I saw
many knots in my body. But as I start to focus on
each one of the knots, the body unties it all by itself,
and I can see it healthy again. It's a miracle."

Noya reacts to her body, "I have never been in
here before. I have only been in my brainy left-brain
mind and seen its idea of the body. What I see and
feel now is fantastic."

"Good, good, good," I respond enthusiastically.
"Now let's explore some movements that are part of
your DNA. They are an important part of who you

are and cannot be changed even if you wanted to. As
we do this exercise, strengthen your awareness of
what the body is telling you.

"First, fold your fingers together with a thumb on
top. Let your folded hands rest in your lap. Become
aware of how they feel. You had no choice in the way
you just did this. Your body always does it exactly
the same way. Now notice which thumb is on top.
Some will be right-thumbed, and some will be left-
thumbed, and it has nothing to do with your
dominant hand. However, everyone in your family
does it the same way because it is in your DNA. Try
changing the position of the thumb. Try to lace the
fingers in the opposite way. Be aware of what the
body is telling you. It is telling you it is wrong."

Everyone starts commenting on what they are
experiencing. Their amazement is universal, and the
awareness deepens.

"Next, place your hands palm down on your
thighs just above the knee. Be aware of how they
feel. Again, this position is in your DNA and feels
right for your body. It likes the way it feels. Now
notice the position of your little finger and the
distance it is from the next finger. That position and
distance cannot be changed. It is part of who you
are, and your body is telling you so."

I walk around and change the position of each
person's little finger about two millimeters.
Everybody reacts on how wrong it feels.

"Look at it. Go ahead and move it back to its
own position. Be aware that it is comfortable again."

Everyone makes the same comment in one way
or another, "It is such a little distance, but an
enormous difference in the way it feels. It is right for
my body." There is a growing confidence in
everyone's body awareness.

I continue, "Next, cross one leg over another. Be
aware of how the body feels. Now notice which leg is

on top and its position. This too is part of who you are and is also in your DNA. Your body is communicating that to you. If you switch them, your body will tell you it doesn't like it."

Everyone starts to experiment with various positions. They comment on their body reactions. Their voices are now in the present and no longer far away.

I explain, "I have tried my whole life to retrain my body to accept the opposite position. But as soon as I'm not thinking about it, my body switches them back automatically. The bottom line here is, the body knows what is right for you, so always listen to your body. Also note that the body is not connected to the ego and as long as you are listening to the body the ego has nothing to say, and the left-brain irrational mind is turned off."

I check each person, before I continue, to make sure they are totally into their bodies. "Now, we are going to tap into your body center. Try to relax your body as much as possible, without letting it collapse into a heap of jelly. Be aware of your inner presence. Go deeper than your muscles, bones and organs. Focus on the cells and atoms. Go into them. Don't think about them. Experience them. What do you see? What do you feel? Be aware of the space, the vast empty space. Go into it, bath in it. Relax. Feel the inner peace. Feel the reality that is you."

Everyone is discovering their inner presence, and their bodies are becoming increasingly radiant. I can see their individual colors creating an aura around them.

"Become aware of the energy moving through your body. There will be an energy flowing up from the earth into your feet and through your body. This is your oneness with the earth. You'll feel another energy flowing up through your body, out the top of your head, and around to re-enter trough your navel.

It will continue to flow in this circle. It will often have a color, which changes according to your mood. This is your life energy.

"As your sensitivity increases, you will feel all kinds of energy around you, from other people, from other organic life, and even some inanimate objects, like a stone. This is your body's center connecting with the essence of being within all things. Your body center is your essence of being. Note that the left-brain ego is quiet because it is completely outside your body center. Also, note that the left-brain irrational mind has no function here."

I study them very carefully to determine if they are ready to go on and take their first real step. The 'Great I Am' chimes in and assures me that they are ready but cautions me to bring them back to the surface slowly.

"Very slowly, bring yourself back to your hands in your lap. Take your time. Stay relaxed. You will feel your body singing to you as you make this journey. This is what Adam and Eve felt in the beginning."

I wait and watch. The 'I Am' lets me know when they are ready and pleased with their progress.

When they're ready, I continue. "So far you have learned to listen to your body without movement, but you can't spend the rest of your life sitting down. Through the next exercises the ego is going to try and confuse your perception. The body has developed unhealthy habits and the left-brain irrational mind and ego likes it that way, because it is familiar and less work. However, you have now learned that your body will not lie to you. When you are ready slowly stand up."

I wait, "You are now about to rediscover your natural body structure."

I wait until everyone is standing. I start to move around among them, adjusting their posture as I speak. "Stand as straight as you can. The outside of your feet should line up with the inside of your shoulders or armpits. Your knees should be slightly bent and directly over the center of your feet. This is called your grounded position, or in yoga the 'mountain position'. Listen to what your body is telling you.

"If the knee is too far forward, you will feel added pressure on the knee, greater tension in your calf and the back of your upper leg. If the knee is too far back or locked, your thigh muscle will go rigged. What you are trying to find is the point of minimal contraction before your muscle relaxes. I call this the 'toned muscle position', which is at rest.

"Now balance the pelvis on top of your legs. Rock it up in the front and down in the back. Your body will tell you that the lower abdomen and butt cheeks are too tight. Rock the pelvis down in the front and up in the back. Your lower back is now screaming at you. Rock it up and down until you find the point at which the muscles are equally toned.

"This is where your ego gets involved. It will tell you, 'You look better with it up in the back. Your butt looks bigger and your stomach flatter,' or it will take the opposite approach, 'Your butt's too big, tuck it. You don't want everyone looking at it.' Your ego doesn't care what your body is telling you or how good your body looks. The truth is you always look the best in the natural body position.

"Continue to focus on your back elongating your spine as you go; move up your neck to your head. Your head should be back, with your ears over the middle of your shoulders and your chin tucked slightly back. Imagine that there is a thread attached to the top of your head in the center. The thread is pulling you up higher and straighter.

"Suddenly the ego will be back again telling you, 'This feels strange. It takes far too much effort. The slouch is comfortable.' In addition to its lies, the ego is lazy.

"Listen to your body. As your skeleton reaches its natural position, your muscles will tell you how effortless it feels. Your inner energy will be flowing stronger and brighter. By ignoring your left-brain ego, the body will become more confident and stronger.

"Next you need to become aware of your trapezius muscles. This is where most people carry the majority of their tension, which causes them to slouch. Your ego likes it that way.

"Slowly role your shoulders in a circle, drop them down, then role them forward, bringing them up to your ears, and back and down very slowly. As soon as you feel the trapezius muscles reach the 'toned position', stop.

"The shoulders will be slightly back, and your middle finger will be resting naturally centered on the side of your thigh. You are now standing centered in your natural body structure. In this position, you have your greatest physical power, balance, and endurance. Work on it until your body feels centered, exactly as it did when you were sitting down."

I watch everyone as they struggle to find their centered position. Slowly moving from person to person, I help them make the needed adjustments.

I explain what is going on, "The left-brain ego will do anything to break your body down, because when you are in this body position you are nearly invincible to its lies. Don't fight the left-brain irrational mind and ego, just focus on centering your body, and the body will shut them down. Take your time. You did it once you can do it again."

Gradually, everyone begins to find their center again.

I wait until they are all relaxed and stable in their

centered mountain pose. Then I caution them, "Unfortunately, the minute you take a step, your left-brain ego and irrational mind will make you revert to old habits. Don't get angry or frustrated. You will simply shut it down again. Ironically, the more the left-brain irrational mind and ego fight you, the easier and quicker it will become to shut them down."

This comment causes everyone to grunt and grown.

I respond, "That's your left-brain irrational mind and ego responding. Listen, what is your body saying?"

They all look inside for a moment. Then they start to smile, and all say at once, "It's laughing!"

I smile and continue, "OK, take a step. Be aware of what is happening. Let the negative reaction go, ignore the left-brain irrational mind and ego, and focus on regaining the naturally centered body position. When you are comfortably centered take another step. Keep doing this routine, making the left-brain irrational mind and ego back off, until you can walk around on the deck."

At first, everybody looks like stiff robots walking in extreme slow motion, one frozen step after another. However, they are all determined, and their vocalization becomes brighter and victorious. Then Ori starts to hum the Beatles' tune "All you need is love." Within seconds everyone joins in, and their walking becomes more natural, upright and effortless. Their inner beings are soaring.

I walk over to the door to the deck and open it. Standing by the door, I say, "OK, put on your shoes and walk up and down the first flight of stairs."

As soon as they started down the stairs, they all began to look like robots again. After repeating these three times their bodies are centering and in control again.

I called out, "OK, down the stairs and run through the lobby, run outside and leap. Let your body fly."

While running, there are some brief hesitations, but their bodies recover quickly. Outside, they start leaping like gazelles. Their leaps are so long and so high, they start to gather an audience. I start to run and fly with them.

After a few moments, I move out in front of them and stop. I motion for them to stop, and they assemble in front of me. With only motions, I ask them to center up. They each elongate and stand radiating their enormous energy.

I say quietly, "Your body has become your temple. Let's go give it some food."

CHAPTER 22
Meditation - Breathing

During lunch, the group starts to come together as a team or even a family. What they experience in their bodies gives them a common bond. This bond opens them up to a whole new world. Their closeness removes all differences, by opening them up to acceptance and understanding. All of them become equal. Even Hanna becomes just another member of the group.

After lunch, we meet back on the roof garden.

I ask everyone, "Roll out your mats and lie down on your backs, with your legs stretched out. Start to become aware of your body again. Avoid left-brain thinking about it, just be aware. As you know now, awareness is your sixth sense. It is different from the other five senses. Although awareness has feeling, it does not use touch; it may experience vibrations, but it does not use the ears; it is the primary sense in all other creatures. Relax and be aware of your body. Be aware of its presence again. Be aware of its shape. You are aware now that it is talking to you, but not with words. Simply, relax and be aware. Start to focus on your breathing.

"Your breathing is totally interrelated with your natural body structure and function. You already experienced the difficulty of shutting down the left-brain irrational mind and ego. Well, your breathing will help you shut them down.

"In this exercise, you are going to find the source of your breath, your body's natural breathing.

"Your body does this all by itself. However, many trainers engage the left-brain irrational mind and ego and make you think you can control your breathing, with comments like, 'Relax and take a breath,' or 'Take a deep breath.' The result is a forced breathing, a heaving of the chest, and an intake of less air. Let's discover how the body breathes NATURALLY.

"Become aware of your body as before. Only now, your muscles are going limp and parts of your body are pressing into the floor. Observe it as you did this morning. Fold your fingers together and place your hands on your abdomen just below your ribcage and let them rest there. Slowly bring your awareness to focus on your breathing. This is natural breathing. In this position, your body does it all by itself. It is what your body does every time you fall asleep. For the purpose of this exercise, try to avoid falling asleep for now."

Everyone chuckles

"Note what your hands are doing. They are rising and falling as your abdomen goes up and down. The natural action of your diaphragm causes this. You breathe in and the hands go up. You breathe out and the hands go down. Let's run a test.

"Move your hands and place them on the upper part of your chest. Continue with your natural breathing. Be aware of the effortless ease of each breath. Take note that your hands are not moving. This is a very important note, because your left-brain irrational mind and ego are going to try and tell you that the best way to breath is with your chest, which is simply not true. The ribcage is not very flexible and can't expand more than 2.7% to take in more air. However, the diaphragm stretches and pulls down expanding your lung capacity considerable. When you try to breath with the chest, the expanded chest feeling is your lungs reaching their maximum capacity within the chest cavity, not a dramatic expansion of the cavity.

"Move your hands back to the abdomen position. Now you are going to take a deep breath using the natural body function. This is the opposite of what the left-brain irrational mind and ego has been telling you for years. On your next exhale, use your hands and push down to force all the air out of your lungs. The more air you force out; the more air you will take in. When you have forced out as much air as you can, do nothing; don't hold your breath, just relax. Your body will take a deep breath all by itself. Your lungs will fill to their natural capacity. You cannot stop it or hold it indefinitely.

"If you repeat this process several times, you may hyperventilate (taking in more oxygen than the body is using). The symptom is a slight dizziness. If you experience this sensation, hold your breath, and let the body recover. Skin-divers and mountain climbers use this technique to their advantage."

I look around and study each person carefully. I notice that Noya is repeating a meditation mantra to herself. I bend down and whisper, "Shut down the mantra and be aware of your body and breathing." Her eyes pop open wide. There is shock and wonder in them. "For now, focus on your breathing. You are about to discover something deeper within you."

I continue to guide the group, "Return to your natural breathing. When you are confident that you are aware of your natural breathing process, get up and sit on your sittable again. Find your body center again and connect your breathing to it. The 'I Am' created the two to work together. However, prepare yourself, the left-brain irrational mind and ego are going to try and tell you to go back to your chest breathing. Whether you are sitting or standing, put your hands on your upper abdomen again and let your natural breathing move them in and out. Simply focus on your breathing, the body will relax, and the left-brain irrational mind and ego will quiet down. As the breath and body-center unite, the left-brain irrational mind and ego will back off. As I said earlier, the left-brain irrational mind and ego are lazy and there is nothing they like better than doing nothing. However, they know that you are not going to sit there forever. It will ally with your unhealthy habits and get you later. Try your natural breathing."

I study each person carefully. Some are having trouble combining the natural breathing and body awareness.

"If your left-brain chatter or ego become persistent over this merger, do not get angry, simply blow it a kiss and push it aside to get back into your body breathing. When you are in your body as you were before lunch, put your hands on your abdomen and relax. You will discover it is already happening. Simply, let them merge by them self. If your left-brain irrational mind and ego try to confuse you and tell you that the merger is complicated. Remember, your left-brain irrational mind and ego will lie to you constantly. Your body will never lie to you. Listen to your body and let it merge with your breathing."

Everyone starts to relax, and their focus becomes stronger, but it is harder for some.

I bend over Ori and whisper in his ear, "Blow it a kiss and move on." He does so literally.

His eyes open like saucers and he says, "It works!" Then he begins to relax. His body and breathing merge.

Hanna and Jacob start to talk to the various parts of their body and carry on a conversation with them. This helps the others realize how natural their awareness really is.

I comment, "Learn to recognize your awareness and how it communicates. It is more than a feeling or touch. It is coming from deep inside you. Be aware. Your breathing happens all by itself."

Talia starts to cough uncontrollably. There are tears running down her cheeks. I move to her immediately.

The 'Great I Am' starts talking to me, "She was a cigarette smoker and has been keeping a secret. She gave it up two weeks ago, when the doctor diagnosed her with lung cancer. Now her left-brain irrational mind is screaming at her."

I support her head in the palm of my hand and whisper, "I know what is happening. Your body can heal you. Shut down the left-brain chatter and cough as hard as you can." I place my other hand on her lower chest. "Go into your body and see your lungs as healed."

She coughs violently for another minute. Then it abruptly stops. She looks in my eyes and smiles, while nodding her head yes. She whispers, "It's gone."

I turn to the others, "Everything is fine. Let's get back into our bodies and breathing. Note how your left-brain irrational minds are taking advantage of the interruption. Relax and push it aside.

"Your breath is the healing tool of the body. Hanna, go into those knots you started working on this morning. Breath into them. Everyone breathe into any difficult or painful area you found this morning.

"Be careful, I can hear your left-brain chatter saying, 'But if the pain is in my leg, how can I breathe into my leg?'"

Everyone looks at me, as if I had read their minds.

"It is a strange phenomenon, but you will actually feel it happening. The pain will decrease, and a healing will begin to take place. Whether it is because you are sending more oxygen to the area, or firing up neurons in the area, or there is a natural healing power in you, we don't know. Yes, it could be all of the above. The fact is, you will soon feel the body moving easier and growing stronger. This is not because you strengthened your muscles. It could be because you are freeing them from unneeded tension. The goal is to be able to maintain this centered state as you move through your daily life. Keep working on it. You will prevail."

I watch them for a moment. Their bodies and breathing need to unify. The radiance they had this morning begins to return. Slowly, they become stronger and more present.

"Now stand up and move about the deck. Pause only when you need to shut down the left-brain chattering mind and ego. Talk to the plants and the insects. Talk to the stones. Talk to each other. Stay centered and enjoy the feeling. Feel your awareness reach out to everything and everyone to whom you talk. Feel your awareness merge with each other.

"You may now experience a lightness of being from your awareness; the entire world will change around you. You will block or neutralize your left-brain ego. You will shut off your left-brain chatter and bring your irrational mind under control. Your body will emerge confident and in charge of your physical being. It will become your greatest ally. Others will see you differently and they will seek your presence. Enjoy this feeling; enjoy the new connection with others; but avoid the mistake of using it to feed the ego. The moment your mind says you're superior, more powerful than others, or you feel you can control others, you will have made that mistake. Remember it is only your awareness.

"Don't dwell on it. It happens to the best of us.

"Simply recognize it and move back to your Love-light side, your lightness of being. The other thing is, from now on you will never be alone. You are now ready to connect."

Everyone stops and turns to look at me. They know what that means.

I study the group and then continue, "What all of you accomplished here today is what most people would be glade to accomplish in a lifetime of meditation. Those that do reach this point usually stop here. They feel that they are fulfilling the goal of meditation, to center the body and shut down the left-brain irrational mind and ego. However, that is only the beginning."

CHAPTER 23
Meditation - Connecting

"You are all here to connect to the 'Great I Am' within you. Now, the 'I Am' wants to use my voice to speak to you before we begin this especially important step. Very soon, you will be listening to the 'I Am' within you directly."

I pause and let the 'I Am' take over.

As usual, the 'I Am's voice is extremely powerful. "You are all ready to take the next step in your meditation. Since you are such an eclectic group, I want you to know the truth from Me. I Am the 'I Am' in each of your cultures. Each of your sacred texts verify My presence if you examine them closely. Yet, in each of your cultures, religious leaders have chosen to hide that fact for one reason or another. My purpose here is to end all war and conflict. To create a new earth where differences are a strength not a source of hatred. To bring Love and unity back into creation. I say this because your left-brain irrational minds and the irrational minds of others will try to shut you down. What I promise you is, if you connect to Me and accept My purpose for your life, I will protect you as long as there is no hatred or violence in your heart."

When 'I Am' gives me the floor, I look up and study the faces of the group. They are all bright eyed and in awe.

I explain, "The goal of our meditation is to center yourself and find the 'Great I Am' within you. Once you find the 'I Am' and are listening to the 'I Am', you have the big Free Will choice to make, to accept 'I Am's purpose for your life, or remain bound to your left-brain irrational mind and ego. That is true Free Will.

"Choose the purpose the 'Great I Am' has for you,

and it will be like a second berth. You will be leaving behind all your old hatreds, false emotions, prejudices and misperceptions. You will be living in the present. You will be living in the Love-light. Once you connect to the 'I Am', you will be making that choice every minute of every day for the rest of your life. You will experience many discussions and debates with the 'I Am', but the Free Will choice will always be yours. Sometimes, you will make the wrong choice, but 'I Am's Love and patience will always be right there with you. Sometimes, 'I Am' may even learn something from you. In that case, brace yourself for 'I Am's overwhelming response of joy.

"Of course, your left-brain irrational mind and ego will try to convince you that the left-brain irrational mind and ego are your only reality and freedom of will. Choose your left-brain irrational mind and ego and you will be bond to all its rules and pseudo-moral laws for the rest of your purposeless life. If you make that choice, you will also get to choose to do or not do millions of don't dos and live in the gray zone. That is what the left-brain irrational mind and ego will have you believe is your freedom of will. Some have even done the unthinkable, by going completely to their dark-side and turning their backs on the 'I Am'. Very few have ever been able to reverse that freedom of will choice and find their way back

"It is your Free Will choice, to live in the Love-light or not."

I study their reaction and listen to the 'I Am' to see if there is any negative response. There is none. In fact, they are eager to get on with it.

As I introduce the next step, I study their faces, but pay a little more attention to Noya. "You have all grown up as part of a Hebrew or Islamic culture. You are all descendants of Abraham and Moses or

Mohamad, who were all connected to the 'Great I Am.' Like Samuel, the Teacher/Prophet, and Jacob, the father of Israel, they simply connected. Yet here we are in a complicated irrational world, which has buried, bared, or hidden 'I Am's presence within us. Thus, we turn to the Eastern traditions to find our way into the 'I Am'. Unfortunately, pseudo-spiritual leaders have and still do pervert those traditions and practices.

"Today, you rediscovered the essence of meditation. You learned to shut down your chattering left-brain mind and ego through inner body awareness. You rediscovered your source of breath, which has been part of us since creation. You learned to combine the two techniques and center your body, finding your inner-being, your place of stillness and peace. Now, to outline your next step on this journey, here is a description of that journey, from the UPANISHADS (The sacred scriptures of India):

> Inside your body is a shrine.
> Inside the shrine is a lotus flower.
> Inside the lotus is a tinny space.
> Inside that tinny space lives the
>   creator.
> Inside the creator is the Universe.
> Find it, and you will be one with the
>   creator and all things.
> Be there, and all things and the
>   creator will be one with you.

"Now, sit on your sittables and get into your bodies and breathing. Do **not** start using a mantra. When you reach your center, I will guide you into the most powerful mantra of all. This will assure the success of your connection. Go ahead and shut down your left-brain chattering mind and ego."

I move among them and watch each person

carefully. I can feel that 'I Am' is waiting. The group, surprisingly, moves very quickly into their inner-bodies and breathing.

As soon as everyone's breathing unifies, I speak in a slow rhythmic tone. "This mantra was first used by Krishna's mother, Devaki, and was later discovered by Patanjali.

He says in his YOGA SUTRAS, (I let Patanjali speak.) 'My mantra is the unutterable syllable ॐ in Sanskrit. The history of the syllable is important for the meditator. The syllable ॐ represents our eternal present. All that we have been in the past, and all that we will be in the future is present in the syllable ॐ. There is nothing that we have been or will be in the future that does not exist in the here and now. If we fully connect with our unutterable syllable ॐ, we will be one in our inner being, our 'Great I Am' center. I (Patanjali) consider this to be the most powerful of all mantras. Can you imagine my surprise when I discovered why no one ever utters this mantra aloud?

'I was practicing my breathing before meditation. I pressed all the air out of my body and relaxed. The air came rushing back in. My ears were listening. I let my body exhale naturally. My ears were listening. I long since had trained my mind and ego to be still. My inhale, with the mouth open, came again all on its own, OOOOOOO. My exhale, with my mouth closed and through my nose, followed naturally, MMMMMMM. My body was saying this syllable ॐ without utterance.

'That night in my meditation, I started the breathing by pressing out all my air. My body took a deep breath, OOOOOOO. Then it exhaled, MMMMMMM. The unutterable syllable ॐ was just there. As I started across the prairie of my daily life, my left-brain mind and ego started coming at me from all directions like a herd of steers. The unutterable syllable ॐ repelled them. I wasn't saying it; my body was. If I became distracted for a second, or any dark thoughts tried to sidetrack me, all I had to do was slide back into my breathing and my body mantra and let the syllable ॐ do the work. As I approached the river of light, a vast darkness and then a silence and stillness encompassed me. When the silence and stillness were total the river of light rushed in, and my breathing became slow, even, and effortless. The unutterable syllable ॐ was now truly one syllable. I felt the 'I Am' laughing and 'I Am' filled me with the joy, love, light, and contentment of that moment.' Thus, said Patanjali."

I listen. Their breathing is now slow, rhythmic and unified. I continue, "Now it is your turn to discover it. Breath in through your mouth and out through your nose."

They start the cycle. I wait for three breaths and say, "Listen with your body awareness." I pause, then I say, "Listen with your inner ear." I wait.

Suddenly, Noya blurts out, "Good God, it's OM!" She catches herself and continues, "Oh, forgive me. I shouldn't say it. But my body is saying it all by itself." She then goes into her deepest meditation ever.

I wait. Soon, I can feel it when each of them starts to connect to the 'Great I Am.'

I wait until everyone connects. I wait a little over twenty minutes until everyone makes their choice. Now, everyone has a purpose for their new life. Then I say, "OK, start to come out of your meditation. I know you would like to stay in there for the rest of your life. Well, I have news for you. You will **BE** in there for the rest of your life."

Slowly, everyone surfaces and sits in silence. Their faces and bodies are radiant with their inner Love-light. They look around and smile at each other. It is as though they are seeing each other for the first time. In actuality they are because each person is a new being.

I ask, "Who would like to share their experience with the rest of the team?

Noya jumps at the chance. Her body is vibrating with excitement. "This is the most incredible experience of my life. When I was a little girl, I wanted to hear his voice calling me, like Samuel. I could feel that he was inside me, but I could never find him. I only thought I was listening. Once, I shut myself in a soundproof room. All I heard was my heart beating. The 'I Am' was not speaking to me, I thought.

"I tried every kind of meditation there is. Some gave me a little inner peace, but none made me aware of my body and breathing. So, I manufactured a connection, which I discovered today was my own left-brain irrational brain chatter. I was my own worst enemy.

"Today, I found 'I Am's presence within me. I expected power and judgment, but I found gentle caring. I expected male dominance but found sensitive insight. I expected to get my marching orders but received the most incredible Love-light I have ever known.

"The 'I Am's purpose for me, as part of this team, is to stop hatred and violence. I'm to help women move past their fear and emotional paralysis. I'm to teach this process to all who truly seek the 'I Am'.

"Hayah, a simple thank you is not enough. For you lead me to a life worth living."

Hanna is the next speaker, "My whole life, I have been living in pain. I thought it was in my body and mostly caused by others. Today, I discovered it was in my left-brain irrational mind and ego, and I'm the cause of it. As soon as I got into my body and shut down my yapping left-brain mind and ego, I found I could heal the pain centers. I have never felt so good and so free. I wanted to stay in that state forever.

"Then I discovered my source of breath, or should I say that my source of breath found me floating inside my body. My yapping mind wanted to break me down and regain control, but I blew it a kiss and it ran away.

"I went so deep in my body, breathing new life into every cell, every atom. I saw the vast space between the electrons and nucleus of each atom. They looked like miniature solar systems spinning around inside me. I went into the vast space. I felt so small. Then a beam of light came racing through the darkness, like a shooting star. The next thing I felt, I was inside the 'I Am,' and 'I Am' was inside me. My whole being was cleansed and made whole by the 'I Am's incredible Love-light.

"We talked for what seemed like days. 'I Am' described the 'I Am's purpose for my life. My role with this team. My goal to help all women. Then to my amazement, 'I Am' said, 'I want you to be my Prophetess to modern Israel, the Middle-East and the world.' In my heart, I felt unworthy, but 'I Am' said, 'I shall put the words in your mouth. And My Love-light shall be your strength.'"

She swallowed to get the words out, "I accepted!"

The group sits in silence for a moment. The 'Great I Am' starts to fill me in on a surprise. I listen carefully. Then I turn to Talia and Jacob. They are looking at each other. I say to Jacob, "I understand you have something special to tell us about your connection."

Jacob reflects for a moment and then jumps in talking a mile a minute. "This past week has been an incredible roller-coaster ride, with many gains and difficulties. Today's high, peaks them all, for many reasons. Some of it, I will leave to your own insight."

He looks at Talia, who nods yes. Then he continues, "Five days ago, I proposed marriage to Talia. She turned me down. She didn't tell me why. I emotionally crashed, and my pesty left-brain mind and ego went into overdrive. I thought she hated me because I asked her to stop smoking. My pesty left-brain mind and ego invented a thousand ways I have been a jerk, or maybe it was another guy. I didn't know what to do.

"This morning, she started to cough, and I thought she was going to die. Then, Hayah helped her.

"I struggled to get past all this in my meditation. Fortunately, I got past it and shut down my pesty left-brain mind and ego. Although, it kept trying to use this issue to get back in. Each time I blocked it and went deeper. Luckily, I managed to connect to the 'Great I Am' within me. The 'I Am' already knew my pain and the whole situation.

"Before anything else, 'I Am' started explaining what was happening. Talia was dying of lung cancer. She didn't want to be a burden on me and my love for her. Then, the 'I Am' and Hayah healed her. The cancer is now gone. Through the 'I Am', our love came together as one. Through the 'I Am', I proposed again, and she accepted. This Love is far beyond anything either of us has ever experienced.

"Besides this wonderful perk, 'I Am's purpose for me is to bring unity between all faiths and all cultures. I would be an idiot to turn the 'I Am' down."

Talia is beaming with the Love-light, "All this happened, because the 'I Am' is alive within us. What the 'I Am' is giving us is beyond description. It is more than intimate. It is beyond compassion. It takes love to a whole new level. You have aptly called it the 'Love-light.'

"This connection with the 'I Am' is so wonderful, I cannot understand how our ancestors could walk away from the 'I Am'. A greater Love does not exist. Compared to the 'Great I Am', our left-brain irrational mind is a joke and even then, only black comedy.

"Yes, I accept 'I Am's purpose for me and will gladly lead all people to the 'Great I Am' within. The 'I Am' is also giving me the ability to help others find healing within themselves.

"Hatred and ignorance ends Here and Now."

"Amen to that, sister," Abbud confirms the sentiment. "My experience of today's events is similar to the rest of you, with a couple of major differences. I doubted that any kind of meditation could shut down the left-brain irrational mind and ego. And, I had no hope that I could connect with the 'Great I Am' within me.

"Yet, here am I, connected and ready to go to work. 'I Am' wants me to lead my people out of the dark ages and into the Love-light. The 'I Am' wants us to live in a word with the 'I Am' at our center. And I want to be part of that!"

Everyone turns to look at Ori. He is sitting on his sittable, back strait, hands in his lap, feet on the floor and eyes closed. He is listening intently.

Without opening his eyes, he asks, "Hayah, how did you manage to glean this effortless process out of the vast sea of meditation mediocrity, misperception, false goals and intentional untruths?" Before I can respond, he continues. "A ha! 'I Am' started guiding you when you were only twelve years old. You were still innocent. You, lucky boy. Thank you very much, with all of my heart."

He opens his eyes and addresses the group. His voice is clear and powerful. "The 'Great I Am' asked me to breath truth and justice back into the democratic political process. All who serve must connect to the 'I Am'. Plus, all citizens must connect and serve in the democracy. With 'I Am's help, I will wipe the words, 'Let someone else do it,' from their procrastinating minds. With 'I Am's help, I will teach people to embrace the differences between each other and the strength in those differences.

"I will be steadfast. I will fulfill 'I Am's purpose for me. I will fill the world with 'I Am's Love-light. I will support you, my sisters and brothers, in all we do to serve the 'I Am'. May 'I Am's Crystal City become a reality in our lifetime."

Everyone responds with, "Yes, yes, yes!"

"From now on we will close each session with a healing exercise," I explain to the team. "This exercise helps one-member to experience extremely deep inner body meditation. The 'Great I Am' will pick one person each time. For this session, you are all getting 'I Am's message that it is Hanna.

"Hanna, lie on your stomach on your mat and relax. Go into your meditation. The rest of us will kneel beside her, three on each side. We have three movements to do. The first is a gentle touch. Work on the area of her body in front of you. Let your fingertips glide across her body at whatever speed suits you. Go for at least a minute. The second movement is a gentle tapping. Change your speed frequently. Go for at least a minute. The third movement is a gentle slapping. Be sure it is not too hard. Go for at least a minute. Now, mix up the touching, tapping and slapping. Go for at least a minute longer... and stop."

Hanna says from deep within, "Don't stop."

I continue, "Hanna, roll over on your back." She rolls over. "Now repeat the three movements the same way. Touching... Go for at least a minute. Tapping... Slapping... Mix it up... And stop."

I pause and then ask, "Hanna, where is Heaven?"

Hanna responds with a distant voice, "Within me."

"After every session one of you will experience the real location of Heaven, the ultimate connection with the 'I Am'."

Hanna slowly comes out of it and sits up. She starts to speak several times, then says, "There are no words to describe it. Can we do it again?"

Everyone laughs.

"Tomorrow morning, we will meet back here. We will start with a story and our meditation, as you will do every morning as a team. After that, I will prepare you for the action in the field."

CHAPTER 24
Field Training

As everyone gathers outside the roof garden, there is a constant buzz. Now that they are all connected to the 'Great I Am' within them, they have the 'I Am's constant presence and their shared experiences to talk about. They also have many personal questions to ask me.

One of these questions may be of interest to you, my readers. "How does the healing process work, with the 'Great I Am' within us?" Here, I will give you the condensed version. I explain it in a little more detail in *A NEW CURTAIN OPENS, Chapter 24.*

"For healing to take place, both the person healing and the person or animal being healed must be connected to the 'Great I Am' within them. Technically, we don't do the healing. The 'I Am' does. We are only 'I Am's hands. The person needing the healing care must be able to see that part of their body healed and whole. This is easier for animals than humans. As in creation, the 'Great I Am' is the chemist/biologist during the healing process. Once the healing takes place, it cannot be explained to a person who is not connected, so don't bother."

After about 30 minutes of sharing their experiences, I ask everyone to get out their mats or sittables, which ever they are going to use to meditate. As they set up, I explain, "Every day or at least twice a week, you should gather for group meditation. This is important for you to function as a team and stay ahead of any problems in the field. Listen to the 'I Am', and 'I Am' will call you together, if you need extra group time.

"You can use the same format that I'm using

now: gather and catch up; set up for your meditation;
someone give an inspirational message or tell a story;
meditate for 30 minutes; and then discus experiences
and action plans.

"Now, settle down in your places. I'm going to
tell you a story initialed, '*Light Out of Darkness.*'

> *Making a Spiritual Journey through
> the darkness of this world is not a simple
> undertaking. However, finding the Love-
> light that gives meaning to life makes it
> worth the effort. To Hoss Proxetter
> finding his 'Great I Am' center was the
> turning point of his life.*
>
> *Hoss was only a boy, when he
> discovered the 'I Am' inside him and heard
> the 'I Am's voice. 'I Am' said to him, "You
> are my chosen one. I need a special
> messenger to the people." The 'I Am' told
> him where he was to go to school and
> what he was to study. the 'I Am' said, 'I
> will be there for you and guide you along
> the way.' Then 'I Am' left him to do as 'I
> Am' asked, but 'I Am' left him with a
> warning to tell no one.*
>
> *Hoss could not believe what happened
> to him. The power of that moment was
> incredible. It was all he could do to keep
> from shouting it from the rooftops. The 'I
> Am' talked to him. 'I Am' gave him signs.
> 'I Am' revealed to him various aspects of
> who 'I Am' is. The 'I Am' said, "In my
> chosen, there is to be no self, because you
> are one with me."*
>
> *However, Hoss began to see himself as
> different. He felt important and over the
> years that followed, he became
> increasingly filled with himself. This*

began to build a barrier between him and the 'I Am'. His meditation became more difficult, with his left-brain irrational *mind and ego controlling him. This led Hoss into a deep despair with many doubts.*

His left-brain irrational *mind became another voice inside his head, "You may be chosen, but where is God when you need Him? Why is God not present?" These questions or doubts were shaking the very center of his being.*

Hoss cried out, "Am I alone?" "Where are You?" "Have You abandoned me?" "Have I done the right thing?" "What have I done, that you have turned away from me, oh... oh God?"

His left-brain *mind fired back immediately, "You see there is no answer from God. Trust me I will be your guide."*

Hoss wept. Even though the 'I Am's Love-light was blazing within him, Hoss let his left-brain irrational *mind and ego take control and misdirect him from his 'Great I Am' center. His mind even had him using the name God instead of his real name, 'I Am'.*

While in his third year of graduate school, Hoss' despair peaked. He passed through the fire. He started to feel that the 'I Am's apparent abandonment was ironic. It was only a childhood fantasy, which he blew into unreal proportions. Who was he to think that God would choose him anyway?

Not long after that, he went through the fire again. He began to see the whole event as comical. He was a joke. God was a joke. His experience was a joke. Life was a joke. He believed and trusted in a childhood fantasy, which made him feel stupid and vulnerable. Nothing had any meaning and life seemed pointless.

This brought him to the fire of death. He went to the schools the 'I Am' asked him to attend. He studied the subjects the 'I Am' asked him to learn. As he finished, there did not seem to be any point to any of it. He hated who he was and planned to destroy himself.

As he knelt in his small room by his bed, with his hunting knife in front of him, he looked up and cried out. "Oh, 'Great I Am' release me from this life." His rational mind was silent. His left-brain *ego hid from destruction.*

At that moment, a tiny speck of light appeared in front of him. It began to grow larger and larger. It moved to his right, beside the bed, and began to fill the end of the room. Within the light, he could see a figure taking shape. As the figure grew clear, he saw that it was Yeshua holding out His arms to him. The figure spoke to him; "You are my chosen one." Tears were streaming down Hoss' cheeks.

The Love-light surrounding Yeshua, then began to grow brighter and brighter. Soon there was only Love-light, and the Love-light grew even stronger. It consumed all the furniture in the room, and then consumed the walls, floor and ceiling. It began to consume Hoss. He could see his hands and legs disappear into the Love-light. In the last instant, he saw himself as a tiny black speck within this bedazzling Love-light. Then even the speck disappeared. His soul was on fire. His sense of self ceased to exist. He became one with the will of the 'I Am'. He could feel nothing but Love, see nothing but Light. He was in the Love-light; the Love-light was in him. He was one with the 'Great I Am'.

As the Love-light slowly faded, he found himself still kneeling by his bed. The knife was no longer in front of him. In its place was a purple flowering sprig of lavender. Its fragrance filled the room. In that moment, Hoss felt a transformation, for the 'I Am' was in him, and he knew his mission.

He must bring the Love-light out of darkness.

(STORIES FOR YOUR SPIRIT, Vol. II)

I paused for a moment and then asked everyone to start their meditation. And I went into my own meditation. The 'Great I Am' was busy with all of us. On a few occasions, 'I Am' united us all at the same time. That unity was a powerful experience for us all.

After 30 minutes, I ask everyone to come out of their meditation. This varies, in the length of time, because of the different communications going on between the 'Great I Am' and a member of the team. When everyone is ready, I start with the field training.

"I picked the *Light Out of Darkness* story because it raises two important questions. What caused Hoss' depression? And how could this happen to a person, connected to the 'Great I Am' within him?

"Let's start with Hoss' depression. What caused it?"

Abbud chimes in, "The 'Great I Am' says 'I do not know anything about depression.' How can that be?" Everyone else responds with verbal affirmation.

"OK, but that in itself should tell you something."

Ori sees it first, "It is not part of who the 'I Am' is. So, where does it come from?"

"Precisely!" I affirm. "It was not part of creation and it is not in the 'I Am'. It only exists in the **human** left-brain irrational mind. The same as all dark emotions, such as hatred, paranoia, or any psychoses. We are causing it ourselves. Even to the point of causing pain in our body, called psychosomatic behavior. Hanna, you discovered that yesterday."

"Yes, I did," Hanna affirms. "But when I shut down the rational mind and ego, my body was able to flush it out. Last night, it tried to come back, and I had to center my body to get rid of it."

"Bingo! So, what caused Hoss' depression?"

Abbud jumps back in, "Now I know why I liked that story so much. Hoss is like us. He connects with the 'Great I Am.' But he is in school. He has the most important experience of his life but can tell no one. His ego says, 'why not? You are important now.' He must shut his mouth and study to learn. His left-brain irrational mind takes it all in. Then it turns around and tells him it's useless. That is when Hoss starts to hate his life. The story is telling us what we can expect as we fulfill the 'I Am's purpose for us."

Jacob adds, "But all we have to do is connect and stay connected to the 'I Am'."

"That's correct, Jacob," I confirm his conclusion and answer to the second question. "But and that is a big BUT your left-brain irrational mind and ego will always be trying to distract you. Make no mistake, they are enormously powerful. You must maintain your awareness at all times.

"To help you maintain your awareness, here are a few tips about the left-brain irrational human brain. Some of you know this in part, however there are some links 'I Am' tells me of which you are unaware. Yes, now you know how I can read your minds. You all know that the brain has many parts, each with a special function.

"The right lobe of the brain we use for inductive logic, with thoughts that are only rooted in facts or observation (all the sciences, including medicine), mathematics, astronomy, all the arts, body awareness, your visual picturization, meditation, and most importantly, your Spirituality, the 'Great I Am.' This is where your brain can experience the 'I Am' in your body.

"The left lobe we use for – deductive logic, with thoughts that are used for conjecture and opinion (philosophy or theory), left-brain irrational thought, the ego, psychology and, are you ready, Theology. However, the rational mind is telling you, IT is the only truth, when it is not.

"The human mind has two sides, the light side and the dark side. They both exist in all humans. The light is positive, and the dark is negative. The positive side contains actions like love, kindness, awareness, generosity, peace, spirituality and forgiveness. The goal on the light side is to connect with the 'Great I Am' within us and live in the crystal city.

"The dark side contains actions like hatred, selfishness, ego, greed, violence, theology and war. The goal on the dark side is to dominate, rule and destroy all others. Contrary to what the irrational mind will tell you, there is no gray in the middle. I need to shatter one more irrational myth. Wars do not end wars. They create endless wars. Wars ultimately produce self-destruction.

"Before I continue, do you have any questions."

Talia quickly respond, "The 'I Am' says I should ask you this question if I want the short answer and want everyone else to learn from it. As you're aware, I'm a descendant of Levi. So, Why is Theology in the left brain and Spirituality in the right brain?"

I laugh, "The 'Great I Am' always does this. I once told someone, 'Don't ask the 'I Am' a question unless you have time for the answer.' (Now, we can hear the 'I Am' laughing.)

This is the short answer. "In Theology, is God an idea or an experience?"

Talia says, "It is the study of God; so, it must be an idea."

"In Spirituality, is the 'I Am' an idea or an experience?"

"An experience."

Ori says, "That is definitely the short answer, and it's clear as crystal. So, how long did it take you to see it that way?"

I laugh and say, "I would rather not count the years. Let's just say an exceedingly long time, lost in the left-brain irrational process.

"Are there any other questions?"

Noya timidly raises her hand, "Hayah, where does this put religious institutions?"

"Noya, that is a particularly good question and very difficult to answer. In most of the religions, the founders and many of the early followers were connected to the 'Great I Am' within. They were in actuality, Spiritual movements. A quick examination of any one of them will reveal a point at which they organized into religious institutions. Once they were institutions, they had to have rules/laws, doctrines and dogmas to control the believers. In the Hebrew tradition, they were a Spiritual family up to and including Moses. Then Moses received the ten positive words to live by, written on two tablets by the 'Great I Am.'

"After presenting them to the people, everything changed. The ten positive words became ten commandments, eight of which were negative. The point at which text manipulation started is easy enough to spot. In chapter 18 of Exodus, Jethro, a priest in Midian and the father-in-law of Moses, visits Moses and convinces him to delegate most of his responsibilities to him and other priests and leaders. In chapter 19, the 'I Am' is no longer within, but up in the sky. In chapter 20, which contains the Priestly cult version of the ten commandments, the people break the inner connection. And, neither Moses nor the 'Great I Am' can mend it. The Priestly cult broke up the narrative of Moses' sojourn on mount Sinai in many places, with their insertions. The actual tablet stories exist on in the end of chapter 24 and chapter 32 through 34, which no longer list the ten words."

Ori quickly asks, "Can you tell us what the ten words are?" The others respond to his question affirmatively and want to hear them.

"Better yet, let the 'Great I Am' tell you, one at a time. Listen and call it out when 'I Am' gives it to you. Remember, these are the ten words of the Love-light of the 'Great I Am.'"

Jacob calls out, "CONNECT (ל֗ח̣ב̣ר)."
Abbud calls out, "CHOOSE (לבחור)."
Hanna calls out, "HONOR (כבוד)."
Talia calls out, "REJUVENATE (ל֗ה̣צ̣ע̣יר)."
Ori calls out, "RESPECTFUL (מוק̣יר)."
Noya calls out, "HONOR LIFE (חיהכבוד)."
Hanna again, "STEADFAST (איתן)."
Ori again, "HONEST (י̣ש̣ר)."
Noya again, "TRUTHFUL (אמיתי)."
Jacob again, "SATISFIED (מרוצה)."

Ori responds immediately, "But some of those can be interpreted in many ways."

"And who told you that, Ori?" I counter immediately.

"Oopps, my left-brain irrational brain chatter."

"If you need clarification, ask the 'I Am'. If your inner awareness has a different message engage the 'I Am' and listen. You may even discover 'I Am' is flexible. When 'I Am' first gave me the 10 positive words, I thought 'HONEST' and 'TRUTHFUL' where the same thing. 'I Am' patiently explained that 'HONEST' was an <u>action</u>, to always do the right thing openly and to be trustworthy. 'TRUTHFUL' describes the <u>things you say</u> as being real and true in fact. Note that this makes things black and white. There is no gray zone."

I change the subject, "Now we need to move on to some important things you need to know before we go into the field. The 'I Am' is already telling me about your concerns.

Hanna asks, "How often should we meditate?"

"That depends on how connected you are. In the field, it is best to connect 24/7. This week, I suggested you meditate three times a day for twenty minutes each time. You may notice, I meditate for a few seconds every hour."

Abbud asks, "How does the Slow-Motion-Perception work? I calculated from the video that you are moving at about 180 miles/hour."

"In any crises, certain people automatically go into SMP. You feel like you are moving in slow-motion. When we connect, we can go into SMP at will. The more you use it the faster you will get." Using SMP, I run to Abbud; take his pen; and run back to my place; and hold up his pen. "It is not magic." Everyone laughs as I throw him his pen.

Abbud catches the pen, "But I couldn't see you."

"Yes, you could, but the brain doesn't register it. The hand is quicker than the eye."

Talia asks, "Can you explain the 'boomerang-effect' and how it works?"

"The 'boomerang-effect' is your major defense. You must connect and be free of hatred. Do I need to repeat that?" Everyone shakes their head no. "This is what you will experience. At all times, the 'Great I Am' has an invisible shield around you. It is around you right now. If anyone commits an act of violence against you, it will boomerang off you and go directly back to the perpetrator, with equal velocity and impact.

"Therefore, if a person shoots at you, the bullet will bounce of you and kill the shooter. If a person attacks you with a knife, their action will end up cutting themselves. It is the same regardless of the weapon, mechanical or physical. Any assault will boomerang back on the attacker.

"There are two changes 'I Am' made since the videos you saw. Any person or persons who order the violence, will also experience the boomerang-effect. Also, it will be the same for robots, drones, or any mechanical device, chemical, or biological weapons. The effect will boomerang back on the operator and persons who ordered it."

Noya responds nervously, "I don't want to kill anybody. Is there any way to avoid this?"

"I feel exactly the same way. The elephants felt exactly the same way. And the message you are getting is, the 'Great I Am' feels the same. If you have only love in your heart, you are not killing them; they are killing themselves. However, that doesn't make it any easier, especially when members of our own family are involved.

"What I do is work hard to convince my adversary to reverse their course of action. The 'I

Am' also does the same. Can you imagine what it is like for the 'I Am' when people don't listen or don't want to listen. It is heartbreaking to the 'I Am'. And very difficult for us to witness. Strangely enough, this never occurs with any other creature on the planet.

I must add, however, there have been times that a person is so deeply lost in their dark-side, and I have little desire to bring them out or waste my breath. But 'I Am' always insists that we try. Every life is important to the 'I Am'."

For the next two days, we will all meet here at 07:00 to start our day with meditation together. This will give us a chance to solidify our connection with the 'Great I Am' and each other. The rest of the day, you will have time to get your things in order before we start our mission. Listen to the 'I Am', and the 'I Am' will guide you.

Welcome to the Love-light.

CHAPTER 25
Testing the Waters

After the team's morning meditation, I pull Jacob
and Abbud aside. "I want the two of you to know that
I'm going to meet with your fathers today. I need to
give them a heads-up and get the warning out there."
Jacob responds, "The 'I Am' has already told us.
We are all going to spread the word to our friends
and family. We also have the school and news
sources covered. Briefly the 'I Am' said, 'There are to
be absolutely NO acts of VIOLENCE against My
Justice Team.' The 'I Am' is guiding each of us."
Abbud hesitates and speaks timidly, "It is a
dangerous idea for you to try and talk to my father.
He doesn't know the meaning of 'nonviolence,' and
he is not to be trusted. Besides, you would never get
over the border and back alive. Why don't I show
you the secret tunnel?"
"That's a great idea. Can you meet me back here
at 13:00?"
"Shure!" Abbud says more confidently.
Jacob cautions me, "You are aware that my
father is very locked into his hatred and set in his
ways? I'm glad you're doing this because I couldn't."
"You soon will be able to, with 'I Am's help," I
assure him.
As we each go our separate ways, the 'Great I Am'
starts filling me in on Jacob's father, Nirel ben Addi.

Nirel is the Deputy Minister of Defense and
Foreign Relations. The Ministry of Defense is in a
very impressive building in the Hakirya section of Tel
Aviv. So, I'm able to walk there from the school.
This will give the 'I Am' a chance to brief me on what
to expect.
As always, 'I Am' starts with the history (which I

already know) of the UN setting up the State of Israel in 1948. Although, I always find 'I Am's slant on things more factual and more accurate, I will focus here on the main point. Within a few minutes, 'I Am' is describing how the leaders of the government are continually departing from the UN agreement regarding land, borders, resources, ethnic rights and emigration. In all these cases they are in violation of the Treaty. Because of the United States' Hebrew support in the UN, all sanctions against Israel have been blocked. Consequently, the Israeli Government keeps pushing the issues further and further. And closer and closer to war.

Then to my surprise 'I Am' begins to talk about the once "Chosen People." 'I Am' says, "My Chosen People..." and pauses for a long time. I can feel the 'I Am' wrestling with some strong feelings. Then 'I Am' says, with resolution, "You already know my love for Abraham and Sarah, Moses, Samuel, Isaiah, Hosea, and those few Hebrew people who are connected to me. They were My Chosen People. But now, I must focus my attention on My Choosing People. Those are the people who are choosing to Connect with Me. Those are the people who are choosing to fulfill My purpose for their lives. My Choosing People will bring the Love-light to the world. My Choosing People will make the crystal city a reality.

"What you are about to encounter, in your meetings with Nirel and Abbud's father, Abdul 'Adl, are two falsely holly men with no connection with Me or the slightest interest in connccting. Their left-brain egos are in full control of them. One will charm you with lies and deception. The other will lure you, like a fox, into a trap. They both choose to live in their dark side. Be cautious. I will be with you."

As 'I Am' finishes, I find myself standing in front of the Ministry of Defense. The building looms ominously over me. I blow all the air out of my lungs and let my body breath the unutterable syllable. After three breaths, I open the door and enter.

The guards confront me. I tell them I have an appointment with Nirel ben-Addi. They have me walk through a security scanner and direct me to the reception desk. I wait at the desk for the Sergeant to finish his cellphone call. After I announce myself, he checks his tablet and motions to a Corporal to escort me to Nirel's office. He knocks and opens the door for me, without saying a word. I respond, "thank you."

As I enter the room, Nirel is busy on his computer. I look around the room. The walls are covered with pictures of construction, a master plan of the State of Israel, a plan for the expansion of the boundary wall, but no pictures of people. At the end of the room there is a model of a future kibbutz (a collective development or community). As I study it closely, I realize it is in the Gaza strip. In a nanosecond, I realize what Nirel is up to.

The 'Great I Am' can feel my anger rising, "It is OK to be angry, but let it motivate you positively."

Nirel stands and walks over to me. "That kibbutz will be the biggest and best we have ever built. Isn't it a lulu?"

I respond in a calm cold tone, "Unfortunately, it is a violation of your UN charter!"

He snickers, "The UN, who needs them?"

The 'Great I Am' says through me, "No more than you need the 'Great I Am'!"

This comment makes Nirel step back. He freezes in his tracks, with his eyes fixed on me. "They are the cause of our suffering."

I look him in the eye. "You are the cause of your own suffering. You turn away from the 'Great I Am.' You respond to hatred with greater hatred. There is not one commandment or law that you keep. You live in a sea of lies and self-perverted justice. You walk away from the Love of the 'Great I Am' and love yourself and power. You disgust the 'I Am' and you disgust me."

Nirel puts on a false smile and tries to be friendly, "Come now Hayah, we can be friends." The evil wells up in his eyes. He shifts and tries to make his way back to his desk. "How can I help you?"

I step in front of him. "I'm here to warn you. Your hatred and injustice end here and now. Your oppression is over. The Justice Team is here to bring the Love-light and peace back to all the people. Any act of hatred or violence against them will boomerang back on the perpetrator and whoever gives the order. Do I make myself clear?"

"Come now Hayah, Israel is not a people of hate and violence." He dodges around me and makes a beeline for his desk. "We are a people of Faith and God is our ally. We are an oppressed people seeking to restore God's law." When he reaches his desk, he quickly reaches around and presses a button on the side of the leg hole. His face becomes maniacal. "You are the enemy here, an enemy to me and the State." He picks up a small bronze Magen David (Shield of David) from his desk, which he assumes has some religious power. "You are an enemy to Yahweh. He shall striii... Aiii... Yiii..." The Magen David terns red-hot in his hand, and he slings it in the air to get rid of it, screaming in pain."

I reach up and pluck it out of the air as it flies up toward the ceiling. It becomes a blinding white light in my hand, and I set it back down on his desk. "Change and enjoy the Love-light." I motion to the glowing Love-light.

Nirel tries to bang the light with a book, with no affect.

At that moment, the Corporal bursts in the room and rushes toward me. He grabs my arm and twists it behind my back.

Nirel's arm is being twisted up behind his back. He shouts in pain, "He tried to kil... Ohy... No... Stop! Pleeease stoppp..."

I turn to look at the Corporal. His arm is also behind his back, and his face is twisted in pain. Slowly, he brings it forward again and rubs the pain in his shoulder. He looks at me and sees the loving calmness in my face. He takes a step backward.

Nirel shouts, "Kill him!" He hesitates, and quickly reverses the order, "No, no, no, that's a ridiculous idea."

The expression on the Corporal's face is total confusion. He looks in my eyes and sees only the Love-light. Slowly, a realization comes over him, and he timidly says, "Your Hayah." He holds up his arms to show me he means no harm.

I walk over to Nirel's desk, pick up the Love-light, and put it in the Corporal's pocket. I pat him on the shoulder, and say, "Find that Love-light within yourself and your life will change." I turn to Nirel and say, "Now you are warned. Get the word out. The lives of thousands depend on it, both officers and soldiers. You now know how the boomerang effect works. Shut down your hatred and violence, or your own actions will destroy **you**."

I go into Slow-Motion Perception (SMP) and move so fast I seem to disappear. Their jaws drop open in awl. I leave the room and building without being seen. Outside, I hear sirens and shouting behind me. I turn and look over my shoulder to see the military chaos in the building. I smile.

I return to the school, while in SMP, to get back as quickly as possible for my appointment with Abbud.

I arrive at the school in plenty of time. As I enter the building, I notice that Abbud, Jacob, and Talia are having lunch. I get a falafel and join them. They are all very hyper.

Jacob is anxious, and super charged, "The 'I Am' has been in our ears all morning. It's like a radio broadcast of a football game. It's fantastic. It's like there are no surprises when dealing with other people. Will we all be able to do that?"

"Yes!" I answer with a smile, "and the longer you do it the faster and better you will get at listening. Just shut down the left-brain chatter and listen."

"Can you tune into us like that?" Jacob is feeling a little embarrassed and vulnerable about his private relationship with Talia, and the others are having the same reaction.

I smile, "Boy that would be fun!" I laugh and then add, "Unfortunately, not. I tune into 'I Am' and 'I Am' tells me what I need to hear. I don't get to share your private moments even though you may be sharing them with the 'I Am'."

Talia feels relieved, then blushes. "The 'I Am's presents when Jacob and I are... are... together is fantastic. I'm glad it is private."

Abbud laughs, "It is a lot more private than your revelation just now."

Everyone laughs. Then we all hear 'I Am' laughing too.

After a few moments Jacob slowly becomes pensive. He says, "I'm beginning to feel like the Justice Team (That's what 'I Am' called us.) is my new family. I'm both embarrassed and annoyed with my father. Although, his actions are not a surprise to me, now I don't know how to relate to him the next time we meet. I'm a different person. How do I deal with the conflict?"

I wait a moment before responding, "You're connected. What is the 'I Am' telling you?"

"Wow!" Jacob exclaims. "The 'I Am' will tell me what my father is going to do beforehand. 'I Am' will help me respond positively and help me remain calm.

I will always see the purpose in everything I say or do. I can encourage my father to get the warning out to everyone and help him see the importance. What?" Jacob is listening to 'I Am'. "You've got to be kidding!" Jacob says to us, "The 'I Am' says that my father may even decide to connect. Now that would be a miracle!" Tears of joy well up in his eyes.

Talia is deeply moved and shares in Jacob's joy. "This is very hopeful for all of us. I would love to see my family get connected to the 'I Am', and I have two sisters and two brothers. This could actually bring us all together."

The 'Great I Am' and I are overjoyed with this. "I would like to see that in all families."

Abbud says softly while reflecting, "I must tell you all that most of my family has gone too far to the dark side. Their hatred is so deeply rooted, I don't fit in anymore. In fact, I'm afraid of what might erupt when they hear about me and the Justice Team."

The 'Great I Am' is talking to all of us, "There is only one way you can truly conquer an enemy. And that is with LOVE. Abbud, your instincts are correct regarding your family, but your love and My Love-light could bring some of them out of their darkness. Because through you, they may now discover they have a choice."

We process this in silence. Then Abbud, Jacob and Talia start writing something down.

I watch them for a moment, and then curiosity gets the best of me. "What are you writing down?"

Abbud says, "That is the best quote ever. I don't want to forget it. 'There is only one way you can truly conquer an enemy.'"

And they all say together, "'And that is with LOVE.' Wow!"

My heart fills with joy for them. I have been with the 'I Am' for so long, I sometimes forget how special 'I Am's words are. Yes, I have heard that theme before, said by Yeshua under other circumstances, but this turn of a phrase is definitely a WOW. I glance at Abbud, who is studying me intently. I can read in his eyes a deep concern and a need to talk to me about something. The 'Great I Am' encourages me to open the door for him. I smile.

Abbud relaxes a little bit, and says, "We need to talk about my father. Is it all right to talk in front of my friends here? They already know most of it."

"Of course! We are all on the same team," I assure him.

He pauses a moment before opening up, "My father is an egomaniac. He sees himself as the next emperor of the Middle East. He thinks of himself as the reincarnated Mohamed. He sees his own hatred as a divine tool to destroy all the infidels, who don't think like him. He believes that his God is all powerful and commanding him to kill all nonbelievers. His vision is to force all people to bow down before him and worship him.

"To him the State is his empire, and he is the divinely chosen ruler. The people are his chattel. A government is his tool to control and rule the people.

"Although, most of the Palestinian people would prefer to live in harmony; my father has a few power-hungry supporters, who see this as a personal opportunity. They want all-out war and destruction.

"When you meet my father, you will not see any of this. You will see a jovial man with a great sense of humor. His broad smile and white teeth will set you at ease. He will agree with everything you say in order to manipulate you to his advantage. He will lull you into a sense of security. The minute you start to like him, focus on his teeth, and remember this. They are very sharp!"

CHAPTER 26
The Lion's Den

I reflect on Abbud's description of his father, and what I should expect, as we head for the secret tunnel. The 'Great I Am' confirms everything Abbud said, with a few details. One of which was Abdul 'Adl setting up a couple of innocent Palestinian young men to confront the border guards. They were both shot and killed. And he used the fear and remorse to stimulate anger and hatred among his people. He cared nothing for the two men.

Abbud asks, "I hope you're not claustrophobic?"

I look at him and smile broadly, "Yes, but I have been in some pretty tight places."

Abbud laughs, "The 'I Am' is giving me a picture of some of those places. Well, I hope I never experience any of the those. This is a piece of cake by comparison." He reflects for a moment to organize his tips. "Once we go into the tunnel we need to avoid talking. In some places, we will pass sections with very thin walls or could be close to another tunnel. The sound could give away the tunnel. If we need to communicate, we will need to use sign-language or whisper in each other's ear.

"The tunnel is quite long, so if you need to relieve yourself do so before we go underground. That problem is compounded by a small spring that runs through a few meters of the tunnel. If you don't have to go before, we enter, you will have to hold it until we come out. I know the trickle gets me every time.

"When we get to the other end, we will come up near the Fallen Dome in Gaza. I'll point out where my father will be. Then, I will show you my little hiding place. When you're done, you can stop for me and we can slip out together. What do we do if my father attacks you?"

"Relax," I assure Abbud. "We can communicate through the 'I Am'. Just stay awake and connected. The 'I Am' will narrate the whole thing. Believe me, it is better than a cell phone."

Abbud remembering, "Oh, yes. Just before we enter the tunnel, we need to turn off our cell phones and take out the battery. They can be detected and tracked even underground. I always feel half naked without mine."

"I take it that you haven't noticed. I don't carry one. I find that it distracts from my connection to the 'I Am'. We have a running thing going all day long." I laugh, "You might say I'm addicted to my connection with the 'I Am'."

Abbud laughs and brightens up, "I can see that happening to me too. But first I need to kick my addiction with my cell phone."

"I have heard that the best way to kick it is leave it home for two months and never carry it with you except on required outings with GPS and emergency communication backup. Once you kick the habit, you will discover there are a lot more hours in your day. And you will be spending most of those with the 'I Am'."

"I think I'll start when we get to the tunnel." He is listening to something and it is not the 'I Am'. "Yes, no, yes, no, yes, no. Yes. Yes. Yes! You won't believe the damn left-brain chatter that just hit me. That one was difficult to shut down. Does it ever get any easier?"

"Nope! In fact, it gets much more invasive. However, you will get better at shutting it down." I pat him on the back.

We are walking up to a street latrine when he says, "If you got 'a go now's the time."

"But we're a long way from the border."

Abbud smiles, "That's why it is so secret."

We both relieve ourselves, and Abbud heads to

an alley next to an old house. I follow as soon as I finish. A few meters down the alley, Abbud is waiting for me. As I approach, he holds up his finger to his lips, for me to keep silent.

Then he turns and opens an old iron coal shut door, very slowly so as not to make any noise. He then gets down on all fours, with his feet facing the opening. He backs in and climes down. As his head disappears, I see his hand gesture for me to follow. I do the same as he did and soon find myself standing in a sealed off abandoned coal room. Abbud climbs back up a few steps on the ladder and carefully closes the iron door.

The old coal room is now pitch black. Abbud turns on his flashlight and checks me out. He then puts it under his chin to make a scary face. I have to put my hand over my mouth to keep from laughing aloud. He then shines the light around the room.

There is no longer any door? I'm connecting to the 'Great I Am' within me. But before I can ask, I can feel his smile. Then Abbud shines his light on a small pile of coal about a half meter from the wall. He walks over to the pile and appears to be sliding his hand under one of the large pieces of coal. He lifts with considerable force; and the whole pile lifts up and stand on its side revealing a small opening and a set of stairs. Abbud shines the light down the stairs and motions for me to start down. After twelve steps, I reach a landing, and Abbud motions for me to stop. He steps down, closing the hatch as he goes.

Around the outside edge of the wall there are sacks of potatoes and turnups. On the opposite wall there are shelves with preserves and some empty jars.

Abbud opens a hidden hatch in the floor. He shines his light down a deep hole, with a very tall ladder. He motions for me to start down. As soon as I'm down far enough, Abbud starts down closing the hatch behind him. My eyes are adjusting to the darkness, so the tiny light coming from Abbud's flashlight seems like a beacon.

The climb seems to go on forever, but then my foot touches soil. I reach out to touch the walls but find none. I step aside and wait for Abbud, with one hand on the ladder. As his light comes through the hole in the top of the chamber, about five meters above me, I can see that the chamber is quite large. There are three passageways exiting the camber in different directions. Each is about two and a half to three meters high. I look closely at the walls of the chamber, expecting to see freshly dug surfaces. But they are granulated and firm from many years of use. I turn to Abbud to ask how old the tunnel is...

When 'I Am' stops me, "Remember, silence! As to how old they are. They were here when I lived here."

Abbud hears the 'I Am' as well and mimes the number 4,000 and a question mark with his hands and shrugs his shoulders. He turns and heads down the middle passageway. I fallow the light out of the darkening chamber.

We move down the tunnel at an amazingly fast pace. The height and width of the tunnel changes all the time. Some places are so low or narrow, I have to bend down or walk sideways. Other sections are quite open, like walking through a long room. After the first hour, I begin to wonder how long this tunnel is. I shut down the brain chatter and stay focused.

The 'Great I Am' starts to tell me that Abbud is concerned for my safety, saying, "I explained to him again about being protected, but his left-brain chatter keeps playing on his fears. This is happening to the others too. We have to coach them to keep them focused. While you are in with Abdul 'Adl, I will let them all see what is happening, so they can learn from it.

"Then when you are done here with Abdul 'Adl, we can take them to one of the refugee camps. There is always a lot of hatred and violence festering there. They can interview some of the people to learn who some of the leaders and perpetrators are in their homeland. The leaders are often blocking me and are not the people in the news."

I suggest without speaking, "That's a great idea. I suggest the Za'atari camp. That is the largest, with over 80 thousand people."

I can feel that 'I Am' is considering it. Often in situations like this, the 'I Am' will check every single soul in both camps in order to decide. Finally, 'I Am' says within me, "The new one in Azraq is smaller, but the people are more current in their troubles and flight. The perpetrators they know will be more helpful. I also learned that Abdul 'Adl has infiltrated both camps to stir up their hatred. But he is now focusing on Azraq for some reason. That is my choice. OK?"

"Azraq it is," I respond affirmatively. Here I want to point out to you, the reader, what it means to be connected to the 'Great I Am' in a dialogue. When 'I Am' makes a choice, it is open for discussion. I often have a different opinion for a particularly good reasons. Sometimes the debate can go on for days. Most of the time the 'I Am' ends up being right, but there are rare occasions when 'I Am' learns something from me.

"And those are the ones I enjoy the most!" the 'I Am' says to you. To me 'I Am' says, "Abbud wants you to know we are almost there."

I feel relieved. On the way back, I'm determined to start training Abbud in Slow-Motion Perception (SMP). Although, it was great to do a regular walk this time, to really experience the tunnel.

At this point I start to see signs of destruction and repair in the tunnel. We also go through what looks like small rooms or hubs, with many entrances and exits. I'm sure glad to have Abbud as a guide because this is now a major labyrinth. 'I Am' then sends me the message that he has been doing this since he was 7 years old.

Finally, we stop in a dead-end. There are no exits that I can see. Abbud walks to one wall and steps on a small stone. A secret door opens on the opposite wall, and he motions for me to enter, while keeping his foot on the stone. As soon as I'm in, he rushes for the opening, while the door is closing. I quickly step out of his way.

We are now in a small chamber, with a ladder going up several meters. At the top there is what looks like a large pipe standing on end. We step into its door. It would be big enough for three people. The pipe slowly turns until the opening is in a hallway. We step out and the pipe turns back concealing the opening.

We are somewhere near the Fallen Dome in Gaza, but still below ground. We walk down the hallway to a large stack of wooden crates. Abbud touches a panel in one of the lower crates and the panel pops open. It is like a little room, with a bed, a chair, a small table, a battery lamp and several books. Abbud whispers, "This is my hiding place."

After he closes the panel, he then walks back up the hallway past the pipe to a stair well. We walk up three flights of stairs, past an exit to the street and one more flight to a steel door. Abbud gently pulls the door open, with a cloth covering the inside. He whispers, "Slip out from behind the flag and walk over to the reception. They will take you to my father's office." He gives me a-thumbs-up and disappears down the stairs.

I slip out closing the door behind me. As I cross the lobby to the reception, I look back to see what flag it is. It is a large Palestinian flag. At the reception counter, I ask for Abdul 'Adl. The clerk is courteous and rings his office to announce my presence. Within a minute, I see him approaching the desk, with a broad smile and white sparkling teeth. He is a stout man, with a huge pot belly and balding head. He is dressed very business-like, including the red tie.

As he reaches me, he extends his large hand in a jovial manner, saying, "Hayah, it is a pleasure to finally meet you. I have heard so much about you and all you are doing to help the animals in Africa and India. You have opened the world's eyes to a serious problem. Come, let's go into the lounge where we can talk in privet."

He continues to flatter me as we cross over to a small comfortable lounge off the main lobby. His friendly manner feels genuine and has me off balance. He actually seems very charming, and not at all like the man Abbud described. I start to relax. Then I remember his teeth, 'they are very sharp.'

The lounge is small and cozy, on one side there is a small table and chairs, on the other side there are two comfortable chairs with a small coffee table and a floor lamp. The large bay window opposite the door looks out on the ruins of the complex. The sight of the destruction brings me back to reality. But in the next moment, Abdul 'Adl invites me to sit in one of the comfortable chairs. I sit and try and get a read on him form the 'Great I Am' within me.

The 'Great I Am' says, "He is blocking me completely."

Abdul 'Adl sits in the other chair and asks, "Ok my friend. Tell me, how can I help you?"

I struggle to move my focus from his teeth up to his eyes. I say softly, "I'm here to bring a warning for you and your people."

He reaches for a tablet under the coffee table and takes out a pen. "I have heard about the warning, and I want to write it down. I'm grateful and flattered that you have chosen me to get the warning out. I will not fail you." He sits with the pen poised over the tablet.

I start slowly, "The hatred and violence must stop here and now. You and your people must find the Love in your hearts to live in harmony."

As he writes this down, he keeps nodding affirmatively, saying, "This is wonderful! Finally!"

"A Justice Team will come to lead the people in a new life with the Love-light, and they will protect them from the hatred and violence of those who would attack them. Those who set aside their hatred and connect to the Love-light within them will be protected. Any act of violence against them will boomerang back on the perpetrator, with equal force."

Abdul 'Adl's pen is flying across the page, "I love this. I want to be part of this."

"Even those who lead with hatred, and order the violence, will experience the force of the boomerang effect no matter where they are or how protected they may be."

He says, "This is really great!" He holds up his pen and asks, "I just want to know. How is that going to work. It defies the laws of physics?"

I smile, returning his pleasantry genuinely, "Good catch Abdul 'Adl. There are two laws at work here. One is the physical law of moving objects, who's physical impact has an equal and opposite reaction."

He interrupts in a friendly tone, "I get that one. The bullet bounces off the animal or person and back on the person who shot it. But what's the other law?"

"The other law is the law of hatred. 'Hatred is the poison you take and expect your enemy to die.' In other words, your own hatred kills you. Now from this time on, how does that work? A hateful Leader orders the death of a person in the Love-light. The hateful General, receiving the order, orders a Soldier to do the killing. The hateful Soldier, sitting in a command room, launches a drone, which flies a great distance to where the person in the Love-light is having lunch. He aims at his forehead and pulls the trigger. Now the bullet bounces off the person in the Love-light and boomerangs back on the drone, the hateful Soldier, the hateful General, and the hateful Leader. The drone explodes. The Soldier, General, and Leader are hit between the eyes. Their deaths are the result of their own hatred."

I look at Abdul 'Adl. He is white as a sheet. He is no longer smiling, and his eyes are nearly bulging out of his head. He swallows deeply and asks, "What is the defense? What if the Leader dives in a bunker?"

I shake my head, sympathetically, "The result will be the same. There is no defense once the hateful order is given. The only defense you have is to shut down the hatred within yourself and find the Love-light within you. Then the order will never be given."

Abdul 'Adl is very silent. Then he puts on his teethy smile again saying, "This is great. I want to be part of this. I can't tell you how grateful I feel that you came here to fill me in on all this. I will see that the word goes out to everyone in the Palestinian community. Thank you."

He doesn't realize that the 'Great I Am' within him is telling me that he means none of this. But I'm hoping that I can win him over.

He quickly adds, "Come, let me show you my meditation and prayer room. I think it will mean a lot to you and help you understand where I'm coming from."

I smile, "Shure. Lead the way."

We walk out of the lounge and across to the elevators. The elevator takes us down many levels. I don't know how many because the light is not working. Finally, the elevator stops, and the doors open. We walk out into a narrow passageway and turn to the left. About twenty meters down the hall, he opens a door on the left that has no lock. He reaches in and turns on a light switch.

He says to me, "Have a look."

I step in. It is a small room. In the corner there is a sleeping mat rolled out on the floor, a stool in the opposite corner and a prayer mat in the middle of the room.

He says with his big smile, "Do you like it?"

"Yes, it is quite cozy. Do you pray down here five times a day?" I take a step back toward the door.

Suddenly there is a click and a rattle as a steel bared door falls down and hits the floor with a loud bang. His eyes sparkle as he sees that I'm locked in the room with my face close to the bars.

He steps up close to the other side of the bars. The teeth and grin on his face are now maniacal. He laughs harshly, "Now you can spend the rest of your life with your damn Love-light and see what it gets you. How do they say it? Three months without food, three days without water. And you shall get neither. Hee-hee-hee!"

I calmly ask him, "Please don't do this. Let go of your hatred and I can help you. Let me show you how to find the Love-light."

He laughs a hideous laugh and turns to walk away. Only now he is facing the inside of the cell. His laugh turns into a scream, as I close the door.

I quickly retrace our steps back to the elevator and go up to the lobby floor. I cross the lobby and turn with my back to the wall next to the flag. I study the room to make sure no one is watching me. I go into SMP and slip quickly behind the flag and out the door. I retrace my steps back to Abbud's hiding place. Before I get there, I find Abbud waiting by the pipe.

He pats me on the back, whispering, "Great job. Thank you very much."

"Don't thank me, thank the 'I Am'. Three days from now you may want to let someone know where he is."

Abbud responds reluctantly, "Why should I do that?"

I quote, "'And that is with LOVE.'"

He laughs, and we use SMP to return.

CHAPTER 27
Ego Minister Warning

In the morning, I meet with the Justice Team on
the roof garden. We do our warm-up, meditate and
connect with the 'Great I Am' within us. The 'I Am'
fills the Team in on Azraq in Syria, and how they
need to find out as much as they can about the
perpetrators responsible for the flight to the refugee
camp. 'I Am' also explains why the people are
blocking the 'I Am', making it impossible to get a
read on the situation.

This means that they need to be prepared for
unexpected violence against them. The 'I Am'
describes what this means, "If you are connected you
are protected. I Am within you, and I will protect
you. However, you must learn to stand firm and send
out the Love-light to those attacking you." It is
interesting to note, the 'I Am' did not have to explain
this to the elephants.

I tell them that I arranged for a UN van to take
them to the camp for the day and bring them back.

I also tell them that I have a meeting with the
Prime Minister, Absalom Mahlonyahu. If they have
any difficulty I will come to their aid at once.

I then start a coaching session with them on
Slow-Motion Perception (SMP). I review with them
that SMP is the natural body reaction in an
emergence or crises. "You are moving so fast that
everything around you seems to be in slow motion.
With the 'I Am', you can call on the SMP mode at
will, to deal with a crisis, to flee the scene, to quickly
act to stop an object from hitting an unprotected
person, or extra fast transportation. The 'I Am' will
help you whenever you need it, even if it's just for
fun."

We start with basic hand movements: moving an

object, catching a ball, removing a weapon from someone's hand or pocket, taking a picture of someone's angry face with their own cell phone.

Next, we practice walking, running and leaping. The speed and height of these leaps depends on one's physical condition. The formula is, if you can run a kilometer in 5 minutes, in SMP you will be 10 times faster, or 10 kilometers in 5 minutes, or 1 kilometer in 30 seconds.

Some of the team are catching on quicker than others. Abbud's SMP walk back from the Fallen Dome is giving him an edge, so the 'Great I Am' recruits him to help some of the others. The challenge begins to produce a joy among the team. They like working with each other. It is all about everybody doing it well. They are pulling together, and the team begins to jell as a cohesive unit.

The 'Great I Am' within them is sending constant messages of encouragement to each one of them. They all can feel 'I Am's joy. The 'I Am' says, "This is the way it will be when 1% of the people connect to Me, and the Crystal city emerges. There is complete and total harmony between everybody."

They all shout together, "Living in the Love-light!"

After seeing them off to Azraq refugee camp in the UNHCR van, I head to Givat Rom in central Jerusalem via the train. I arrive punctually at ha'knesset (the Parliament building) and go directly to Mahlonyahu's office. His secretary informs me that he is out of the office and should be back any minute. I sit in the waiting area and browse through some of the magazines laying on a coffee table.

There is still no sign of him after 30 minutes. I look at the secretary and catch her eye. She simply shrugs her shoulders and goes back to work.

I start to meditate and listen to the 'Great I Am';

who starts to fill me in on the situation with Absalom.
He has sexually assaulted a young woman, who sits
in The Knesset. They are in a custodian's mop closet;
he is threatening her to keep silent about this
business. His threats range from political
destruction to sever bodily harm and disfigurement.
The woman spits in his face, snaps a picture with her
cell phone, pours a cleaning solvent over his penis
before he can zip up and exits the closet. Absalom
screams in agony and tries to wash it off in the slop
sink.

The 'Great I Am' feels outrage toward this man.
Then 'I Am' says, "I Am a hairs-breath away from
writing these people off completely. Now, this man
will suffer. Normally, he would be able to wash the
solvent off, but I Am going to damage his penis'
blood circulation. He shall never have another
erection for the rest of his life. **Let all men know
this shell be the boomerang effect of this kind
of action form this day forward.** You can tell
Absalom I said so!"

I stand and walk around the waiting room
looking at the pictures on the wall. It is going to be
some time before Absalom manages to get here.
Slowly the pictures begin to tell a story. They are all
about power and authority. They picture a man's
grand ego and self-importance. There is not one
humanitarian, self-giving picture in the lot.

The secretary gets up from behind her counter
and walks over to me. She is about to apologize for
the delay. I put my hand over my heart and say,
"There is no need to apologize. He is on his way. He
will be here in four minutes. Thank you for your
kindness."

Her jaw drops open with total surprise written all
over her face. She looks at her watch to check the
time and returns to her desk. Precisely four minutes
later, a disheveled Absalom enters the office. The

Secretary checks her watch and looks at me with question marks in her expression. She says, "Mr. Mahlonyahu, your appointment is here."

Absalom barks back, "Give me a minute to collect myself. Will you!" He inters his office without looking around, slamming the door behind him.

The Secretary walks over to me, and asks, "Who are you, Mr. Hayah?"

"Just a messenger, ma'am." I give her a friendly smile.

"I thought so. I have seen some of your news clips. Thank you for what you are doing for the animals." She pauses, and I can see fear come into her eyes, as she looks at Absalom's office door. Then she adds, "Things need to change around here, don't they?"

"Yes, ma'am. They do. The 'Great I Am' insists on it."

"Well, it's about time, if you ask me. Tell the 'I Am' that I'm backing everything 'I Am' is doing."

I smile and say, "Tell the 'Great I Am' yourself. The 'I Am' is right there within you. The 'I Am' has already heard you, but you don't hear the 'I Am'. Stop talking to the 'I Am' and start listening. If you must say something, use Samuel's words, 'I'm here. I'm listening. It would give the 'I Am' a great deal of joy."

"Thank you. I will do that."

I glance toward Absalom's door.

She quickly adds, "He is coming. Isn't he?" I nod yes, and she hurries back to her desk. But takes out her cell phone and starts videotaping what is happening.

Absalom comes bursting through his door, tugging on the crotch of his pants. Within seconds his face is in mine. He is so close; I can feel his spittle spray on my face. "Look Mr.... Mr.... Mr. Hi ho, I'm a busy man. I don't have time for your nonsense. I don't know who th..."

I cut him off, stepping forward a few inches until our noses touch, "Mr. Prime Minister, are you sure you want to do this out here? Maybe we should go into the privacy of your office." He backs up, but I stay in his face talking calmly.

He puts his hand on my chest and pushes hard, but his effort causes him to stumble backwards. I'm the brick wall in front of him. He cowers to the side cursing in Hebrew under his breath.

I say calmly and softly, "Come, let us go into your office. You need to hear what I have to say. The well-being of the Hebrew people depends on it. Your own life depends on it. Calm yourself and let us go into your office."

He goes into a rage, "You son-of-a-bitch! You can't tell me what to do!" He picks up an old wooden chair and swings it violently at my side. The chair breaks apart on his own side, sending him flying across the room and landing on a pile of broken pieces. He grabs his arm and whimpers in pain. "It's broken! You broke my arm!"

"Correction, you broke your own arm." I'm now standing over him. "Have it your way. Let's have this warning in public for everyone to see and hear. Remember it is your choice no matter how damaging it is going to be to your left-brain and ego.

"You govern this State with fear and power. You sow the seeds of hatred everywhere you go. You put on a show of worship only to glorify yourself. The word 'peace' on your lips means 'domination' not the end of hatred and violence. Well now, you shall answer to the 'Great I Am' within you.

"From this day forward every act of hatred or violence will boomerang back on you personally. You personally are now responsible for every act of hatred or violence in the military chain of command, in the political system and your personal contacts. All the hatred and violence will boomerang back on you. No matter how vaguely you may give the orders, it will boomerang back on you.

"If a soldier shoots to kill one of the Justice Team at the border, his or her bullet will boomerang back to kill the shooter, everyone up the chain of command and finally to you. The only way to save your life is to stop the killing.

"You saw what happened when you tried to shove me. You shoved yourself. You saw what happened when you tried to hit me with the chair. You actually hit yourself. That is how the boomerang effect works.

"You want to stop it and protect yourself, then get the word out now, no more hatred and violence. The same holds true for everyone in the military, every policeman, every politician and religious leader. Get the word out to them.

"Now let all this be known to the public. The boomerang effect is enforced. You are now held responsible, just as this busy man is responsible for the act which delayed him from this meeting. A young woman from, the Knesset, who is in charge of the cleaning staff was showing you the shortage of cleaning equipment in the custodian's closet. Without warning, you shut the door and raped her. You then threatened her to keep silent. In defense, she soaked your still naked private parts with a caustic cleaning solvent. While you were washing yourself off, she managed to escape. On returning to this office, you made several calls to have her fired. To those you called, be warned, any act against this woman will boomerang back on your own head. You shall never have another erection for the rest of your life."

Absalom screams and kicks his feet, like a child, "Have you no sense of privet decorum? You stupid asshole! Shut your mouth, or I'll shut it for you!"

Still on the floor, he picks up a broken chair leg and whacks me on my leg. Only it hurts his leg instead. "No! Stop! Stop!"

"That's the boomerang effect, my friend." I can't help but laugh at his stupidity. "I hope you have the good sense to get the word out. Your life depends on it."

The Secretary holds up her cell phone, "I'll see to it; that it goes out." She then calls the infirmary to bring up a wheelchair for the Prime Minister. And says to me quietly, "Can you stay for a few minutes? I would like to talk to you about... the 'Great I Am' within me." I nod in the affirmative.

I gather up the bits and pieces of the broken chair using my handkerchief, so as not to get any splinters. If I did, they would just end up in Absalom. Poor man. I can tell from his moaning that he is in enough pain. Although, there are many women, who would disagree. The wheelchair is here in less than two minutes, and he is rushed off to the infirmary.

The Secretary looks after him. I speak to her as she turns around, "Mary, what do you want to talk about?"

She stops, with her face showing surprise, "How do you know my name? I don't wear a ..." Her face broadens into a big smile, "Of course you know my name. The 'I Am' told you." She sits down and motions for me to sit in the chair next to her. I sit down and study her face. She is deeply moved.

She continues, "I stopped and listened, just as you said. Suddenly, 'I Am's voice was inside me and told me to take out my cell-phone and record what was about to happen. I did. 'I Am' then explained everything to me as it unfolded. 'I Am' explained why the boomerang effect was necessary because people have lost their integrity and have no sense of the positive rules that govern our behavior. I watched it play out in Mr. Mahlonyahu's actions.

"Then the 'Great I Am' let me see what happened to the young women. 'I Am' showed me who it was, poor girl. Her name is Ruth. My hart ached as you described what happened to her. Tears filled my eyes, and my mind swam with distorted images playing out the events. It took all my efforts to hold the camera steady. My body started to shake and... I felt..." She paused.

I could see her body trembling. I started to reach out my hand to comfort her, but 'I Am' tells me to wait, because it will only produce a negative reaction. Any man's touch would be threatening. I wait. My heart goes out to her.

She tries to continue, "You see... Oh..." She takes a deep breath, "I never... I'm... I'm a Me Too." She burst into tears. While sobbing, she continues, "He did this to me, the abuse, the assault, the threats. For years I have kept it inside me. I can't stand to feel any man's hand on my body. Not even my father's." She pauses again.

"Is it wrong of me to feel good that he got what he finally deserves?"

I shake my head, "No. It is possible that the boomerang effect will not only stop him from ever harming anyone else, but make other men think twice about committing this atrocious behavior ever again."

She is looking down at the floor, "I hope so." She pauses again, but her countenance changes as she raises her head, "But how does the 'I Am' feel about this? The 'I Am' is gone."

I smile, "the 'Great I Am' is not gone. Your left-brain clutter and left-brain deception are blocking you from hearing the 'I Am'."

She jumps in, "What's that, 'left-brain clutter and left-brain deception? I know about brain chatter, but not those."

"Left-brain clutter is when you let the mind dwell on the past. They can be things that happened to you, or someone you know, or in history. Picture an attic in the family house. There are mementoes stored there from many generations. Everything is piled there without order. It is total clutter. The same is true of your past left-brain thoughts and experiences, only the left-brain tries to tell you they are important when they are nothing but clutter. Let them go.

"Left-brain deception is when the senses experience one thing and the left-brain tells you that it is something else. You see parts of a log floating and rolling on the lake, but the left-brain tells you it is the 'Loch Ness Monster.' Institutionalized religions have been using it for many millennia, making a person believe that 'God' is a supernatural being up in the heavens. When in reality, the 'Great I Am' is right there within you. The 'I Am' is your essence of being, a real living, immortal part of you.

"Left-brain clutter and left-brain deception do not want to lose their power over you."

"So, what do I do?" She asks.

"You need to shut them down, but you can never get rid of them completely. Here, I will show you how.

"Blow all the air out of your lungs and relax, let your body breath all by itself. Note that the brain has no function in the process. Let the body blow all the air out through you nose. Then relax and let the body suck in the air through your mouth. You are now shutting down the left-brain irrational mind." I watch her silently.

As she becomes aware, I can literally see her light

up. She says, "The 'I Am' is there. The 'I Am' is talking to me again."

The 'Great I Am' says to her, "Mary, I miss you. It is great to have you back. I Am always here. There is much that we need to talk about, but right now we need to get the word out to all the people, so their hatred and violence does not kill them. Share with Hayah your ideas."

"Yes."

"There is no need for the formalities. I Am part of you and know your affirmative response before you say anything." 'I Am's words are kind and loving.

Mary looks at me, "The 'I Am' wants me to..." she pauses. "But you already know that." We both smile and laugh. She continues, "I will send out thousands of Priority Notices. They will have the picture of an American Indian and his saying, 'Hatred is the poison YOU take and expect your enemy to die.' These will be posted all over the State. By using the State system, they will be up within twelve hours. I will then compose a warning letter to be sent to all the military outposts, the military command, the news services, email addresses, schools, public organizations, offices, factories and foreign neighbors."

The 'Great I Am' interrupts her, "Can I help you write individual letters to each one of those groups? I can give you the key words that will resonate with each group and have much more meaning to them."

Mary pauses and looks at me, "Is 'I Am' asking **me** for permission to do something?"

I laugh, "Get used to it. The left-brain mythical domination is gone forever. In fact, you will discover, the 'I Am' values your opinion."

"Wow!" she is a bit overwhelmed. She then says to the 'I Am', "Yes, thank you, but You already know that. We will make the letters more personal to the people and make the people more likely to pay attention."

"Then let us get started," the 'I Am' says.

She responds apologetically, "I just need to ask Hayah one more question." She turns to me, "Hayah, I want to follow you."

I smile, "It is not me you will be following. It is the 'Great I Am'. In fact, you will discover that the 'I Am' has a purpose for your life. If you wish to connect with the 'I Am'."

The 'Great I Am' starts to laugh, and says, "Hayah, that is not what she meant."

CHAPTER 28
Sexism

That night, as I fall into a deep sleep, I begin to see myself standing in a huge crowd of people all standing shoulder to shoulder, back to belly. The crowd is still and silent while listening to a loudspeaker. Most of the crowd are women, with a few men scattered among them. I can see that we are outside a courthouse in India and listening to a trial in progress. Slowly, I begin to feel an internalized intense concern and fear building up in the people.

Then I recognize one of the voices on the loudspeaker. It is Uddatla, speaking out for women's rights. She is one of those I trained in India. Her voice is overpowered by a man arguing the biological and social superiority of men. She snaps back, "But a woman's body is sacred and not the chattel for any man's sexual desires and pleasure."

The young man standing next to me says, "Hayah, you better go in there. This is not going well." The young man, talking to me is Shaik T also from the India group. "The defense attorney is playing up the cultural rights of men, and the Judge is buying into it. All these people around you are here to support the rights of women. They are all connected and part of the India movement. But the political insiders are not listening to the 'Great I Am's message. Uddatla needs your help."

I start to take a step forward toward the courthouse, and a path opens miraculously through the crowd. I enjoy all the loving, connected faces as I walk past. The Love-light is so powerful, it is hard to believe that those inside cannot feel it, or don't want to feel it.

The crowd continues to part as I climb the steps to the courthouse and walk through the large double doors. The security guards do nothing to stop me. If anything, they back up a step. I walk down the crowded corridor and turn to enter the courtroom.

Here the crowd changes. It is mostly angry, haughty men parading and vocalizing their superiority. Their hostility is dominating the mood in the courtroom. Uddatla is a beacon of light in their midst.

Next to the wall, I see Dick from the *National Geographic*, shooting pictures. Then I feel a hand on my shoulder. I turn and see Abby, his wife. We hug, and she whispers in my ear, "It is a good thing you came."

I ask, "What's going on? Is this a trial about women's rights?" She pulls back and studies my face, with confusion in her eyes.

She says, "No. I'm surprised She is not telling you what is going on."

"She?" I ask.

"You know, the 'Great I Am' within us. Are you sure you are Hayah?"

Suddenly, I hear the 'I Am's voice, "This is not a dream. You need to be here, and this is about to become very ugly. Incidentally, Abby and most of the women here, see and hear the 'Great I Am' as feminine. In actuality the 'I Am' is neither... Or should I say both. Well, we can save all that for later. Right now, we need to turn all this around, or this case will set us back two hundred years.

"The case is about the rape of this young woman by those six men. The judge is famous for ruling in favor of the defendants, the rapists. Unfortunately, they have no clue as to what I'm about to do, and you need to enlighten them. Otherwise, it is just another sexual disease."

I turn to Abby, "Yes, it's me. It seems I have been asleep on the job. Take me up to Uddatla."

As soon as the defense attorney sits down, we

move quickly up to Uddatla. Uddatla calls out to the Judge, "Your Honor, if it please the court, I would like to add a colleague to my team. His name is..."

The Judge cuts her off, "I know who Hayah is. But I don't see what he has to do with this case. This has nothing to do with wildlife, and it is not a life-or-death situation."

I say to the Judge, "May we approach the bench, Your Honor?" He motions for us to approach.

He looks down on us, "This better be good. I want to rap this case up today."

I say quietly, "I assure you we have your best interest at heart, Your Honor. Could we meet with you and the defense attorney in your chambers? And we could rap this up in ten minutes."

"Look, Hayah, I don't know what you are trying to pull here, but you have no power in this legal system. I will recognize you for the prosecution, but your request is denied. Anything you have to say will be said in open court, and what you say will be held legally accountable." He waves us back.

As I return to Uddatla's table, I study the six men. Their ages range from 26 to 52. They are all ugly and disfigured. Three are overweight, and one of those is obese. Their faces and body language reveal an egotistical, bully and dishonest nature. Each is a prince of the dark side. Emotionally, they are all struggling with a hidden truth they have not shared with each other let alone here in court. I study their attorney. He is a dashing looking man in his early 30s, with a muscular phasic. Then the 'Great I Am' fills me in on what he is hiding. "He is as guilty as the other six. He has raped or assaulted 13 women, and all are afraid to come forward. And one of those is his sister. All of these men now have permanent erectile dysfunction."

I ask Uddatla, "Have you presented all your evidence?"

"Yes, but the Judge is paying no attention. His mind is made up. What can we do?"

"That is why I'm here." Behind me I hear a voice. I spin around and see Rohan, the Conservator of Forest & Field Director of Nagarjunsagar-Srisailam Tiger Reserve.

"Your Honor, as a friend of the court, I'm here to tell you that the message you are about to hear is the TRUTH. I verify the validity of its source and the accuracy of the information. Hayah has come here to protect you, not to threaten any of us. I also believe you should adjourn for five minutes so you can look out the window. There is over ten thousand women and men standing outside in a vigil to assure justice is done in cases like this. As your friend, I ask you to listen carefully and take precautions."

The Judge bangs the gavel, "Court is adjourned for five minutes. Rohan, will you accompany me?"

The two men exit the door behind the bench.

Everyone in the courtroom is sitting in total silence. Normally there would be an erupting buzz between all the people. But all the men sense that something is about to change their lives forever.

I start to meditate and connect. Uddatla sees me and does the same. Abby joins us. Our collective energy sends a positive wave of the Love-light through all the people in the room, including the six perpetrators and their attorney. Dick sees it visually and captures it on the faces of the people. The Judge returns with Rohan.

He addresses Uddatla, "Do you have any other evidence you want to present to this court?"

"Yes, Your Honor. I call Hayah to present the conclusive evidence to the court and the people."

I stand before the Judge. "I stand before this court to reveal the conclusive evidence against these seven men, not only of their crime, but their deliberate deception of the boomerang effect of their crime on their own bodies."

The Judge asks, "You mean <u>six</u>?"

"No, I mean seven. Their attorney is equally guilty of the same crime, of which he is yet to be tried, with 13 women, including his sister. He too is experiencing the boomerang effect and concealing it from this court."

I turn to the people, "Be it known to all. The 'Great I Am' within you has created a boomerang effect against all hateful sexual assaults. Any man committing such an act, and any man or women ordering such an act, or any man condoning and encouraging such an act, will be rendered impotent with permanent erectile dysfunction. It is important that this be made public, so every man will be aware of the consequence of his actions. Women are no longer your toys. They are your equal and deserve your respect. They are all, your sisters in the 'Great I Am'."

I turn back to the Judge, "Your Honor, with all due respect, the warning says you too will be held accountable if you condone and encourage sexual abuse. I recommend, that you examine these men regarding their deliberately concealing their condition. If they deny it, it is easily confirmed."

Their attorney shouts, "Objection!"

"Overruled! And, Sir, I'm holding you in contempt of court." He says to the attorney.

He then calls each of the defendants by name and asks them to stand one by one. He asks each one the same five questions.

1. Are you having erectile dysfunction?
2. When was the last time you had an erection?
3. Do you want to change your plea?
4. Why did you try to deceive me and the court?
5. Did anyone put you up to this?

It is no surprise that all the defendants had the same answer to all the questions. Yes, on the first. The date of the rape was the second. They all were shocked at each other's loss of sexuality as a result of what they did and changed their plea to guilty. As to the fourth question, they were all guaranteed that the Judge would find them not guilty. Yes, was the answer to the fifth question, and his name was Mahar, their attorney. As it turns out Mahar had tried seven other sexual misconduct cases before the Judge, who acquitted them all. What was behind this we do not know. However, he became a different Judge and a major advocate for sexual equality and prosecutor for sexual abuse.

Uddatla was ecstatic for the results, as was Abby and all the women there in silent protest. Shaik T was also pleased and said, "This puts us one step closer to having the 1% for the Crystal City. The word will spread like a wildfire through a dry prairie."

The Judge, Rohan and Dick came looking for me, but I was nowhere to be found. The Judge turned to Rohan and Dick and asked, "Who is that man? And I don't mean his name."

Rohan and Dick look at each other with a big smile. Rohan says, "Besides being the man that just saved your sex life, he is the man that can help you connect to the 'Great I Am' within you and help you find the Love-light."

Dick adds, "You have no idea what dimension 'I Am's Love-light will add to your marriage."

The Judge says, "I would really like to take one of his classes and connect. If he can help the two of you, he can help me." They all laugh.

Rohan adds, "Shaik T can help you with that class."

The next thing I know, I'm reclining on my bed

having a discussion with the 'Great I Am' about the gender specific question. I know it sounds confusing. And when the 'I Am' says that it does not matter, that does not help any.

The 'I Am' says, "That is better than calling Me an 'It' even though I Am in all things. Most of those things do not like being called an 'It' either. They like to be called by their proper names. Now the proper name you use, the 'Great I Am,' is the best so far. But for some people that is a mouth full. I do not like the name 'God.' It is confused with every false deity ever created by man. Not to mention that it is the noun in most foul language."

"So, what do we do?" I ask.

"Well, now that 'I Am' is not gender specific, what does it matter which gender they feel 'I Am'?"

"The problem is that to one person you may be a Him and to another person you may be a Her, and that sounds a lot like two different beings."

"Well, we cannot have that!" the 'I Am' says emphatically. "Even when the Devine Mother (the name you use) and I are together, we are one." There is a long pause here.

At first, I assume 'I Am' is wrestling with the problem. Then I can feel that 'I Am' is dwelling on the possible unity of Them being together again. The 'I Am' would really like to have creation continue. It takes a long time for 'I Am' to come back to the problem.

"Consider who I Am. I Am the Essence of Being (another mouth full) in all things. A look back at creation might help us unravel this problem. I Am the Sphere of Light. I unite with the Sphere of Love. In Light are all the detailed images, right down to each atom, of all to be created. In Love is the energy and all the life fluid to make it happen and give them life. In our unity, a powerful eruption occurs (which you know as the 'Big Bang), and Word is born.

Through Word all things, from stars to plants, are created. Word can see all that is in Light, and all that is in Love. Through Our unity all creation happens. Together, we become the Love-light. We are one." (The details of this we already covered in THE MEDITATION BIBLE.)

The 'Great I Am' continues, "Now note there is no gender specific between or within our Oneness. In the early part of creation, all the elements, plants, a few non-gender creatures, who could reproduce without mating, and many things that no longer exist were non-gender. Gender only came into being when we started creating all the creatures and eventually humans. I Am the Essence of Being in it all."

I jump in to clarify a point, "O.K. you are 'I Am'. You are the Love-light. What happened to the Word?"

'I Am' laughs, and I love it when 'I Am' laughs, because it is filled with the Love-light. I can feel 'I Am's smile as the 'I Am' says, "And what did you just use to say, 'Love-light'?"

I smack myself on the forehead, "The Word!" Then I add, "So Word in this context is a none and not gender specific. It is so in all languages."

"More," 'I Am' says. "Word is all communications. It is the communications used by all creatures on the planet, except humans. When you see a bird hovering over your empty birdfeeder and looking at you, there is no physical Word spoken. Yet it is perfectly clear what the bird is saying, 'The birdfeeder is empty.' When your dog sits by the door and looks you in the eye, there is no mistaking that he or she needs to go out and do their business. When you are listening and aware of My presence within you, you feel the Love-light; and you **experience** what 'I Am' telling you. That is also the Word; We are one. The Word is all communications.

The Word is unity. The Word is oneness. The Word is life, for I Worded all things into being."

The 'Great I Am' reads what I'm about to ask. "OK, let us look at that situation. 'Word became flesh.' There is no specific gender in Light. There is no specific gender in Love. So, when people are connecting with the 'Great I Am', they are connecting to the Love-light and our Oneness. Now, let us look at what all religious institutions have done to the Word become flesh.

"All of a sudden Word's presence as Yeshua, a boy, erupts into a divine hierarchy which is gender specific. This is true of the Greeks, all cultures to the West and all to the East, North and South. Suddenly, 'I Am' no longer Light, but Father. Love becomes the Devine Mother, who's hatred transforms her into the Dragon Lady. And Word becomes our Son. Can you see that all this is nonsense?"

"Yes, I can," I respond instantly. "Yeshua, a male, is conceived by Mary through the Love-light. Yeshua is Word. Yeshua is united with the Love-light within him. Through Yeshua You are able to experience the human dilemma. Yeshua's life is your life. You are One in life. Yeshua's death and resurrection are the Love-light's victory over Hatred. Yeshua's life is only gender specific for thirty years. As Word, Unity is as in the beginning. So, how do we unravel the Love/Hate female gender specific? My use of Devine Mother and Dragon Lady."

The 'Great I Am' ponders for a moment and then summarizes the situation. "Once Love flips to Hate, creation pauses. It is Our Unity that made creation possible. Hate was not able to see that.

"Hate creates the dark-side. Hate creates the left-brain irrational mind, with deductive logic and gives it to humans. Hatred and Darkness are non-gender. One is a poison and the other is a place or existence without the Love-light. Neither is an entity or part of who 'I Am'. Neither is who Love is.

"The act of Love is still alive and well with Me and Word. The Love-light is still who we are. But humans are looking in all the wrong places. Humans are left-brain irrationally searching for a Heavenly Myth. Only humans can shut-down the left-brain deception and bring Love back into the Love-light. Then and only then will creation continue."

I reflect on this for a long time.

I enjoy these conversations with the 'I Am', "Wow! I finally see the importance of nongender specific. And you are also resolving another issue. Contrary to Augustine's Trinity, one God, three persons, You are saying that You are one person, with tree parts."

"Bingo! Go to the head of the class. I had a difficult time getting through to Thagaste (Augustine). That is why he could never get the Holly Spirit part right. His memories of his many wives and mistresses kept muddying the waters. He never knew the real meaning of Love. He never found the Love-light."

"OK. Let me summarize this for our readers. The 'I Am' is the Light, One Being, the Essence of Being in everything. Love is the Life Force in all things. The Word is the Unity of all things from the inside to the outside, the force that assembles all things and holds all things together, the Love-light. Love is still part of the 'I Am', even though Love has turned to Hate and gone to the dark-side. When We bring Love back to the Light, they shall be one again. When the Love-light is whole again in the Word, creation can continue. The three parts will be whole again.

"Regarding the gender problem, Light, Love and Word are non-gender, so the whole 'I Am' is a non-gender issue.

"Then it came to me when you caught my use of

227

'Divine Mother' and 'Dragon Lady'. This may be the way I see Her, but that doesn't mean that my image needs to be the standard. In English, why not simply use 'I Am' for your pronoun?"

"That is a brilliant idea. Could you go back and change all the He, Him, His and Her references?"

"Shure, it's a lot of work, but worth doing. It will make the whole story more universal." (Now it is done. As you the reader knows.) The nicest thing about the non-gender 'I Am' is people can experience the 'I Am' with their own personal feelings, whichever way produces the best connection. It is the connection that matters most. The 'I Am' is an experience, your experience.

"Hayah, I want you to know; I really enjoy these discussions too. Now, you better get some sleep."

CHAPTER 29
Syria - Civil War

After several months and many meetings, I finally convince the UN High Commissioner for Refugees (UNHCR), Phil Dandy, of our non-violent and positive intentions for an end of the Civil War in Syria. Phil is a good man and an excellent speaker. His work with the United Nations is outstanding, and his humanitarian efforts to help the refugees are making a difference. Although, the 'Great I Am' said he was close to connecting, all my efforts to help him connect came to nothing. His mind was so filled with family, the UN problems and other diversions in New York City, he could not shut them down and listen long enough for the 'Great I Am' to get through to him.

However, Phil managed to get us transportation while we are in the Middle East. The UNHCR has arranged a flight from Tel Aviv to Deir ez-Zor in Syria. Where, we will meet with Hydia Sabba the former Speaker of the People's Council (the legislative branch of the Syrian Government). The Team departs in the early hours of the morning, so as not to attract too much attention. I have asked the Team to wear sturdy casual clothes, shoes and a plain hat, but no fatigues. They are to carry only a small fanny-pack, with their 10 essentials and a bottle of water.

We use the flight to meditate and confirm our unity with the 'Great I Am' within us. Within moments the seven of us are all one. The Love-light feels bright and powerful.

The pilot, Bill, calls back, "Wow, that's some powerful stuff. I can feel it all the way up here." Then he exclaims, "Oh, oh, yikes! Even the plain can feel it. We just got an incredible boost of energy."

I laugh, "How would you like to save some fuel?"

"Shure. The UNHCR would appreciate it," He laughs.

"Ok! Turn off the engine fuel lines," I say calmly.

"What?" He is stunned.

"Be sure and let us know if you start to go too fast." I turn to the Team. "OK shift your focus over to the engine rotors. Picture it is going faster and faster." Without question everyone clicks in and within seconds they have control of the rotors.

The piolet is holding his breath as he shuts the fuel valves. Then... With the fuel completely off, the Team has full control. The plane starts to pick up speed.

"What? What!" Then Bill exclaims. "That can't be!"

I call out, "What is the maximum speed for this plain?"

"I don't know!"

"Look it up in your manual. It should be about 913 kilometers per hour."

"That's it. Your almost up to that now!"

"Let us know when we need to slow down to land."

"I think you better start slowing down now. We are almost there."

I tell the team, "Slow it down a little bit." I then tell Bill, "Just keep telling us 'slower' until you are going at your landing speed. When you land call out stop. We will stop the engines and reverse for a few seconds."

"Roger, that."

Within ten minutes we are on the ground and taxiing toward a group of people waiting for us.

Ori is vibrating with excitement. He says to everyone, "Do you realize what this means. This is going to revolutionize the transportation industry! Wow! It will change every industry, every life.

Natural gas and oil will soon be obsolete. They will be nothing more than a worthless gooey thing to avoid."

Noya chimes in, "Your right. It will become worthless. In fact, if the truth were known, most of the wars for the past two centuries have been caused by a need to control the oil and natural gas empire. That is definitely the case here in Syria. The 'Shiites' (Shia Muslim Arabs) are only 12% of the population, yet the al-Ass family controls the government, because they control the natural gas and oil."

"That means Russia has backed the wrong horse, by taking over the oil and natural gas," Ori adds. "They will soon be useless and worthless."

Jacob asks me, "What does that mean for the Syrian people? Oil and natural gas are their major industry."

I smile, "They go back to agriculture. And with the over population of the planet, their produce will be in extremely high demand. The people will be wealthy again and without war."

Talia reacts, "I'm really going to like this job. Let's share the Love-light."

We pull up to the waiting crowd and shut down the engines. The Justice Team gives each other high-five.

Bill says, "I'm looking forward to our return trip. Do you know when that will be?"

"Tonight. But I wouldn't tell anyone what happened here just yet. One, because you would have a tough time explaining it to a rational human being. Two, because it would make you a candidate for the loony bin. If you want to, you can tell your dog, Wicke. He will understand. Soon, Bill, the time will come when you can tell everyone."

As we scramble out of the plain, Hydia Sabba extends a greeting hand of fellowship to everyone.

She is a stout woman with a kind face and strong personality. As the former Speaker of The People's Council of Syria, she was slowly leading the people of Syria into a peaceful coalition. Within a year she was wrongfully attacked and maligned by a secret alliance of Russia, the United States CIA and the al-Ass regime. As a result, she lost her post, and that is why Russia now controls the oil and gas production.

Finally, she greats me, and asks, "Hayah, welcome. How are we going to do this?"

I look over her group. There are only a little over a hundred people. Yet, I can see the flags of all the Syria factions, but one, the Shiites. Some are bearing arms. I ask, "Is this everyone?"

"No, these are the leaders. The main body is in those three large aircraft hangers. We didn't want their drones seeing our strength. We are about 10,000 strong. I know we are not as many as the elephants were, but we are unified."

I smile, remembering the elephants, "If everyone can connect as the elephants did, then this will be a tremendous success. The only problem I see is that a few are still bearing arms. Why is that?"

Hydia looks at those bearing arms, and says, "They don't understand your directive that if they are connected, they are protected. They all say they are connected, but they don't see how it will work."

"Fair enough," the 'Great I Am' confirms their connection and describes their insecurity, because it has never been tried out. The 'I Am' has reservations with only one person in the group. I say to Hydia, "Have all those bearing arms or having doubts to step forward. Also, ask everyone in the hangers to assemble on the runway in six groups."

She gives the order and it happens.

The 'Great I Am' assigns a Justice Team member to each group. I move to one side to meet those in doubt.

As each person steps up, I greet them and thank them for the honesty. When they are all assembled, and I have their complete attention, I explain. "There is nothing wrong with having doubts about your own behavior, but never doubt the protection of the 'Great I Am' within you. Now lay down your weapons in front of you. When you get angry, I don't want you to try and take a shot at me, because you will only end up killing yourself. Believe me, this is going to hurt you more than me." All but one lay down their weapons, he hesitates and then lays his weapon down slowly, but in a ready position.

I walk up to the biggest man and stand in front of him. I say, "You are about to strike me as hard as you can, but you are going to feel the full force of the blow on your own face. Do you understand?"

Without hesitation, he swings with a closed fist at the left side of my face. The blow passes my face but connects with his left jaw. He stagers back, with his left hand coming up to feel his sore face.

I ask, "Do you want to go again?"

He says, "No way, you made a believer out 'a me."

A third of the group steps back with him.

I step in front of two women, one tall, the other with a cunning look on her face.

I say to the cunning woman, "You are going to tell this woman to slap me as hard as she can. But be aware, the boomerang effect also strikes the one who gives the order."

The cunning woman gives the order. The tall woman's slap passes my face but connects with her own face and the face of the cunning women. Both are doubled over in pain. The two women and another third of the group step back.

I step in front of the man, who left his gun in a ready position. I'm getting a message on him. His grin reveals that he has slipped to his dark side. I say, "Take your best shot, Hero!"

He snaps up the pistol and fires at my chest. I quickly move the back of my hand in front of his chest. The bullet bounces off my chest and back at the palm of my hand. The velocity drives my hand back against his chest and he flies backward. I catch the bullet and walk back to where he has fallen, clasping his chest. I bend over and press the built into the pam of his hand, saying, "That is the bullet that could have killed you. Take it home Mr. Hero and tell your family that their hatred nearly cost you your life. A new dawn is rising. Hatred and violence end here and now. It's a pity, Mr. Hero, you could have been a part of it."

I turn to the rest of the group, "Does anyone else want to challenge their doubt, before we get down to the business of saving this country."

Everyone steps back and returns to their group, leaving their useless weapons strewn across the ground.

Meanwhile, the Justice Team has been hard at work with their groups. Their objectives are to stabilize their connection with the 'Great I Am' within; to increase the power of the 'I Am's Love-light between them; to produce a sense of unity among them; and prepare them for the attack that will soon be upon them.

Hydia and I survey their progress through the 'Great I Am', who asks us to evaluate their change in mood.

Hydia observes, "There is a distinct change taking place. Their military discipline and seriousness of purpose is slipping away. Is that a problem? How quickly will they follow orders?"

"Hydia, they are becoming a new family, and this is their first gathering. It feels like a party to them. That is a strength, not a weakness. No one will be barking orders at them. They will be listening to the 'Great I Am' and Me."

I add an interpretation to help Hydia understand, "The elephants and all creatures but humans are in complete sync with the 'I Am'. They respond to the 'I Am' without question. Humans, however, have 'Free Will' and can choose. You just saw the results of human doubts, which are produced by the human left-brain irrational mind. As everyone here shifts into their right-brain, they have an absolute awareness of 'I Am's presence. This will make them all of one mind with each other and one mind with the 'I Am'. And that is something worth celebrating."

"Wow," Hydia takes it all in, "Thank you. I get the picture." She then turns to the 'I Am', "Where did you find this guy?"

"Actually, we found each other when he was twelve."

We all laugh.

Suddenly, there is a drone hovering overhead. There is no panic among the groups. The 'Great I Am' explains to everybody, "The drone is out of Damascus. The operator is sitting in a control room, with six supervisors behind him. Two are from the al-Ass regime. Two are from Russia. And two are from the CIA. They are discussing the purpose of this assembly. One of the CIA knows about Sabba's non-violent gathering of the Syria people. All of them start to declare that you are a threat to the oil and gas fields.

"Now the drone spots the group of leaders, with Hydia Sabba and Hayah. They all scream repeatedly at the same time, 'TAKE THEM OUT!'

"Be prepared."

The leaders all focus on the drone. The drone opens fire on the group of leaders. The bullets fly down like an angry swarm of hornets. The leaders open their arms to receive the bullets. Within two seconds the bullets are on their reverse course back to the drone. On the bullets impact, the drone explodes and falls to the ground in many pieces. All the Syria people stand in silence.

The 'Great I Am' sighs in sadness, and then reports, "The operator and all the supervisors are dead in their chairs. The computer system is totally destroyed."

There is a feeling of remorse flowing through everyone. To the 'I Am' any death is a loss.

A moment later the 'Great I Am' is back in our ears. "A large Division of 17, 000 ISIS soldiers are approaching from your Southwest. They have been tipped off by an American CIA operative that if they take you out, they will have control of the airfield and the gas and oil fields in the vicinity. Form a long half-moon arch to greet them and fly your colors."

'I Am' then says to me, "Hayah, you have to approach them and warn them to lay down their arms and leave the area. Be prepared, their hostility is totally unpredictable."

I look to the Southwest. I can see their force slowly moving in our direction. Beside the soldiers, I can see a few armored vehicles and several open pickup trucks with mounted machineguns. All are flying the ISIS flag. As they slowly move forward across the open land, they spread out, so their fighting line is over a kilometer long.

I wait until they are within two kilometers of us and then begin to walk toward them carrying a white flag of truce. When I'm within a kilometer five of their men rush out to capture me and drag me back to their line, leaving the flag of truce in the dirt.

I demand to speak to their Commander, but a mob of them strip me and beat me. Every blow boomerangs back on them, but they assume that it is me fighting back. They are a pretty bloody bunch before they stop and realize I don't have a mark on me.

Finally, one of their leaders steps forward in his Balaclava Mask. I can see the blind hatred in his eyes, but give him the warning, "Lay down your weapons, for every act of violence you take toward us will boomerang back on yourselves." As I finish the warning, he hits my face with considerable force.

He stumbles back from the blow and assumes I hit him even though my hands are bound behind my back, because I allowed them to be tied. He then orders me to kneel down in front for all to see. I do so willingly. The camera people rush in to set up for the best shot. He unsheathes a large-bladed knife. He makes a short speech, which could be considered a prayer. But the 'Great I Am' assures me that it is an ego raving. The blade swings down past my head and falls to the ground.

I stand up, removing the ties from my hands, and walk away.

A friend of the leader calls out to him. He doesn't answer. The friend tugs on his arm, and the leader's head rolls to the ground and his body topples over.

I can hear the thud and the deathly silence that follows. I can feel the terror running through them. I do not look back. Normally, I feel a great remorse for the loss of life and the human refusal to listen. In this case my heart is rejoicing as a reaction to this group's arrogance, religious insanity and self-righteousness. I secretly don't want them to listen and then annihilate themselves in a battle. The 'Great I Am' makes me check these dark thoughts, and I turn to look at them, shouting, "YOU HAVE BEEN WARNED!" I turn around and continue to walk back.

The 'Great I Am' says, "Thank you for giving them the final warning. Even I know that feeling. You cannot imagine the billions of times I have seen humans do this." Then the Word speaks for Himself, "Even Peter could not connect with Me within. I fed the 10,000. I explained the similarity of Me and the bread within. Everyone walked away, and he sat there. I asked if he wanted to walk away too. His response showed that he was locked into his rational perception and not capable of connecting. He said, 'You are the Messiah. I shall follow you.' (John 6) I knew from that moment on he would betray Me. He went fishing, and I went North for a year."

As I reached the group of Syrian people, I could hear the religious cleric in the ISIS group shouting in a rage, "He is a Warlock. He has no real power. Kill him! Kill them all! Kill, Kill, Kill." I turn to face them, and they are now only 100 meters away.

I open my arms as do all the Syrian people.

ISIS opens fire. The silence ruptures with the continual gun REPORT. In an instant the air is full of led, of every size and shape, flying toward us. A roar of laughter rolls up in their Company. In their chattering left-brains and ego, they imagen a victory. The next instant all the flying led boomerangs back at them. They cannot see it.

We watch as every shell and bullet returns home. The impact is silent as blood and brains fill the air. Armored vehicles blow apart in every direction. Pickup trucks flip and tumble backwards, like dominoes on a board. Ten seconds later there is a deathly stillness. And we all take a breath.

The 'Great I Am' sadly speaks to us all, "The CIA operative has been blown apart by 17,000 bullets while sitting in his hotel room. He will not be found by his Handler for a week." Then 'I Am's mood shifts, and continues with a sense of urgency, "Quickly form yourselves into one tight group. Three

Russian officers sitting at the airport in Damascus have plotted to take you out with an airstrike. Six Russian Sukhoi Su-57 fighter jets are scrambling as I speak. Have no concern. You are protected. And they are warned."

We quickly come together in a tight group around Bill's plane on one end of the airstrip. As we turn and look to the Southwest, we can see the jets approaching low on the horizon. They are three abreast in two waves.

As they fly in, the first wave opens fire, with their guns blazing. Instantly, the bullets return and riddle the jets full of holes. The two on the outside veer off to the side and crash. The one in the middle explodes flipping end over end and crashes 100 meters down the runway. The second wave has released their rockets before they realize what is happening. All three pull up sharply, but the rockets take them in their undercarriage. Their jets explode into a million pieces and are scattered down the runway about 200 meters away.

The 'Great I Am' adds, "And the three Russian officers are riddled with bullets sitting in their chairs. Hopefully, this will be a wakeup call."

We are standing in silence for the longest time, trying to process what just happened. The only sound we hear is the fluttering of the tribal flags. Slowly, without a word, the flags are taken down and folded up. I turn to the Kurd standing next to me, as she respectfully slides her flag in its pouch, and ask, "What are you doing? Why are you striking your colors?"

She stands tall and smiles, "We are one People in 'I Am' now! We are one Family, all brothers and sisters.

Hydia slips one arm through mine and the others slip their arms through the arm of the person

standing next to them. Soon we are all 10,008
strong, linked in one chain. She says in silence,
through the 'I Am', "This chain is forever, 'I Am's!"
In silence we become one brilliant Love-light and
outshine the setting sun.

As we board the plane, Bill asks, "Can I become
part of your team? I would like to connect to the
'Great I Am' within me."
I smile, "The 'I Am' would like that, Bill."

On the return flight to Tel Aviv, a major interest
began to turn into an attraction. Hannah sat in the
co-pilot's seat to give Bill a crash course in breathing,
listening and connecting. Before we landed, there
was a lot more energy between them and that was
very personal. It was a beautiful thing.

CHAPTER 30
Holy War

As we gather on the roof garden this morning for our meditation together, Bill is waiting for Hanna and me. They warmly greet each other and try to be nonchalant about their attraction. Everyone smiles as they arrive and go about their business. Hannah guides Bill through the steps.

Bill manages to connect with the 'Great I Am' during that first thirty-minute period. We all get the message loud and clear. His inclusion is warmly received by everyone.

I quickly get everyone's attention, saying, "The 'Great I Am' needs to take us on a special mission this morning. I have only done this once before but found it to be an incredible experience on many levels. There is a secret meeting about to take place in Iran between five religious leaders, who are not connected to the 'Great I Am' in any way. They are, Ila Mahenie, the Ayatollah and Supreme Leader in Iran; Mahum Idomha, the head of the Supreme Council in Iraq; Ila al-Nisista, the Ayatollah in Iraq; Cardenal Mashentie, of the Arab States; and Bishop Fredric, of the Armenian Apostolic in Iraq and Iran. The purpose of the meeting is to create religious domination and control of the people of Iran and Iraq. Since they are blocking the 'I Am' and are too far to their dark side, the 'Great I Am' cannot get an accurate read on what they are up too.

"This may seem irrelevant, but the Ayatollah Mahenie has an aviary of twelve birds in his office where the meeting will take place. As with all things in nature, the birds are connected with the 'Great I Am' within them. Eight of those birds have each agreed to host a member of the Justice Team within themselves during this meeting."

The group is silent. I study their faces with bulging eyes and total amazement, and some with open mouths. I smile and continue.

"This is how it works. While your physical body sits here in the roof garden, your essence of being (your 'Great I Am' center within you) will become one with the essence of being of one of the birds. The birds have already chosen who will be joined with them. When you are one with the bird, you will be able to see and hear everything that takes place in the meeting. Your greatest advantage, however, is your heightened Awareness. You will be able to feel what the clergy are feeling, even though the clergy may be concealing it.

"The reason we all must take part in this is because we are all witnesses and our collective recollections of what transpires will be more accurate and complete than a single accounting. Your individual perceptions and awareness will give the 'Great I Am' what is needed to plan a defense.

"OK, ask your questions."

There is a long silence as the group recovers from their shock. Soon everyone reflects and connects with the 'Great I Am' within them.

Noya is the first to respond, "I really love birds, so this is going to be a lot of fun for me, but..." She hesitates, "Who is in charge while we are in the bird?"

"The bird is," I say, and then explain, "The bird actually knows a lot more than you do. Like all-natural tings and creatures, they don't have the handicap of a left-brain irrational mind."

Abbud chimes in, "I have nothing against birds, but wouldn't it be less conspicuous to be something like a fly?"

"Oh, yes, the proverbial fly on the wall."
Everyone laughs. I add, "I don't know about you

Abbud, but I wouldn't want to be a fly in a room with twelve birds."

"Oopps," says Abbud, "good point."

Ori asks, "What if the birds are attacked?"

"The birds are connected..." I start.

Ori answers his own question, "If their connected, they are protected. But then, the fly is connected too."

I quickly add, "Yes, and what is the boomerang effect for a fly eaten by a bird? Indigestion or an acute case of Diarrhea."

Abbud responds, "I could have lived without that analogy. Forget that I said anything about the fly."

Everyone is cracking up and the whole room is in a great humor.

Bill is feeling insecure, "I'm new at this. Shouldn't I have more experience before going on a field assignment?"

Hannah smiles and answers his question, "You are so filled with the Love-light, the birds are going to Love you."

Everyone continues to laugh and a warm positive feeling spreads through the group. I feel relieved because no one finds the mission ridicules. Now the 'I Am' is laughing.

"Great!" I say to everyone, "start your meditations, breath and connect with the 'Great I Am' within you. The 'I Am' will take you to your bird." Within a few seconds, all eight of use are singing and chirping in the aviary. Some of us are testing our freedom and joy of flight. The aviary takes up the whole end of the room with two large windows, a large bird house and many tree branches. A wire net divides the aviary from the room.

Ayatollah Mahenie is filling the feed container and then the water container. When finished, he carefully stows the bag of feed and bottle of water.

He then stands in front of the aviary and admires us, trying to whistle our tunes. He is not even close, though he thinks he is.

A young servant boy shows in the four guests and leaves. They join Mahenie in front of the aviary to enjoy the birds. Everyone has only positive comments and praise for the aviary and Mahenie's care of the birds. Their enjoyment is very genuine.

After several minutes, Mahum Idomha suggests that Mahenie open their meeting with a prayer. Everyone focuses on Mahenie, who moves away from the aviary and turns back to face Mahum.

"And to whom should we pray, Mahum?" Mahenie says with a haughty air.

Mahum responds with sincerity, "Why, Allah, of course!"

Mahenie motions for everyone to fallow as he walks into the other end of the room where five comfortable chairs await them. He motions for the others to be seated, while remaining standing behind his chair, which is more like a throne than a chair. He grasps the back of his chair like a pulpit, and says, "It is my wish that we wear no masks during this meeting. There should be no pretenses to cloud our goals and intentions. We all need to be open and tell it like it is." There is absolutely no sincerity in anything he is saying, and his left-brain ego is about to reveal that. He addresses Mahum, "To which Allah shall we pray, my friend? It appears that there are five Allahs in the room."

Mahum says cautiously, "But there is only one Allah."

"No masks, my friend." He says waving a finger in the air. "We are not talking to the people here. The people are our pawns. They do our bidding and fulfil our purposes. We are their leaders. And I'm your leader!" The others squirm in their seats.

"I will make myself clear, and I expect each of

you to do the same." There is a growing haughty undertone beneath what he is saying. "My brother ruled Iran with an iron fist. I'm doing the same. My son will do the same after me. I'm the Supreme Leader. This chair is not the throne of a King or Emperor, who rules by Devine right. This is the throne of Allah." He moves to stand in front of the chair and looks directly at Mahum. "And I'm **ALLAH**, Mr. Idomha! And don't you forget it, my friends." He turns to the others, as he slowly sits, "And I expect all of you to be the same to your people. Be their Allah. Be real. Be greater than the mystery. A leader leads. A King rules. Allah is absolute power demanding total obedience. Be Allah!" He sits back in his chair studying the others.

The first to break the silence is Cardenal Mashentie, "No mask! For centuries, the Catholic Church has claimed the same thing. The Church is God, with absolute authority. The Pope is God. I'm God. The Church has one purpose, to control the people. I'm here to unify that effort jointly with all of you."

Bishop Fredric opens up, "I'm so accustomed to wearing the mask, it may be difficult for me to take it off. As a young priest, I worked constantly to help the people with their faith and belief in an unseen God. Only to watch them lead two lives, one holy in church and another very worldly. When I became Bishop, I had to face the reality that the Church needed to control the minds of the people and suppress their perceptions. So, in this company I can take off the mask. The people are not the flock. They are the means by which the Church can survive. And we must control them."

Ayatollah al-Nisista, with his head slightly down, is studying everyone in the room, looking out from under his eyebrows. He is constantly frowning. At this moment, his focus stops on Mahum. There is a very slight negative shake of his head. Then his gaze shifts to Mahenie and back to Mahum. When Mahum makes no effort to speak, he starts in, "Thank you Ayatollah Mahenie, I welcome the opportunity to take off the holy mask. Like you, I see myself as Allah. I'm his presence. I'm his voice. I'm his judgement. I'm his authority. The only purpose the people have is to follow and fulfil my will. They must support the institution and give their lives to Allah, ME!

"That said, we must establish an alliance with each other not to challenge but to support the holly supremacy of each other. This is of paramount importance at this critical time facing us now. And because of the crises facing us, I question the motives and purpose of Mahum's presence in the group." His gaze falls directly on Mahum.

"Of course, you would say that al-Nisista," Mahum quickly responds. "You are not elected by the people. And they barely recognize your holly authority.

"For the sake of the people, an alliance is important for our two nations. It is the strongest way to stand up to Russia and the United States. However, I question your ability to dominate the people and bend them to your will. You may see yourselves as Allah but betray the people and they will desert you quicker than one of those birds in that aviary. You have no idea of the power behind the movement that is challenging your holiness.

"I suggest we turn our attention to the movement that is changing the lives of our people. What do you plan to do, when Hayah comes here?"

Ayatollah al-Nisista flashes in a rage, "You are a pagan foul! The government has no power over the people. The Church has power over them. They will do as we say and die doing it. I don't even know why you are..." Mahenie cuts him off.

"Mahum, your point of view is well taken. Who is the power behind this movement? And who is this Hayah character?" Mahenie speaks in a friendly tone, but his head is back and chin up. His eyes gaze off in the distance.

Mahum starts cautiously, "As I understand it, their 'Great I Am' is the source of their power."

"And who is that? You fool!" al-Nisista snaps.

Cardenal Mashentie responds, trying to contain himself over Nisista's ignorance, "In Abraham's world, what is the name Allah calls Himself? Is not Abraham still the father of Islam? Where did you get your theological education?"

Nisista snaps back, "From my father!"

"It shows," Bishop Fredric says with an evil grin.

Mahenie stands and tries to regain control of the meeting, "Please, my friends, control yourselves." Turning to al-Nisista, "Put a lid on it! My friend." Now walking behind his chair again, he focuses on Mahum. "Tell us, Mahum, are they using the 'Great I Am' name in another way than Abraham?"

"No sir." Mahum continues cautiously, "They use it exactly as Abraham and Moses used it. But– But not as the Hebrew, Islamic and Christian Churches use it today."

Mahenie's eyes wander around the room to the birds and back, "And how is that? Please explain."

Mahum continues with a reflective tone, "To Abraham and Moses, the 'Great I Am' was within them. They had an intimate relationship with the 'I Am'. The 'I Am' was, what we call today, their essence of being. Then the institutional churches turned the 'Great I Am' into a sky God like the Greek pantheon. Thus, making God a mystery, a deity up in heaven."

There is a general murmur and mumble running within the others. Now the birds are singing loudly and fluttering from branch to branch. Mahenie turns and commands them in a loud tone, "Hush!" There is an immediate silence that fills the room.

After a moment Mahenie continues with the same wondering look, "Continue, Mahum. And how is this Hayah character taking advantage of this?"

Mahum resumes in a very left-brain irrational way, "Hayah's method is very spiritual. He teaches them to breath in a secret way in order to shut down the left-brain irrational mind and ego. They then sit in silence. A Love-light comes into that silence and stillness and the 'Great I Am' begins to speak to them as the 'I Am' did to Abraham. They actually hear the 'I Am' and can see 'I Am's Love-light. It all seems a bit psychotic to me. Right now, I really don't know what to think."

Mahenie shakes his head, "Mahum, that doesn't begin to explain how ten thousand unarmed Syrian people could stand up to an ISIS Division and six Russian jets and wipe them off the face of the earth. They must have some secret all powerful weapon, some forcefield. Your logic be damned!"

Mahum continues, "There is, but it doesn't make any more sense. They say if they are connected to the 'Great I Am' within them they are protected. They can have no hatred or violence in their heart. Then 'I Am's Love-light will cause any act of violence or aggression to boomerang back on the perpetrator with equal force. Their leader, Hayah calls that the boomerang effect."

"That's it!" exclaimed the Cardenal. "All we have to do is lure him in. Lock him up and throw away the key."

"My friend Nirel, from Gaza tried that and ended up trapped in his own prayer cell without food and water for three days," warns Mahum.

A deep silence falls over the room, including the birds. During the minutes that follow one or another leader opens their mouth to start to say something, but no sound crosses their lips.

Finally, Bishop Fredric, confesses, "Over the past week, I have lost over half my priests and their flocks to this 'Great I Am' movement. If we don't stop them, we will be out of business. What are we going to do? This could be the end of our control over the people. The end of our respective churches."

"I will die first," al-Nisista exclaims.

Mahenie says with resolve, "I'm going before the people and will give them my 'Victory' speech. I shall talk about the past victories. Their victories over Americans and the Saudis. I shall praise their martyrdom because that is why they are victorious. For victory, they are willing to make the sacrifices.

"In that speech, I make no command for violence or aggression. Therefore, there is nothing to boomerang back on me.

"Yet the message will fire them up to defend the cause and achieve victory. And the victory will be mine! I shall remain in control, and I shall thrive."

Mahum says softly, "Only there is a major flaw in your plan."

"What did you say, Mahum? Speak up man!" Mahenie barks out.

"I said there is a major flaw in your plan!"

"What flaw? It is perfect. I hide my hatred. I order no violence or aggression. Yet the people will lay down their lives without hesitation. I'm safe. I'm victorious."

"I'm surprised you don't see it, Mahenie. You are an intelligent man."

"For Allah's sake tell me, Mahum!"

"You will end up with no people. They will all be dead." Mahum sits back and ponders the other's reaction.

"Some victory," says the Cardenal.

"A Church without believers," says Fredric

"That's a frightening thought," says al-Nisista.

250

"OK, OK, I get the point!" says Mahenie. "So, what do we do? We must do something!"

Mahum reflects for a moment, then says, "Could we sit in silence for a few moments and listen to the birds?"

Bishop Fredric looks at Mahenie and then the others saying, "That is an excellent idea!"

Within a few seconds all agree. As the silence deepens, the birds singing increases, and they flit and fly about the aviary. Then even the birds settle down. They begin to chirp back and forth to each other as though they were carrying on a conversation. This ends in another chorus of bird song. Finally, even the birds are silent.

Out of the stillness, Mahum hums to himself and then says, "Maybe we should invite this Hayah to come and talk to us or we can go to him. No trap. No tricks. We should listen to what he says and see what he is doing. Just maybe he can help us.

"From everything I have heard, he seeks no power for himself, even though everyone sees him as a superhero of some kind. What harm would it be to just listen? We have nothing to lose.

"Who knows, we may even discover a new way of doing things. Or it is an old way of doing things that got lost somehow. That would explain the Abraham and Moses connection to the 'Great I Am', he is always talking about."

The others sit looking at each other. Then one bird begins to sing the most beautiful tune anyone had ever heard.

When the bird's song ends, Mahenie says, "I have never heard him sing that song before. It's a message. Let's call the meeting, with no monkey-business."

Everyone agrees.

CHAPTER 31
Holy Meeting

Back in the roof garden, we all come back into our selves. It is like awakening from a dream. At first, we look around and study each other. The sky is cloudy. But the radiance on the deck is extremely bright and powerful.

It takes some minutes before Jacob asks, "Which one of you was the bird that sang that beautiful song? I have never heard a bird song like it."

One by one the question goes around the group and everyone says, "Not me."

Everyone ends up looking at me. Jacob says, "How did you do that?"

I smile and say, "It wasn't me."

Then the 'Great I Am' within us all says, "I was inspired. This is a major breakthrough. I never would guess that any of these men are ready to take this step. I have been waiting for this for thousands of years. Thank you. Thank you. Thank you."

There is a silence before I open the discussion.

"Let's start with the most difficult person first; the one that is deepest in their dark side. Would that be, Mahenie or al-Nisista?"

Abbud responds, "That is a difficult call. Mahenie's family is so intrenched and conservative as religious leaders it is hard to picture him as being open to anything else. Al-Nisista is not the brightest lightbulb in the box, but that might work in his favor."

Talia says, "They are all going to be difficult, so let's start with Mahenie. His left-brain ego is out of control and a product of many generations. It blew me away when he said he was willing to listen."

"Go ahead, Jacob." I can see he is anxious to speak.

"Regardless of his past and outward image, I sensed a genuine connection with him as a bird. He really loved us and was listening to us."

Noya adds, "I felt that too."

Hannah says, "His ego is just another mask. The real Mahenie is the bird lover."

"Great! Then that is the way we get through to him." I add, "Perhaps it would be best to meet with him by himself at his place, with the aviary."

All agree, and I move on. "What about al-Nisista?"

Ori jumps on this one, "I really like him. I sensed he has an inferiority complex and compensates with aggression. He is secretly at odds with his father's dogmatic rules, but feels he is left with nowhere to hang his hat. If we can help him find the Love-light within, it will turn his life around."

Bill adds, "I had the same feeling about him, but couldn't put my finger on it. Ori, great catch!"

I ask, "Should we meet him by himself on his turf as well? He might feel more secure."

"Yes, but not at his fathers' palace," Ori adds. "Maybe his own prayer room. I'm sure he has one."

"This is good. What about the Cardenal?"

Noya starts with a hummm, "I felt a common feeling in the Cardenal and the Bishop. It is complex. They both have risen in their church hierarchy because of their obedience. Yet both institutions are experiencing a spiritual crisis due to biblical errors and dogmatic inconsistencies. The Bishop is looking for answers, but in all the wrong places. The Cardenal does not feel that his institution needs a major overhaul."

"I felt the exact same thing, Noya. We should meet them together, out in nature some place," Hannah says. "The harmony in nature will give them a clue as to where the truth can be found."

Everyone agrees with her suggestion.

I pause, and reflect, "There is something about the Cardenal that is making me cautious. We need to keep our guard up when dealing with him." I can feel that the 'I Am' is having the same reservation. Now everyone reflect.

"That brings us to Mahum. What reading did you get on him?" I ask.

Abbud starts cautiously, "I know you are assuming that he will be the easiest of the group. My take on him is just the opposite. He is so intellectual; it is going to be difficult to get him out of his left-brain irrational mind. Even though he is sympathetic to those connecting with the 'Great I Am' within, I don't sense that he has any interest in making that connection. He is only curious. He is rooted in René Descartes', 'I think, therefor I am.' We have two problems. First, we need to help him see the limitations of his left-brain irrational mind. Second, we need to help him become aware of his essence of being within his center. Only then will we be able to get him to meditate and connect."

Talia looks at him lovingly, "Sometimes you amaze me, Abbud. I didn't see that one at all. But you're dead on."

"Wow! You are right," I exclaim. "How are we going to solve the problems? I doubt that an attack on his left-brain intellect would be expedient. Any suggestions?"

Bill raises his hand. Hannah whispers to him warmly, "You are connected. We all know you want to speak."

"Why not invite him as an observer to one of our meditation sessions or a plain ride? That's how you got me." He looks at Hanna and smiles, "Well partially any way." We all laugh.

"That's a brilliant idea." I suggest, "Maybe we should do both. We can invite him here, and then we can all fly him home. We can let the experience do the work to open him up. Then, we can coach him if he is interested."

We all agree, including the 'Great I Am' who fills us with the Love-light. The 'I Am' says, "I have learned so much from this team today; I Am truly overwhelmed with joy. I like your solutions. Abbud, contact your friend Zephan in Iran. He is eager to pull a group together and be part of this."

I contact Ila Mahenie and set up a workshop at his aviary meeting room for the next day. He is excited about that possibility and asks how he should furnish the room. I request only prayer rugs. Abbud and Talia agree to help me with the training.

The Team then divides up the rest of the meetings. Ori and Jacob will work with al-Nisista in his private prayer room.

Hannah suggests that she, Bill and Noya take the Cardinal and Bishop to Shanadar park in Erbil, Kurdistan, Iraq.

Mahum will be the guest of all of us on the roof garden. Abbud will contact him. The 'Great I Am' assures us; there will be no conflicts in scheduling.

Early the next morning, we meet at the Tel Aviv airport and board Bill's plane. He will fly Abbud, Talia and me to Iran airport, where we will meet Zephan and three others to go to Mahenie's estate. Bill will fly on to Iraq airport and drop off Ori and Jacob to be met by al-Nisista. Bill's last stop will be a small airstrip in Erbil, where he, Hannah and Noya will meet the Cardinal and Bishop to go to the park.

Zephan warmly greats Abbud with a powerful hug and much back slapping. He then introduces us to his three friends. Boaz is a tall, muscular man in his late twenties. He has a soft gentle manner which is a contradiction to his appearance. Shay is short and built like a tank. He seems quiet and shy, though his eyes are bright and alert. Yan is average height and very thin. His movements are lightning quick, and he is exceptionally jovial. The young men react on Talia's presence and her casual clothes and a soft cloth hat with a medium brim.

The 'Great I Am' is immediately in our ears, with what they are thinking. Then, 'I Am' focuses on Talia to strengthen her self-confidence. With the 'I Am's guidance, she then greets each of them separately with a handshake.

Talia says, "Welcome, Zephan, to women's equality. It is just like your mother told you, only now the day has come." Zephan is taken by surprise at her intimate knowledge of him.

She offers a hand to Boaz. He cautiously takes her hand, and she shakes it vigorously. "Welcome, Boaz, don't worry, I won't tell your girlfriend the thoughts you are having." He blushes and smiles.

"Well Shay, you are the man with eight brothers." She takes his hand before he offers it. "Welcome, this will be a new experience. I'm glad to be the sister you always wanted in a house full of men." He is both stunned and aglow with brotherly love.

Yan is holding out his hand with a big smile, before Talia steps in front of him. To his surprise Talia does a quick complicated handshake that he created only days ago, and no one could master it yet. "Welcome, Yan." She smiles.

Abbud and I are laughing really hard, which starts the others laughing. After, a minute, Abbud says, "I'm sorry guys. She is taken." Now, Talia is laughing.

When the laughter subsides, Zephan asks Talia, "How do you know so much about us?"

"That is one of the advantages of being connected to the 'Great I Am' within you," she answers him. "When you connect, you will experience it too. The 'I Am' is right there inside you all the time."

Shay says, "I can't wait."

****

When we reach Ila Mahenie's estate, we are escorted to the aviary, were Mahenie greets us warmly. I can see by the expression on his face, that he too is reacting to Talia's attire. But he says nothing about it. The young men in the group are fascinated by the aviary, and Mahenie is overjoyed to give them an introduction to the birds.

I ask the 'Great I Am', "Did you set this up? Because this is where I planned on starting the class."

The 'I Am' assures me that it is Mahenie's connection to the birds, which makes him want to show them off to everyone and introduce them.

After the introduction, Mahenie turns to me and says, "Hayah, shall we begin?"

"We already have," I reply. "Ila, do you feel connected to the birds?"

"Yes, I do, very much so," is his instant response.

"Do you feel that they feel connected to you?"

"Yes, I do. There is a great love between us."

"Which connection is stronger, your connection with them or your connection with Allah?"

Ila hesitates and then slowly says, "I wish my connection with Allah were, but it is not."

I look at Ila and then at the others. "Let's see why that is the case with most people. Do you realize that the birds are all deeply connected to the 'I Am'?"

"I have felt that" Ila responds.

And all the young men say the same.

"Look at the birds, everybody," I point toward them. "Now I'm going to ask the 'Great I Am' to ask the birds to all turn around and face the wall."

The birds instantly turn around and face the wall. Ila and the young men gasp.

"Now 'I Am' will ask them to turn back." They all turn back. "Ila, which are the females?"

"I can only tell the males who have the blue seer above their beaks," Ila says.

"Fair enough. I'm going to ask the 'I Am' to have the females fly up to that top branch." All the females fly up to that branch. "Now, anyone, why are the female plumes the same as the male's plumes?" I motion for Talia to hold back.

Zephan looks at Talia and then at the others, then says, "They are equal."

Ila looks at me, "How did we get this so wrong?"

I pass 'I Am's message on, "The 'I Am' says, over 1700 years ago an angry husband went into a rage because another man looked at his wife lustfully. Women have paid the price ever since. What the 'I Am' does now is neuter the man."

Ila says, "That will solve the problem."

"I ask the 'Great I Am' to tell the females to go back to their mates." They all return to their mates. I ask Ila and the young men, "Would you say that these birds are connected to the 'Great I Am'?"

They all respond, "Absolutely, yes, without a doubt!"

"The 'I Am' is telling me that you are all thinking, 'What do they have that we do not?' That is the wrong question. You should be asking, what do we have that they do not?"

Ila and the young men look at each other with a puzzled look on their faces. Finally, they look at Abbud and Talia to see if they know.

Abbud and Talia say at the same time, "A left-brain irrational mind and ego. The gift of the fallen Hate, to lure us into the darkness and away from the Love-light."

Ila turns to the birds, and asks, "Is that TRUE!"

The birds all burst into a beautiful song, which lights up the heart of everyone present.

After they finish, Ila turns to me, "Hayah, you know how to get us back on track. Will you teach us?"

"That is what I'm here for. Lie down on a prayer rug and put your hands on your abdomen just below the ribcage. Just relax, let your body breath all by itself."

The birds become still and silent. They are breathing with us. Soon everyone's breathing is in unison.

****

Al-Nisista meets Ori and Jacob in a very secluded area of the airport. He takes them to his car, which he is driving himself. Jacob gets in the front seat and Ori in the back.

As they pull out, Jacob starts to ask, "Don't you have a chauf..." Al-Nisista cuts him off with a finger to his lips and honks the horn while mumbling something. The remainder of the drive is in silence. After a twenty-minute drive into a remote area, they approach what looks like a humble farmer's home, with an attached storage shed. To Jacob and Ori's surprise, Nisista presses a remote-control button and the shed door opens. As they pull in, the place appears to be deserted. Nisista gestures for silence as they get out of the car and enter the one room house.

Nisista says, after he closes the door, "The car is bugged. I have told no one about our meeting. I hope that is all right with you."

Jacob says, "We understand."

The room is very sparsely furnished. Nisista motions for them to sit at a small table. There is an awkward silence as they study each other. Ori breaks the silence, "Why don't you tell us about your problems with the doctrine and dogma of your father and grandfather?"

He smiles shaking his head, "Does it show that much?"

"No," Jacob responds quickly. "The 'Great I Am'

feels you are way ahead of the rest of your family. Tell us what you are going through."

Nisista ponders for a few minutes. His emotional pain and frustration are written on his face. Finally, he takes a deep breath, and says, "My father and grandfather were hell bent on their total rule of the people, and they ruled absolutely. They twisted their faith to suit their political lies and control of the people. The law was not a Devine law; it was their law.

"As I studied the sacred texts to prepare for my succession, I began to discover their deliberate misinterpretations in order to maintain their power. Before long, the texts made no sense, and I began to question the existence of Allah. He was a heavenly myth, no different than the Greek Pantheon.

"So, I looked deeper, only to discover a word here and a phrase there, that revealed a Devine presence within us. But then my left-brain irrational mind kicked in and filled me with doubts. I couldn't fight it off. I even questioned my own sanity.

"Now, I hide behind the family mask, and I don't know what to do. When I heard what you were doing with the people, all my questions flooded back. Can you help me?"

"Yes," says Ori. "That is why we're here. The first thing we need to do is shut down your left-brain chatter. Lie down on the carpet and put your hands on your abdomen. Relax, and let your body breath all by itself."

****

Meanwhile, the Cardinal and Bishop are meeting with Bill, Hannah and Noya at Shanadar park in Erbil. They are sitting under the hanging branches of a large tree, deeply engaged in a theological discussion. Bill is hanging back in the discussion, feeling new to the group.

The Bishop says, "But, the Church says that the 'I Am' is up in Heaven, an aethereal Being."

The Cardinal adds, "And we must follow what the Church says. It is our law, our doctrine."

Hannah is losing patience with them, and says, "The 'Great I Am', as the burning bush, says to Moses, 'I Am Hayah I Am,' which correctly translated means 'I Am your essence of being I Am.' How many times did Yeshua say, 'I Am within you' or 'I Am in the Father and the Father is in me' and 'the Father is in you.' Your doctrine is misleading you."

The Cardinal snaps back, "Who is this Yeshua you talk about? Do you mean Jesus?"

Noya patently says, "The 'I Am' says to Mary and Joseph, 'His name is to be Yeshua'. Jesus is the Greek translation of the Aramaic Yeshua. Would you like to know the Greek translation of Mashentie?"

The Cardinal is silent. Bishop Fredric is experiencing an epiphany, "Have you experienced this?"

Bill blurts out, "Yes, we have! Would you like to find his presence within you?"

Fredric is struggling to shut down his left-brain irrational mind.

The Cardinal's jaw is set as he looks up into the tree.

Fredric responds, "Yes, I would. What do I need to do? Can I do it right here, right now?"

"You sure can," replies Noya with enthusiasm. "Just, lay back on the leaves and put your hands on your abdomen just below the ribcage. Blow all your air out, relax and let your body breath all by itself."

Cardinal Mashentie gets up and walks away. The scowl on his face reveals a deep anger and hatred.

****

Over the next thirty minutes, all those trying to connect with the 'Great I Am' within are finally able to shut down their left-brain irrational minds, experience the Love-light and connect to the 'I Am' within. Mahenie and the young men are filled with joy, and the birds sing, welcoming their connection. Nisista weeps with praise and thanksgiving, while experiencing a new sense of self confidence. Fredric is humbled and in awe, while filled with repentance and new courage to bring a new message to his colleagues and church members.

The 'Great I Am' rejoices in their connection, with a purpose for each person.

262

CHAPTER 32
Left-Brain Deception

As Mahum arrives at the roof garden in Tel Aviv, he has the mat and sittable we asked him to bring. We all welcome him warmly with handshakes, sensing he is not a hugging person. We invite him to join our circle, with his sittable. Once he is settled and everybody introduces them self, I ask.

"Mahum, we are glad you agreed to come here and learn about the connecting process we are using. However, you have a major roadblock to achieving that end. Would you like to overcome that roadblock?"

He quickly responds, "I'm an open-minded scholar. What is the roadblock?"

Hannah responds warmly, "You have already identified it. It is your Left-brain Irrational Mind." She smiles and adds, "I started with the same roadblock. So be patient with us and we will get you past it. Hayah is particularly good at untying Gordian Knots without a sword, and he has taught us a lot."

I say, "I'm going to put your Left-brain Irrational Mind to the test, but please avoid being angry or defensive, consider it a game. So, let's have some fun. Do you agree with the logical syllogism premise, 'I think; therefore, I am?'"

"Yes, I do." He says confidently.

"Have you ever challenged that premise?"

"No, I have not," he responds cautiously.

"Well, let's put it to the test. Without using any of your senses or our senses, would you please prove to us that you exist. Take your time to <u>think</u> about it," I say smiling.

Mahum responds quickly, "I'm thinking!"

No one responds. Some are looking right

through him. Others have their eyes closed,
meditating.

After some time, Ori asks, "Are you sure that
your thinking? I can't tell. Share your thinking."

Mahum ponders for a few minutes. Then he
opens his mouth as though he is about to say
something and closes it again, saying nothing. This
happens several times.

Noya interjects, "Maybe you just think you are
thinking. Have you ever had any Left-brain
Chatter?"

"Yes, lots of it, sometimes all the time. Like right
now." Mahum blurts this out in frustration.

Abbud adds, "So what makes you think that you
can trust your thinking? Maybe your thinking is
Left-brain Deception."

Mahum reflects on that possibility.

Bill asks calmly, "Has any of your Left-brain
Chatter ever been true or helpful?"

Still frustrated, he says emphatically, "Never! It's
a damn nuisance. It's in my head all the time. I wish
I could get rid of it. The person who invents a way to
shut it down will be a millionaire overnight."

Jacob laughs, "You're looking at the guy who
found the way to shut it down, and it will cost you
nothing."

Talia gets Mahum's attention, and asks, "Is there
any other creature or thing on the planet that has a
problem in knowing their own existence?"

"No," Mahum responds quickly. Slowly the
frustration leaves his face, and he adds, "And, none
of them have a Left-brain Irrational Mind. Allah be
praised! We have done this to ourselves." He looks
at the light on everyone's face. As his eyes stop on
me, he asks, "Your connecting process will really shut
down the Left-brain Chatter? As well as the Left-
brain Clutter, Left-brain Chaos and Left-brain
Deception?"

I respond with a simple, "Yes!"

"When can I begin?" He asks instantly.

"Right here and now! Roll out your mat and lie down."

We are all super charged with this breakthrough.

As everyone lies on their mats, I sit next to Mahum. The Team immediately goes into their breathing, with the goal of creating a positive environment for Mahum's journey. I explain to Mahum, "Lie on your back and put your hands on your abdomen just below your ribcage. Now, relax and let your body breath naturally."

Mahum starts to do a forced breathing with his chest. He is telling himself to breath in through his nose and breath out through his mouth.

"OK, put your hands on your chest. You can only feel them going up and down a little bit. You are letting your Left-brain Irrational Mind tell you how to breath with your chest. And you are not relaxing. Now, put your hands back on your abdomen. Good, don't think about what I ask you to do, just let your body do it. On your next exhale, push down with your hands and force out as much air as you can. Now, just relax and do nothing. Let your body do what it wants to do. It is exactly what you do every night when you fall asleep. Relax, listen to your body."

Mahum does this, but the relaxation is difficult for him.

"Be aware of what your body is telling you. It will never lie to you like your Left-brain Irrational Mind does."

Slowly, he starts to relax bit by bit, breath by breath. Then like a switch, his body takes over, and his Left-brain Irrational Mind is shut off. His breathing becomes natural and even. He is breathing in through his mouth and out through his nose. In less than a minute, his breathing is in unison with the rest of the group. This lasts about three minutes. Suddenly his body becomes tense, and Mahum screams out, "I've lost control of myself. I've lost control of myself!"

I lay my hand on his shoulder to help calm him down, saying, "That's your Left-brain Deception screaming at you. For the first time in your life, your body shut it down, and it lost control of you. Don't be angry. Don't fight with it. Just focus on your breathing and relax, feel it going in and out. Your hands are going up and down."

Quicker this time, Mahum slides back into his natural breathing. A smile slowly curls up on his face. This time it lasts for five minutes, before he is attacked again.

I see it coming and whisper to him, "Blow it a kiss."

He physically blows it a kiss and slides right back into his breathing. Again, it synchronizes with the Team's breathing. This happens a few more times, but less often, and each time he becomes stronger.

When I sense he is ready, I say, "You are now breathing in harmony with the Team. Stay relaxed and keep breathing, while I show you a little secret. Without your Left-brain Irrational Mind knowing it, you have been using the Unutterable Syllable ॐ. This syllable has been used and abused for thousands of years, without realizing its power. Without vocalizing the syllable, the body says it. On your next inhale, draw the air in through an open mouth. On the following exhale, close your mouth and breath out through your nose. Listen as your body says it, OOO, MMM. You don't say it the body does. The ॐ Syllable is the most powerful mantra to shut down the Left-brain Irrational Mind. All one-pointed mantras use the Brain to slow down the Brain. But if you are going to connect, you need to shut it down."

Suddenly Mahum starts to blurt out, "Allah be praised. It's the..." I put my finger over his lips saying.

"It is the Unutterable Syllable ॐ."

I move everybody to the next step, "Continue your breathing and stand up and move about the deck. If your Left-brain Irrational Mind sneaks back in, blow it a kiss and glide back into your breathing. Avoid getting upset with yourself, because then you will have to start all over.

"As you walk or run, center yourself by using your breathing, and you will feel like you are flying."

Mahum is walking on air.

I bring Mahum back to his sittable. "Now, use the Unutterable Syllable ॐ to find the vast space within you. Once you are there look for a speck of light and move toward it."

I can feel the Team doing the same to create the communal feeling, with Mahum. Some are enjoying the renewal of their own experience. I do this every morning to embrace the Love-light and start my day.

Because of our connection with the 'Great I Am' within us, we can see Mahum's progress. When Mahum reaches the vast space within, he first sees the light as a cluster of stars. The Brain Chatter kicks in and he shuts it down with the ॐ Syllable. Each time he reaches the vast space, the specks of light are waiting for him. As he moves toward them, his Left-brain Irrational Mind attacks, and he starts again.

I gently lay my hand on his shoulder and whisper, "Be patient, be persistent you will break through."

It takes three more times, before he breaks through and moves into the Love-light. The 'Great I Am' embraces him and fills him with more joy than he has ever known. From this point on their meeting becomes very private.

Every member of the Team turns to look at each other. We wait quietly and watch the glow around Mahum.

After many minutes, Mahum opens his eyes and looks around at us. There are tears in his eyes and his mouth is trying to find the words. Finally, he says, "There are no words to describe what I just experienced. I met the 'Great I Am' within me, in my essence of being. It is an experience beyond words, beyond thought. The 'I Am' gave me the purpose for my life. Every fiber of my being wants to say yes, but my left-brain is filled with doubts. The people of Iraq need me. And what will my family say? How can I tell them what just happened? How can I tell anyone when there are no words to describe the experience?" He looks into our eyes.

We all smile and lay our hands on him, uniting the Love-light within us all.

Abbud says, "We all had that experience, but it can't be described in words. It must be experienced. As Hayah likes to say, 'The 'Great I Am' is an experience, not an idea.' When you are ready, you will make your choice."

Hannah says, "Ok, my new friend, how do you prove that you exist?"

Mahum smiles and responds quickly, "The 'Great I Am' is within me. Ask the 'I Am'!"

We all laugh. Hannah responds, "That is the best answer yet."

Bill changes the subject, "Mahum, we have a number of groups to meet in Iraq and Iran. I scheduled the plane. May we have the pleasure of flying you home?

Mahum responds warmly, "The pleasure would be all mine. When will we leave?"

I respond, "Let's all have lunch. It is always better to travel on a full stomach."

Everyone immediately agrees to that suggestion.
During lunch, Mahum asks a lot of questions
about Syria and the large-connected group there. He
wants to know if that is going to happen in Iraq and
Iran. Without hesitation, he is pleased to learn from
the 'I Am' that it is.

He says, "I can see that, with people connecting
to the 'I Am', we might see the end of war as we know
it."

We all share-in that vision.

Aboard the plane, we put Mahum in the middle
of us.

Bill gets us off the ground and the conversations
wind down. All the Team is waiting for the
invitation.

Bill finally asks nonchalantly, "How would you
guys like to take over the engines and save me some
fuel?"

Ori says, "I thought you'd never ask.

Within seconds, we have control of the engines
and the plane picks up speed. Bill turns off the fuel
lines. Mahum sees this and grasping firmly on his
arm rests. Slowly he begins to relax as he breaths
and connects. The 'Great I Am' explains to him what
we are doing; helping him see and feel it. Mahum
looks around and studies our concentration. The
'Great I Am' helps us see all the ways this can be
used, and Mahum begins to see how this will change
the world for ever. The experience is setting him
aglow again.

Bill is laughing as we land at the airport near
Mahum's home. We taxi up to the terminal to let
him off. The 'Great I Am' tells us that Mahum has
something to share.

He says, "That was the second most incredible
experience of my life, and both on the same day. And
by the way, I accepted 'I Am's purpose for my life.

Maybe you can help me to get my family on board."

I answer, "We sure can. Bring them to one of the rallies we have scheduled tomorrow in this area."

"Will do," he says and gives everybody a high-five as he gets off the plane. We wait to make sure he is in the terminal. He opens the door and turns to wave us off.

Bill is on the intercom with flight control to get clearance for our departure. We have seven rallies scheduled, three in Iran today and four in Iraq tomorrow.

Al-Mahenie and Zephan will attend and be guides at all the rallies in Iran, which will also include as guides Boaz at the first, Shay at the second and Yan at the third. The goal of each rally is to help as many people as is possible to connect to the 'Great I Am' within (The last thing we want to create is a new institution, but we need to discover the unity of all those connected to the Love-light.); and to identify the potential leaders or guides, who can help others connect. At each rally, Mahenie and I will do opening remarks, to prepare everybody for the connecting process. The large group will divide into smaller groups of 25 to 30, led by a Team member or a new leader. For closing remarks, everyone will assemble in a spirit of unity, and we will hear individual's testimonials about their connection to the 'Great I Am' within and their accepted purpose.

The first rally opens with an earth-shaking round of applause for Ila Mahenie. The people realize that his presence marks a new beginning for the people of Iran. His opening remarks are all about our connection with the 'Great I Am' within us being the fulfilment of Mohamed's Islamic promise, not a replacement of it. He says, "Allah (the 'Great I Am') is alive and well, living within you right now. I have walked this path of the connecting process. I connected with the 'I Am', and now my heart sings like a thousand birds. Empty your heart of all the anger and hatred from the past. Shut down the chatter of your negative left-brain mind. Discover the Love-light within you, embrace it, and let it embrace you. Then your heart will know that you are one with the 'Great I Am' within you. Be aware of 'I Am's voice and presence, and 'I Am' will tell you the purpose of your life. Although you have a choice in the acceptance, I recommend that you choose positively and embrace your given purpose. I have. And my life has changed. I now experience more Love-light than all my days before, combined. Now, I offer that Love-light to you."

There is a stomping of feet, which grows louder and louder. Over this, there is a low chant, Yiii Yiii Yiii Yiii Yiii Yiii Yiii... which grows into a loud crescendo and explosive YAAA! This is followed with more applause.

Ila Mahenie works for 3 minutes to calm them down and then introduces me. They start to applaud, but I gesture for them to cease. When they are still.

I say, "When you connect to the 'Great I Am' within you, I would like you to applaud yourself and your new life in the same way.

"In a moment we will divide into small groups, where you will connect to your body's breathing, connect to your inner body awareness, connect with the Love-light and connect with the 'Great I Am' within you.

"There is one point I need to emphasize as you begin this connecting process. Women and men are equal. That fact may have a changing effect on your culture. Al-Mahenie will answer your questions regarding that issue."

I turn and look at Ila, and he gives me and the people a smile and thumbs up.

I point to the person in the front row on the far right, "Please start counting, each person calling out one number, from 1 to 10. The next person in the row, from front to back, call out the same sequence 1 to 10. Please remember your number." Soon all the groups are formed.

I walk over to the Team and Guides. I have ten bits of paper in my hat, with the numbers on them and their location. They each draw a number from the hat. I tell them, "Please announce your number and everyone who has that number can follow you, their Guide, to the group location. I plan on drifting from group to group."

I smile as this is being done, because the first minute or so is total chaos. Then in a click, there is perfect order.

All the groups are making great progress. The positive energy in the building is growing stronger every minute.

As I'm walking down the hall to the next group, the 'Great I Am' is in my ear, "Make your way to Ila's group. We have a crisis blooming. There is a Thug from the Russian Mafia, who is about to attack Ila. He is colluding with his Grandson, who wants to see his Grandfather dead and assume the power of his office and take control of the wealth. They are both so far to their dark side; it is impossible to get an accurate read on them."

I slowly open the door to Ila's room. The people are deep in their breathing. Ila is walking among them, laying his hands on those that need help. He is only five steps from the Thug and his Grandson. I immediately go into Slow-motion Perception, and I'm at his side in an instant, whispering a warning in his ear.

His first reaction is, "Shall I call my bodyguard."

I respond, "You no longer need a bodyguard.

Stay connected and their violence will boomerang back on them."

The Thug sees that we are aware of them, and springs into action. He has a cattle prod and a pistol. The Grandson has a large double-edged knife. I call out a warning, "Any act of violence here will boomerang back on you. Lay down your weapons before it is too late." The whole group is now watching. Ila calls out to his Grandson, "Oas Stop!"

The Thug attacks Ila with the cattle prod, trying to send a powerful jolt of electricity into his body. The jolt boomerangs and the Thug flies backward five meters. Oas moves in raising the knife over his head. The Thug takes aim with his 45 and fires three shots at Ila's head in an instant the bullets explode in his own head. Oas' blade appears to come down on the crown of Ila's head, but actually passes through his own head cleaving it to his shoulders. Oas' body remains standing for a moment, with his hatred frozen on his face.

I look around the group and see the fear on their faces. I say, "There is nothing I can say that will remove the horror of those images from you minds. Your breathing will shut them down, but they will always be there. The one thing I can promise you, is 'If you are connected; you are protected.'" I see their fear gradually change to wonder.

I change the subject, "Come let's find you a new room."

CHAPTER 33
A Changing Iraq

Yesterday while we were running our three rallies, Mahum and al-Nisista were having a private meeting about their new connection with the 'Great I Am' within. This was the first productive meeting they ever had. And, for the first time they were both on the same page listening to each other. Al-Nisista explained that for the first time he experienced self-confidence. In addition, Mahum's story about the fuel free plain ride blew al-Nisista away. He said, "For once in my lifetime, I'm looking forward to a decent future."

Also, at their meeting, they plan their introduction for their rally. They will both speak to the people as unified leaders, each taking different sections of the intro. Al-Nisista will start with how this connection is part of creation and Mohamed's promise. Mahum will introduce the three steps of the connection process. Al-Nisista will explain the equality of men and women. Then Mahum will introduce me.

When Mahum gets home he calls his Wife and children together and tells them about his day and connection with the 'Great I Am' within him. To his surprise, his two children already know about the rallies and are planning to go. His Wife became extremely interested when she hears about women and men being equal.

She immediately asks, "What do you mean equal? In all things or just spiritual things."

Mahum responds, "In all things. There are even three women who will be leading groups tomorrow."

"Can I come?"

"It would give me boundless joy. If you connect,

then we will be in perfect sync for the rest of our lives."

She throughs herself in his arms, with a powerful caress between them. She feels a strong positive energy and light emerging from him. She pulls back slightly to look in his eyes, and says, "You are a different man."

"Yes, for sure. And I love you more. I was afraid you wouldn't accept me."

"Silly man. I only hope I can connect too. I want that Love and Light in me too. I'll go with you tomorrow."

Their two children stand smiling and admiring them.

Mahum says, "Then we'll all go together tomorrow."

What follows is a powerful family hug.

Later that evening the 'Great I Am' tells everyone, who needs to know in Iran and Iraq, about the tragic event at the rally. He ends by saying, "Have no fear. If you are connected, you are protected. But, be alert, be cautious."

As soon as Mahum gets the news, he calls al-Nisista, "I'm concerned about you brother. I assume you got the news. How are things sitting with your family?"

"Thank you for calling. I have already informed everyone. They took one look at my strength and backed off. I have never experienced that before. All my Grandfather could say was, 'Do what you think is best.' This has given me more strength of purpose than I have ever known."

"Great, see you tomorrow brother."

"Thanks," he smiles warmly, "brother."

The next morning in my meditation, I connect instantly and greet the 'Great I Am,' "I'm here. I'm listening."

To my surprise the 'I Am' says, "There is a plot unfolding for today. I need to give you a heads up. A CIA operative out of Azerbaijan is planning to assassinate you. He has followed you carefully from Syria, to Iran, to Iraq. He has a strong negative reaction to the growing connection group. He is determined to stop you. He has a very dark background. He is anti-Semitic, has a violent racial hatred, and he has an ethnic hatred which runs very deep toward his dark side. He is a member of the KKK in the US, and he is part of Donald Dump's and Russia's mafia movements. He has murdered many Muslims without trial, men and women alike, all only convicted by his own hatred.

"He has an ex-military sniper with him, who is a paid gun for hire. She is taking up a position on a tall building overlooking the park, where you will have your third rally.

"It appears that the CIA operative plans to follow you through the first two rallies. I will help you to spot him. But I recommend that you do not approach him.

"I have a plan to send them both a warning. I want you to write two warning notes one for each of them, and I will have the notes delivered by two Rooks. The first Rook will take the note to the Sniper. The second Rook will take the note to the CIA operative.

"Take the time to write the notes now. You may sign them from the 'Great I Am' within."

I get some paper and a pen from my backpack and sit down at the table. I ponder for a moment and then start writing; "THIS IS A WARNING! Any act of violence against any connected person will boomerang back on you with equal deadly force. YOU ARE WARNED! The 'Great I Am' within."

I ponder the next message, and then write,

"STOP WHAT YOU ARE PLANNING TO DO! Your part in any act of violence will result in that violence boomeranging back on you as well as the Sniper. CONSIDER YOURSELF WARNED! The 'Great I Am' within."

The 'I Am' says, "Very well, let us hope it has the right effect on these people. It would give Me immense joy if they listened. Now, wipe your fingerprints off the notes. We do not want law enforcement to trace them back to you. However, I would love it if they came after Me." We both laugh. "Ok, fold each note three times, and I will send the Rooks."

I fold the first note and the Rook arrives. He sits on my balcony railing waiting for me to put the note in his beak.

I fold the second note and another Rook arrives. She calls me, and I go out on the balcony to put the note in her beak. I watch, and she flies toward the first rally site.

I finish my exercises, meditation and head for breakfast.

We all meet in a large hall of the facility that Mahum and al-Nisista have selected. The hall is packed, with standing room only. The buzz among the people is overflowing with positive energy. The team is moving among them answering questions and spreading the Love-light. From the sidelines, I watch with enthusiasm.

As al-Nisista and Mahum enter with an arm around the other's shoulder, the crowd goes instantly silent at the sight of them. They have never seen this before.

As they reach their places on the platform, they part and shake hands, each placing their other hand on top of the handshake. At this sign of unity, the crowd breaks into a vigorous cheer and applause.

The crowd's excitement does not taper off as al-Nisista approaches the podium and stands behind it. He smiles broadly and enjoys their enthusiasm, thanking them repeatedly. Then, he turns and gestures to Mahum and applauds him. Mahum gestures back and applauds him.

The audience loves it. Al-Nisista struggles to try and quiet them down. After a few minutes, he raises both hands as a gesture for them to be silent. The joy of the audience continues.

Finally, al-Nisista begins to speak very softly, so he can barely be heard, "The 'Great I Am' is within you. Be still and listen for 'I Am's voice. The 'I Am' of Mohamed is within you. Listen, listen, listen." Before he could repeat this word three times, the crowd became completely still and silent.

He studied the crowd and began, "You are all here to learn how to find the 'Great I Am' within you. Let your goal be to connect with 'I Am's presence. The 'I Am' is as real as the heart that is beating within your breast.

"When I connected this week, my life changed forever. I now have a purpose in my life. The Love-light now fills me, as it fills my brother Mahum. We are here now to help that happen for you.

"But, first let me tell you how this connection changed my life. I was lost in a sea of doubts, confusion, ignorance, and insecurity. My hatred was poisoning me. The negative controls of my left-brain irrational mind were leading me down a path that did not exist. Yes, I thought it looked real. My Left-brain Chatter told me it was real. Yet not one step was positive. Not one step was taking me anywhere. It was all, blah-blah-blah Left-brain Chatter. I'm sure you all know it well.

"Then the Left-brain Chatter became Left-brain Clutter, which was leading me toward meaningless goals, one false step after another, dozens of left-brain thoughts jumbled together. This went on until my mind was worse than the disarray of my house and uncleaned swimming pool.

"Next came the Left-brain Chaos. Not one thought led to a logical conclusion. Not one list of facts added up to anything real or true. While the Brain Chaos kept telling me, 'You're doing fine. Chaos is a good thing. It will all work out in the end. You'll see. Go with the flow.' Shure! All it was doing is leading me away from the 'Great I Am' within me. It was encouraging me to chase a fantasy, a myth, a false dream.

"Finally, Left-brain Deception attacked me. Yes, it was lying to me all the time. It was filling my head with false conclusions that had no basis in fact. It tried to convince me that a good argument never hurt anybody. It was trying to keep me as far away from the 'Great I Am' as it could. It turned my left-brain intelligence into a monster. It wouldn't let me listen to anyone else's ideas. It encouraged me to attack anything they said and never apologize.

"Well, I apologize here and now!

"A few weeks ago, I started watching and listening to nature and all its creatures. Suddenly, I was aware that none of those creatures have any of these Left-brain problems. They are all in perfect harmony with nature. They don't have a RATIONAL MIND.

"Then Mahum and I met Hayah. I listened and a whole new dimension opened up to us. Suddenly, we experienced the truth, the 'Great I Am' is right here within in us. (He puts his hand over his heart.) All the theological doctrine and dogma, which troubled me for years, fell away like dust from an ancient book. At last, I could feel..."

Al-Nisista is interrupted by a shouting voice from the audience, "Are you trying to tell us you're going to start a new religion? Are you trying to tell us that you are God? The Church is the Body of Christ! Not you!" It is Cardenal Mashentie, with two priests. They turn and start to walk out, pushing their way through the crowd.

"Stop, Cardenal. Take the time to listen. Shut down your Left-brain Deception. Yeshua is not an institution and never was. Mohamed saw that. Open your heart and listen to 'I Am's voice," al-Nisista calls after him.

Cardenal Mashentie turns at the door and shouts back, "Blasphemy!" shaking his fist. He turns and walks out of the hall. The two priests slam the door behind them.

"As I was saying," al-Nisista continues, unshaken, "I could feel the presence of the 'Great I Am' within me. Just as you are going to discover for yourself. In a moment Mahum will explain how.

"But first, let me make one thing clear. We are not here to start another new religion. That mistake has been made too many times. You are here to learn how to shut down your own Left-brain Chatter and find the 'Great I Am' within you. Only then will the 'I Am' be able to show you the truths in your own self. Through the 'I Am', Mohamed assures me that my connection and yours to the 'Great I Am' fulfills his promise.

"Now, I present to you my brother Mahum." He gestures to him and steps down.

The audience applauds energetically. Mahum steps into the podium and turns to applaud al-Nisista. After a moment, he motions to the audience to be quiet. They quickly settle down.

"Welcome friends and neighbors. We are all here to learn the three steps to finding the 'Great I Am' within you. Hayah and his team will lead you through these steps. For some this may go quickly. For others it may take time. For all of you, it will happen. You will find a new life.

"So where is Love hiding? Where is the Love-light? Well, they are right here," Mahum gestures to his heart, "in my heart and yours. Like me, your awareness has been trying to tell you that there must be something else to life. There must be more than just pain and suffering, wealth and poverty, war and obliteration.

"In the first step you will learn the language of your body and learn to listen to it, shutting down the left-brain chatter. Your body will never lie to you.

"In the second step you will learn the source of your breath. Your own natural breathing will become your mantra. It too will help you shut down your left-brain chatter.

"In the third step you will find your inner peace, then you'll find a light in the darkness. As the Love-light embraces you, and you embrace the Love-light, you will have the choice to Connect with the 'Great I Am' within you.

"I know that seems to be incomplete, and you want to know more. In a few moments we will divide-up the group, and you will be immersed in all the details."

Mahum steps out in front of the podium, "But now, I want to share with you what happened to me as I started to take these steps.

"I started step one thinking I knew it all. I keep my body well trained. I'm its master, and it does what I tell it to do. But what my Left-brain Chatter is telling me is a lie. Then I discovered, as you soon will discover for yourself, that my body is talking to me, and it doesn't lie. The war between me and my Left-brain Chatter was hard to shut down. All I can say is that it is worth the effort to shut it down. I now listen to my body and feel healthier than I have ever felt.

"Next I discovered that my left-brain irrational thoughts were making me breath wrong. My intellect assumed that it was all powerful, and it controlled me with lies and deception. It kept saying, 'Take a deep breath. Take a deep breath.' I puffed up my chest but took in only a little air. No matter how hard I tried, I was still short of breath. Then Hayah had me lay down and put my hands on my abdomen. When I started to exhale, he told me, 'Push down with your hands and push all the air out of your lungs. Then do nothing, just relax.' To my surprise, my body took a deep breath all by itself. My chest didn't even heave up, my abdomen did. Then I learned an ancient secret. You will learn that secret today. Your body says the mantra, which will shut down your Left-brain Chatter, all by itself. Listen only to it, and I guarantee that you will break through.

"I don't care how smart you think you are, and my left-brain ego had me thinking I was the smartest kid on the block; you need to let it go. Shut it down! It is worth the effort. As hard as it was for me; it was worth the effort. It is the best thing that ever happened to me. At first, I was afraid of the vast empty dark space within me. Then I feel a peace come over me that is unlike any peace I ever experienced before. I can see the vast space between the cells in my body. I can see them at work and feel the blood pumping threw my body. This wasn't something I was doing. My body is doing it all by itself. Then in the midst of the splendor, I see three specks of light floating in the empty space. I move toward them and meet the 'Great I Am' for the first time in my life." Mahum pauses, holding back a powerful emotion welling up within him.

He concludes, "I only hope and encourage you to find the Love-light within yourself."

The audience is silent, and al-Nisista joins Mahum. They hug, patting each other on the back. The audience brakes into applause. Al-Nisista motions for their silence and says, "There is one more little detail, which is not minor in any way. From this day forward in Iraq, Women and Men shall be equal in all ways, public and private. It is agreed. It is the will of the 'Great I Am' within us all." A cheer goes up in the audience and Mahum and al-Nisista shake hands on it.

Mahum quiets the audience and introduces me. I step to the podium and start before the applause can start again. I divide them into groups and introduce their group leaders. Everyone eagerly proceeds to their assigned locations.

CHAPTER 34
In the Cross-Hairs

There is a general excitement as everybody assembles in their respective groups, spread-out in various locations within the beautiful gardens. Bill is working with Hannah to learn how to guide others to finding the Love-light. We are all aware that theirs is more than a developing friendship between them.

I circulate among the six groups, mostly as an observer and only answering the occasional question. With the aid of the 'Great I Am' within me, I'm aware of the progress of everyone who is trying to connect with the 'I Am' within and the Love-light.

I'm also aware of the number of times that I'm close to being in the cross-hairs of the Sniper. I can hear the chatter between the Sniper and the CIA operative. After some time, the 'I Am' lets me see that the CIA agent is in his car speeding away from the scene. He is desperate to protect himself from the boomerang effect of what they are doing. I can see by his surroundings that he is already over 50 kilometers away, speeding back to Azerbaijan.

After several close calls and more than three rounds of the groups, I decide to cut the tension short and deliberately walk out into an unsecured area.

Within seconds I hear the voice of the Sniper, "I have a clear shot to the middle of the target's forehead."

The CIA agent shouts back, "Take it and get the hell out of there!"

I pause and look up at the Sniper, clearly mouthing the word NO. I hear the pop of a silenced shot as I go into slow-motion perception. I watch the bullet boomerang off my forehead and speed back at the Sniper. Before she can blink, the bullet passes through her forehead and blows out the whole back of her head.

At the same moment, the same thing happens to the CIA agent. His brains spray into the back seat. The car speeds off the road, down an embankment and crashes into a concrete wall. It explodes into flames and a million pieces.

As I come back to normal perception, I walk over to a nearby bench and sit down. In spite of my protection, these events always take a lot out of me. The experience of death and destruction are never pleasant. I look around at the reverberating joy growing in all the groups. No one is aware of what just happened.

I feel the Love-light of the 'Great I Am' well up within me. 'I Am' says, "I need to prepare you for something that is unexpected. This has been percolating for several centuries. Now the pot is about to boil over. While many in the Hindu, Judeo, Islamic and Christian communities are seeing the ancient truths hidden in their texts and are eager to connect with Me and find the Love-light, there are those in the Roma-Catholic movement that find YOU a major threat to their institution. To them God is their institution. To them God is the fantasy that makes them billions. To them YOU are the one who will destroy all that. This has happened before, as you know; well, it is about to happen again. I need to prepare you."

"I sensed this was coming," I whisper sadly. "Your will is my will. I will do whatever you ask."

"I know you will," 'I Am' responds confidently. "Unfortunately, we will have a problem communicating. Tonight, they are planning on drugging you before you return to Israel. You will need to finetune your awareness to feel my presence. Of course, I will be right here within you. I wish you did not have to go through this. Remember, whatever they do, I will protect you."

After a bright Love-light moment within me, 'I Am' begins to fill me in on some people who need my help to connect in three of the groups.

I quickly hurry over to Talia's group. There is a 19-year-old woman, who is the daughter of Ahmed Jannati from Iran. She is having a battle with the hatred within her. Her body is shaking. Her Brain Deception is screaming at her. She is silently screaming back in confrontation. It is an inward battle of great violence.

I sit down next to her and take her hand. She opens her eyes and looks into mine. Her contorted face begins to relax. I whisper softly, "breath out all your air and relax. Let the body breath all by itself. Listen to what your breath is saying." Her breathing starts to stabilize, and the unutterable syllable calms her down. I notice a twitch at her temples. I whisper, "Yes, here it comes again. This time blow it a kiss after each breath. Do it three times. Then listen to the syllable." Her heart jumps as she sees it retreat, and she smiles. Slowly, she begins to relax. As she discovers her inner peace, I let go of her hand.

I sit quietly and watch, as she discovers a bright light in her heart. As I silently slip away, the Love-light fills her inner being. I look back and see a radiant glow on her face.

Through a tight stand of trees, I come upon Ori's group. All but one young man are deep in their connection with the 'Great I Am'. The young man is off to the side, rolling with silent laughter in the grass. I watch him for a few minutes, while the 'I Am' is filling me in.

At first, I cannot comprehend why he would be laughing. I have experienced boundless joy, deep and abiding Love and a blinding light. These have given me an uplifted heart, but never laughter. I say to the 'I Am', "O.K. I'm here. I'm Listening. Why is he laughing?"

The 'Great I Am' lets me stew for a couple of minutes, while I feel a smile and joy. "Hayah, this young man has been deeply lost in the Dark Side most of his life. He has lived under the Dragon's wing. Before today all he knew was hatred, violence and darkness. He came here today to disrupt and destroy what he calls, 'The idealistic clap-trap.' When he starts to listen to his body, he is amazed at how much it is telling him. He was the first to break through. Then he embraces his breathing, and the unutterable syllable blows him out of all the deception and darkness he is living with. He flies into the light and finds Me instantly. Now, he is in the Love-light. He is connected with Me. Suddenly he realizes that the Dragon was once Love. He sees the human choice and finds it ridiculous. He sees the human hesitation and self-made dilemma and finds them comical. He finds it laughable."

Suddenly, Sam, the young man, sits up and shouts out, "We can bring the Dragon back!"

Now the 'I Am' and I are both laughing.

I walk around the pond to Noya's group. Noya points out a woman, in her mid-fifties, sitting in a lotus position. Noya tells me, "She insists that she needs to talk to you."

I walk toward the women and study her pose. Her back is straight. Her head is erect with the chin tucked. Her legs are crossed, and the soles of her feet are facing up. Her arms are relaxed, and her hands are resting on her thighs with the palms up and the middle finger touching the thumb. It is a perfect classic pose.

I sit down next to her facing in the opposite direction. I pull my knees up to my chest and embrace them. I study her face and body. It is as stiff as a board, and no light is radiating trough or from it.

She opens one eye to look at me. She asks without moving her lips, "Hayah, I cannot get your method to work. I'm in nirvana, but nothing happens. All I see is blackness."

"I can see and feel that" I say calmly and warmly. "Focus your attention on your hands. Is there any energy flowing through them?"

"Yes, it is flowing in a perpetual circle." Her eyes are now open and looking at me.

I smile, "Now simply open your hand and let them relax palm up."

She does so, and after a moment her eyes light up, "The energy is flowing out from me."

"Exactly, but you said that nothing was happening, so that energy is negative. Is that the energy you want to send into the world?"

"Of course not!"

"So, use that energy to heal yourself. Turn your hands over palms down and relax." I watch as she does this and her eyes grow brighter.

"The energy is moving through my body, but then it gets stopped by some very tight muscles." Her face shows a disappointment.

I wait until she looks into my eyes. Then I say warmly, "I want you to very slowly come out of your Krishna pose, which, by the way, is absolutely perfect." When she is sitting comfortably, I ask, "Of what skill was the first person who captured that pose?"

"It was Krishna," she responds, listening to and being led by her Left-brain Chatter.

"No, he was not even the first person, because he learned it from his mother. It was an unknown painter and sculpture, who captured him in that pose in his mid- twenties. When he was your age, he could no longer do it, but the painting and sculpture have survived many millennia. Now you have discovered that this pose or any pose is not the meditation.

"Meditation is shutting down the left-brain irrational Brain Chatter and learning to listen to your body and breathing. The goal is not in finding nirvana (absolute nothingness) which takes you only halfway, but to find the Love-light within you, which is absolutely everything.

"After you accomplish this, you can go back to your Krishna pose and embrace the energy of the Love-light within you."

Her face is filled with excitement, "Can you help me with those steps?"

"That's what Noya is doing," I say kindly, as I gesture to Noya. I know this woman is angling to get special one on one attention for some reason, but right now I'm facing a much bigger problem. I conclude warmly, "I know you will do very well and hope to see you again soon."

As Noya takes over, I move to a small-secluded spot in the park. I immediately start to listen to what the 'Great I Am' starts to tell me.

(In case you haven't figured this out, we no longer need to chatter endlessly with long lists and endless requests and orders to a higher power. We simply do the Samuel thing, saying, "I'm here. I'm listening.")

"Hayah, I still do not know everything that is going to happen. There are a lot of different power levels in the Roman Catholic Church, and each level has its own agenda; but as soon as one level passes their plan up the chain, the plan begins to change along with the agenda. Right now, all I can prepare you for is what will happen today. But you need to know; their intentions are hostile.

"The first thing we need to do is prepare the team

for your coming absence. There is no need to alarm them, and Hannah can manage the Team. I, of course, will lead them and keep them informed of what they need to know about you. Fortunately, they will have plenty to keep them busy with the rising holy war in Syria, Iran, Iraq and Israel.

"The Shiite Houthi rebels are moving in to support the right-wing Islamic clerics opposed to al-Nisista, Mahum, Hydia and Mahenie. The Houthi support from the billionaires in Hodeida has made them the most heavily armed force in the area. Their goal is to destroy the Love-light movement and the people of Israel."

I focus on the now and suggest, "I can simply tell the team that You have a mission for me in Rome, and it is hard to determine how long it will take. As soon as it is accomplished, I will be back to assist them."

"That sounds good," 'I Am' agrees. "Right now, their plan is to drug you and secretly carry you off. Do not resist or try to stop them. Do not try to WARN them. They wrongly think that your Warnings are a trigger to the boomerang effect, and by silencing you their actions will have no repercussions. This behavior tells me they are already warned and know that what they are doing is wrong.

"It is important for you to remember that I Am right here and will always protect you. The situation and circumstances will not alter that new law of Physics."

I focus on the problem, and I cannot imagen any circumstances which would prevent me from feeling 'I Am's presence within me. Our connection has been so strong for so many years.

"You may think that Hoss," says the Word, "but I know from personal experience, it can happen."

That comment leaves me silent and reflecting.

After some moments, I see the groups returning to the lecture hall. I follow to sum up the days experience.

As I look over the assembled group, the 'Great I Am' fills me in on the few people who still need to connect. I start with them to comfort and encourage them. "I understand that some of you are still working to connect to the 'Great I Am' within you. Focus on how far you have come and celebrate the progress you make every day. Mohamed once told me how many years it took him to connect, and I was shocked." I listen to his voice in my head. "And he says, 'You don't need to go live in a cave to do it.'"

The crowd laughs and begins to relax. "You now have a map to show you how to get there and stay connected. Make it your first priority, and you will get there. It is worth the effort. What is the opinion of the rest of you?"

There is a huge shout goes up among the rest of the crowd, "YES, YES, YES!"

I continue to address those still connecting, "For now, don't go into harm's-way. Keep your focus on finding the Love-light and connecting with the 'Great I Am' who is your essence of being. Once you are Connected you are Protected."

There is a big question mark on the faces of many of those Connected. I answer, "Protected means much more than the old Spiritual shield of protection. The 'Great I Am' is within you, and now 'I Am' is creating an invisible shield around you. Any act of violence against you will boomerang off you and back on its perpetrator with equal force and destruction. That is why we say, 'If you are Connected, you are Protected!'

"Basically, the 'Great I Am' is redefining a law of physics, 'Every action has an equal and opposite reaction.' This would have been part of creation, but at that time humans had not gone to their dark-side. Now all the animal kingdom is protected, and only humans lag behind. As for Nature it has always been in effect, we call it the balance of nature. At the present moment we are experiencing its powerful message through climate change. If we do not reverse our addiction and greed toward fossil fuels, we will wipe ourselves off the face of the earth.

"Those of you, who are newly Connected, are hearing those words differently than you have ever heard them before. Why? Because scientists have talked themselves blue in the face, and you were not listening. Now, 'I Am' is shouting it in your heart, your essence of being.

"Make no mistake, the enemy that you will soon face, the Shiite Houthi rebels, are supported and manipulated by the Hodeida billionaires and their oil interests. They are allying with the old Islamic clerics, who do not want truth and change, but would prefer to turn their hatred into a Holy War. BUT THERE WILL BE NO WAR!

"In a few days you will have a chance to stand side-by-side with your neighbors from Syria, Libya, Yemen, Iran, Iraq, and many from Israel. You will stand together as one family Connected to the 'Great I Am' within you. You will stand together in the Love-light.

"Feel the LOVE-LIGHT within you. That is your strength. That is your newfound unity. Alone or together, if you are Connected, you are Protected."

The crowd erupts with applause and a cheer. As Hayah steps down from the podium, al-Nisista and Mahum join him. They join hands and raise them in unity. Then all in the crowd join hands shouting, "Love-light, Love-light, Love-light."

It takes several minutes before the crowd settles down and breaks into smaller groups. Mahum's family rushes up onto the stage to embrace him. Al-

Nisista's family, mother, brothers, sisters and relatives come up to embrace him. His father stands to one side, with pride written on his face. He too has found the Love-light.

I motion for the Team to assemble backstage. This message is also communicated to them by the 'Great I Am' within them. They all move quickly to a backstage room.

After congratulating each member of the Team on a job well done, I say apologetically, "Now, I want you to know that I'm being called away on a special mission to Rome. You will be returning to Israel without me. While I'm away, the 'Great I Am' will be preparing you for the largest Islamic confrontation to date. Hannah, I'm counting on you to shepherd the Team while I'm gone." The 'Great I Am' captures their attention immediately.

I take advantage of the moment and slip away to the men's room. Afterwards, as I'm standing washing my hands, two men dressed in black enter. One stands on each side of me, and I feel a prick on my neck. As I look in the merroir, the 'I Am' turns me back into Hoss saying, "I will be with you".

I feel my brain start to fade. My body senses start to numb. I lose control of my breathing. I feel my awareness, my presence slipping away. The 'I Am' slips away with my consciousness.

The transformation takes the two men by surprise. One asks the other, "Is this the right guy? He looks old."

The other man looks around the lavatory, "He's the only one in here."

Hoss passes out and starts to collapse. The two men grab him and carry him out unseen.

CHAPTER 35
Out of the Frying Pan...

*Black magic
A dance at Stone Hinge
The goddess of light,
    which is darkness;
The goddess of love,
    which is hate;
The goddess of peace,
    which is war and violence.
Clay bodies being tortured;
    the loved ones of many.
Hoss taken prisoner,
    to destroy and kill.*

The two men in black dump Hoss on a stretcher and wheel him over to a phony ambulance. He is quickly loaded, and the ambulance speeds off without sirens. Several minutes later the ambulance pulls into a private airport, with its lights now flashing. It pulls up to a private jet waiting on the tarmac. Hoss is carried onto the plane and buckled down. One of the men returns to the ambulance and drives off. The other man sits down across from Hoss and buckles up. The pilot, also dressed in black, checks that they are both secure and returns to the cockpit. The airplane taxies out to the runway and waits for clearance to take off. Within minutes they are airborne. The plain climes quickly to 30 thousand feet and soon breaks the sound barrier.

The flight is incredibly quiet. The man in black is in his early thirties, clean shaven and quite obese. He checks Hoss several times; each time he checks his pulse, temperature and finally slaps Hoss hard across the face twice, with a forward swing and back swing. This gives the fat man a great deal of

pleasure, and he laughs hysterically. Each time he
rhetorically asks, "Where's your boomerang effect
now buddy?" The rest of the time the fat man spends
most of his time flipping through a magazine, using
only his left hand. In his right hand, he holds a
Rosary, which he quickly moves through his fingers
without thought or feeling.

Soon they are making their approach to Rome,
Italy. The pilot asks the fat man to buckle up. First,
the fat man makes a short cellphone call. Then, he
gives Hoss another injection in the neck. He slaps
Hoss twice and buckles up.

They land at the public airport and taxi to a
private section. As they approach a hangar, the doors
slowly roll open. A small tractor tows the airplane
into the hangar and the doors close. Another man in
black approaches the airplane. He is tall and gaunt.
His face is so sunken in that he looks like a walking
skull. Even though his lips are so thin, they reveal
the outline of every tooth. He rolls a set of steps up
to the cabin door. The door swings open, and he
climbs abord the plain.

A moment later, the skull man in black and the
fat man in black are carelessly carrying the limp body
of Hoss off the airplane. Hoss' body is sagging like a
limp hammock. They carry him to a nearby black
van. The pilot rushes ahead of them and swings open
the rear doors of the van. Hoss is thrown in the back
like a sack of potatoes. A garage door opens and the
van speeds out into the murky night.

The van makes its way through the narrow
streets of Rome. The skull man is driving. He is
constantly cursing about illegally parked cars, trash
in the street and homeless people wandering around.
Finally, they reach a back entrance to the Vatican.
The skull man pushes the button on the automatic
garage door opener fastened to the visor. They pull
into the underground garage and park among several

other vehicles.

The two men in black awkwardly pull the unconscious Hoss out of the back of the van. They lose their grip and he falls to the concrete floor with a thump. They laugh, and the fat man takes out a coin saying, "I'll flip you to see who gets to take the feet end."

"You're on," says the skull man. "I call tails."

The fat man flips the coin. It falls on Hoss' chest. They both look down. The fat man cries out, "Best out of three!" He snatches up the coin.

"No way!" shouts the skull man. "Get your fat ass up here and take this end."

They switch ends and lug Hoss over to the elevator. They drop Hoss and push the button. When the elevator arrives, they slide Hoss in on the elevator floor. The skull man pushes the bottom button, 6. Skull man starts to whistle a hymn. The elevator stops and they pick Hoss up and carry him off.

They start down the stairs right next to the elevator. Two levels later, they go out into a dingy corridor. Thirty meters down the corridor, the single light becomes further and further away. Finally, the fat man says, "This is it."

Hoss is dropped on the floor, and the fat man takes out a large old key and opens the rusty steel door. The two men each take one of Hoss' arms and drag him into the cell. There is no light in the cell. As they drag Hoss to the corner opposite the door, they hear something moving toward them. The fat man says loudly, "Step back John. We brought you company."

John is a tall, lanky thirteen-year-old boy. His face is round with a long nose and big ears. John's eyes are adjusted to the darkness. He asks, "Is that Hayah?"

The fat man is uncertain, "We think so, but it

doesn't look like him. We have him drugged."

"What are you bastards up to Fat Jack?" John follows skull man and Fat Jack as they exit the cell.

Fat Jack laughs, "Let's just say we are going to give him a warm welcome. You can join him if you want." He pushes John back and slams the cell door in his face.

John saw Hayah in India. He saw the truth in everything he was saying. He embraced the awareness and struggled to follow the program. He kept struggling to break through but could not connect with the 'Great I Am'. He felt close many times but found it impossible to shut down his left-brain chatter and anger over being imprisoned for verbally confronting a Catholic priest. Now, here he is with an old man who is supposed to be Hayah. He stands over him studying his features as best he can in the dim light coming through the small window in the door.

He says to himself, "It sure doesn't look like him."

He bends down and checks his vital signs. Talking to himself, "What have they done? You're not dead. The bastards! They have drugged you! Why? Don't worry pall. I'll take care of you."

He walks over to get his water bottle and returns with it. He lifts Hoss' head and pours a little water into his partially gaping mouth. His body drinks the water automatically. John adjusts Hoss' body to a sitting position, propping him against the wall. His head falls limply, with his chin resting on his chest. John realizes that this is not going to work and lays him in a prone position again. John arranges his body to make him as comfortable as possible. He gives him another sip of water.

The cell has no furnishings, nor does it have any raised places to sit or use as a bed. It is 5 meters square with a 5-centimeter hole in the middle of the room to be used as a toilet. Consequently, the cell always smells of human waste. John is now used to what he calls the "aroma," and no longer walks in circles around the room to avoid the hole. In fact, when he does his walking exercises, he walks in an extraordinarily complex pattern in order to get the maximum exercise both to his body and his mind.

John is now sitting across the room watching Hoss, lying motionless. Without realizing it, his focus becomes increasingly intense. All he seems to see is just Hoss. All he seems to feel is just Hoss. Then, that intense focus shifts over to his awareness of his breathing and how his body is just settling and focusing on one thing, Hoss. Without realizing it, he has shut down his left-brain irrational mind. Now, he is focusing entirely on his breathing. Hoss disappears from his conscious mind. As he settles into his new rhythm of breathing, he becomes aware of a dark space within himself. Then without thinking, feeling only peace and stillness, he notices a single tiny speck of light. The light of the spec is pulsing and growing stronger as it moves through the space coming closer and closer. At first, he feels that he recognizes the rhythm. His left-brain chatter kicks in and tells him that it is a tune from the past. A tune that he loved. His mind shifts, and he tries to remember the tune. The light comes closer and stronger. The pulsing goes in and out, in and out. He can feel that the pulsing is part of him. Then suddenly an awareness comes over him. He can feel that the pulsing is the same as his breathing, the same as his pulse, the same as his heartbeat. It is part of him. Slowly, he can feel this speck of light is in him, in his inner space, in his inner being. The light becomes stronger and stronger brighter and brighter.

It is Light, brighter than anything he has ever felt or seen before; it is present; it shifts and floats in the dark space within himself. He waits. He hopes. Then the Light becomes stronger still. It consumes the dark space within him, and he moves toward it. And then without any conscious thought at all, the Light fills him. The darkness within him disappears and the Light becomes extremely powerful and strong. He feels a Love unlike anything that he has ever felt before in his life. He now embraces what he is experiencing, the Love-light, and out of that Love-light comes the 'Great I Am' within him. John is aware. John is silent. He listens.

"Well John you finally did it. At this critical time, you finally found me. I cannot begin to tell you how much it means to me that you have broken through the left-brain chatter and distractions which have kept us apart.

CHAPTER 36
The 3 Spirits

The Justice Team, Hannah and Bill, Jacob and
Talia, Abbud, Noya and Ori, are gathering at
Mahenie's aviary in Iran. Mahenie greets them with
open arms. The birds instantly recognize them and
greet them with excitement and song. Mahenie
marvels at the bird's response while he is standing at
the door. The site fills him with extraordinary joy.
The birds fly toward the net and hover in front of
their mate. They communicate through the 'Great I
Am'.

The 'I Am' explains everything to Mahenie.

He smiles and says to the 'I Am', "That is why I
have become even closer to them and know what they
are saying to me and feel their love so strongly."

'I Am' explains, "Now you will have that
connection with all living creatures. They are all
connected to me and through me you are connected
to them and all of nature."

"Thank you, thank you, thank you. It fills my
heart with joy," says Mahenie with a broad smile.

"I know. I Am in here, and I share your joy."

Mahenie laughs, "Of course. I'm still getting
used to your constant presence."

"Heads up. Your other guest are arriving."

Mahenie turns to greet Hydia Sabba from Syria.
They have known each other for many years, but this
is the first time that they have seen each other since
they connected to the 'Great I Am'. They each feel a
warmth that they have never known before, which
brings them together in a strong embrace. As they
pull back and look into each other's eyes, they both
feel like brother and sister.

They both say at the same time, "Wow, it is nice

to see you!" They both laugh.

Mahenie steps back and gestures for her to come in, "Welcome, Welcome Sister." He reacts on the intimacy of his remark and quickly corrects himself, "I apologize. I mean Hydia, or Mrs. Sabba."

Hydia smiles and says, "I share in the new feeling brother. And the 'I Am' seems to approve."

"I feel that too." Mahenie takes her hand as she walks in and their arms are fully extended as their hands slide apart and she enters the room.

Hydia looks over her shoulder with a smile. Then she turns to greet the others.

It is no surprise that Mahum and al-Nisista, from Iraq, arrive together. They are like two peas in a pod now. They're 'Great I Am' radiance is very visible.

As they greet Mahenie, Mahum and Nisista draw him into their radiance; the glow becomes brighter. There are hugs all around, with a lot of back slapping. Mahenie says, "I feel like I'm taking a bath in the Love-light."

The other two men respond at the same time, "I know the feeling."

They enter the aviary and mingle with the others. There is a powerful energy that fills the room. The glow becomes brighter still. There is unity and oneness. And the birds are included in that oneness. Suddenly, everyone freezes. They each feel an overwhelming joy in the 'Great I Am' within them.

The 'I Am' says, "This is the Love-light that can change the world we live in. There are 3 Spirits that would like to share this moment with you. Like all Spirits they are part of Me all the time and I'm part of them. The first is Devaki, the mother of Krishna."

A small ball of swirling bright light begins to form in the midst of the room's glow. When it is 5 cm, it begins to pulsate. Then small bits of light begin to shoot out from it and take the shape of a middle-aged woman, with long black hair which falls gracefully over her left shoulder and down past her waist. She is wearing a multicolored fabric raped tightly around her body, with many ties. Her glowing light brown face is round with a warm radiant smile. In less than a minute she stands among the others in her original human form. Without hesitation, she moves among them, embracing them and greeting them warmly.

Devaki's main topic of conversation is family. She stresses not only the importance of the blood family but of the human family. She treats everyone in the room as if they are part of her family. This creates an instant bond between her and every person to whom she is talking and between the other people in the room. She is also stressing the role of women in society, their equality, their leadership ability, their strength and their sensitivity to the needs of others.

This theme on the role of women produces an open and heated debate between Devaki and Ila Mahenie. At one point the debate captures the attention of everybody in the room. Mahenie takes the traditional position of the Islamic state. Devaki, with the 'Great I Am's help, focuses on Mahenie's intimate relationship with his mother as a child. The memory of these moments brings him back to the feeling of immense joy and love. Within seconds, he is laughing and giggling like a little boy. Then to make her point, Devaki askes him a question, "Mahenie do you have as a man or a father the ability to bring that kind of joy out of people?"

Mahenie is silent.

Devaki leads him over to the aviary. She points out the family of birds, and says, "Which kind of world would you like to live in, a world of joy and song or a world of hate and sorrow?

Mahenie embraces her, and says, "Thank you for your wisdom. Very well put. I have already chosen the life of joy and song."

Devaki continues to work the group and engage those that she meets.

A small new sphere of light begins to swirl just as with Devaki. It to shoots out small bits of light as the image begins to form. This figure is a tall male with long hair and a full beard. He wears a flowing tunic which shows signs of wear and soil. His feet are clad in open sandals. His face looks kind and caring and bears a gentle smile. These Spirits are the real people, not just ghostly images. They can be seen and touched.

'I Am' says, "This is my faithful friend Abraham. I call him a friend because of his constant closeness. Throughout his entire life, he listened carefully to everything I asked of him. He followed my will without question, and he is indeed the father of many of you here."

Many in the room begin to bow toward him. He quickly motions with his hands for them to raise their heads, and says, "Please, please, please, we are all blessed with our connection to the 'Great I Am' within us. I'm only a simple man, who did what he was told. Hopefully, you will do the same."

Abraham walks among those present, spreading the simple message, "You have Free Will. It is your choice. I recommend that you go where the 'I Am' leads you. That choice has made all the difference in my eternal and physical life."

Abraham moves among the group greeting each one and asking about their connection with the Love light. With the women, he gently reaches out and softly lays his left hand on their cheek.

Noya responds to his touch in a whisper, "I have never felt so much Love from the touch of any man. Thank you." She reaches out and rests the palm of her hand over his heart.

He smiles and moves on.

The third Spirit begins to emerge in the center of the glowing room. Like the other Spirits, it is first seen as a small ball of intense swirling light. As the ball increases in size and begins to pulsate, the sparks shooting out from it are more numerous and a bright yellow color. They begin to form another male figure of medium height with his head rapped in a white turban and a long white beard. His tunic falls loosely around his body. His hands and arms are already open in an embracing gesture.

The 'Great I Am' introduces him, "The energy and love of this man you should recognize. I present to you Mohammed. He brings you an especially important message for the task you are about to undertake."

The entire group turns to face Mohammed. Some begin to kneel.

Mohammed, still with his embracing gesture, says, "Brothers and Sisters, don't disgrace me with your physical homage. You already honor me with your oneness in the Love-light, of which I'm a part.

"I asked to be here this day to clarify my main message and its oneness with the message of the 'I Am' within you. Everyone on the face of this planet is our brothers and sisters. Embrace them with love and help them find the Love-light. Help them find the 'Great I Am' within them. Help them connect, in Free Will, with what the 'I Am' is asking of them. Our purpose here is to share in 'I Am's purpose for us all.

"Listen, listen, listen to 'I Am's voice. Stop assuming you know. Stop interpreting what I say, or what any other leader says. Stop worshiping a religious movement, a hierarchy, a social/political entity. Start listening to the 'Great I Am' within you. Start leading all others to the Love-light that you have found within yourself.

"Other leaders have misinterpreted my word

'infidel'. Simply put, an infidel is any person who turns to their dark-side and refuses to see the Love-light and listen to the 'I Am's voice. Yes, I reacted on the Roman Catholic Church as a dictator of faith to control their people. The institution is the infidel, not the people. The people are your brothers and sisters. Even 'Islam' has become another institution leading people away from their 'I Am' center and using 'infidel' as a hate mantra to kill and maim others. If you need a mantra, use this, 'Live in the Love-light and let hatred destroy itself.'

"Why do I say we are all brothers and sisters, when we are not of the same blood? We are one family, the human family. We are one race, the human race. We are one in the 'Great I Am' along with every other creature and thing on this planet.

"As brothers and sisters, you can argue and discus your different points of view. One is not right and the other wrong, listen to each other. You might learn something. Have you ever noticed that when you work or live alongside another person of color, ethnic background, or nationality that you eventually forget there is a difference? You know them and accept them as a brother or sister.

"The bottom line is, 'See the person'! They are your brother and sister."

Mohammed begins to move among the group. Of course, there is a lot of hugging. There are also a lot of questions, mostly about The Qur'an. These he fields with a great deal of skill and insight. However, he ends every textual comment with the same question. "Which is more important, the written word or the word you hear from the 'Great I Am' within you?"

Oddly, the common response is, "Aren't they the same thing?"

To this question everyone hears laughter, and the laughter is from the 'Great I Am'. Who then responds in a light tone, "Not even I can dictate something without listeners making mistakes or misinterpretations. I consider it sheer luck when they get it ten-percent correct. It is always better to get the Word directly from me."

Out of the clear blue, Bill asks the 'I Am' a serious question. "Are you going to send Yeshua to meet with us some day?"

'I Am's laughter rings in everyone's ears. After a moment, the 'I Am' says gently, "This is Him, Bill. This is the Word. He is always the one who speaks for me. The only time you and I can directly communicate is when your own awareness is able to sense my message within you."

"I have felt that many times," Bill responds. "Thank you, Yeshua. That makes our communications incredibly special to me. Though, I suppose I should have figured that out for myself."

Hannah whispers reassurance to him, "That's OK, dear, I didn't see that either."

Hannah then turns to the group and tries to get their attention. "Can I have your attention please?" The three Spirits give their attention first, appearing anxious to participate. They encourage the others by pointing toward Hannah. Without another word the group responds and there is complete silence.

Hannah takes a deep breath, "You all know the crisis our countries are in and the backlash we are getting form our own clerics, who are threatened by our connection to the 'Great I Am' within us all. They are about to launch an assault on us, and I'm sure the 'Great I Am' is giving you a heads up with your local groups. Now, the 'I Am' has a plan."

The group, including the three Spirits, pull the chairs in the room into a large circle. They each settle into their chair, filled with the glowing Love-light within them. A stillness and silence fills them as they listen intently.

The 'Great I Am' begins with an upbeat suggestion, "Let us create a positive outcome from a very nasty problem. Your neighbors in the south, from Yemen, are experiencing a cholera and malnutrition epidemic. Let us make them our mission. You and your people can take them food and Vaxchora (the cholera vaccination drink). I can bring them fresh clean water.

"Yes, this is like taking a lam into the lion's den. The Shiite Houthi rebels' stronghold is in Hodeida, their richest and largest city. The Islamic clerics that want to destroy you have hired the Shiite to help them. They see their mission as a Holy War against the Connected People, the Yemen tribes and the Israeli people. (And I Am telling you, no War has ever been Holy, ever is Holy or ever will be Holy.)

"I Am not about war, never have been and never will be. I want to offer the Love-light to everyone. I want to help the lost rich, the poor, the sick and the starving. This shall be our mission. However, make no mistake, we will be the targets of the Shiite and Dark Hateful Clerics. But, if you are connected, you are protected. They will be warned, and they will destroy themselves.

"Hannah and Bill have worked out some details for our peaceful humanitarian mission. I'll let her explain." All eyes turn to Hannah.

Hannah leans forward in her chair, while Bill walks around to each person to deliver a small packet. When this is done, he sits down again.

"Each of you will need to return home and recruit those who would like to participate in this mission. They must be connected to the 'Great I Am' within them. They are to bring no arms. You will need to organize them into small groups to make the trip together. It is important that the groups travel separately, so this does not look like an invasion. We will camp in tents, so bring the right gear and clothes. Each of the groups should put together as much <u>fresh</u> food as they can transport.

"The packet Bill gave you contains Vaxchora, a vaccine drink against cholera. Thake it now. Bill has arranged with UNHCR, that each of you has as many cases of vaccine as you will need for each person, who will participate. It is important that they take the vaccine 10 days before they arrive in Yemen. Next week you can start sending groups on their trek, a few each day and at various times. We will assign groups their tasks as they arrive. Please bring any leftover vaccine for the Yemen people.

"Our rendezvous place is Aleetmh in the Al Jawf Governorate, between Sa'dah and Al Abr, North of Khab on N556. The 'I Am' will guide you to the exact spot.

"The Justice team and I will be flying down to Sa'dah air strip in a couple of days. Bill says the air strip has been bombed-out, but he thinks he can manage a landing with the small plane. If you have any questions or problems, send them via the 'I Am'.

"It has been wonderful to meet with you all, including the Spirits." She approaches each Spirit, "Thank you for wanting to meet with us. We shall draw great strength from all that we have learned from you and especially the feeling that our own connection is truly eternal."

Everyone says farewell to the Spirits, and they slowly resume their Light form. After visiting and singing with the birds, they depart like shooting stars into the glowing Love-light in the room.

CHAPTER 37
Vatican Darkness

John slips his hands under Hoss's armpits and slides his body up the wall a little bit, until his head and shoulders are resting on the wall.

Hoss is still unconscious. His body is limp. He is not capable of doing anything for himself, not even eat or drink.

John puts a piece of his bread in his own mouth and chews it until it is soft and moist. He removes a portion of it and puts it in Hoss's mouth. He strokes Hoss's throat until his body swallows the bread. He then gives Hoss a sip of his water. John repeats this routine several times until the bread and water are gone. This is the only nourishment Hoss gets.

John says to the 'Great I Am' within him, "That seems so gross. I'm not sure I would like it if someone did that to me."

"That is exactly what a mother and father bird do to feed their chicks. Like the birds, if Hoss does not get a little food and water, he will die. The body needs the food and water."

John responds, "When you put it that way it doesn't seem so gross. How can they do this to him? What has he done to them? I'm the one who attacked their bigotry and their theological bullshit."

"He is a threat to everything they believe, their power over the people and their future income." 'I Am' sighs deeply, "That's the way they have been for the last two thousand years. They just do not want to listen. They would not even listen to Yeshua. All they could see was money and power." 'I Am's words taper off to a whisper.

John sits in silence for a long time. His mind races over everything Hayah had taught him, the sacred texts, the breathing, the body, the Love-light.

The difference of freedom of will and real Free Will.
He finally asks, "How did Hoss find you?"

"Hoss found me when he was only 12 years old.
He was playing a Halloween prank on the police chef.
While waiting for a cat to find the fish head, he was
sitting in a hideout up in the dunes. He emptied his
head of all thoughts and was sitting quietly. I start
talking to him, and he responds. The next thing I
know we are having a discussion as if it is the most
natural thing in the world. In many ways he reminds
me of Samuel. After that, we become very intricately
connected, and he accepts My purpose for him and
becomes part of My Love-light. There has not been a
day since, that we have been cut off from each other,
until now."

John sits in silence for several minutes. Then
jumps to his feet urgently, "Their coming! I got to lay
him down again."

'I Am' says, "You got that one the same time I
did. Be gentle."

John quickly slides Hoss back into a prone
position and races to the opposite side of the cell, sits
and pretends to be asleep.

The door opens.

Fat Jack and Skull man enter the cell, with
flashlights. They observe John sleeping and move on
to Hoss. They walk over to him and give him a kick.
His body jerks. Fat Jack says, "He's still alive."

Skull man responds, "Just barely."

"Help me get his clothes off," Fat Jack says to
Skull man.

Skull man doesn't move, "Are you sure that is
what the Cardinal wanted? Do you have something
else for him to ware to the party?"

"Shut-up and help me get his clothes off!" Fat
Jack orders Skull man.

Skull man slowly moves in to help. The two men
pull off Hoss' clothes jerking his body this way and

that. They have absolutely no consideration or kindness toward Hoss. As Fat Jack twists and pulls off Hoss' underwear, Hoss is left naked and face down on the stone floor.

Fat Jack stands over him motionless staring at his buttocks.

Skull man stands at the door with the large wad of Hoss' clothes in his arms. He watches Fat Jack and grins at his lustful expression. Finally, the wait gets to be too much, he shouts, "Jack give him the shot and let's get out of here. The smell is getting to me."

Fat Jack snaps out of it and takes out the syringe. He bends over Hoss and gives him the shot in his butt cheek. "There, Mr. Superhero, you don't look so powerful anymore."

Skull man and Fat Jack disappear out the steel door, slamming it shut with a bang.

John goes over to check on Hoss. He rolls him over on his back and arranges his body in a comfortable position. He takes off his own t-shirt, curls it up in a tight roll and puts it under Hoss' head. He mumbles to himself, "Why are they doing this to you?"

The 'Great I Am' explains to John, "They are afraid of him and think he has great powers. Since he was a young boy, we knew this day would come."

"Don't they know that it is you, who has the powers? Don't they see that the Love-light is within them too?" John shakes his head.

"To them it is witchcraft. Throughout history, anything that diminishes their control over the people is a threat to their very existence. I watch them fill the people with hate and fear, just to maintain their control. Yet, in all Yeshuah's life, not once did he use the word hate or ask people to fear me. It has been the same since the beginning with every religious group ever formed by the human species. The reality is that their hatred and fear is a product of their own dark thoughts and actions. It is like they have trapped themselves in a vicious cycle they cannot end. Nor do they want to end it."

John asks, "What do we do, now?"

"We wait. They have called together their cardinals, bishops and arch deacons from all over the world. They are assembling every secret order of their church, every powerful and enforcing entity of their institution. They will take action."

John responds with confidence, "We will be ready for them."

The 'I Am' agrees, "We are ready."

CHAPTER 38
Peace Gathering

Bill is flying the Justice Team to Sa'dah, Yemen. As he approaches the air-strip, he makes two low passes to check out the tarmac. With a plan, he has the Team cut the power, and he glides in at a right angle to the runway. Then he banks the plane and slides into perfect alignment with the runway. His speed is half what it would normally be, and they role to a stop seven meters from the first bomb hole. The whole Team takes a deep breath.

Abbud calls to Bill, "I have never seen that one before. Where'd you learn to do that."

"My Grandpa taught me that one in his by-plane. This was my first try with this plane. It was a little faster than I would have liked. Next time, I'll have you all slow us down a bit. The important thing is that it works. It is excellent for emergency landings, and you can land on a dime."

Hannah is all business, "OK Team. We need to hop out and see if any of those hangars are empty."

Everyone disembarks and runs toward the row of hangars along the side of the runway. Most of them are loaded with junk or crippled planes. Ori calls out to the others. He has found one with only a couple of drums in the way. Jacob and Abbud go to help move the drums out of the way. Bill immediately starts to taxi toward the hangar.

A UN van and a small UN truck approach from the south end of the runway, weaving around the many bomb craters. They approach the hangar, while Bill parks the plane. Noya motions for them both to back into the hangar on the cargo side of the plane. As soon as they park, Bill walks over to greet them. There is a friendly exchange.

The rest of the Team immediately goes to work

unloading the cargo. They load all of the Team's gear, three cases of vaccine and a few cases of fresh food into the back of the van. Then, they load the rest of the cargo into the truck. There are over thirty cases of vaccine plus fifty some cases of fresh food of all kinds. After they secure everything, the Team squeezes into the van.

Hannah greets the two drivers and cautions the truck driver for his trip back to Hodeida. "Don't stop for any disabled vehicles on your way back. There are several traps being laid for you as we speak."

The driver asks, "How do you know that?"

Hannah smiles, "A little birdy told me."

Bill laughs and shakes hands with the Truck driver, "Be safe. And don't stop for anything. I'm going to call in and have a helicopter sent out to escort you. What you are carrying is worth more than gold. Good luck my friend."

The Truck driver gets in and pulls away, waving. He drives out of the city and turns South toward Sana'a and Hodeida.

Hannah is standing and surveying the bombed-out ruins near the airstrip. She marvels that the buildings are from the fifteen hundreds. There is an eerie expression on her face.

Bill walks over to her, "What do you see?"

"Besides the sad destruction of the ancient buildings, I have an eerie feeling that someone is watching me. I'm trying to get a read on them from the 'I Am', but there is a lot of mixed emotions."

Bill responds, "You are aware that Sa'dah is one of the most heavily bombed cities by the Shiite rebels. I'm sure they have a strong defense militia."

Hannah nods, "I see them, and they are armed. They keep popping up in a dozen places. But what I feel is quite different."

Bill is about to say something, when the 'Great I Am' interrupts him. "It is a little girl. I got her now.

I thought it was her left-brain chatter, but it is not. She is running back to her mommy. Listen to this."

The rest of the Team jumps out of the van, to check it out. "She runs into their poor damaged house. She finds her mommy in what is left of their kitchen. She is tugging on her apron, to get her attention, saying, 'Mommy, Mommy, I have seen them!' Her mommy is looking down at her, with her face all lit up, 'What have you seen, Sweetie?'

"The little girl, Mia, sings out, 'I saw them, Mommy. The Angels are here! The Angels are here! I saw them! They are here to save us!' The mother takes off her apron and takes Mia by the hand. 'OK darling. Show me.' They are on their way to the entrance to the airstrip. I guess you better get going if you want to meet them."

Hannah responds, as the Team starts to squeeze back in the van, "I'm no Angle."

Bill responds, "Yes you are, my Dear."

Hannah smiles and gives him a kiss.

Hannah and Bill take the last two seats in the van, and they pull away toward the road at the south end of the runway. The Driver playfully weaves the van around the bomb-holes. When they reach the entrance to the road, 12 armed men meet them, with their weapons hanging down under their arms.

The Driver is petrified. The Team quickly climbs out of the Van.

Hannah says to Bill, "What do I do? Shall I hold up my hands?"

"No. Greet them with open arms. Here comes Mia. Start with her."

Hannah throws her arms around Mia as she rushes up, "Mia, it so nice to meet you."

They hug for a moment. Then Mia turns to her mommy, "You see I told you they were angels. She knows my name!"

The Sa'dah men offer open handshakes to

everyone. They are friendly and start to mingle, with one common gesture, clasping the Team member's shoulders between their open palms, and a purr.

Mia's mother greats Hannah, "We were told that you were coming. You are the Justice Team."

Hannah is surprised, "Yes we are. How do you know that?"

"We have heard of you. Everyone here has been hoping that you would come. We are tired of the fighting, illness and death. To us you are angels."

Hannah responds warmly, "We are no more angels than you are, but we are connected to the 'Great I Am' within us. If you are interested, I can send a couple of people back here to teach you how to connect."

"Could you? I know a hundred people who would sign up in an instant." Her response was genuine, and she added, "Can Mia and other children sign up? It would mean a lot to them."

"That would be wonderful. In fact, Mia is almost connected already." Mia overhears this.

Mia jumps up a down, singing.

Hannah asks, "How many people have survived here in Sa'dah?

"Only about 75000."

"Can I leave you a case of cholera vaccine for the children? It is not much, but it will help some."

"Can you? That would be a blessing."

Bill was already on his way to pull out a case of vaccine.

Hannah explains, "We are on our way to Aleetmh, where we will be setting up base-camp. If you need anything you can reach us through the Fuel Station. It has been a pleasure to meet you."

There are farewell hugs all around, with Mia insisting on hugging everybody. The Team climbs back in the van. The driver pulls out on the highway and turns Northwest toward Albuqa, over the mountains. The Team is very silent and listening to the 'I Am's instructions preparing them for their desert visit. 'I Am' tips Bill off to a pistol in the driver's door cubbyhole. The 'I Am' does not read any hostility in the driver, but he should head back to Hodeida as soon as they unload. He may be able to intercept the Truck driver as he goes through Sana'a and give him assistance. The Truck driver may need his help.

"Hannah," Abbud tries to get her attention, and then asks, "I don't know if anybody else has thought about this. But what are we going to do about a latrine? We can't dig one the old-fashion way, because of the sanitation issues."

Hannah responds with a smile, "I never thought you would be the one to ask that question. But it's covered. Noya has an invention for us to try out. We applied for the patent yesterday. Noya, would you explain how your porta potty works. If it works, it will revolutionize the camping industry forever."

Noya is a bit shy and starts off slowly, "the small black collapsible tank we loaded holds the porta potty, a deflated truck tire innertube, a set of compression valves and hoses. After we unpack the tank, we will assemble and install it.

The porta potty is in two halves. The top half, with the seat and lid, has a two-liter water container and a compression apparatus. When you sit on the toilet, your weight will cause the compression apparatus to put the water under pressure, so when you flush, a jet spray will clean the bowl instantly.

The bottom half, with the holding tank, has a pulverizing processor, which grinds up the waste into small bits. We will also use it as our garbage disposal. Every day, we will empty the holding tank into the waste tank, using the filling valve.

The waste tank, which will be one-third full of water, will fill naturally with methane gas. When the compression gauge reads between 3-5 psi, we will fill the innertube with the methane gas and use it to cook all our food.

When we pack up, to move on, the contents of the waste tank can be used as a fertilizer. Thus, completing the natural cycle of life.

There is only one disadvantage for all the men. You will have to learn to urinate sitting down.

There is complete silence in the van.

After a moment Abbud breaks the silence, "I'm speechless. That is the most incredible thing I have ever heard. The urinating sitting down is nothing. Doing it in a bottle is what I don't like. Have you tried it out?"

"Yes, I have. It works."

Abbud's eyes are popping, "It Works!"

Hannah reminds everyone, "This is the most important contribution to end the crises here. Vaccines will help. Fresh vegetables will help. But they won't clean up the polluted rivers and water supply. Every household, wandering tribe, and place of business can have one, along with free heat and fuel to cook by. They won't need to wait years for large sewage plants. They can have this now and make the whole thing out of recyclable materials."

The whole van becomes a buzz with possibilities.

Hannah asks the Driver, "How long do you think this drive will take."

The Driver checks his notes, "It's about 220 km, and it will probably take 2 hours 50 minutes. The mountain part will take the longest. I have programed the GPS."

Jacob laughs, "My internal GPS says the same."

Talia pokes him in the arm, "Cool it!"

A chuckle roles through the van.

CHAPTER 39

Endless Time

Hoss is still in the same location, only lying on his back naked, on the cold floor. The rolled-up t-shirt is no longer under his head. His breathing is so light and slow that it is hard to detect if he is breathing at all. Not even his eyes move under his eyelids.

John is now wearing his t-shirt again. He is sitting on the floor, leaning up against the wall sound asleep. His head hangs heavily on his chest. His body is twitching and jerking; his voice is mumbling and yipping, like a dreaming dog. His head jerks erratically from side to side and up and down.

Suddenly, his eyes pop open, and he scream, "No, no, no don't do that! Get off him! Leave him alone!" He is now standing and flailing his arms about, like he is fighting his way through a pile of debris. "Stop, stop, STOP it!"

In an instant, he is consciously awake. He stands facing a wall, unaware of where he is. A shiver runs through his body, and he shakes it off as he turns around. Slowly, his face shows his realization of where he is. He studies Hoss for a few moments. John's breathing is irregular.

His Left-brain Chatter starts in on him, "Look at him. Is that the way you want to end up?"

"No. But he's a good man."

"Shure he is," his Left-brain Chatter says sarcastically. "And look what it got him. You deserve better."

John shouts, "He's a super-hero! He is everything I want to be!"

His Left-brain Chatter laughs, "He is an old fart, naked and soon dead to the world. What does he got that you ain't?"

John sits next to the wall, pulling his knees up to his chest and whimpers, "He's a good man. He's a good man." He repeats this over and over again, until he falls off to sleep. Even then, his mouth keeps forming the words on his lips, he's a good man, he's a good man. John heaves a deep sigh and drifts into a deep sleep.

> Time passes.
> Time?
> What is time in a place like this?
> What is a day?
> When did it start?
> When does it end?
> A day starts when you wake up in the morning.
> A day ends when you fall asleep at night.
> But here there is no morning.
> Here there is no night.
> You sleep.
> You wake up.
> An hour can feel like a day.
> A day can feel like a week.
> A week can feel like a year.
> Time passes.?!

John opens his eyes, looks around without moving.

The Left-brain Clutter starts to kick in again, "Steel door closed and locked, check. No light, check. Waste hole full, check. Floor dirty, check. Ask the food person for a broom, check. Ask for a T-bone steak and three ears of sweet corn, with butter, check."

John reacts, "Why don't you shut up?"

"I just want to give you something to hope for," the Left-brain Clutter insists. "Just think about it. If she gives you a broom, you can ask her for a dustpan. If she gives you a steak, you can ask her for mashed potatoes. If she gives you all that, you can ask her for a TV. If she brings a TV, you can ask for a date."

John shouts, "Shut the F up. She's not my type. She's a Nun."

"What do you care if she's your type. The more friends you have on Facebook the more popular you are. The more popular you are, the better chance you have to find the right mate. If you find the right mate, the better chance you have to clean up..."

"To clean up the mess you always make of my life," John finishes the Left-brain Clutter's sentence. "S H U T up! Go clean your swimming pool!"

"That would be a waste of time. It would only get dirty again."

"S H U T up! S H U T up! S H U T up!" John pauses. There is complete silence. He mumbles to himself, "That's a blessing."

In silence, John walks around the cell. Each time he passes Hoss, he checks on him.

John sits down and starts to meditate.

As soon as he starts, the Left-brain Chaos pops into his head. "You know that meditation is a total waste of time. It creates a total distraction to your left-brain irrational mind. Your left-brain irrational mind is all powerful. If you learn to use 100% of your left-brain irrational mind, you will control the universe. You will be all powerful. Your left-brain irrational mind has made you the higher species."

John cuts it off, "Shure Dodo head, name one human who has done that since the beginning of Time, with his or her left-brain inductive Logic."

"You may be the first!"

"Bull! The only positive contribution humans have made is in Science trough deductive Logic. Science can build off its mistakes with new data. Your left-brain irrational thoughts compound errors based on one false premise after another."

Brain Chaos pushes the issue, "Name one!"

"I'll name one. There is not one positive conclusion made by your left-brain irrational thoughts that is not contaminated by assumption, theory and misperception. It is called religion or theology. You know nothin about Spirituality."

Left-brain Chaos starts, "But... But..." There is a long pause. "But..." Then there is silence.

"Your silence says it all. In fact, it reminds me of a single piston engine, put, put, put."

Left-brain Deception kicks in, "Look, John, do you want to get out of here? Do you want to escape whatever is waiting for him?"

"Of course, I want to get out of here, with him."

"John, you know that is not possible, but I have a way to get you out of here, if you just listen to me. I know these people. They will listen to me. They always do."

John asks, "How will you do that?"

Left-brain Deception says confidently, "I'll tell them you are not part of his conspiracy."

"But I'm part of his mission now!"

"They don't know that."

"You mean, I just have to lie about my connection with Hoss."

"It's not a lie. You tell them you are not part of him. Which you are not. You are part of me. You are steadfast in the faith. You are steadfast in whatever they want. Just ask and it will be done."

Suddenly, John remembers what Hayah said about shutting down the Left-brain Chatter and not getting angry. He blows it a kiss and it disappears.

John starts to meditate again. His breathing becomes slow and rhythmic. Slowly, he goes deeper and deeper. Finally, he reaches the point of stillness.

The feeling of time ends. Time is meaningless. He is in the present moment. The present moment fills him. He is full of peace. He is bathing in the Love-light. Then he hears a voice.

The 'Great I Am' is filled with concern, "Wow! I almost lost you there. Welcome back!"

John embraces himself, "Thank you, thank you. Your Love-light is filling me again. I want to hold onto it for all eternity. It is so easy to slide into my dark side. It is terrifying." He then feels the 'Great I Am' embracing him.

"I Am always here. You are sensing a loss of time awareness. That is quite normal under your circumstances. However, humans have turned time into something it is not, allowing the left-brain irrational mind to dwell on the past and worry about the future. All that really matters is the present moment and what you are doing now. Right now, you are connected to me. That connection to me in the present moment produces the 'eternal present'. All that you were in the past is in your 'eternal present'. All that you will be in the future is in your 'eternal present'. So, the 'eternal present' contains all that is past, all that is, and all that is yet to come. Time becomes irrelevant. Focus on the 'eternal present'.

"Now, I need you to rouse Hoss. His body is fighting off the drugs. There is bread and water at the door. Eat and drink for the two of you."

Without hesitation, John replies, "Yes. Whatever you want, I will do it."

John goes to the door and collects the bread and water from the hatch next to the floor. He goes over and sits on the floor next to Hoss. He picks up Hoss' head and shoulders and cradles them in his lap. As he feeds Hoss, he notices that his body is responding more quickly than before. The 'I Am' is pleased with that development.

CHAPTER 40
Base Camp

The Justice Team arrives at the place where they would like to set up their base camp. Hannah has the driver continue down N556 to the Fuel Station, which is only a 100 meters further South. She wants to see if she needs to get permission to set up the base camp. She instructs Bill to walk to a house, which is 196 meters across from the Fuel Station, and ask if they have any problems with them setting up the base camp on the other side of the stone hill. The intended base camp is to be 485 meters West of the highway, on the North side of the stone hill.

The Justice Team gets out to stretch their legs, and the diver takes advantage of the opportunity to fill up the gas tank of the van. He also makes a quick check of the oil, water and air in the tires.

The owner of the Fuel Station warmly greets Hannah. She too is already aware of the Justice Team and their mission. She is flattered that Hannah is so considerate to ask for permission to set up camp. She says, "Most people would pull in and set up camp, without a word. You know, you don't need to be that far off the road."

Hannah responds, "Thank you, but our spot will put us closer to the water supply."

"What water supply?" the woman asks. "There is no water anywhere near there, never has been, never will be. All of the water holes and rivers around her are badly contaminated."

Hanna smiles, "Today there will be a water hole. If you or any one in Aleetmh need pure water, we will gladly share our water."

The woman's mouth falls open and her eyes are as big as saucers. She timidly says, "You are angels!"

"Not angels. We are just people trying to do the

right thing and living in the Love-light. We will gladly share that with you as well. We will also help anyone interested in connecting with the 'Great I Am'. Yes, that's the same 'I Am' of Abraham."

"How did you know I was going to ask that?"

"The 'I Am' is in you too. Also, spread the word, if you or any of the Aleetmh families need the cholera vaccine we have enough for everybody. I must go now so we can set up camp."

"You are most welcome. I'll spread the word. And I'll come out to visit." The woman sees her out.

When Hannah gets back to the van, Bill is already there. His report fallows that of Hannah. Everyone climes back in the van, and they head back up the highway about 100 meters.

They turn left on a track and head to the rock hill. Hannah says to the driver, "Do you see that tall tree on the edge of the hill? Head for it."

"Got it. Is that where we are going?"

"Yes, it is. Park about twenty meters from the tree. As soon as we unload the van, you can head down to Sana'a. Hopefully, you will be able to connect with the Truck driver."

The Team is intensely watching as they get closer and closer to the tree. When they reach the tree, they all hear the 'I Am', "This is it."

Hannah says, "Stop." And the driver stops. Everyone quickly gets out of the van. With unspoken organized precision, the van is quickly unloaded and stacked neatly in separate piles on the dry sand.

Bill thanks the driver and sends him on his way.

A moment later the Team stands looking at Hannah. She stands tall, holding a 3-pound sledgehammer, with a noticeably short handle.

She says, "You all should be part of this. The 'Great I Am' is telling us we shall have water. So, listen as I follow 'I Am's directions."

'I Am' says to Hannah, so everyone can hear,

"Turn and walk to the large tree. Bill take the shovel." Everyone walks to the tree. "Now, Hannah, look on the rock in front of the tree. You will see a white crystal bit imbedded in the stone, about 70 cm below the tree. Put your finger on it, so all can see."

Hannah does so.

'I Am' continues, "Now, Bill and everyone, dig a trench in the sand about 1-meter round and 70 cm deep. Throw the sand to the left and in front of the trench so the water can run off to the right."

Bill digs three shovels full of sand and hands the shovel to Jacob. Jacob digs three shovels full and passes the shovel to Talia. She digs three shovels full. And then the shovel is passed to Abbud, Noya and Ori and each digs three shovels full. When done, the hole is 1-meter around and 70 cm deep. They each dig another three shovels full to create a shallow runoff ditch to the right. Ori packs down the sand on the two sides, with the back of the shovel. They form a slight mound to control the water flow. Then he steps back with the others.

The 'I Am' says, "Hannah, with one hard blow of the mallet hit the white crystal bit. Use a full swing over your head and bring the mallet down. Let its weight do the work and focus on the spot."

Hannah stands to the side of the white crystal bit. She focuses intently on the spot and swings the mallet high above her head. Everyone is breathless as the mallet seems to come down in slow motion. When it hits the white crystal bit, a loud crack can be heard. The sound of the crack seems to go deeper and deeper into the earth. Hannah steps back.

All is still. They wait. They wait some more.

Hanna turns and looks at Bill. Bill returns the glance and is about to say something.

The 'Great I Am' says to them all, "Stop the Left-brain Chatter. Make yourselves one with the earth. Feel what is happening."

They all do as directed. Soon, they all feel a vibration from deep within the earth. It moves up through their legs and gets stronger and stronger. The vibration seems to become longer and longer, rolling like a wave. As it gets higher in the earth, it gets higher in their bodies. Soon they feel a low-pressure building. They can feel the water seeping up the crack in the rock deep within the earth. When it reaches the surface, it spouts in a steady stream about 7 cm high.

A cheer goes up among the Team, and they all shout, "Thank you!" filled with joy as they watch the trench fill up with water. Then, they all become silent as they bathe in the joy of the 'Great I Am' together. Slowly the trench fills and runs off. They each scoop up a handful of water and drink it. Now their bodies are rejoicing.

Hannah gets the message that the daylight hours will soon close. She calls on the team to pitch the tents and set up camp. There are three large tents. One for the women. One for the men. And, a mess-tent, with a cooking table and an eating table with seven chairs. On the cooking table is a two-burner gas stove, a cutting board, two dish tubs and a cooler. There is also a small tank of methane gas to cook with until the innertube has gas enough. There are also two small tents you can stand up in. One is for the latrine, in which Noya is putting up her porta-potty. The tank is nearby, with the innertube. The other is a small teepee tent for showering. The canvas only covers the middle five feet of the teepee. In the top is hung a five-liter bucket with a valve and showerhead. They keep the bucket full all the time, so the water warms up in the sun. Consequently, the last person to shower is always getting a cold shower or showering later in the day.

Bill is busy in the mess-tent, fixing their first

meal. It is a bit decadent for the camping environment, but most of it was pre-prepared the day before they left. It starts off with a baked-apple with chopped nuts. Next there is French onion soup, with a tossed green salad and bread. The finale is a rich carrot-cake, with a sweet cream-cheese topping. The meal is a remarkable success, and Bill receives high praises from everyone including Hanna.

Unfortunately, they all knew that from that day on it would be a limited camping diet for everyone. They intended to share their fresh vegetables with others from the area, who were suffering from malnutrition, especially the children.

After dinner, some took their chairs out to watch the sunset, others sat in the sand. As with all sunsets, it was quite spectacular. While the last shooting rays filled the sky, the owners of the Fuel Station, Asiya and Fahad, and their neighbors, Zaina and Saeed, came walking into camp. For a few moments they shared the setting sun.

In the afterglow of the sunset and stillness of the air, Asiya hears the running water. She leaps to her feet calling out, "I hear running water! I thought you were kidding!" Her husband Fahad and the others are on their feet in a flash.

Zaina says to Saeed, "This can't be! It's a miracle!"

Hannah calmly asks, "Would you like a drink of water? I'll get you a clean cup. They walk over and everybody fills their cups with water and toasts the new miracle. Hannah says, "You are welcome to come anytime and take what you need. It is the 'Great I Am's gift to Aleetmh.

CHAPTER 41
Body Strength

Hoss has started to show small signs of body movement. The 'Great I Am' sees this as an incredibly positive sign and is encouraging John to help him recover. This has motivated John to try and get Hoss up and about.

John has Hoss' right arm around his neck and is holding Hoss' hand at his own shoulder. John has his left hand under Hoss' left armpit. This way he can support most of Hoss' weight and attempt to get him walking again. Right now, John is only dragging Hoss along, with the top of his toes sliding on the floor. John keeps telling him, "Take a step. Use your feet. Take a step."

John stops and using his hip, he swings Hoss back and forth, until Hoss' feet are flat on the floor. He balances Hoss and tries to get him to use his own strength to stand up. He says, "Come on now, you already did this once. Find your balance." He relaxes his grip a little bit at a time. Slowly, Hoss' legs become rigged and start to support his body. There is no sign on Hoss' face that he is even conscious, but his body is trying to do as directed. Slowly the balancing rigidity moves up his body. His hips are moving up and down trying to find the position of strength. Then the focus moves into his lower spine. At first his back is very wabbly, but John's support helps him build the stability one vertebra at a time. Soon, Hoss' focus reaches his shoulders and neck. This seems easier at first, but his head is wobbly on his neck and takes a lot of extra effort to balance. But the blank expression on his face never changes or registers the difficulty. Once again, he is standing erect. John's support is now minimal.

John encourages him, "That's it. Feel your strength. Don't hold your breath. Breath into it."

Hoss stands stronger and taller.

John says, "OK let's try again. Take a step." John takes a small step, with his right foot, while fully supporting Hoss' weight. He notices a very slight movement. "That's right. Take the step. You can do it."

Very, very slowly Hoss' right foot moves forward, until it is equal with John's step. Now, the process of shifting his weight onto that foot begins. This too is terribly slow.

"You're doing it. You're doing it." There is a slight wobble, which John stabilizes. "That's ok. I got you." As soon as Hoss is secure, he encourages him, "That's good. Keep going."

Hoss soon has his weight on his right foot.

"Ok, now bring up your left foot." John slides his own foot at the same pace that Hoss moves his.

Suddenly, Hoss moves his left foot quickly up to his right foot. This causes him to lose his balance, and he cannot recover.

The surprise overtakes John and he struggles to stabilize him. He is unable to regain control and they start to fall. John twists himself in the direction of the fall and pulls Hoss to fall on top of him. This protects Hoss from injury, but they go down with a thump. It takes John a minute to recover, and they lie there in a heap.

The 'Great I Am' says to John, "He is exhausted. We need to give him a chance to rest. He has been at this for hours, and the drugs are taking their toll on him as well."

"I agree," John says as he is crawling out from under Hoss, who is not moving. "I think I'm still in one peace. I'll check him to make sure there are no injuries." He quickly looks him over, in front and back. "There are no cuts or scrapes, but that doesn't mean that He isn't going to end up with a bruise or two."

"If he has, he will not feel them today."

"Are you able to reach him yet," John asks? "Or should I say, is he able to reach you?"

"The latter is always the case. I can always read and know everything that is going on in your body and mind. In this case Hoss' mind is badly numbed. His body is struggling to free itself from the drugs. Right now, his body is listening to you more than to me." The 'I Am' studies the heap of flesh that is Hoss. "Would you be so kind to arrange his body in a sitting position against the wall? That would make him more comfortable, and he can practice holding his head up."

John does as suggested. When done, he starts to do some exercises. When he finishes these, he goes right into his meditation.

Hoss is struggling against the drugs. The little body awareness he has is very shaky. He is not able to control many of his movements. He has no feelings inside his body or on the skin of his body. All nerve sensations are numbed. In addition to this, his mind is completely numb. He has no emotions. He has no thoughts. He has no mental awareness. Right now, he is a blank slate.

John opens his eyes and studies Hoss. There are two repeating movements accruing. His feet are moving from side to side. His head keeps falling to his chest. Then Hoss labors to lift it again and press it against the wall. The 'I Am' makes it clear that these actions are totally within the body instead of being mentally directed. The body wants to move and function again.

The 'Great I Am' says, "The drug they used may end up working to our advantage. It has a stronger effect on the brain than on the body. What they do not realize is that humans have a problem shutting down the brain in order to focus on the body. Now Hoss can focus all his attention on recovering the body functions, without having to fight the Left-brain Chatter."

John asks, "Is he ready and rested enough to give the walking another go? I want to see him make a breakthrough."

"Try it. We can always make other pauses to let him rest."

John stands up and walks over to Hoss. Picking him up is like lifting a giant bag of Jell-O. He puts his hands under his armpits and slides him up the wall. Then holding Hoss' body against the wall with his own body, he manages to get Hoss' right arm around his neck again. Supporting Hoss' weight across his shoulders, he is able to slide his left arm behind Hoss' back and get his hand under Hoss' left arm pit. With his left hip against Hoss' right hip, he can now support all Hoss' weight.

He pulls Hoss out into the cell and helps Hoss to get his feet under him. Now the walking lesson starts again. This time, there are two big differences. John no longer needs to tell Hoss what to do. His body simply does it and is doing the movements much quicker (meaning slowly, instead of very, very slowly). Hoss is standing erect and supporting increasingly more of his weight. It is a shuffle walk, with a sliding step, instead of a step, involving a leg lift and slight bend at the knee.

They cover half the cell before Hoss' step gives out and John ends up dragging Him on his toe tops again. This time, John bounces Hoss on his hip, with one swing, and gets Hoss back on his feet again. Instantly, Hoss starts the shuffle walk again, and they move on.

The 'Great I Am' explains, "This is all in his body memory and not his mind. That is a good thing. His body wants to do more, so keep going until the body

remembers how to do a slow, knee lifting, walk.
John, you also need to slowly let Hoss bare more of
his own weight. However, it will take a lot longer
before Hoss will regain his sense of balance.
Therefore, keep a good hold on him.

"John, you are doing a wonderful job. I sense
you are enjoying this."

"I sure am! I feel like a physical therapist healing
a patient. Every meter is a new landmark. I believe I
may have found my calling in life."

"I would say you have. You are a born healer.
When this is all over, we will have to get you the
training. Plus, I can add a whole new dimension to
your healing touch."

Hoss' strength, balance and movement steadily
improve. Then Hoss pauses. John senses it and
stops with him. John can feel an energy moving up
Hoss' back. Hoss starts to stand straighter and
stronger. His body is finding its balance. John can
feel it and encourages him, "Go ahead. Lift our knee.
Take a step."

The shift of Hoss' weight from one foot to
another takes some effort. Then with John's support
and stability, Hoss' body takes a knee lifting step.
Slowly, he takes another and then another. They are
about to reach a normal pace. Every step is stronger
and stronger. Hoss is walking.

Slowly, John eases off his support. Hoss' next
three steps are perfect. Then Hoss loses his balance.
He stumbles, and they go down as before.

John laughs, this time, as he craws out from
under Hoss and checks him for wounds. John says,
"You're all in one peace," and pats Hoss on the
shoulder. He slowly untangles his body and sits him
next to the wall.

John turns away and checks his body, saying to
himself, "Well, your all-in-one piece too." Then to
the 'I Am' he says, "Should we give his body another

break? Or maybe stop for the day?"

The 'I Am' laughs, "I Am not going to answer that. You should turn around and see for yourself."

John turns and sees Hoss sliding up the wall all by himself. When he is up, he stands erect, with his right arm held out straight from his side.

"It looks like he is all ready for you and another round." The 'I Am' and John both laugh.

CHAPTER 42
A Growing Presence

The arrival of the many connected teams has already begun. There is a large community of tents, and the parking area is filling up. Hannah is assigning teams to assist with the cholera epidemic and malnutrition in different areas needing help. (The UN and the Red Cross are focusing on Hodeida.) Hannah's teams are reaching out to the many northern tribes, the smaller cities, and the few large cities, like Sana'a and Sa'dah.

In many of these areas, there is a growing interest in meditation classes to connect to the 'Great I Am' within. Hannah assigns each member of the Justice Team to one of these groups to help the people connect.

The only exception is Noya. Her sole responsibility is to collect as much of the recyclable materials to make as many porta-potties as possible. In the words of the 'Great I Am', "This is equal in importance to connecting with Me. It not only creates a positive and permanently lasting solution to the sanitation problem; I have had more people connect with Me while sitting on 'the thrown' than at any other time." Noya also ropes off a potentially fertile plot of ground 20 x 30 meters. Here she will spread the fertilizer from the decomposed waste in the methane gas tanks.

It is no surprise that, those connecting to the 'I Am' all want to come to the Aleetmh camp site to experience the community. Of course, the fresh water is also an attraction. Bill tries to keep track of the size of the group but loses track after it passes ten-thousand people.

This information soon becomes public

knowledge which reaches the Shiite and Islamic clerics. Their debate to attach the many small groups or wait until they gather into one large group seems to go on endlessly, until they hear from Russia's leader Poopin. He will deploy 12 jets and 30 tanks to assist in the assault if they wait until they are all gathered in one place. He wants to end this interference with one quick blow. The Shiite and the Clerics quickly decided they will attach at Aleetmh.

Those connected with the 'Great I Am' know this information as it happens. They immediately follow the 'I Am's guidance to get prepared. They have only two problems, those with weapons and those that have not connected yet.

Bill goes to work immediately, with the help of the 'I Am', to identify these people. Those with weapons have three choices. They can leave. They can go home, store their weapons and come back. Or they can turn over their weapons, and Bill will bury all of them until after the attach. Those not connected with the 'I Am' will need a bunker for protection and a chain of connected people around them. They can build the bunker with sandbags.

There is an irony in all this; there is absolutely no panic. Those connected to the 'Great I Am' are exercising their Free Will to do what 'I Am' asks them to do. Those not connected are following the internal order of the group.

The primary focus of the gathering remains steadfast, to help the people hit with the cholera epidemic and malnutrition. The connected families are distributing the vaccine, mostly to the children. They are cooking the fresh vegetables and serving them to the hungry people.

Most importantly, there is a long, but steady, line of people taking water from the new spring. The people of Aleetmh are truly rejoicing at this incredible wonder. They open their hearts and tell the story of how Hannah struck the rock with the short-handled mallet. And the water miraculously sprang forth from the earth. Needless to say, the word of mouth spread throughout Yemen.

After the arrival of Hydia, Mahenie, Mahum and al-Nisista from Syria, Iran, and Iraq, everyone wants to hear what the difference is between the Islamic religion and the spiritual connection with the 'Great I Am' within. As they meet in large groups, the subject always begins with their faith in the doctrine and dogma of the religious institutions. In that context, Mahenie raises the questions concerning everyone's personal experience of faith. Their feeling is in their heart, not their mind. Mahum shares his struggle with his rational perception. These create a very heated debate. It is Hydia, who brings everyone to a quite unique perspective by asking two questions. "Are you the institution? Or is the institution you?" This brought everyone to a deep silence. The Love-light begins to fill this pause.

Out of the silence, al-Nisista begins to speak quietly, with the Love-light filling his voice, "The Islamic family is one people. The Hebrew family is one people. The Christian family is one people. All Believers are a family and one people. In the 'Great I Am' we are one family of all people. For we are all in the 'I Am' together and one in the Love-light. For the same 'I Am' and Love-light is in us all. Let us be ONE!"

In silence the Love-light fills everyone. Those connected are all a glow. Those not connected want to be part of the Love-light. Those not connected organize themselves into groups of 30, with three instructors in each meditation group.

Into this positive environment comes the whole of one of Yemen's Northern Tribes, including their livestock. They heard the word in disbelief. Hannah knows they are coming and stands on the outskirts of the camp to greet them.

Those assisting her give each of the children the vaccine packet to drink. Hannah leads them to the water. She shows them one of the new latrines and explains how it works. She points out where they can camp and put their livestock. There is a strong positive communication which passes, like a wave, through the Tribe.

Out of a tight knot of the Tribal members emerges their Chief. He stands at a slight angle in front of Hannah, studying her face and smiles.

He finally says in a very business tone and manner, like he is about to negotiate a deal. "How much is this going to cost us?"

Hannah's smile broadens, "Nothing in money."

This puts him off balance, "What then?" He looks at the ground and waits for the bomb to drop. Then he looks into Hannah's sparkling eyes.

She says, "Only your good behavior and good wishes." Her smile communicates her sincerity.

"That's a deal," he smiles broadly. "Is there anything we can do to help?"

"Not right now. Get your Tribe settled in and make yourself at home. I'll let you know if there is anything to do latter."

The 'Great I Am' is in Hannah's ear, "Well played. I want you to know, this whole Tribe is remarkably close to connecting with me. The children are the closest. They are all meditators and spiritual seekers. I will let you know when they are ready."

Hannah asks, "Where is Bill?"

"Working on the bunker. He is always asking about you as well."

She smiles and heads in that direction.

On her way, Talia and Jacob stop her. Talia says, "We want to let you know that the camp is now free of cholera. In a couple more days we'll have the malnutrition licked as well."

"That's fantastic. We're right on schedule then. Can you see that the new Tribe gets whatever they need? Jacob, you and Talia will be the ones to help them connect. Check out the children first."

Jacob says, "Wow! You know what this means?"

"No. What?"

"You get one Tribe to connect; you will have all the Northern Tribes connected within a year."

"That'll mean a lot for Yemen," says Talia.

Hannah adds, "Why don't you get Abbud to help you. I sense that he would like an excuse to get off the latrine detail. The rest of us can take turns helping Noya. I have never seen anyone so filled with joy over building latrines. She says we now have enough methane gas to power some of the cars. She is trying to get the valves."

"Wow! Everyone in the camp is anxious to see that. I hope it works."

Hannah says confidently, "It will work! The need for oil will be history."

Poopin, in Russia, is ecstatic to hear that his enemy is so stupid and naive to put all their eggs in one basket and be in one place. He says to the news reporter on the TV, "I will take magnificent pleasure in wiping you off the face of the earth. The Middle East will be mine." He searches through some papers on the table next to him. He finds a small note pad and thumbs through the pages. When he finds his note, he reads it allowed, "I do not order the attack. I'm just telling the officers to do what they think best."

CHAPTER 43
Into the Fire

Hoss is struggling to connect to the 'Great I Am' within him. The drugs are still numbing his body senses. His sight is blurred. His hearing is faint, and everything sounds like it is a mile away. His nose smells only the foulest things. His fingers and skin have hardly any feeling at all. The taste in his mouth is very dry and undefinable. His mind is a blank screen in a black room. Only his frustration is growing.

Slowly his inner body, muscles and natural instinct, have started to come back. However, he has no conscious awareness of them and what they are doing. They are functioning on their own.

Right now, he is trying to focus on his breathing, with John's help. He is lying on his back. His body is breathing all by itself. John is teaching the teacher. He moves Hoss' hands onto his lower abdomen. "Do you feel them going up and down?"

The expression on Hoss' face and in his eyes reveals a futile struggle. His body twitches and jerks uncontrollable.

John describes it to him, "Your hands are going up. Now they are going down. You're breathing in. You're breathing out."

The 'Great I Am' says to John, "Your description is only frustrating him. It is like his body knows what it should be feeling but cannot feel it. I want to help, but he is not aware of me at all."

John asks, "What should I do?"

"I do not know." The 'I Am's words leave John dumbfounded. After a moment, 'I Am' continues, "Try getting him up and walking again. He was doing well with that, and the walking may lessen his frustration. Then we can try the breathing again when he is relaxed."

John starts to help Hoss up. Hoss helps and then starts walking by himself. Soon he is well balanced and moving quite quickly. He makes several circles of the cell by himself. Suddenly, he stops and stands still. After a few minutes, he lays down again and puts his hands on his abdomen all by himself.

John watches in silence. He can see that Hoss' struggle is more controlled. After some time, he sees Hoss' lips start to synchronize with his breathing. He is breathing in with his lips open and out with his lips closed. He shouts, "You're doing it."

Hoss is finally shaping the unutterable syllable ॐ with his lips, breathing in and breathing out. Fortunately, he does not need to shut down any brain chatter, because that part of his brain is not working. Very slowly his body finds the dark space within him. Then his face lights up with a brilliant light, as the Love-light fills his inner body. His awareness tunes in to the presence of the 'Great I Am' within him. There is one-hundred percent communication, which is without words.

This is the way the 'I Am' prefers to speak to us. There is no need of any brain function to interpret words and calculate meaning.

Hoss' captors have made a major mistake, with their mind-numbing drugs. Unlike their Theological minds, or left-brain irrational thinking, which are constantly forming false assumptions, Hoss is connecting directly with the 'Great I Am' who is his essence of being.

The 'I Am' communicates to John what is happening. "We are connected again, and he knows he is protected. You are also protected."

"Thank you," John responds. "But what about the Warning? Will Hoss be able to Warn them of what will happen?"

"Their use of the drugs on him already indicates that they are Warned. They think the drugs will cancel out his powers. They do not want to hear the Warning. Then again, they have never wanted to hear one word from Me. They can pray for hours with many requests, directions and orders, without listening for two seconds to my response. They have laid the trap and are in for a shocking surprise."

John is frightened. He does not know what this means. Strangely, Hoss reaches out and takes his hand. Instantly, his fear disappears, as they sit down on the floor.

There is a rattling of keys, as someone prepares to thrust a key into the steel door and throughs the bolt. The door squeaks open, and four Vatican Guards march into the cell. They tie a blindfold around Hoss' head and bind his hands behind his back. Two men pick him up and carry him to the door. The other two men bind John's hands behind his back and carry him out.

Some of Hoss' senses start to return, but he allows his body to hang limp as they carry him. John does not struggle against them either, but asks, "Where are you taking us?" There is no answer. The guards carry them to the end of the dimly lit long corridor. Then they start up a very narrow spiral stone stairwell. They pass 6 landings, but keep going up, without stopping. Finally, they reach a normally lit hallway and an elevator.

On the elevator, the guards lay their bodies on the floor, while they go up several more levels. Soon the door slides open. The guards pick them up and carry them to the end of the corridor. When they reach a set of double steel doors, the first guard backs into the panic-bar and pushes the door open. The second guard holds it open with his foot until the third guard has it.

They are now outside. They turn to the left and
go down a walkway to the end of the building. Soon
they are clear of the buildings and are crossing a
large undeveloped area.

John looks around in all directions trying to
place where they are. His eyes struggle to focus, but
the light is blinding. He can only crack them a little
bit. All he can make out is a lot of construction or
scaffolding or something. None of it looks familiar at
first. Then, he sees a fountain that looks vaguely
familiar. He can't place it.

Hoss' skin senses starts to return. He starts to
describe what he is feeling to us, through the 'Great I
Am', without the guards hearing. He says, "I
welcome the sunlight as it dances on my skin. The
air is cool, but the sun warms my naked body.

"Now I feel my body being hoisted up until my
feet can rest on a small platform. They yank my body
around and press my back against a large steel pole.
Someone unties my hands and pulls them around the
pole and binds them securely. Then they bind my
ankles and tie them to the pole."

I can feel them hoisting John up and lashing him
to the same pole, so we are back-to-back. I can feel
his fear.

Neither of us say anything until the guards are
gone. It seems like it takes them forever because
there is a lot of noise below us. They are tossing
things about, with a lot of crashing and smashing.
When they finish, I can hear them walking away,
while talking to each other.

I can hear work still going on all around us, 365°.
They are building something, but I can't tell what.
John's fear is growing stronger. I can feel his body
shaking.

"John, can you see what is going on."

John turns and looks over his shoulder. Hayah
senses his action and turns to him. They are now

face to face. John cannot believe his eyes. They grow really big as he exclaims, "You're Hayah!"

"Who did you think I was?"

"The 'Great I Am' said you were Hoss. I was hoping you were Hayah, but when I saw you up close you were just an old far... Never mind, I literally thought our goose was cooked."

Hayah smiles, "Well, you are one of the very few people who knows that secret. If 'I Am' can trust you so can I. One day you can tell me all about it, but right now, I need you to tell me what is going on out there with all the construction. Where are we?"

"We are in the Vatican Piazza. They have taken down the Obelisk in the center. I can see it lying in the exit, Papa Pio XII, with the cross removed. They are building bleachers all around us, which are so high they are covering the two Bernini fountains. They're both turned off. We are tied to a post, which is exactly where the Obelisk used to be. You are facing the Basilica, Piazza San Pietro."

Hayah takes a deep breath, "And what did they build underneath us?"

"Nothing." John sighs, "It is a very large stack of firewood and kindling!"

"Oh, boy! So, we **are** the cooked goose." Well, my brain chatter is back, and I don't need to tell you what it is saying. There is no way that a fire can be boomeranged. A spark can fly 2 or 3 meters, but a fire cannot jump a defensible space. I blow the left-brain chatter a kiss and realize why John is scared. I say to John, "Is that why you are so scared? I could feel the panic racing up and down your back."

"Not now," John says confidently. "I know you have the power."

I love his confidence, but haven't the heart to tell him the hot spot we are in.

I hear the heavy breathing of the workers around us. They are being incredibly quiet, working in silence and making as little construction racket as possible. Every now and then a plank or something falls, and I hear a boss slapping or beating the worker, which makes more noise than the falling thing. The Church has absolutely no concern for the people. In fact, the planet is reaching the point of over population and starvation, but the Church will not approve of birth control.

Oopps, I'm getting off point.

I can feel the sun wain as it begins to set in front of me. The joy of the last moments of warmth on my skin makes it fell all aglow. As the Love-light within me sets my inner body aglow. I bask in this serenity for several moments. I let the feeling in my body drift back to John.

His body purrs with excitement.

Suddenly, I'm aware of a deep silence around us. The workers are gone. The birds and creatures have fled the unholy area. The chill of the darkness creeps over my skin. I stop this from going back to John.

At last, my body feels free from the drugs. I race into the safe space within me. The Love-light is within me and all around me. I shout, "I'm here! I'm listening!" Those four words are the only words Samuel ever prayed. The 'Great I Am' and I are together again, we are connected. This is the greatest of all feelings.

In spite of our current predicament, my joyful oneness with the 'I Am' is overwhelming. It takes several minutes before I can ask, "Can you protect us from the fire?"

The 'Great I Am' assures me, "Fear not, I Am with you. I Am here. We can do this. Fill yourself with the Love-light. Make sure there is no hatred in you. No matter what they say or do. We are one.

"I explained this to John, but you must constantly reassure him. Because this will be terrifying. The Fear could lead him off center.

"What is about to happen is a just end for what they have done. They bring it on themselves. Their own hatred starts the sparks. Their lies blow it into flame. Their deception of others kindles the fire. Their greed and avarice turn it into a blaze. Their desire for power, control and domination drives it into a raging inferno. The Hell they preach shall be the HELL they find. It is of their own making."

The unusual silence continues. Not even the wind is stirring. Then at a distance I hear the running footsteps of a young boy. He is approaching from St. Peters Basilica toward us. They grow closer and closer. When he reaches the pyre, he climbs up the pile of wood, until he reaches the platform. He pulls himself onto the platform in front of me. The next thing I know, the boy is untying my blindfold.

As my eyes try to focus, I look at his face. All I see is sadness and eyes filled with tears. He whispers in my ear, "I knows who you is. I connects trough you at Kinigi." He pulls back slightly.

I recognize him. "Bosco! What are you doing here?"

"When mom dies, I ends up in an orphanage. Afte year, dey tinkt I should bes a Priest and sends me here. I bes dese guys sex toy. When I hears whad dey're going ta do ta you, I decides it be better ta die wid you dan live dis nightmare. I will stands here by you. Please don't sends me back ta dem."

I comfort him as best I can. "Can you let go of all your old hatred and anger toward them?"

Bosco responds without hesitation, "I ready has. I lives in de Love-light."

I turn my head to John and say, "John, this is Bosco, the saver of the White-back Mountain Gorillas. Bosco, this is John, who saved me from the drugs they gave me."

John says to Bosco, "Are you sure you want to do this? It won't be a pretty sight. If you leave now, you can escape down Piazza Papa Pio XII."

Bosco says confidently, "I's safer ifs I stays rond yous all."

A drum begins to beat inside the Basilica.

I look about to see as much as I can, but I cannot move. My body is bound so I can't move. I turn my head and study the bleachers. They are 18 rows high, with a back railings. There is a set of stairs at each end of the bleachers. There is a gap bout 20 meters wide in front of me. I ask, "John do the bleachers go all the way around back there?"

"Yes, they do."

"No staircase? No exit?"

John hesitates, "None! They built their own trap." He searches for a positive response. "Well, they will make a beautiful sight to see, intimidating but very beautiful."

In front of me, in the middle gap is a stage, 6 meters wide and 2 meters high. It has tall hanging carpets on three sides and a railing across the front, with an opening and steps in the middle. In the front center is an elevated throne. There are no other chairs. I cannot see if they elevated the back section of the platform.

Six drummers appear at the door of the Basilica in two columns. They each carry a large kettledrum, with a very deep ominous sound.

Following them are two columns of the Vatican Guards in fancy dress uniforms, carrying burning torches. Fat Jack and Skull Man are among them in uniforms.

Then in the middle, the Pope appears in his beautiful gold trimmed miter and most elaborately decorated robes carrying his gold Shepard's crook.

Behind the Pope are two columns of all the Cardinals, processing to the drumbeat, step by step.

The Bishops follow them and then the Arch Deacons. As the two columns reach the center behind the raised platform they split, one to the right and the other to the left. The Drummers circle around the platform and take their position in front of it. The Vatican Guard take their places in front of the bleachers.

The Pope and selected Cardinals take their places on the platform.

The remaining Cardinals, Bishops and Arch Deacons split to the left and right side, filling the bleachers from the bottom to the top.

I can't believe how long this takes, but it feels like it is much longer than an hour. As the last Arch Deacons ascend the stairs and take their places, the Drums start a dramatic pulsing drum-roll. They finish with a unified exploding Boom.

The First Cardinal steps forward on the platform and begins to read from a book of Exorcism. As his voice reaches its height of volume and emotion, it cracks, leaving him speechless. Two others try to take over from where he ended, and the same happens to them. The Pope motions for the Second Cardinal to resume. The Second Cardinal begins to read from an incredibly old large leather-bound book THE POWER AND AUTHORITY OF THE CHURCH. After the introductory passages, he begins Article I. His voice is clear and regular until he reaches the word, 'Absolute...' Here, he starts to cough uncontrollably. He cannot continue. Two others try but cannot utter the next word. One gags and throws up. The other starts to sneeze until blood sprays form his nose.

Finally, the Pope, rises from his throne and steps forward. He motions to the six Cardinals, in their drastic states, as if to sweep them off the platform and out of his way. He shouts at the top of his lungs,

"You are Guilty of Heresy against the Church and ..." The word does not come out of his mouth. He struggles to say the word, but the 'G' always catches in his throat.

Bosco screams at the top of his lungs, "U-alls de HERETICS here! Yous oughts ta bes ashams of yous-all!"

The Pope glares at Bosco and motions for the Guard to light the pyre. A drum-roll begins. The Vatican Guard steps forward and thrusts their torches into the kindling at the base of the pyre. It slowly catches and small flames begin to dance through the tinder. Suddenly there is an explosion of white-hot leaping flames.

But it is not the logs around the poll. The robes of the Pope, every Cardinal, every Bishop, every Arch Deacon, every Drummer and all the Vatican Guard have burst into flame. In an instant they are all ingulfed in the blaze.

I can feel the heat from where I stand, and Bosco turns his face into my chest and tries to shield my body. John looks down at the logs around us, and shouts, "We are not burning! The fire is out!"

As we look around the bleachers, all their faces start to turn black, and their one and only deafening cry goes up all at once. **"NO!"** The sound echoes in the air for several seconds. In less than a minute their robes and bodies are reduced to ashes, which slowly falls into a heap where they stand. It all happens so quickly that the fire does not even scorch the boards on the bleachers.

Suddenly, a strong updraft, caused by the fire, rushes in and blows away the ashes. The only thing left is their jewelry and the Shepard's staff.

Bosco unties us, and we climb down. As we stand in a circle looking at each other, we are all aglow with the Love-light. We embrace each other.

I ask, "Are you all-right?"

They say, "Yes! And you?"

"I feel a little naked."

The 'I Am' reacts, "What do you mean? That is the way I made you."

We all laugh.

Sadly, some days later, the news media reports that the Vatican has been deserted and there is no trace of anyone, not even the Guard. There is no clue that would help resolve the mystery of their disappearance. The Church around the world now seems to be in chaos. The local people have already started to help themselves to the gold and jewels left behind. The police and authorities are part of that group, so it is not likely that anything will be done about it.

CHAPTER 44
Unholy War

As the gathering grows in Aleetmh, the issues of cholera and malnutrition begin to slip away. The vaccine prevents any new cases, and a quick cure awaits those sick on arrival with fresh water and fresh vegetables. The added presence of the Love-light is creating a miraculous feeling. Everyone can feel the presence of the 'Great I Am' in so many people.

In the midst of this environment many healthy debates keep springing up throughout the camp. Instead of confrontation, people are listening and then talking. Not everyone agrees, but at least they understand why their neighbor has a different point of view. Thus, creating a nonviolent community, with everybody working together.

Throughout the tent city, small groups are emerging with common interests. One of those is agriculture. The people used to accept the infertile lands and vast deserts of the country. They thought they had to learn to live with it.

Now, all that is changing. The used-up compost, when they extract all the methane gas from Noya's Latrine Miracle (It's new name), is turning the desert into a blooming field. The garden patch, cultivated by Noya's team, is now growing food. The Tribe is now collecting the livestock's feces and putting it into the Latrine Miracle. And that is only half the miracle.

The Latrine Miracle is now producing all their cooking gas, and tent heating gas on chilly nights, And fuel for the vehicles. They accomplished this with a minor change of the heater's and car's gas valves. The adaptation on all the motor vehicles causes the greatest positive response. The Chief of the Northern Tribe is reported as saying, "The fact is, my camper literally now runs on my own crap. And I shall never runout of that!"

There is no sewage, and this is all done in a highly sanitary way. There is no need to drill one oil or gas well.

Al Mahenie, from Iran, was ecstatic to learn that the feces of birds produces the greatest quantity of methane gas. He immediately started organizing his people to develop this change in Iran. Bill told him that he knows a chicken farmer in Massachusetts, USA, who runs his whole farm and a fleet of vehicles on the bird's methane gas.

Things like this are bringing people together. All of a sudden, wealth is worthless. When we work together productively, we produce plenty. Together we have all the riches we need.

In every small group debate, the Love-light is always present. Listening to your neighbor has a positive effect on everyone. Suddenly, one group discovered that their prosperity was fake. It was a left-brain illusion created by the ego, selfishness, greed and a lust for power. Finally, they ask the question, "What does might, domination, authority, total rule and class supremacy ultimately give us?" The answer is clear, "Division and chaos."

With that realization a different view of community begins to emerge. They all started talking about giving, caring, unity, sharing and living in the Love-light.

This is the community that the Shiite Houthi rebels and the Islamic clerics are about to attack, with the Russian aid. There is no preparation for war. Yet they are ready.

Hannah asked everyone to rise early this morning before sunrise. They are taking down their tents. They may leave Latrine Miracle tents and mess tents up. They are stowing all gear and bagged tents around the bunker. Those not connected to the 'Great I Am' gather in the bunker. This only amounts to 79 people.

They accomplish all this in 12 minutes before dawn, and everyone is walking into the center of camp. When they are all together, Hanna reminds them, "No weapons of any kind! No hatred! Only those connected and without weapons and without hatred are protected.

"As we stand together as one body, we remove all hatred from your mind and heart. Breath in the Love-light, connect, connect, connect."

Hannah surveys the situation. The 'I Am' says, "All is in order."

She turns to face the attackers. She takes Bill's hand and all the Justice Team steps out front holding hands. When she looks over her shoulder, everyone is holding hands as a community. When she turns back, she can see the first rays of light and the approaching army. They are 10 kilometers out.

At an extremely high altitude there is a large bomber moving in quickly. At that altitude there are very few visual details, but the 'I Am' helps the connected to hear what is going on in the plane.

The Bombardier says in Russian, "bomb's a way!"

After 10 seconds of silence, the Bombardier shouts in Russian, "Veer off! Veer off! It's not falling! It's coming back! Veer..." There is a sound of ripping metal as the bomb rips out the tail of the plane. The plane is veering north. The Bombardier shouts, "We're lucky it didn't detonate!" The piolet shouts, "Luck be damned! We're going down!" There is a lot of screaming and hollering as the pilot struggles to control the plane. Then after a few minutes a voice is heard from their base, "What have you done! You have bombed our ba..." There is a loud **EXPLOSION** as the line goes dead with static. Seconds later the bomber crashes into the desert floor and bursts into a ball of flame.

The next second, Jacob glimpses a fleet of jet fighters hidden in front of the rising sun. They are approaching fast at a low altitude.

The connected group focuses on them as they grow nearer and nearer. Everyone goes into slow-motion perception.

They are Russian Sukhoi Su-57. The first 6 fly in low and try to spray the large body with machine gun fire. The bullets race toward the group in slow-motion. When 30 cm away, they boomerang back on the six planes, ripping them to pieces. All 6 disintegrate in midair and fall in small pieces all around their troops. The second 6 fly in a bit higher intending to employ their rockets at a distance. At 600 meters, they each fire two rockets. The rockets race in till about 5 meters and then boomerang back. They anticipate this and try to pull up, but one of each of their rockets takes them in the under belly and the plane disintegrates with the bits falling on the troops below. The six returning rockets head straight for the third wave of 6 Su-57s. This is unexpected and all 6 are caught off guard. The rockets hit their target, with six huge explosions raining down debris on the charging troops.

Everyone has been so busy watching the air show, they missed the next threat. There are 3 Armata T-14 Russian tanks in front of the troops. When they are within 100 meters their machine guns start firing. The spray of bullets flies in and boomerangs back on the tanks. The armor on the tanks deflects the bullets, but they ricochet toward their troops, killing many. The three operators of the tanks do not realize this and end up killing hundreds of their advancing troops. Ten minutes later, they get a call ordering them to stop the machine gun firing.

All the tanks stop. All the cannon turrets quickly swing forward and take aim on the Justice Team. Someone commands, "Fire!" All the shells fire, but the slugs never leaves the end of the cannon. The operators don't know this, and the cannons automatically reload. The cannons fire again. This time the shells explode, backfiring and exploding all the shells in their magazine. The explosion shoots the cannon turrets into the air, ripping them off the tank. The self-defense system automatically triggers all their rockets to attack the flying turrets of each other's tank. The turrets are blown to pieces and all the operators are killed.

The troops pause to regroup.

While this was going on, there is an argument building back in the bunker of the community. A mother is having it out with her teenage daughter. The daughter has told her mother that her boyfriend is one of the soldiers with the attacking troops. She wants to rescue him from a now certain death. The mother does not want her to risk her own life in this horrific conflict. But she loves him!

Mom calls this "puppy love," and says, "you don't know what love is."

Aafreedn screams, "You have forgotten what love is! You drove Papa away!"

Mom screams back, "Grow up! You can't leave and that's it."

"I don't want him to get killed! Have you no heart!" Aafreedn is in a total rage.

Her Mom tries to restrain her.

Aafreedn tries to fight her off. Screaming, "I have more love in my little pinky, than you have in your whole body."

Mom struggles to hold on to her.

Aafreedn stomps on her foot and springs free. She climbs over the back of the bunker. When she is out of reach, she turns and screams at her mother, "I hate you! I hope you die!" She starts to run around the group to get to the troops.

Ori turns and looks to his right, trying to locate Aafreedn. The 'I Am' has made him and the team aware of this development. When he spots her, he sets an intercept point and slowly starts to walk to that point. When they meet Ori casually ask, "Aafreedn, would you like some help to find your boyfriend?"

Aafreedn smiles, "Yes, I would."

"First off, you need to shake off that hate bit." Aafreedn looks at the ground. Ori continues, "I know you didn't mean it."

Aafreedn looks up sadly, "I should never have said it. I wasn't thi..."

They start walking toward the Troops, who are still trying to regroup. It seems they are having a command debate as to who is in charge.

After a moment, Aafreedn stops and points. There on the edge of the group, stands a young soldier about three meters in front of everyone else. He is looking directly at them with his gun hanging by his leg. Ori waves for him to come.

He drops his weapon and slowly starts to walk toward Aafreedn. Gradually his pace gets faster and faster until he is at a full run.

Ori stops her from running toward him, interrupting the classic romantic meeting. Aafreedn stands still, and Ori takes a few steps forward. The young man is about 10 meters away before anyone sees him. He is now at full speed.

A Sargent lifts his rifle, screaming, "Deserter! Deserter!" He takes aim.

Ori raises both hands, palms forward, and steps in behind the boyfriend as he passes. Ori goes into slow-motion perception. Before he can shout a warning, there is a flash and a bang. The bullet is on its way. Ori watches it coming in and adjusts his position slightly. The bullet boomerangs off of Ori and heads back to the Sargent. Ori quickly urges the embracing couple to hurry back to the group and the safety of the bunker. Fortunately, because of his speed they are virtually invisible.

The Sargent's death causes a major stir among the Troops. Some said he was ordering them to desert. Others said he was hungry for a sweet dessert.

As the couple jumps down into the bunker, Aafreedn embraces her mother and begs her forgiveness. After Mother and Daughter fully exchange their abiding love, Aafreedn introduces her boyfriend to everyone.

Ori looks on with admiration. After a few sighs, he heads back to the Justice Team.

Back on the battlefield, the Shiite Houthi are assessing their losses. They lost their General and half their men from the bouncing bullets of the planes and their destruction and the ricochet bullets off the tanks and their explosion.

The 'I Am' is making their discussion audible to the Justice Team and Connected Community.

The Shiite Captain says, "I don't know what they got, but it's a whole lot more than we got. Look at them. They just stand there. And nothing can touch 'em."

The leaders of the Clerics chime in, one says, "We need to take control."

"We have the power of Allah," says another.

"We have the authority of Islam behind us," says the third.

The Shiite Captain is outraged. He challenges them, "Have you no concern for human life. Look at the dead around us. Look at our fallen leader. What control do you have? Where is the power of your

Allah? Where is the authority of your Islam? Your empty words fall on the deaf ears of the dead around you. And you don't even have the decency to offer a prayer for them."

A Cleric responds in a heated hateful tone, "You must Believe in Allah, His church's power and Authority. You must have Faith in the scriptures, our doctrine and rules. These men died in obedience. They died in the name of Allah. They died in the name of our Holy cause."

"I challenge you," cries the Captain. "Let just one of you Clerics prove to us, with all your phony left-brain irrational assumptions, that you have one concrete example of your God's existence. Look over there. (He points to the Justice Team and Connected community.) They have met Allah. They know Allah and listen to the 'I Am'. They say that Allah is in them. After today I believe them and not you and your rubbish."

Another Cleric shouts, "Our Allah is all powerful. We Clerics are His reality. We Clerics are His authority. We Clerics represent His power. You are an infidel and deserve to die."

The Captain restrains his anger and says calmly, "OK. Then show us His power. You take the lead." He motions for them to take the front line.

On the other side of N556 in the Connected Community, the 'Great I Am' has four connected leaders stand forward, Hydia, Ila Mahenie, Mahum and al-Nisista. They cross the highway and walk shoulder to shoulder toward the front line. They stop when they are 50 meters from the battle debris. They extend their arms in peace.

Meanwhile, the lead Cleric has been giving a fiery speech to the other clerics. He is calling them to arms to defend their belief in their Supreme Allah to defend their Faith in the Church of Islam. They must kill all those who stand in their way. They must kill all the infidels. "In the name of Allah, Allah, Allah..."

All the other Clerics join in, "Allah, Allah, Allah, Allah, Allah, Allah..."

The Shiite hold back from the chanting and move well back from the Clerics, who are now moving to the front line. The dead still lie before them, ignored by the Clerics.

Suddenly, the lead Cleric spots the four Islamic leaders before them. He raises his rifle over his head and shouts to the others, "This is our power. This is our authority. Watch as I kill that Syrian bitch!" He leans on one of the destroyed tanks and sights on Hydia. Before he shoots, he mumbles, "In the name of Allah, die!" He fires.

The 'I Am' allows everyone (including the Clerics and Shiite) to see this in slow-motion perception. We see the bullet racing toward Hydia. She stands with her hands stretched out in peace. The bullet comes within 10 centimeters of her forehead and boomerangs back toward the lead Cleric. Before he can blink his eyes, the bullet hits him in the center of his forehead, and he is thrown back several meters.

Everyone comes back to real motion perception, and al-Nisista calls out to his father, "How would you like to find the Love-light, Papa?" His father drops his weapon to the ground.

This action causes a wave response that flows back through the Clerics and Shiite as they all drop their weapons and cast off their hatred.

This reaction and the 'I Am's response brings the Justice Team and Connected Community forward to their former enemy. There are friendly handshakes. There are warm embraces of broken families. There is talk and hope of finding the Love-light. Slowly, the Love-light brings them all to the solemn realization of the many dead.

Together, they all bury the dead with respect and

great care. And everyone can feel the 'Great I Am's sense of loss for the many lives.

As they finish the burial and everyone starts to walk back to the Community campsite, al-Nisista's father asks, "Ila, why is your 'Great I Am' killing all these people? Do we all have to live in fear from now on?"

Ila stops and studies his father's face. He can see the fear in his eyes and a concealed tremble in his body. He reaches out and puts his hand on his shoulder, and says, "Papa, the 'Great I Am' never kills anyone. That would be like killing part of 'I Am's self. The 'I Am' is the essence of being in every one of these men who died. That part of the 'Great I Am' is now dead and gone. In reality, each one of these men has killed himself. Their own hatred killed them, along with their lies, greed and lust for power and control of the people. If you were to look at the ballistics of the bullet that killed your leader and friend, you would learn that it was his own bullet that killed him. It was his own hatred."

"I could see that, but I could hardly believe my eyes. So how can I find this God you found."

Ila laughs, "Papa, when I was a little boy, you used to tell me, 'Ila, one day you will be a great man.' Where did that come from?"

"I felt it in here." His father lays his hand over his heart. "It was like a little voice inside me. I didn't hear anything. I just knew."

"Papa, you were feeling the 'Great I Am' within you. The God you worship up there," he points to the heavens, "does not exist. The 'Great I Am' is in here." He points to his heart. The 'I Am' is your essence of being. I will help you find the Love-light within you."

The father and son embrace each other with great vigor.

CHAPTER 45
Summit Meeting

Hayah is back in Israel. John has returned to his friends in India. Bosco is now with a connected family in Finland, where he can get the best education in the world. The Justice Team is also back in Israel, and they are meeting with Hayah on the roof garden. There is no need for a debriefing, because the 'Great I Am' has kept them all posted. The 'I Am' has even filled Hayah in on what happened after the Catholic Church drugged him.

Right now, there are some key questions they need to resolve before they take their next step. The first question they are dealing with is their protection in a vulnerable situation, like Hayah experienced. As it turns out, the boomerang effect is only effective in a physical attack. Increasingly, those committing hateful or abusive acts are using drugs and other substances to subdue their victims. The 'Great I Am' is actively participating in this discussion. In India it was the same question concerning sexual abuse.

The 'I Am' says, "Our choices are limited here. How do we preserve your Freewill Choice while attacking the human freedom of will? Humans need to learn that their freedom of will leads only to their dark-side. Look at how many learned that at Aleetmh. That put the Middle East well on their way to 1% of their population.

"As for the ingested substance problem, I can adjust the chemistry of the body to reject them. When the body experiences them, it will remove them and urinate them off. This, however, cannot be reversed. When Hayah was a young boy, he saw so many drunks; he never wanted to get drunk. I made the adjustment, so he could never get drunk. Years later, his girlfriend broke off their relationship, and he wanted to get drunk. He bought a liter of Southern Comfort, 100 proof. He downed the whole bottle in thirty minutes and felt nothing. However, he did have to spend the night on the toilet.

"As for the drug problem, you need to know the exact chemistry and inject an antidote. Otherwise, the body needs to fight it off, which is not pleasant. You will have vomiting, sever perspiration and diarrhea. The knockout type, that Hayah had, is only overcome by sleeping them off. The body can fight them off and shorten the knockout time, like we did with Hayah. All I can do by being there is help you through it."

Hannah asks, "What about miracles? You have performed many wonders; the water at Aleetmh, the parting of the red sea, the manna in the desert. You did them all."

"They are actually not miracles. They are natural phenomena. Remember, I Am in everyone and everything. I was in you and guided you to the right spot, the right rock and its weakest spot and in the water that wants to come to the surface. I was in the Red Sea, every molecule and we simply parted. It was no Higher power. I was in the manna, an eatable fungus that grew only at night. I was in Moses and helped him find it. You see, no miracles. It may be a wonder to the unconnected human mind, but no miracle. Go ahead, Hannah, ask it."

Hannah hesitates and then responds, "OK. I don't understand."

"And what part of your brain is telling you that?" Says the 'I Am'. And everyone can feel 'I Am's smile, and they smile themselves including Hannah.

"My left brain's irrational thought, of course. OK. Let's look at it scientifically. How can you do those things? And will we ever be able to do them?"

"As I said, I Am in everything. Pick up that rock over there. Up here it is a decoration."

Hannah picks up the rock. It is a mixture of many different glittery things and quite attractive as rocks go. It is about 12 cm in diameter.

The 'I Am' asks, "Guess how heavy it is, no numbers, relatively."

Hannah moves it up and down before responding and then passes it around, "I would say it is slightly on the heavy side."

When it comes back to her again, she weighs it and reacts, "Wow, now it is heavier than gold." She passes it around and everyone has the same reaction of complete wonder.

When she takes it again, she squeezes it tightly. "What the? It is light as a feather. It feels like it wants to fly away." She and the others pass it around carefully, so it doesn't float away.

"I Am part of the rock and can determine its weight. Will you ever be able to do that? Yes, when your Spirit comes home." With that, the rock floats out of Hannah's hand and back to where it was sitting on the deck. Everyone's eyes follow it.

A deep silence falls over the group.

Hayah tries to get everyone's attention. He says softly, "It is difficult for me to move on after what I just went through. I actually had to witness the self-destruction of the entire hierarchy of the Roman Catholic Church. For 2 thousand years the 'Great I Am' has been trying to get through to them, with little success. What will become of them now? No one knows.

"I'm sure that the loss of life you experienced was the same. The deaths never get any easier. So, let us focus on the lives you saved at Aleetmh. The Middle East nations now have a positive connection with each other. The Russian's presence is wiped out. Congratulations to you all for that.

"Now we face a similar challenge. Only this one

is your home. The question is, are you up for the
challenge? These are **your** friends and family.

"Add to this personal intimacy, the fact that the
political climate is so corrupted there is no longer any
resemblance of integrity, ethics, and caring for the
people and their lives. They keep seizing land that is
not theirs under the UN charter. They want to
destroy their neighbors, wall them out and not live
with them. And it seems like this conflict goes back
to the beginning of time.

"As if that is not enough, the Hebrew clerics are
in a worse state than the Islamic clerics. They have
totally lost any awareness of the 'I Am's presence.
While the Hebrew people long to connect to the
'Great I Am', the clerics want to crack the whip on
their backs to keep them in line. They'll pray for
hours on end, asking, ordering, demanding. Then
without listening to the 'I Am' for 2 seconds, they get
up, take off their tallit (prays shawl) and walk away.

"The Israeli military is another problem. They
are a well-organized force, with a noticeably short
fuse. They shoot first and ask questions later. The
breadth and quality of their might is second to none.
While the threat of that power means nothing to us,
it could mean the destruction of the Hebrew people.
The 'I Am' wants to avoid that, if at all possible.

"The 'Great I Am' has a plan and needs to know if
you are up for the task. You are all aware of the plan.
You made your connection by choice. You are living
in the Love-light by choice. The Hebrew and
Palestinian people have not been able to live without
hatred since the beginning of recorded history.
Negotiations have always proved futile. Are you
strong enough to avoid getting sucked back into that
ethnic hatred and self-destruction?"

There is a profound silence and stillness that
shelters the Team as they connect to the 'Great I Am'.

After several minutes, the 'Great I Am' says to

everyone. "This is not going to be easy for the people to accept, but it will be quite easy for us to accomplish as a unified Team. I need your feedback on some of these changes. Firstly, any weapon picked up to maim or kill will immediately destroy or permanently injure the perpetrator and anyone ordering the action. Any person resorting to any violence ends here and now.

"Examples: a Lieutenant orders a Sargent, who orders a Soldier to kill someone. When the Soldier picks up his rifle, I will ignite all the powder in the magazine, killing all three. A Commander orders a Piolet on a mission to take out a group of people or destroy a building, which may contain people. The moment the piolet starts the engine, I will ignite all the powder, destroying the Commander, piolet and plane. In short making all weapons a death trap."

Talia responds instantly, "Isn't that a bit severe? The Soldier and Piolet may not have a choice. Weapons become a booby-trap." She stops, "Oops that is a irrationalization." Everyone chuckles.

"Your right. It is severe," the 'I Am' admits. "But not even the severest deterrents have stopped the killing. I started off with a total ban on weapons, which is a good thing. But would that stop the black-marketing of weapons? This would stop it cold. You pick it up. Your dead! How long would it take to get that word out?"

Noya suggests, "These days, most women have a problem with sexual abuse. Can you insert the word 'harm', so it would be 'Any weapon picked up to harm, maim or kill...'? It's a shame you can't define a man's sexual organ as a weapon. I would like to see that explosion."

There is a hearty laugh in the group.

The 'I Am' says, "I'll make the change, Noya. Thank you. And we all need to find a way to stop the sexual abuse problem, which is my second issue. We

will get to that next. Although, the exploding penis
would be an interesting deterrent. I could actually do
that. An erection that kept filling with blood until it
bursts. That would guarantee no repeat offenders.
Hmmm."

Hannah speaks to the first change, "I can see the
necessity for the harshness concerning weapons,
because laws no longer work in our world. People got
the warning about the boomerang effect, but they
thought they could beat the odds. It didn't stop
them. However, I raise some issues. What about law
enforcement? What about self-defense for those not
connected? Where does that put humans on the
hierarchy of natural survival of the fittest?"

"What about hunting and livestock farming?"
Bill quickly adds.

The 'I Am' responds calmly, "These are all points
I considered. Law enforcement has changed over the
last decade. In many cases, officers no longer keep
the peace, but use their power and authority to back
up their own hatred and greed. Follow the weapon
rule, and no police officer will ever face an armed
assailant. They will only need to remove the dead
body.

"With the weapon rule, self-defense will need to
be redefined. No attacker will ever come at you with
a weapon. So, all the marshal-arts become excellent
defense tools.

"Your survival of the fittest question also gave me
a lot to sort out. In the beginning humans were not
high on the predator list, and they had to avoid those
creatures that were higher. Also, humans were not
fast enough or strong enough to catch most animals
or escape the ones attacking them. They depended
on most game to give their life so they, a human,
might live. Many did this, as humans became part of
the environment. At first this was mostly fish and
fowl, but soon others followed creating my intended

harmony.

"All that changed when humans started inventing tools. First it was the stone knife. Then the stone axe. Then the stone spear. After that it was the bow and arrow, with stone arrowheads. All of these, humans used in relationship to building and food. This moved humans up the food chain. Humans helped each other. Survival was in the sharing. I was part of all this.

"Then in a split second, one human was filled with hate and greed. Suddenly these tools became weapons and another human died, and another, and another, and another. The weapons became power among humans. The weapons power gave them more of everything, and everything that belonged to anyone else.

"I do not need to tell you how far it has come. It is no longer the survival of the fittest. It is the fit weapon of the survivor.

"Any good and connected hunter or farmer will know when the animal is ready to give their life so a human can live. They will respect the animal and treat them humanely. What they use is a TOOL.

"Any trophy hunter, or any cruel, profiteering farmer will take the animals because they can and as many as they can. They have no honor for the life they take. What they use is a WEAPON.

"I Am in them both. I will know what is in their heart. There will be no more splitting hairs."

Ori raises a serious question, "What about Atomic weapons? Triggering them in this way would be disastrous to a lot of innocent lives."

"Thank you, Ori. I have considered that problem. The Atomic Age is about to come to a screeching halt. Until science figures out how to eliminate or control the radioactive fallout for domestic use, they need to eliminate themselves. This is how it will work.

"Any weapon, atomic or chemical, designed to harm, maim or kill, will be triggered in the laboratory before it is employed. Thus, destroying the laboratory and all those working on it. I will know their intent long before they try to discharge one in the lab. All such weapons in storage must be dismantled and launched into outer space, within 30 days of this warning. From there, I will dispose of them. Any attempt to trigger one of these weapons, in the interim, will result in the immediate radioactive destruction of the military and responsible political leaders in that country."

Jacob asks, "What is the best way to get this warning out to everyone?"

"When we finish here, I will get the word out to all those connected to me. Then, you will need to alert the militaries, politicians and press. It is understood, there will be those skeptics who think it is a hoax, and they will try it out. I will alert a bystander to video the perpetrator at a safe distance. They will take that video to the press and receive a handsome payment for it. My estimate is that it will be out there regionally to everyone in 24 hours."

Hayah, who already was aware of most of this, has a question, "It has always been our basic goal to help people find the Love-light. What is making you take this sever step?"

"In the battle of Aleetmh there were thousands killed by ricocheting bullets and shrapnel. None of these soldiers fired one shot. The planes and tanks did it all. Some of these men could have connected if given a chance. Their loss deeply saddens me."

"I can feel that. It is a great loss to us all. Especially after the turn-a-round we had with the rest of the troops. Only one Sargent and one Cleric killed themselves, with a boomerang shot. Most of the other survivors may be connecting with you.

"If we used your new warning, all those troops

and Clerics would be dead. They all picked up their weapons with the intent to kill off the Connected Community at Aleetmh." There is dead silence. After a moment, Hayah continues, "I can see where the new warning is better in the Israeli vs. Palestinian situation we are currently facing. It is better that no battle takes place. It is better that no one takes up arms, ever again, and the new warning will do that.

"However, sometimes the boomerang warning is better, and we need to make that choice for the crisis at hand. You made the right choice for the battle of Aleetmh."

"Hayah, Hayah, Hayah, I really missed you." 'I Am' says to the others, "Learn from this. I always need your help. We will follow Hayah's suggestion. Now let us deal with the sexual abuse problem. We made a major step forward earlier. This is my position incorporating what we said.

"Women and men are equal in all respects, (PERIOD). All societies, businesses, organizations and families must honor this basic premise. Both men and women must honor this premise. Failure to honor this premise is a step toward the Dark-side. (The Dark-side exists only in humans and is ruled by Hate.) To honor this premise is a positive step towards the Love-light and a positive step towards connecting with Me.

"Sexual abuse of either women or men is not acceptable and is considered a step toward the Dark-side. Sexual abuse is the infliction of sexual contact upon a person by forcible compulsion, or by sexual contact with a person who is sexually immature or who is incapable of giving consent because of age or mental or physical incapacity. Any man committing sexual abuse will experience an over enlarging penis which will burst and never function again. Any woman committing sexual abuse will experience an explosive uterus and never be able to experience sexual pleasure.

"What is your response?"

Noya answers quickly, "That should end the nightmare. But I had no idea women participated in sexual abuse."

"More than you know," replies the 'I Am'.

There were no other comments.

The 'I Am' says, "Next are Lies and deception. This is a worldwide epidemic including most people, and especially clergy, politicians, lawyers and the justice system. The solution I propose is a boomerang response. Every time a person lies or deceives someone, I will make them automatically and uncontrollably say, 'That is a lie!' Or 'That is a deception!' They will even consciously hear themselves saying it. Do you have any suggestions?"

Jacob starts to laugh, "That's even better than the flashing red light on the screen."

Hayah adds, "Perfect! That'll work instantly."

The 'I Am' says, "At this time, My last problem is with power and authority. This has evolved over millenniums, from military might, to religious dogma, to royal blood, to political control and now to a wealthy few. Unfortunately, they are now destroying the planet. Nature is out of balance; pollution is deadly, and the planet will be lucky to survive until 2050. The only survival will be the emergence of the many Crystal Cities. These will be a balanced eco systems and only those connected to Me will live there. Unfortunately, 1% of the population in any area must be connected to Me before they can emerge. This has always been the plan, but now we are running out of time." The 'Great I Am' is silent.

A Deep silence falls over the group.

Finally, Hayah says, "LET'S GET TO WORK!"

CHAPTER 46
A New Military

To get the word out quickly, Hayah divides the Team into three groups. Jacob, Talia and Abbud will give a wakeup call to the Palestinian people. Noya and Ori will give the Press a heads-up as to what is going down. Hannah, Bill and Hayah will speak to the Israeli parliament and military. The 'I Am' will help each group to communicate the message as clearly as possible and navigate any hostility.

Fortunately, the Justice Team has already acquired a powerful no-nonsense reputation. The self-destruction of the Russian military in Aleetmh, Yemen, is a number two topic. The number one topic is the quickly growing union of the Middle East states, and they are soon to be free of an oil dependence, because of the Miracle Latrine. Ila Mahenie has gone crazy in converting himself and many others to this unlimited methane fuel from birds, human and animal excrement. As he loves to say, "Excrement, is the one thing we will never run out of." Of course, he uses the crud version of the word excrement and always gets a rolling laugh.

Noya and Ori quickly put together a comprehensive Press Kit. The Kit contains all the warnings specific to the Military, the Israel Parliament, and the Palestinian leadership. It also contains all of the 'Great I Am' commands, with specific examples.

They are enclosing the schedule of all the meetings and the meeting times and location. The enclosure also contains a map with the Gaza meeting location.

The press has invitations and passes to all the meetings and contact numbers to the Justice Team.

Following the meetings there will be a special debriefing for the Press in Tel Aviv.

Bill arranges, through his UN connections, a meeting with all the top officers in the Israeli military. Hannah, Bill and Hayah take their places at the end of an exceptionally large oval conference table. At the head of the room are two flags. One is the flag of Israel. The other is the fag of the Israeli Army (Zro'a ha-Yabasha); on top of the center shield, in the center of that flag, is a sword, with an olive branch entwining it. Between the two flags stand two military guards bearing side arms and a rifle.

As the room fills with officers, there are several small group greetings taking place. These set a tone of friendly comradery. As some of these men and women take their places at the table, they acknowledge Bill, but not Hannah or Hayah. On the appointed hour, a young female corporal steps in the door, then to the side and snaps to attention. Everyone still milling about, rush to their places. Everyone seated, stands, including the Justice Team. The Chief of the General Staff, Viav, a lieutenant general, of three-star rank, enters and takes his place at the head of the table. Everyone sits at the same time.

There is complete silence in the room. Viav opens in a very casual way, "I think we can dispense with our usual formalities. We are here to listen to what Bill and the Justice Team have to tell us. As I understand, they have a new peace proposal. Bill, you have the floor.

Bill stands in his place. He smiles and studies the faces of all those at the table. He begins, "I wouldn't call it a new peace proposal. It is more like the ultimate peace proposal. The 'Great I Am' wants to end all hatred, war and violence. Yes, this will produce the ultimate peace. And it is about to change everything you know about defending your Nation and yourself. Essentially, you will never be threatened again by any hostile force." Bill pauses for a moment to study the change in their faces. On some there is awe and wonder, on others elation, but some are skeptical.

"If you look at your army flag, you will see a symbol of a sword entwined with an olive branch. From this day forward that will no longer be a dream or idea. It will be a reality!

"The 'Great I Am' is sending you this message. Listen carefully and we can discuss it afterwards. 'Any weapon picked up to harm, maim or kill will immediately destroy or permanently injure the perpetrator and anyone ordering the action. Any person resorting to any violence, ends here and now.' There is complete silence in the room. But then a Captain begins to chuckle, and the chuckle spreads through the room.

The Captain says, "Your kidding, right?"

"No, I'm not!" Bill responds emphatically. "All violence ends here and NOW. Today and for all time to come. Your enemy will never be able to lift a weapon to harm, maim or kill you. Just as you will never be able to lift your weapons to harm, maim or kill someone else. I suggest that you lay down all your weapons, to protect yourself."

Bill starts to get a message from the 'I Am'. The male guard standing next to the Army flag, thinks it is a farce. He is about to prove it. Bill calls to him, "Corporal, the 'I Am' knows you are about to challenge the order. Put down your weapon, so you won't be tempted."

The Corporal says slowly, "How do you know what I'm thinking?"

Bill responds, "I don't. But the 'Great I Am' that is in you does. Please put down the weapon."

The Corporal starts to put down his weapon.

The Captain screams out an order, "Don't you dare Corporal! Take your shot! Kill this bastard!" He starts to laugh.

Bill, Hannah and Hayah all yell at the same time, **"NO!"**

The General ducks.

The Corporal starts to raise the weapon and it explodes, ripping off his arm and the arm of the Captain. Both men scream in pain. The female corporal at the door spins out of the room to get medical help. The others in the room start to get up in a rage.

General Viav screams out, "Sit down everyone." They hesitate. "NOW!"

Everyone returns to their seats. Hannah goes to the Captain. Hayah goes to the Corporal. They help them out the door, where they are met by the medics and taken off on stretchers. They return to the room. Everyone is sitting in silence, frozen in shock. Hannah and Hayah return to their places and wait. General Viav is staring at Bill.

Bill finally tells him in a very steady voice, "Go ahead General ask your questions. There is no such thing as a stupid question. The only thing that is stupid is a question never asked."

"How did you know I was thinking that?" asked the General.

"The 'I Am' that is within you is the same 'I Am' that is in me. When you are connected, 'I Am' can tell you things you never dreamed possible. Yes, and you can connect as well. Just like everyone else at this table." Bill smiles with his face aglow.

Viav takes a deep breath and asks, "OK, is this the 'I Am' of Moses?"

"Same one," says Hayah.

One of the Lieutenants at the table asks, "Are you talking about God?"

Hayah smiles, "No. The 'I Am' does not like that

name. That is a mythical spiritual being up in the stratosphere some place, worshiped by ancient cultures and religious institutions. When Moses asked the burning bush, 'What shall I say your name is?' The bush answered, 'I Am האיה I Am'. Many translate the Hebrew word as Hasha, which is <u>who or what</u>, but the real root word is Hayah which means essence-of-being, 'I Am your Essence-of-Being I Am'. Now you not only know who 'I Am' is, you know where 'I Am' is." There is a gasp of breath. "That's right, 'I Am' is in everything and the only species that has lost that connection is humans. Yes, we can help you connect, and that is our ultimate goal. However, right now we need to get 'I Am's message out to you. There are too many lives at stake right now." Hayah nods to Bill.

Bill asks, "Do you have any more questions regarding the first order?"

One of the officers asks, "Would you go over again that bit about us not needing to defend ourselves? What about our protecting the people?"

"Your enemy is bound by the same order. You may want to give him or her a warning to save lives. But their ignorance is not your problem. You are unarmed. If they so much as touch their weapon, it will explode and maim or kill them. After that, your only responsibility is to clean up the mess.

"As to protecting the people, you now have an even greater responsibility. You must make sure they are unarmed, and if not, you will need to help them to lay down the weapon, with no intention to harm anyone."

The officer responds, "Wow! We will need to completely retrain the troops. Not that I mind, thank you."

Another officer asks, "Does this make us responsible for someone else's hatred?"

Hannah takes this question, "No, not at all. Everyone is responsible for their own dark-side and their own hatred. The celestial war of good vs. evil is a myth. The only war against evil is within yourself, within your own dark-side. The only hatred you are responsible for is your own hatred."

General Viav jumps in, "These questions could go on for weeks. I think we need to move on to the next in order, Bill."

Bill makes a face with raised eyebrows, "This one may be hard to take, but it follows the same premise as the first order. If a pilot is ordered to harm, maim or kill, and he or she boards the plane, with that intent, the moment the switch is thrown all the plane's armament will explode, killing the piolet and all those who give the order." Bill takes a breath.

"No surprise." Viav responds positively. "So, we disarm the planes. We won't get blown up for doing that, I presume." He smiles, "What about the drones?" His mood changes the mood at the table.

Bill smiles, "The 'I Am' knows your intentions, so you're safe. As for the drones, disarm them. Use them for surveillance."

"I like the consistency of your 'I Am'. I look forward to our meeting," says Viav.

A "here, here" is heard around the table.

Viav presses on, "OK, what's next?"

Bill continues, "this one is slightly different, but the same theme. There is to be No Atomic or Chemical weapons of any kind, designed or made! The explosion will take place during early development while still in the lab, to minimize the collateral damage. As to the Atomic and Chemical weapons that already exist, they must be disarmed, and all the radioactive or chemical components rocketed into outer space, where the 'I Am' will dispose of them. Compliance must take place within 30 days."

"I like this 'I Am', always consistent and thorough," says Viav. "Is there anything else?"

"Not that we need to deal with here, Sir," Bill sighs in relief, having expected more conflict. "The rest are all behavioral and will be introduced to the general public."

"We thank you for giving us these heads up. It is my assessment that this will change things positively forever. The success of your work proceeds you." General Viav looks around the table, "I for one am very serious about connecting to the 'Great I Am', how about the rest of you?"

There is a show of hands including all but one person. "There you have it," says General Viav.

Hayah replies, "We will call and schedule a group for next week."

Everyone stands, and a buzz begins.

Viav turns to the guard behind him and nods while looking at the weapons.

The guard quickly lays down his weapons and stands at attention with a smile on his face.

CHAPTER 47
6 Second War

Hannah arranges for Hayah to do a special address before an emergency assembly of the Israel parliament. This is happening in the afternoon, following the military briefing. The Chairman introduces Hayah, who is already known to the general body. Hayah approaches the lectern in silence. Then he studies his audience. He can see general uneasiness, which is confirmed by the 'Great I Am'. Right now, they are borderline hostel.

Hayah steps to the side of the lectern and speaks in a clear commanding voice. "Wake up O-people of Israel. I bring you a gift of the Love-light. Wake up O-people of Israel. I welcome you to a new era of the 'Great I Am', the 'I Am' of Moses and your founding fathers. Wake up O-people of Israel. A new dawn is shining brightly within you, and for all your days to come. On this day, all anger and hatred ends. Violence shall be no more. Come out of your dark-side and embrace the 'Great I Am' that is within you.

"The 'Great I Am' wishes to speak to you, so now I let the 'I Am' take over my heart and voice."

The voice that comes out of Hayah's mouth is deep and powerful. "Sons and Daughters of Abraham, why do you turn away from Me? Why do you fill yourselves with anger and hatred? They are not part of Me. Why do you let hatred drive you into a violent rage? That is not part of the heart I gave you. Why do you let your left-brain irrational mind deceive you and deny My presence within you? I Am here! I should not need to use another's voice to speak to you. Why do you pray endlessly with all your demands, orders and give-me things? Be like Samuel with his four words, 'I'm here. I'm listening.' I know the things in your mind. I know the things that need to be done. I know what you want and what you need to have or should have. You need to stop talking and learn to listen to Me. 'I Am your essence of being I Am.' Those are the words I said to Moses.

"There once was a time, when I called you My 'Chosen People', but NO MORE! Now I shall love and protect those who connect to Me. That is your choice. You can be a stiff-neck-people estranged to Me. Or you can connect to Me and be one of My Choosing People. The choice is yours.

"Now open your heart and be aware of my words. Take them into your heart and let them be part of who you are. These are My commands, that you must keep or reap the repercussions. There will be no interpretations, no rewording, no editing, NO CHANGES! Follow them and abide by them."

At this point a few people get up and start to leave the chamber. The 'I Am' can read their dissention. Their attitude is extremely haughty.

The 'Great I Am' shouts, "Sit Down!"

They continue, ignoring the command.

"SIT DOWN, or Fall Down, and I will determine when your body gets up." There is no anger in the 'I Am's voice, only firmness.

Most of those leaving return to their seats. Six stumble in the isle, fall and scream in pain.

'I Am' waves Hayah's arm in an arch and says, "Silence, lay there and suffer in silence." Their mouths are closed, and no sound can be heard.

The whole mood in the hall changes. The majority of the people feel they are in the presence of the real 'Great I Am'. The others are obedient and borderline terrified. A stillness falls over the hall. Those fallen in the isle are silent. 'I Am' allows them to get up and return to their seats.

"There is no need for fear. You are not in any danger. I Am not angry. The goal here is that everyone connects to Me and becomes a part of the Love-light. Together, you will discover we can do some pretty amassing things. The choice to connect is always yours. However, it is mandatory that everyone follows these commands.

"Firstly, any weapon picked up to harm, maim or kill will immediately destroy or permanently injure the perpetrator and anyone ordering the action. Any person resorting to any violence ends here and now.

"Secondly, any weapon, atomic or chemical, designed to harm, maim or kill, will be triggered in the laboratory before it becomes available. Thus, destroying the laboratory and all those working on it. I will know their intent long before they try it out. All such weapons in storage must be dismantled and launched into outer space, within 30 days of this warning. From there, I will dispose of them. Any attempt to trigger one of these weapons, in the interim, will result in the immediate radioactive destruction of the military and responsible political leaders in that country.

"Thirdly, Women and men are equal in all respects (PERIOD). All societies, businesses, organizations and families must honor this basic premise. Both men and women must honor this premise. Failure to honor this premise is a step toward the Dark-side. (The Dark-side exists only in humans and is ruled by Hate.) To honor this premise is a positive step towards the Love-light and a positive step towards connecting with Me.

"Sexual abuse of either women or men is not acceptable and is considered a step toward the Dark-side. Sexual abuse is the infliction of sexual contact upon a person by forcible compulsion, or by sexual contact with a person who is sexually immature or who is incapable of giving consent because of age or mental or physical incapacity. Any man committing sexual abuse will experience an over enlarging penis which will burst and never function again. Any woman committing sexual abuse will experience an explosive uterus and never be able to enjoy sexual pleasure.

"Fourthly, lies and deception. This is a worldwide epidemic including most people, and especially clergy, politicians, lawyers and the justice system. Every time a person lies or deceives someone, I will make them automatically and uncontrollably say, 'That is a lie!' Or 'That is a deception!' They will even consciously hear themselves saying it.

"Fifthly, power and authority. This has evolved over millenniums, from military might, to religious dogma, to royal blood, to political control and now to a wealthy few. Unfortunately, they are now destroying the planet. Nature is out of balance; pollution is destroying the planet and the planet will be lucky to survive until 2050. The only survival will be the emergence of the many Crystal Cities. These will be a balanced eco systems and only those connected to Me will live there. Unfortunately, 1% of the population in any area must be connected to Me before they can emerge. This has always been the plan, but now we are running out of time. These commands are for every nation throughout the world, including Israel.

"Now, I give you the specific instructions for the people of Israel. The border walls, barbed wire and wire fences MUST BE REMOVED. They are a disgrace to the Promised Land I gave you. They are a symbol of your anger and hatred after World War II. You have become worse than the people who persecuted you. You are a better people than that. These walls are a defiance of My command, 'You shall Love your neighbor as yourself,' in Moses' book of Levi. The WALL MUST GO.

"The BORDERS of Israel shall go back to the UN

Armistice lines of 1949. The lines you created after the 6 Day War, in 1967, are now Null and Void. If you wish to live peacefully outside your borders, you must do so under the laws of that State. If you are connected with My Love-light, this will fill you with boundless joy.

"The State of Israel must recognize and honor the State of Palestine, which includes the Westbank, the Gaza Strip, and the East section of Jerusalem, which is their Capital. The greater harmony you create between you, the greater your neighborly love will grow, and the more you will fulfill your promise to Me and the original positive 10 words, which I carved in two stone tablets for all to see.

"Now I return you to Hayah and the Justice Team. They speak with My authority."

Hayah smiles as he comes back to himself. He asks the crowed, "Do you have any questions?"

Slowly several people start to stand in order to be recognized. Hayah looks over the standing people, studying their faces. He picks a young woman with a broad smile.

She says, "I'm deeply moved by the presence of the 'Great I Am' and hope that I might connect with the 'I Am' within me. I also agree with what the 'I Am' said about the boarder wall. It is an eye sore and a false symbol of who we are as a people. Can we still have peaceful checkpoints to welcome people and keep track of who is coming and going?"

Hannah answers the question, "The 'I Am' says, 'Yes, you can, Ruth', and my Team will be setting up groups to help people to connect with the 'I Am' within them, so you can find the Love-light."

Ruth is a bit surprised that she knows her name, but then puts it together. Of course, the 'I Am' knows her name. "Thank you," she says.

Hayah picks out a Rabi, with a full white beard

and white hair dune up in the traditional orthodox way. His suit is black, and his fiery eyes are full of anger. He steps into the isle clutching his large briefcase to his chest.

With a powerful voice, he shouts out at Hayah, "Who the hell do you think you are? You come in here laying down the law, without making one proposal for us to vote on. You think your theatrics can replace our GOD, the God of Abraham. He makes the laws we follow. Not You! I hate worthless men like you and..."

"SILENCE!" rings out the voice of the 'Great I Am' again. "SHUT YOUR MOUTH, Zadok! Yes, it was your ancestors who carried the Arch of the Covenant. But your ancestors were also the ones who took the gold of the people and cast a golden Caffe to worship, while Moses was on the mountain. Your ancestors' actions caused Moses to throw down and break the tablets I wrote, the tablets in the Ark. Yes, Zadok, you come from the lengthy line of the Priestly Cult, but you are still leading, what I once called, 'My People' astray and away from Me. Because of you they are no longer 'My Chosen People', they are not even my Choosing People. You start a 6-day war and steal your neighbor's land. Well, consider this a 6 second war and I take the land back."

Rabi Zadok is slipping his hand into the briefcase he is clutching to his chest.

"Zadok, I can read your hatred and malice toward my disciple Hayah. HEAD MY WARNING! DO NOT RAISE A WEAPON IN ANGER AND HATRED! The rule is no longer voluntary!"

Hayah motions for people to move away, as Zadok steps toward him. Hayah says, "Don't do it Zadok, this is no longer a commandment that you can manipulate to suit your purposes."

Zadok slides his hand out of the briefcase clutching a 45 pistol. Before he can move it away from his chest, it EXPLODES, and rips a huge hole in his chest. His body becomes rigid and very slowly starts to topple forward, like a falling tree. Security guards quickly move in and remove his body.

Hayah steps back and looks at the assembly. All but one of those standing sits back down again. The Youngman left standing is 23, clean shaven and long black hair. He is wearing a blue pin-striped suit. His body is trembling.

Hayah says gently, "There is nothing to fear. The 'I Am', who is within you knows that you mean well." The Youngman stops trembling and straightens up, with a smile. "Go ahead Sam, the 'I Am' wants you to ask your question. It is especially important."

"The 'Great I Am' said that the original commands were 10 positive words. Can you tell us what they are?" Sam's sincerity is very touching.

"Yes, I can," says Hayah, "but 'I Am' is telling me that the rest of you want to hear them also. The 'I Am' originally wrote them in Hebrew for the Hebrew people, and now the 'I Am' wants to tell them to you. So, I will turn over my voice again."

The 'Great I Am's voice comes booming out of Hayah's mouth, "Hear O' people of the Word:

1. CONNECT – <u>Connect</u> to me; I Am within you.
2. CHOOSE – Every day, <u>choose</u> my purpose for your life and be faithful to my will.
3. HONOR – <u>Honor</u> my name, and who I Am, and where I Am, within you and all things.
4. REJUVENATE – Every week or every day, <u>rejuvenate</u> yourself in meditation.
5. RESPECTFUL – Be <u>respectful</u> of your family, your neighbors and all creation.
6. LIFE – Treasure all <u>life</u> as if it were your own.
7. STEADFAST – Be <u>steadfast</u> in all your relationships.
8. HONEST – Be <u>honest</u> in all your dealings.
9. TRUTHFUL– Be <u>truthful</u> in everything you

    say.
10. SATISFIED – Be <u>satisfied</u> with what you have
        and all that you receive.
These are the ten words to live by."

While Hayah recovers, Bill steps up, "On that note we would like to close our session. The Team will linger off to the side if you have any other questions. We will also take your contact info if you are interested in connecting with the 'I Am' within you. Thank you for giving us the chance to get the word out to you. Please, spread the word to all those you meet or text. As you have learned, lives depend on people knowing what is going down."

CHAPTER 48
Palestine Restored

Abbud is contacting his father to set up a meeting with the Palestinian Militia, Political Leaders and Clergy. He starts off with three questions to evaluate the situation. Is he ready to set aside his hatred in order to get a lasting peace? Will he give up all his violence and learn to live without his weapons? Finally, does he really want a democratic State of Palestine?

It is no surprise to Abbud that his father's only problem is the weapons. Unfortunately, this problem is the most dangerous. He will welcome a lasting peace and a democratic State of Palestine. In the end of their conversation, his father agrees to set up the meeting.

When the Team arrives at a remote location in the Southern tip of the Gaza Strip, they are surprised to find over a hundred important leaders. It is an informal gathering, so the introductions are personal and sealed with a handshake. Talia is surprised to see the number of women who turned out to the meeting. Many of them crowd around her to soak up some of the positive energy.

As the group settles down, Abbud sits on a large stone to address the group. "We are here to bring you an important message from the 'Great I Am', but first I want to share with you some particularly good news. As of today, all the land that Palestine lost in the 6-day war, the 'I Am' is restoring to Palestine. The borders will return to the 1949 UN Armistice lines, with no exceptions. You can now form your State of Palestine and seek a seat in the UN." The shocked look on their faces causes Abbud to pause. "It's true! The 'I Am' calls it the 6 second war, and you are the winners." A cheer goes up among the group. "All the Israeli occupied land, in your State, is now under your control. Our recommendation is that you keep the people living there as your tenants and only replace them when they move on. This way you will have a steady income for your new State. It is the 'I Am's wish that you 'love your neighbors as yourselves.' The next bonus is the Israel border barrier must come down. There will still be a border security but unarmed.

"The 'Great I Am' is doing all this for you and expects you, and all people, to keep all the commands I will read to you. It is the 'I Am's greatest hope that most of you will try to connect to the 'I Am' within you.

"Now, the 'Great I Am' feels that it is best that I read the commands to you and make them available to you in print. That way you can follow them to the letter.

"First, any weapon picked up to harm, maim or kill will immediately destroy or permanently injure the perpetrator and anyone ordering the action. Any person resorting to any violence ends here and now.

"Second, any weapon, atomic or chemical, designed to harm, maim or kill, will be triggered in the laboratory before it can be released. Thus, destroying the laboratory and all those working in it. (I know you don't have any, but be warned, you don't want to go down that road.)

"Third, women and men are equal in all respects (PERIOD). All societies, businesses, organizations and families must honor this basic premise. Both men and women must honor this premise. Failure to honor this premise is a step toward your Dark-side.

"Sexual abuse of either women or men is not acceptable and is considered a step toward your Dark-side. Sexual abuse is the infliction of sexual contact upon a person by forcible compulsion, or by sexual contact with a person who is sexually immature or who is incapable of giving consent because of age or mental or physical incapacity. Any man committing sexual abuse will experience an over enlarging penis which will burst and never function again. Any woman committing sexual abuse will experience an explosive uterus and never be able to experience sexual pleasure again.

"Fourth, lies and deception. This is a worldwide epidemic including most people, and especially clergy, politicians, lawyers and the justice system. Every time a person lies or deceives someone, I will make them automatically and uncontrollably say, 'That is a lie!' Or 'That is a deception!' They will even consciously hear themselves saying it.

"Fifth, power and authority. This is now in the hands of a wealthy few. Unfortunately, they are now destroying the planet. Nature is out of balance; pollution is destroying the planet and the planet will be lucky to survive until 2050. The only survival will be in the emergence of the many Crystal Cities. Only those connected to the 'Great I Am' will live there. Unfortunately, 1% of the population in any area must be connected to the 'I Am' before a Crystal City can emerge.

"OK, do you have any questions?" There is a long silence. Abbud studies the group and is surprised to see just blank faces. Finally, one of the women timidly raises her hand to ask a question.

She stands and says, "Does equal men and women apply to a married couple?"

Talia responds confidently, "Yes it does."

"Even the sexual abuse part?" Asks the woman. Her husband pulls her down. He immediately experiences a sharp pain in his groin and releases her. He tries to conceal the pain.

Talia looks the husband in the eye, "Especially the sexual abuse part! Are you getting the message?"

Their silence seems to grow deeper.

The Justice Team looks at each other, and they all have the same doubts. Within seconds, the 'Great I Am' is in their awareness. The 'I Am' tells them that the entire group is blocking any connection and it is difficult to get any read on their thinking or emotions. The 'I Am' says, "This is very unusual. These people should be overjoyed with the outcome so far. They have not been able to get this far for the past 52 years. Something is amiss. Go ahead Jacob ask your question. It might trigger something."

Jacob asks the group, "Well, I'm interested, how do you plan on disposing of your weapons, so they don't explode and kill you?"

Abbud's father Abdul 'Adl answers, "We plan on digging a deep hole in the desert, where we can throw all our weapons, so no one will ever get hurt by them." He smiles broadly, but suddenly says uncontrollably, "That is a deception!" Shocked, he realizes what he just said and quickly looks at his comrades. Their glaring eyes are drilling holes in his soul. He stammers, "but... but... I mean... Ah..."

Abbud shakes his head in shame.

Jacob stands and speaks very clearly, emphasizing every word, "This is a Warning. If you so much as think in anger or hatred in regard to your neighbor, your exploding weapons will send you instantly to the BLACK DOOM that awaits you."

The group freezes in silence. After several minutes they start to look at each other. Every expression of doubt is met with threatening anger. Every look of fear is met with disgust. Every movement suggesting retreat is met with a cut-throat gesture. Soon over 80% of the people are staring blankly at the ground.

The 'Great I Am' says to the Justice Team, "The only way you can break the leaders' control over the others is to order all of the leaders to go home. At least then My command will empower most of them

to follow their conscience. The others will go their
own way and do whatever they plan to do."

Talia stands and says, "I believe that it is time for
everyone to go home and deliberate on what has gone
on here today. Picture the peaceful State of Palestine
as a thriving peaceful community in which your
children grow up without fear." As she talks, she is
raising each of those families with their heads down.
"Picture the schools you can develop, with a better
educational process." Soon some of the families are
in their cars and driving away. "Picture a State with
Parks and Nature Reserves. Picture open Beaches,
where you can peacefully sun yourself." Talia waves
as the last bully family pulls out. She turns to the
others glaring at her. "Picture..." She is interrupted
as one of the leaders springs to his feet.

"To hell with your Picture! I'll give you a picture!
I know what you're trying to do."

Talia steps toward him, but the 'I Am' stops her.
"Waite! He is going to use his car as a weapon to
attack one of the families."

The angry leader shakes his fist at the last family
to pull out and jumps in his Land Rover. He turns
the key. The car explodes in a huge ball of flame.
The other leaders recoil from the blast.

Talia turns to the other leaders and starts to say,
"A weapon..."

Jacob and Abbud join her in chorus, "...is a
WEAPON in any form! BE WARNED!" They walk to
their car and drive away.

CHAPTER 49
Breaking News

Back in Tel Aviv, the Press Conference is under way. They are in a small classroom at the University. Noya and Ori are sitting on stools in front of the group. The opening struggle with everyone trying to talk at the same time is over and they are now standing to ask their questions one at a time. In the back of the room, two networks are videoing the Press Conference.

All of the Press members present here have covered at least one of the meetings, including the one in Gaza. At the start, their main focus was on the violent maiming or killing of those supposed innocent soldiers, political leaders and clerics. All their heated questions were focusing on the angry, violent God who was striking down these supposed innocent, defenseless people. The Press is an angry mob ready to lynch Noya and Ori.

With the help of the 'Great I Am', Noya and Ori are able to quickly learn what was causing this problem. All the Press members had read only the schedule and locations of the meetings, but none of them had read the rest of the material, the cautions, the warnings, or the commands. They have no clue that the main purpose here is to find the Love-light. So patiently they bring them to order and make them read the material.

This is the point at which we join them.

A long-term experienced reporter is apologizing for herself and her colleagues. Then she asks, "Who is this 'I Am' you talk about so much? Is that just another name for God? And what does it mean when you say He is within?

Ori looks at Noya, she nods to him, and he takes the question. "Taking your last question first, the 'I Am' is not a he or gender specific. Everyone experiences the 'I Am' in their own personal way, because the 'I Am' is within you. 'I Am' is not up in the heavens or a myth. 'I Am' is real and present in there." (He points to her heart.) "The 'Great I Am' said to Moses, 'I Am your essence of being I Am', that not only tells you who or what 'I Am' is but where 'I Am' is. The 'I Am' does not like the tag God. God is a left-brain irrational thought word, from left brain theology, which leads us away from our essence of being. The Indian, Greek and Roman cultures all had many Gods, all up in a heavenly domain, or so we thought with our left-brain irrational minds. Then came the Zoroastrian, Hebrew, Christian and Islamic people telling us there is only one God. Then the left-brain irrational thoughts of the Hebrew people divided Him up into twelve groups. Then the Christian's left-brain irrational thought divided Him up into three persons and thousands of different pieces of a pie-in-the-sky. One of which is Islam. I hope you find this as confusing as I do.

"Well, the 'Great I Am', who is not a left-brain irrational thought, but an experience, also finds it confusing. Every creature, plant and stone on the planet is connected to the 'I Am' and thriving. Only humans are uncoordinated with nature, mostly unconnected and slowly destroying the planet."

All the reporters are busy writing in their notebooks. The reporter who asked the question, without looking up, asks, "Are you some kind of Biblical Scholar?"

Shyly looking away, Ori says, "No ma'am. I get it directly from the 'I Am'. If you connect, you can get it firsthand as well."

Another reporter stands and asks. "The command about weapons seems to be a very sever version of the 6th commandment, 'you shall not kill'. Why is the 'I Am' getting so tough on us?"

Noya asks, "Has the 6th commandment stopped or even slowed the killing among humans?"

"No. Now we kill without compunction."

"Precisely!" says Noya, "and the 'I Am' says, 'the original word written on the tablet meant honor life' meaning all life. At first, they interpreted it as 'do not kill'. Then they changed it to 'do not murder' so they could freely kill in war. Now they ignore the command all together."

Another reporter clarifies what he saw, "This means that what we saw was caused by the people, who were about to harm you." Ori nods yes. "Wow, which will make an attacker think more than twice about attacking someone. This just might work. We need to get the word out. Only a fool would pull a weapon to heart someone, if he or she knew it would heart themself."

A young reporter asks, "does this mean the 'I Am' is all knowing?"

Ori responds, "No, not the way you are thinking. The 'I Am' is your essence of being, within you, part of who you are, seeing every thought you have, aware of every move you are about to make."

"Yikes!" The young reporter reacts, turning very red in the face, "That means 'I Am' knows everything I'm thinking when I look at a **woman**!"

Everyone in the room laughs.

An attractive woman stands and asks, "I'm having a tough time getting my head around what it says here about sexual abuse. Is this a LAW, like ME TOO? And who will enforce it?"

Noya smiles, "It is not a law and the 'I Am' will enforce it. You are protected 100% of the time. The second a guy comes on to you with malicious intent or a husband tries to dominate you, the 'I Am' within that person, will cause the penis to have severe pain immediately. No judge. No police."

"Holly maceral! I never thought I'd see the day!" the woman says. "I have to meet this 'Great I Am'. Where do I sign up?"

"We'll be taking names when we're done."

A nerdy looking reporter stands and asks, "Has anyone on the connected Justice Team ever asked the 'I Am' the disposal plan for the atomic weapons sent into outer space?"

Ori responds quickly, "I don't know. Let's ask." Ori appears to go deep within himself, breathing in and out. Then, his face lights up. "Ori is letting Me use his voice. David, I apricate your question. More people in the space industry need to be concerned as to the amount of junk they are leaving in orbit. I have two purposes for the atomic weapons in outer space: one is to consolidate and destroy the space debris; two is to blow up the meteor fields, where the meteors are too big and potentially harmful to the Earth.

"As to your unasked question David, yes, you should pursue a career in the Space Program." Ori slowly comes back to himself.

Everyone in the room is silent for several minutes. Their eyes are locked on Ori. Noya is smiling at him.

David finally tries to say something, "Was that... Was that really... Was the 'Great I Am' really talking to me?"

"Yes, David," Ori replied.

"Oh, boy! I must make that connection!"

Another reporter stands, who has been writing like crazy. She asks, "How often do you communicate with the 'I Am' within you?"

Ori says, "About two times every hour.

Sometimes a little more."

Noya adds, "For me, it is about once every ten minutes. The fact is 'I Am' is always there ready to help and guide us. We have agreed to fulfill the purpose the 'I Am' has for us.

"Do you have any other questions for us?"

The group is silent, and no one stands.

"OK, all those how want to go, may do so."

No one gets up to leave.

"Who would like to learn about our group classes on Connecting to the 'Great I Am' and finding the Love-light?

Everyone's hand goes up.

Noya continues, "Let me give you an outline of what you are getting into. There are three steps you will take: 1. You will learn how to shut down your left-brain irrational brain-chatter; 2. You will find the Love-light within you; 3. You will have the choice to connect to the 'Great I Am' within you and accept 'I Am's purpose for your life."

The experienced reporter asks, "What do you mean, shutdown our left-brain irrational thought? I have spent my whole life developing my left-brain irrational brain power."

Ori responds, "Yes you have, and look what it has given you. When you got up this morning and were given this assignment, you brain chatter told you the assignment was beneath you, and you didn't need to read the lengthy press release."

"How do you know that?"

"You know how I know. Then you went to the Military Briefing and saw two soldiers get an arm blown off. Your left-brain irrational brain-chatter told you that some phony divine power was attacking humans. So, when you got here, your left-brain irrational brain-chatter told you we were responsible, and so you attack us. Now what have you learned?"

"That my left-brain chatter is lying to me," she answers. "I get it, but…"

Ori cuts her off, "your left-brain chatter is telling you IT is your higher intelligence, which is also a lie."

"Yes, I need to learn how to shut it down!"

All the group eagerly signed up. Their group class, with Ori and Nora, starts immediately.

CHAPTER 50
The Stiff-Neck People

Late in the afternoon, I'm sitting in a deep meditation, basking in the Love-light of the 'Great I Am'. Suddenly the 'I Am' says, "Hayah I need you to listen. The Israel Parliament is having a secret meeting, with only the key negative conservative leaders led by Nittin Whoya.

"I have nothing against positive conservatives, who are cautious, careful and thoughtful people toward themselves, other people or society. But when negative conservatives are the greedy wealthy, lawless people and dominating power mongers, I Am dead set against them.

"Nittin Whoya just returned from a summit meeting with Russia's Poopin. (What Whoya doesn't know is that the Russian Mafia is secretly trying to destroy the world's democracies. Of which, Israel is one.) In their meeting Poopin has pumped up Whoya's ego by calling him the Middle-East's Emperor.

"This secret meeting begins with a verbal attack on the Justice Team. Nitin Whoya lets their anger and hatred reach a white-hot peak, without saying anything. I know he is up to no good. As soon as their hatred peaks, Whoya says, without any consideration of My commands, 'I fully know and sympathize with your reaction to these people, but I cannot be part of your hostility. This Justice Team is worse than an infestation of termites on our society and spirituality. You must do what you must do, but leave me out of it. May Yahweh bless you and keep you from all harm.' We both know why he is saying this. What he does not know is that it will no longer work with My new commands.

"Now the subject shifts to the Border Wall. They

are saying that it is their first line of defense. They do not get it. The wall is defending them against nothing. If anything, it is preventing them from fulfilling My old neighbor command. The border wall is now becoming a wall between them and Me. They do not get it. What must I do?"

I'm sympathetic, "They are the same old stiff-necked people they have always been. If the new commands don't bring them around, then they will end up destroying themselves."

"I know. I know," the 'I Am's feeling for them persists. "Why must they constantly turn their backs on Me? I know. They always have, and they always will. But those that are with Me now, were not like this. I want them to listen to Me. The new commands will destroy them."

"Not necessarily," I respond comfortingly. "Your new commands will only destroy those who will not listen. Those that listen will pay you back 100 times over. That's a lot better than the spit in the face you are getting here, remember, David."

"Oh, David, one minute connected. The next minute a million miles away." The 'I Am' is silent for a moment. "Hayah, your right. I need to focus on those that are trying to connect with Me, and those that are connected to Me.

"Now, they are saying without the Border Wall; they are vulnerable to a hostel enemy. That is Not true anymore! The only hostel enemy here is them. The new command makes that clear. The hatred in their hearts is going to blast them to the Black Place, where David can moan with them."

The 'I Am' hears more: "Their discussion now shifts to their land problem. They need more land to accommodate their growth. And the only way they can get it is like they did in the 6-day war."

The 'I Am' reacts. I can feel the deep sorrow. The 'I Am' says, "They are not listening at all. The only way to grow is by being good neighbors spreading the Love-light."

"I agree," I say, "but the new commands do not cover that they are willfully ignoring the new commands You laid out for them. Remember, they are experts at reinterpreting and redefining."

The 'I Am' blurts out, "Will they ever learn?"

I respond, "Now what are they doing?"

"They are off on their GREEDY rocket. Nothing is ever enough. They always need to have increasingly more and the most. Nitin Whoya is telling them, they need to seize all the water rights. It will make them the wealthiest people in the Middle East. It will not only make them wealthy; it will give them the most power over the people. I Am sure you know where that is coming from."

"There's no doubt," I answer. "Poopin and the Russian Mafia."

"Precisely. That man has no moral compass at all. With the new commands, he and the Mafia are in for a major surprise worldwide." Suddenly, the 'Great I Am' is silent.

I hold my breath. Then...

"Oh, no. No. NO!" The 'I Am' is at a loss.

"What?" I ask.

"They are stumbling around the nuclear question; they decide to do nothing; they will not send the weapons into space. From their discussion it is obvious that Israel has not denuclearized according to the Treaty." The 'I Am' is silently processing the information.

I react to their decision, "They don't have a clue about Your command. The hatred and violent intent of just one of them could trigger the whole arsenal and blow the Middle-East off the map."

There is a long silence. I wait. I can feel that the 'I Am' is considering something else.

Then the 'I Am' responds to my comment, like it

is a secondary issue. "I know!" says the 'Great I Am'. "They are turning their backs on Me yet again. They worship and pray to a false God. They never stop or pause to listen to Me." The 'Great I Am' remains silent for some time.

I can feel that something is cooking. There is no fear. That is not something 'I Am' ever feels. Not even in a situation like this. I wonder what it could be. Then I shut down the left-brain chatter and wait. I simply enjoy the Love-light while waiting.

Finally, the 'I Am' breaks the silence, "Hayah, I worked it out. Thank you for your help as always. I have a plan. It has been a long time since I have done anything like this. Sleep well tonight."

I meet with the Justice Team and we go over our progress. Fortunately, there is a lengthy list of people wanting to connect to the 'Great I Am' within them. There is enough to make up 8 full groups. One group for each of us.

I fill everyone in on the secret Parliament meeting of the conservative leaders. Their anxiety increases very quickly. I manage to calm them down, by trusting in the plan of the 'Great I Am' and creating a curiosity about the wonderous thing that none of us have ever seen. I share 'I Am's final wish, "Sleep well tonight." We all go home.

That night, I fall into a deep sleep quickly and without concern. I don't know when, but suddenly I start to have an incredible dream.

I see these balls of light emerging out of nothingness. They sparkle and glitter as they fly through the air. Each one is filled with the Love-light. Soon there are thousands of them. They swarm about me then fly off in different directions. It seems like I know them, or they know me, like each of them has touched my life in some personal way. I reach out, but they avoid my touch. However, I still feel their Loving power.

I look up and see that they are hovering over a sleeping Israel. All is quiet. All is calm. Stillness abounds. Then each ball of light darts in on a specific target. I expect an explosion, but there is none. Then in an instant each section of the Border Wall lifts into the air. Like feathers on a string, they carry them away.

They take some to the home of Nitin Whoya. In seconds, a wall surrounds his house and huge blocks create a roof over the top of it. Barbwire seems to rap itself around it, led by a ball of light. When done, it looks like a fortified bunker, without armament, without entrance and without exit. It seals off those who want to get out, and those who want to get in.

I look around in all directions. The balls of light fortify all the homes of the negative conservative leaders and clerics, who attended the meeting, the same as the others, with no way in or out. Suddenly, I realize that these balls of light are the many living Spirits connected to the 'Great I Am'.

Then, I see many Spirit balls heading to the North. I look closer. Each one is towing a border barrier block. Soon there is a tower in the making. Every other block reverses so they stack level and securely. A broad base is formed, and a tower begins to rise. My mind's eye follows them in wonder.

To the West another tower is forming.

To the South there is a third tower forming.

I start to look back and forth between the three towers. I'm impressed when they are 100 meters tall. I'm flabbergasted when they are 200 meters high. I'm shocked when they reach over a quarter of a mile high, with blinking red lights on top.

When the job is done, all the Spirt balls disappear. I look as far as I can see. The Border Wall is gone, every block, every wire, every poll.

I smile and open my eyes, with my arm raped around my pillow. I look at the clock. It is 5 AM. Oh bother, was it just a dream? I get up and prepare to write it down. As I sit at the desk, I feel the presence of the 'Great I Am' within me.

The 'I Am' says warmly and with confidence, "I want you to go up to the roof patio of the hotel and have a look-see."

I dress. I climb the stairs. When I walk outside, I see three towers, one to the North, one to the West, and one to the South. And the border wall is gone.

My dream has just become a miracle.

I say to the 'I Am', "Thank you!"

CHAPTER 51
Finding the Love-light

Yesterday, the group class of the news and media reporters was a complete success. All the reporters are now connected to the 'Great I Am' within them and fulfilling the 'I Am's purpose for them. When they go home, they have no idea what the 'I Am' has in store for them.

Last night, they were all alerted to the biggest news story in modern history. The 'I Am' assigned them to different sections of "The Spirt-ball Miracle" and the end of the Israeli Border wall. They captured the entire event in word, photo and video.

This morning it is breaking news along with the 'Great I Am's commands delivered to the Military, Israeli Parliament, the new State of Palestine and the press. Special additions of all the newspapers are on the street. Every radio is announcing the news. Every TV is interrupting their broadcasting to break the news. All the news programs are showing videos and special interviews.

One of those interviews is with Chief of the General Staff, Viav. The Reporter ask him, "Are you connected to the 'Great I Am' within you?"

"Yes, Sir." General Viav smiles warmly. "I was lucky to meet Hayah at our Military Briefing, and he agreed to coach me privately. It is the most powerful experience of my life. I don't know how we, the Hebrew people, could screw up something so simple. The 'Great I Am' is not an Idea, or a Theological ethereal being; the 'I Am' is an experience. The 'I Am' is our essence of being. The second I shut up, the 'I Am' within me started to talk to me. The incredible thing is that 'I Am' has been there for my whole life. Now we are in each other."

The Reporter asks, "What is your reaction to the

new Commands the 'I Am' is giving us?"

Viav responds without hesitation, "They are 100% positive! To make them negative, we must do something stupid and hateful. Let me explain. Any person living in harmony with all others, family, friends and neighbors (which includes all others personal or international) is free of any harm. The commands totally protect you. The reason they protect you is because any hateful person who tries to harm, main or kill you will end up destroying themselves. This happens the second they touch their weapon. In other words, the 'I Am' has your back all the time."

The Reporter asks another question, "Would you tell us what your reaction is to the removal of the Border Wall?"

"The mindboggling fact that the 'Great I Am' did this while we slept is a major wakeup call. The hatred and violence end here and now.

"The wall was not protecting us. It was controlling us. There is not one minute in any day that it made me feel safe. Yet, I had to send my solders to protect it and not the people.

"Furthermore, the cost of the wall was costing the taxpayers more than you can possibly imagine. That is money that none of us have to spare.

"Now that it is gone, I look around and see the possibility of a new and beautiful Israel emerging."

"I see that too!" says the Reporter. Then asks, "Do you have any idea why Nittin Whoya and some of the leaders in Parliament have been boxed in by the wall segments? And should we try to rescue them? I feel that everybody needs to hear this.

"You're right everybody needs to know the truth. Only then does any of this make sense. Late yesterday afternoon Nittin Whoya was meeting with these leaders. They were planning to ignore the 'I Am's commands. This would have caused in time their own destruction. Sad but true. Then their meeting turned to the commands regarding nuclear weapons. They did not want to lose the power and authority that these weapons gave them. Therefore, they decided to ignore that command as well. However, under the new commands, if any one of them started to have a hateful thought regarding the nuclear weapons it would trigger the whole arsenal of nuclear weapons to explode. That would wipe the Middle East of the map and cause fallout for thousands of miles. Now Nittin Whoya and these leaders have no access to the trigger.

"They definitely should NOT be released until we have disposed of the nuclear weapons and the labs where they are made. After the disposal of the weapons and labs you may want to release them, but they should be tried for the risk they put us in. If it were not for the quick action of the 'Great I Am' and The Spirit-ball Miracle, we would all be dead this morning."

The Reporter says, "I have one more question, General Viav. Do you have any suggestions as to what we should do to celebrate this Miracle?"

Viav reflects for a moment, "You're right. We should be rejoicing. For the first time in our lives, we have a lasting peace not of our own making. The 'Great I Am' has given us the treaty. The 'Great I Am' has given all humanity the peace. All we need to do is live in the Love-light with each other. All we need to do is behave ourselves and love our neighbors.

"Yes, let us celebrate this day. It is a day more important than the Passover. For on this day, we are all free. Free of fear. Free of hatred. Free of oppression. Now everyone has the chance to connect to the 'Great I Am' within. It is your Freewill Choice. There is no authority requiring it. There is no institution demanding it or else. For on this day, we are absolutely FREE. Let the bells ring. Let the cheers go up. Embrace your neighbor in peace. Let us start living in the Love-light. Today, you can open your eyes. You can open your heart. You can start to listen, with your awareness, to the voice within you. You can see the Love-light within you. You can experience the 'Great I Am' within you. You can embrace the true purpose of your life. You can find the Love-light.

"Yes, let us celebrate this day!" Viav stands and salutes the Israeli flag, with his back to the camera.

The reporter does the same. We can see a glowing white light in the middle of their backs. Seconds later, the light starts growing within the flag as well. A cheer goes up among the crew.

The image fades to black.

From that date on the Miracle spread throughout the State of Israel and the State of Palestine. The Love-light created a feeling of equality between them. That feeling washed away all the hatred and mistrust between them.

An economic equality was born. The differences of rich and poor faded away. The strength of the economy doubled and then tripled. The whole idea of a world bank went right out the window because no economy was as strong as theirs. They became the model for the world.

A Social equality and Sexual equality were also born. Families became stronger. Businesses became stronger and functioned in harmony. Schools became better, with a higher learning level and pure joy in the process of learning. The Government ceased being an institution. Professional politicians became history. The Government became a voice representing the people. Every citizen was required to serve in the Government for two years, without a salary and only room and board. The Military became a service organization to the State and soon changed its name to Peace Corp. Any need a community might have, the Peace Corp stepped in and made it happen, building a new school, building a bridge, creating a park or nature reserve, running the border check points and keeping the peace.

There also emerged a great need to set up small groups to help people connect to the 'Great I Am' within them. These are not institutions and are never more than 30 people. They are meditation groups, for people who need to learn how to connect to the 'I Am' or need to improve their connection to the 'I Am'. They also become a social means to meeting real people, free from the AI (artificial intelligence). In fact, it is these small groups which help people shut down their left-brain irrational thoughts and brain chatter.

So, the connected human race are the only ones that will survive, because they are the only ones that can function without their left-brain irrational thoughts and AI.

CHAPTER 52
Connect

If you asked me, "Hayah, what is the best way to survive in this modern chaotic world?"
I would say...

Before I answer that question, you need to know what happened on the Western border of Jerusalem 90 days after the three towers went up. In the history of the two States, it is only a blip. Some would say it is not worth mentioning. They say that it is because I did nothing. The connected people did nothing. And it was over in a flash.
All humans also have a dark-side within them. Everyone knows the things that draw us into it: the lies, the hatred, the greed, the lust, the ego, the desire for power to dominate others. If those are your choices, you will go deeper and deeper into your dark-side, until it is next to impossible to get out. Yes, no matter how deep you are, you can make the choice to get out. It is not easy, but you can do it. Obviously, it is best if you are not drawn into it in the first place.
This is what happens if you chose to go into your dark side.
Shortly after the three towers went up, a military coalition began to form, made up of negative renegade soldiers, clerics and citizens from Israel, Palestine, Syria, Iran, Iraq and Yemen. They saw the unarmed connected human family as sitting ducks.
For example, Abbud's father, Abdul 'Adl, organized the negative leaders that were at the meeting in Gaza. He saw this as an opportunity to become the Supreme Leader in Palestine. He had no trouble convincing them as to how easy this would be, with so little effort.

Capitan Menahem, of the Israeli army, went to General Viav to recruit him to their cause. Viav heard rumors of what he was up to and did not like it. He flatly turned him down and ordered him to stand down or face a military tribunal.

Menahem saw this as his opportunity to overthrow Viav and become Supreme Ruler of Israel. He was able to recruit a sizable number of soldiers to his cause. All of them were convinced as to the weakness of General Viav.

The outrage of many of the oil barons and clerics from Syria, Iran, Iraq and Yemen over the lost war at Aleetmh was over the top. The influence of Poopin from Russia fueled that outrage. But he was not able to be involved.

Thus, one night 90 days after the three towers appeared, the secret military coalition of the two groups began to assemble West of Jerusalem. Actually, it was only a secret to them. They were all heavily armed. As daybreak began to push back the blackness of night, the military coalition could see that the press was standing on elevated platforms, with mounted cameras. Around the military coalition on all sides was a ring of countless connected people at a safe distance.

The connected people were silent and unarmed.

Before the sun could rise, the military coalition panicked, and they all went for their weapons. In that instant every weapon exploded, shooting streams of blood into the air. The sound echoed off the building. Then all was silent as the sun rose to greet the day.

When the sun was hugely full and dancing on the horizon, the connected people, in silence, moved in to remove the bodies and clean up the debris. There was no rejoicing; for the loss of life, any life, is a sadness to the connected heart.

Before 7 AM, the area was clean and functioning

as normal. The sadness soon passed. The blip on the news was only 30 seconds long. The connected people moved on.

When I first started my journey with the 'Great I Am', I felt that the 1% goal for connected people was difficult but possible. Over the years with the rapid growth in population, it began to look doubtful. Now in recent years, the Over Population has made it impossible. But...

Now we have two forces working in our favor. One is the number of people destroying themselves, like the Middle East Military Coalition. The other is the AI. Artificial Intelligence is expanding so rapidly it is dehumanizing the planet.

How does AI do that? The growth of our technology becomes faster and faster every month, no longer every year. Right now, it is almost impossible to get any human assistance to resolve technical internet problems. A computer that once upon a time would last ten years or more, now barely lasts as long as three years.

The birth of the cellphone has allowed AI to take over. Humans think they must carry their cellphones with them all the time. Humans are quickly becoming the servant of their cellphone, rather than the other way around. It is no longer just a phone. It does everything. It tells time. It's your alarm clock. It's your GPS. It Swishes your money. It does your research. It plays your computer games. And... And... And it does your dating.

Yesterday, I was climbing up a mountain. It was a beautiful sunshiny day, with a cool breeze. As I came out of the dense forest into a rocky section of the trail, there sitting on a large bolder was an attractive young woman texting on her cellphone. She was oblivious to the beauty around her. One hundred meters away, on a lower level of the same

trail was a handsome young man texting on his
cellphone. He too was oblivious to the beauty around
him and also appeared to be oblivious of the beautiful
woman behind him.

What a pity I thought. It would be much more
fun to come upon this young couple locked in a
passionate embrace. So, I decided to introduce them
to each other, only to find out that they were texting
each other. Their passionate embrace was taking
place in the text message.

The AI was steeling all their pleasure, and they
were oblivious to that too. Unfortunately, in today's
world this is common. Cellphone zombies are as
common as sand on the beach.

AI robots are also developing at an alarming rate.
Some of them look exactly like living human beings.
Will they replace us? They are designing some of the
robots to provide us sex without emotion. That will
resolve the Population problem. BUT it allows AI to
get rid of us altogether.

Recently, I was speaking to a meditation group of
young millennials. I asked, "How many of you are
connected?" To my surprise everyone raised their
hand. I didn't know whether to be overjoyed or what.

In a second the 'Great I Am' was in my ear,
"Hayah, none of them is connected to Me. They are
only connected to the Artificial Intelligence."

I responded, "Now what do I do? Will they listen
to me?"

The 'I Am' says, "TELL them a story. That is
something that Artificial Intelligence cannot do. AI
can only read them a story, without emotion or
human expression. Sometimes the ancient oral
traditions can bring the human race back to their
human senses."

Oddly enough, this Story did just that, and 30
millennials began to shut down their rational

thoughts and brain chatter. They are even turning off their cellphones.

Now, I'm on my way to the United States of America, to unravel their chaos.

So, what is the best way to survive? I say, connect to the 'Great I Am' within you, find the Love-light and live in it! The Crystal City will survive and so will you!